D0672137

DEATH
AND THE
SISTERS

Also by Heather Redmond

The Dickens of A Crime Mysteries

A Tale of Two Murders
Grave Expectations
A Christmas Carol Murder
The Pickwick Murders
A Twist of Murder

Heather Redmond

DEATH AND THE SISTERS

A Mary Shelley Mystery

KENSINGTON
PUBLISHING CORP.

www.kensingtonbooks.com

This book is a work of fiction. Names, characters, businesses, organizations, places, events, and incidents either are the product of the author's imagination or are used fictitiously. Any resemblance to actual persons, living or dead, events, or locales is entirely coincidental.

To the extent that the image or images on the cover of this book depict a person or persons, such person or persons are merely models, and are not intended to portray any character or characters featured in the book.

KENSINGTON BOOKS are published by

Kensington Publishing Corp.
119 West 40th Street
New York, NY 10018

Copyright © 2023 by Heather Redmond

All rights reserved. No part of this book may be reproduced in any form or by any means without the prior written consent of the Publisher, excepting brief quotes used in reviews.

All Kensington titles, imprints and distributed lines are available at special quantity discounts for bulk purchases for sales promotion, premiums, fund-raising, educational or institutional use. Special book excerpts or customized printings can also be created to fit specific needs. For details, write or phone the office of the Kensington Special Sales Manager: Kensington Publishing Corp., 119 West 40th Street, New York, NY, 10018. Attn. Special Sales Department. Phone: 1-800-221-2647.

The K with book logo Reg. US Pat. & TM Off.

Library of Congress Control Number: 2023938819

ISBN: 978-1-4967-3799-1

First Kensington Hardcover Edition: October 2023

ISBN: 978-1-4967-3800-4 (ebook)

10 9 8 7 6 5 4 3 2 1

Printed in the United States of America

May is the sweet month
Yes, we all dreamed of it once
A poet's embrace

Cast of Characters

Mary Godwin*   Child of fame, a writer

Jane Clairmont*   Mary's stepsister

William Godwin*   Mary's father, a philosopher

Mary Jane Godwin*   Mary's stepmother

Percy Bysshe Shelley*   Atheist. Lover of humanity.
                        Democrat

Harriet Shelley*   Shelley's wife

Eliza Westbrook*   Harriet's older sister

Reverend B. Doone   A clergyman

Fitzwalter Abel   A Bow Street Runner

John Hocke   A handsome young poet

Cecil Campbell   A handsome young poet

Mrs. McAndrew   Cecil's sister

Sophia Campbell   Cecil's cousin

Peter Corn   A handsome young poet

Claude Barre   A book collector

John Williams*   A Welsh man of business

Willy Godwin*	Mary's half brother
Fanny Godwin*	Mary's half sister
Charles Clairmont*	Mary's stepbrother

*Real historical figures

"Beware; for I am fearless, and therefore powerful."
—Mary Shelley, *Frankenstein*

We drifted o'er the harbour-bar,
And I with sobs did pray—
O let me be awake, my God!
Or let me sleep alway.
—Samuel Taylor Coleridge, *The Rime of the Ancient
Mariner*

The rose is fairest when 't is budding new,
And hope is brightest when it dawns from fears;
The rose is sweetest washed with morning dew
And love is loveliest when embalmed in tears."
—Sir Walter Scott, *The Lady of the Lake*

Chapter 1

London, Thursday, May 5, 1814

Jane

"I'm calling my tale *Isabella, the Penitent; or, The Bandit Novice of Dundee*," my stepsister Mary explained, tucking the notebook she'd brought back from Scotland under her pillow.

"I wish I had your talent for writing." Fanny, my elder stepsister, seated on the edge of the mattress, bit off the end of the thread from the hem she'd just repaired. Mary's shift fixed, a trade for the story she'd just read us. "You're going to be as famous as Mother and Papa someday."

"It's just one scene, really," I pointed out from the end of the bed, irritated by the excessive praise always attached to Mary and her parentage. How could my mamma, mere translator Mary Jane Godwin, compare with their late mother, the famed philosopher and writer Mary Wollstonecraft? "Where is the rest of the story?"

"I don't know yet." Mary tapped her pencil stub ostentatiously against her cheek. "I have to decide if Fernando is the villain, or Diego. One has to be the hero."

"They could both be villains," Fanny said, her pockmarked cheeks flushing. Her skin was pale like Mary's, but not in the same ethereal way, though she was only nineteen, three years older than us. She neatened her sewing box and closed the lid.

Fanny rarely left Skinner Street. Not a healthful environment, it showed on all of us. Fanny, pale; Mamma, fat; Papa, old before his time; and Mary, suffering with bad skin and pains. Of my half brothers, Charles stayed away as much as possible, not wanting to run the business he'd been educated for at great expense, and Willy was a petulant child. The doctor had been so worried about Mary that she'd been more away than at home these past years. Even I'd been sent to boarding school when we had the money.

"They could both be the heroes. She can love them both, and they can fight over her." I winked at Fanny. "Isabella can explore love with both of them. She isn't tied to outdated morality and the demands of a dead faith."

"She's literally a nun in training," Mary said, frowning at me. "Hundreds of years ago."

I ran my hands over the soft blanket on her bed. "Your mother and Papa had to have come up with the ideas they presented in their books from somewhere. Maybe atheism and free love were the style in Scotland hundreds of years ago."

Fanny shushed me, spittle landing on the edge of her lip. "Mary Wollstonecraft? William Godwin? Geniuses don't need some style from hundreds of years ago to find their ideas. They read and think and, well, write." She threw up her hands.

"I wasn't being disrespectful," I insisted. "That Percy Bysshe Shelley insists community is the way to move forward."

Mary's lips, not full, but charming in their shape and blooming color nonetheless, curved. "This Mr. Shelley does not know Papa as well as he thinks, despite being his devoted disciple. Papa is not a social being at all. He believes in philosophizing alone."

"He went to see the Shelleys, though," I said. "In Wales."

"And didn't find them," Fanny said with a giggle. "Oh, you'll see, Mary. Shelley, as you must call him, is terribly handsome, with a pretty wife, but I don't think she's coming tonight."

"What does handsome have to do with anything?" Mary asked, picking at the tip of her pencil.

"When you're rich, you can be careless," Fanny said. "And when you are handsome, you can ruin everything around you."

"La." I laughed at her. "Which of us will be known as a philosopher?"

I heard Mamma's voice then, calling us down to the dinner table. We'd been sent upstairs to dress. Must not embarrass ourselves in front of the Godwin family benefactor, this rich Shelley, who had promised to take care of Papa since he was *such* a disciple of the great man.

We collected our younger brother from his room and went down the creaking stairs. Fanny admonished Willy not to run his hands along the walls. They were damp, and the divots from his fingers were starting to show. Plus, during the drier months, the plaster tended to flake off.

In the dining room, where we did most of our entertaining, the walls were papered and dried daily, so they didn't look as bad. Papa had been angry about the expense of the paper, festooned in classical style with columns, grapes, and vine leaves, but Mamma had insisted we needed a room fit for guests. Papa didn't mind accepting the compliments for the redecoration.

They were already in the room, Papa and Shelley. He greeted Fanny and me, very friendly, but spluttered a bit when Papa introduced Mary. She didn't seem to notice but looked at him under her lashes after we'd all seated ourselves.

Mamma practiced *service à la francaise*, of course. Papa ignored us as Thérèse, our cook, and the kitchen maid brought in the dishes and placed them in the center of the table, but Shelley's eyes often drifted in Mary's direction. I was bored and merely wanted to get through the meal and back upstairs, where hopefully, I could talk Mary into choosing Diego as the hero so she would continue the story.

I noticed the peonies we had picked on my birthday last week were sadly faded now, despite the sugar I'd added to the water. They filled the air with the scent of decay, almost over-powering the burnt stew. I didn't know why Mamma hadn't tossed the bouquet; Mary and I had been busy minding our bookshop downstairs all day.

Mary glanced at the wilted blooms, the flowers drooping over the chipped jug, then glanced at me sideways. I knew that expression. Judgment, as always. I jumped up from the table, ignoring my mother's hiss, and grabbed the jug. Mary laughed as I opened the window and tossed the flowers onto the pavement below. It couldn't make the street smell any worse. We were across the street from Newgate Prison, after all.

The last public hanging, just out of eyeshot from our front windows, had been over a month ago, but at Smithfield Market nearby, the gutters ran red with animal blood most days.

Time passed, with a discussion of Napoleon that went over my head and floated away without me learning anything.

Shelley delicately pushed his stew aside. "'Man forsook the path of nature, and sacrificed the purity and happiness of his being to unnatural appetites.'"

Mary's eyes went bright. "You are so right." She quoted lines from his poem *Queen Mab* back at him:

> *And horribly devours his mangled flesh,*
> *Which, still avenging nature's broken law,*
> *Kindled all putrid humours in his frame.*

Mary pushed her bowl away with an air of triumph.

Shrugging, I pushed my dish away, as well. "What shall we eat instead?"

Shelley's brown curls danced around his high-colored cheeks

as he tilted a plate of sliced bread toward me. The underside of his blue velvet coat sleeve nearly slid through the butter. He would not have cared, I suspected, unlike many gentlemen.

"'Man is of soul and body, form'd for deeds of high resolve,'" Mary said, quoting again, and took a piece of bread.

"I am flattered by your recollection of my work," Shelley said, taking the next slice.

He started to pull the plate back, perhaps to offer it to Willy, but I stopped him with my fingers on the edge. "Me too."

His look slid from me to Mary again. Who could blame him? The pallid, injured girl she'd been when she first went to Scotland two years ago had returned with blooming cheeks, spun spiderwebs of golden hair, and limpid hazel eyes. It was no wonder she'd already had one Scottish marriage proposal, which Papa had turned down.

I bit into my dry slice of bread. Mother tried to keep an elegant table, but she simply wasn't elegant and always fell short somewhere.

Mary and I were sixteen and positively dying to be anywhere but here, but Papa had insisted we be at home. Neither of us wanted to be shopgirls, which was all Mamma desired for us, so she didn't have to mind the bookshop herself. She still fancied herself a French-to-English translator, like she'd been before marrying Papa.

Papa and Shelley launched into a spirited discussion about the peace talks that were shortly to begin in France. My mother interrupted occasionally, spouting little phrases in French that added nothing to the stimulating conversation. Our French was very good since we used to live in the Polygon, a collection of thirty-two houses around a garden square, positively teeming with French émigrés.

Papa turned to our visit earlier in the day with Mr. Constable, who published Sir Walter Scott. He and Shelley discussed the *Encyclopædia Britannica* while my thoughts wandered.

Would Mary accept a new Scottish proposal if it came? Would I ever see her again if she returned to Dundee? I had no interest in Scotland, but given the opportunity to go to Switzerland, I would be first in line. Mamma said I was half Swiss.

Finally, Papa pushed back his bowl and rose, making a shooing motion with his arm. "I'll speak to Shelley alone now."

My mother went pink with outrage. My father smiled genially at her. "I'm certain you need to close up the office, Mrs. Godwin."

Mary gave Shelley a sidelong glance, then rose, putting her arm around Willy.

I followed them out of the room, the floor squeaking and settling beneath us. Sneaking about was close to impossible in this ill-built house. Our steps on the staircase rattled the entire house. Papa paid no rent on the place since the ownership was in dispute, but as a result, no one maintained it, either, leaving us in a precarious situation.

"Change into your nightshirt," Mary told Willy after pulling it from a peg on the wall and handing it to him.

I picked up his water jug and went downstairs to refill it, trying to keep my footsteps quiet. Papa was attempting to negotiate funds from Shelley, who was heir to a deliciously wealthy family. As a disciple of my father, he had promised to care for the family financially, but as he had little readily available, he had to raise the money by some kind of complicated process I didn't understand.

When I returned with the water, Mary and Willy were sitting on the bed. Mary's slender arms were weaving the air as she sang:

> The red-coat lads wi' black cockauds
> To meet them were na slaw, man,
> They rush'd and push'd and bluid outgush'd,
> And monie a bouk did fa', man!

I rolled my eyes. "More Burns?"

Willy stuck out his tongue at me. He had reached the age where he wanted to hear about nothing but soldiers and brave deeds of yore. I battled a stew stain on Willy's waistcoat while Mary finished the song. Her voice did not have my skill, but she overcame her weaknesses with the power of her recitation.

Fanny poked her head in. Mary stopped so our eldest sister could give Willy a kiss.

"I see why you were in love with Shelley now," she told Fanny.

Fanny's painfully plain face went pink. "That was a long time ago."

"I was too little then to notice him," I said.

"I don't remember meeting him," Mary said.

"Your Scottish friend Christy Baxter did." Fanny pulled up Willy's sheet. "I think you were ill from the return trip."

"I usually am," Mary said ruefully. She swept the filaments of her hair off her cheeks. "He does have the most piercing eyes."

"Just like you." Fanny's voice was soft. "I like that he worships Mother."

I rolled my eyes. I could admit my mother was an embarrassment, but no one ever sainted the living, right? Mary Wollstonecraft was my spiritual mother, in any case, even if I couldn't claim her flesh as my own. I would have experiences and adventures, just as she had. Fanny had not inherited any of the Wollstonecraft fire, though she, like Mary, had traveled more than I had.

"What?" I suddenly realized all three of them were staring at me.

"You stamped your foot, Jane," Willy said.

I shrugged. "I was thinking I'd like to travel."

"That's all very well," Fanny said, "but if you stomp about, the entire house will shake, and Mamma will come."

All four of us shuddered at that and giggled.

"Mrs. Shelley is very pretty," Fanny said conversationally.

"I don't like how she dresses," I said in a tone of dismissal. "I'm glad she stayed in Bath this visit."

Mary curled a lock of her hair around her finger. "Shelley though. I like height in a man, and sensibility. Did you hear how rapturously he described Bath?"

"He is nothing like Papa, for all that he claims to be a disciple," I agreed.

"Papa is old," Willy said.

"He is bent over by all the writing he does, poor thing." Fanny ran her fingers down Willy's discarded socks, feeling for spots where the wool needed reinforcing. She tucked one into her apron.

Mary's gaze slid over her workmanlike attire. "I don't think Shelley will grow old and bent. His spirit will keep him upright and strong."

I snorted. "Who cares, as long as his lips stay full and soft, right?"

"Jane!" Fanny cried, though still in that soft tone she never rose out of, no matter the provocation.

"He is very attractive," Mary agreed, "but his best quality is his mind."

Chapter 2

Mary

Mary, Jane, and Fanny perched on Willy's bed while Jane sang a ballad she had heard on the streets about Jack Sheppard, that famous criminal who had escaped from Newgate.

She had a lovely singing voice. When Jane finished the tragic tale with the folk hero's hanging at Tyburn, she had tears in her eyes. Fanny had gone very pale. Mary worried about her stoic older sister much more than she did about dramatic Jane. She leaned over and squeezed Fanny's cold hand.

"Go to bed, dearest. Mamma has made you work much too hard today."

Fanny smiled. "It was worth it, to see Shelley enjoying the bread I baked."

"Be careful," Jane warned. "Papa won't like too much sighing over the poet. Besides, what is wrong with bread from a bakery?"

Fanny stood, though her eyes stayed downcast.

"I think you daydream as much as I do," Mary observed.

"Can you blame me?" Fanny asked. "This is not the life Mother wanted for us."

"I hate that woman for making us leave the Polygon," Mary agreed. "Sometimes I think I will die for the sight of a healthy tree and a patch of green grass underneath."

As if in answer to her words, the sounds of drunken male singing grew as men passed by the house. Though the juncture of Skinner Street and Snow Hill was a neighborhood of prisons, warehouses, and manufacturers, people lived above their businesses like the Godwin clan did.

"Some nights, we can even hear the prisoners wailing," Mary said aloud, twitching back the curtains to glance into the road.

"I never can," Willy piped from his bed.

"Haps when I hear them, it's the voices of the dead," Mary said. "Rather than the living who are locked behind those walls now."

Willy sat up in bed as if propelled, marionette-style, by strings. "Do you think so?"

Fanny blew out the candle. Mary took the hint and smoothed the curtains, still winter wool.

"I'll write down my thoughts and read them to you," Mary assured her brother. She caressed his cheek, then followed Fanny out. Jane came last.

The floor rattled as the front door opened and closed. Fanny took Mary's hand and pulled her upstairs into Jane's bedchamber, a narrow room that spanned the length of the house, so they could see the poet moving into the street.

"I wonder where he is staying," Fanny said.

"Somewhere grander than this," Mary told her.

Curiously, Shelley didn't wear a hat. He slouched into the street, and his long, lean, loose-limbed stride ate up the cobbles as he grew smaller and vanished into the darkness.

"A fine figure of a man," Fanny said, her nose touching the window and leaving a mark.

Mary agreed but didn't say so, enjoying the peaceful respite before Jane appeared. Fanny fussed around the room, straightening the clothes on their stepsister's pegs, until she came in.

"Come, Mary." Jane flopped onto her bed. "Tell us a story about the prisoner ghosts wailing."

"I'll have to think it up," Mary said and then began to quote. " 'This relation is Matter of Fact, and attended with such Circumstances as may induce any Reasonable Man to believe it.' "

"What's that?" Jane asked. The floor creaked as she kicked off her slippers and knocked them to the floor.

"Defoe, I think," Mary said, already considering the form of her story. If only Mother had written such fanciful tales, to give her ideas on how to construct them. "I'll consult his works in the bookshop for further inspiration. It seems like quite a good start to a ghost story."

Mary placed her slippers next to Jane's and walked down in her stocking feet, hugging the wall so as not to set off the worst of the creaking stairs. If Mamma heard her, she'd be set to mending something. Her stepmother never thought about the cost of candles when she could make her daughters work themselves into exhaustion after dark.

The bookshop's interior door hung open. Very odd, as Mamma was particular about making sure that the smells of domestic life, particularly cooking odors, did not damage the books.

Mary shrugged, glad she had come downstairs, because if Mamma had been the first to notice, she'd have no doubt blamed Mary. She lit the lantern kept in readiness for customers who wanted to browse in the dark corners.

While she knew exactly where Defoe was kept, she first went to a back corner of the shop and dropped to her knees, then pulled out a much-loved volume that Mamma kept in stock because she knew that it sold, even though it was anything but highbrow or philosophical. Ann Radcliffe's *The Romance of the Forest*. Feeling a little breathless, like a Gothic heroine about to swoon, she opened the book to her favorite page. With the lantern held over the engraving, she examined the bare legs of the man removing a blindfolded girl from a house.

She bit her lip as she looked over the engraved musculature, feeling a familiar shiver dance up through her body. Did Shelley have legs so magnificent? He certainly possessed the broad shoulders and narrow waist of the figure on the page. She set down the lantern when it shook in her hand.

"Oh, to see a form like that," she whispered to herself. None of her Scottish suitors had possessed a body she wanted to caress. As such, none of them had enticed so much as a kiss from her. After a last heated glance, she closed the book and tucked it away again.

The next shelves were in front of the bow windows. The Juvenile Library was shelved there, at the perfect height for children. Works of historical merit were on the other side. Mary rose.

Her foot twisted as she took the first step. She grabbed for the edge of the bookcase with one hand, the other gripping the lantern tightly. Her fingers were trembling by the time she righted herself. She reached down and swiped at her foot. Something sticky coated her fingers. What was on the floor?

"Honestly," she muttered to herself. More cleaning. She set the lantern on the bookcase and walked past the windows. Slatted lines from the shutters were illuminated by the oil lamp that burned all night at the corner of the road.

Distracted by the sudden reflected light, she tripped again. "Blast," she cried.

When she tried to take another step forward, her way was blocked by something solid. Confused, she prodded it with her foot. It felt warm, dry, and slightly yielding. She backed up to take the lantern in her hand again, then cupped the side of it with her hand to keep the illumination from the road. When she reached the mass again, she held the lantern out over the floor.

Her mouth dropped open when she saw what lay in front of her. A man, like something out of a painting of the French Revolution, was sprawled on the floor. Facedown. She swept the lantern over his body. Her hand shook as she saw first one knife, then another.

The first was impaled in his back. The other, in the mysterious recesses between his legs.

"Faith!" Wobbly, Mary blinked hard, then forced herself to kneel down beside the sprawled figure, to touch the man's hand.

Still warm. She squeezed it, feeling that strange sensation of callused male flesh under hers, then dropped the hand. What was she doing? Molesting a corpse?

She scooted back, her eyes closed, then opened them again, feeling her lips tremble at the sight of the dark blue velvet coat, the dark stain around the knife gleaming wetly in the light. She knew that coat. Shelley! That fine figure of a man, ended so cruelly. They had just seen him leave not twenty minutes earlier. Had he been accosted in the street and dumped here?

"I could have loved such a being." Tears sprang to her eyes, and she let them fall, keenly feeling her sensibility. Hadn't he said he was a new father? And his poor young wife, not even twenty yet, a widow.

"Mary?"

Drat that Jane. Could she not offer up a moment's solitude to anyone?

Her stepsister's footsteps came closer, along with the bobbing of a candle flame.

"Don't come any closer," Mary warned. She set the lantern down.

Ignoring her, Jane came down the space between the bookshelves and turned in the nook in front of the windows.

"What are you doing?" she asked.

Mary scrambled to her feet, hoping to block her sister's

view. The candle wavered as Jane took in the scene. She gasped loudly.

"What," Jane asked, "is that?"

"Knives," Mary said. "Murder has been done here."

"What?" Jane repeated, some frantic power coming into her voice. "Papa?"

"No," Mary said, grabbing the candleholder before the candle dropped. "Shelley."

She saw what was going to happen and held up her other hand, hoping to forestall it. But she failed, and Jane, coming closer, screamed. Mary bent under the onslaught and grabbed her sister's hand.

"Hush," she begged, pulling her away. "We have to tell Papa before the watch comes."

Though Jane resisted, Mary pulled her through the bookshop, then forced her to sit on the steps and hold the candle while she went back for the lantern. She set it on the table in the hall.

"Stay here," she commanded.

"But," Jane whispered. "But the body."

"Papa will know what to do."

"But the watch."

"Papa should call them, not us. Do you want him surprised?"

"The bookshop," Jane said next.

"Yes, it's very bad," Mary agreed.

"It isn't S-Shelley," Jane stuttered. "He just left."

Mary pulled the handkerchief from her sleeve and tucked it into Jane's unresisting hand. "It must be," she said. "Who else? Cry quietly, please." Hoping her sister obeyed, she picked up her skirts and ran up the steps to her father's library.

Her father was not at his desk, though a candle still burned under her mother's portrait. Mary blew a kiss to the serene figure. The painting included her, since her mother had been in an expectant condition when Opie painted her. Loathe to do so, she blew out the candle. Her father never thought of the expense. As always, the family was mired in debt.

She went up past the next floor, which contained the schoolroom, and to the third, where the boys and their parents had their rooms. The arm that had given her so much trouble these past years twinged as she knocked. She suppressed the feeling, not wanting the old troubles to return. Older now, surely, she had some control over her body?

Mamma opened the door, holding a candle, still dressed in brown silk, which creased and pulled over her porcine curves.

"Mamma," Mary said, "I need Papa."

"Whatever for, girl, at this time of night? Get to your bed. You have the shop to mind tomorrow."

"It's important," Mary said. She didn't want to explain, but she was afraid of what Jane might do if she tarried. It wouldn't surprise her to find her stepsister supine over the body, sobbing dramatically. Jane was simply unmanageable.

Mamma huffed and turned into the room. Mary heard her father rumble; then he appeared in the doorway, hurriedly thrusting his arm into his coat. His wife helped him pull it on. Though he still dressed plainly, like the dissenting minister he had once been, fashions for men were tight.

"What is it, Mary? Is someone ill? Do I need to fetch a doctor?"

"It's past that, Papa."

Mamma gasped theatrically and put her arms around her husband. "Willy? My son?"

"No, ma'am," Mary said. "Shelley is dead."

Even in candlelight, Mary could see the color drain from her father's withered cheeks.

The Godwinian philosophy was that anyone who needed funds was entitled to them, and her stepmother's bad business decisions over the years had brought them to this calamity. A rotting house, a rotting business, and unpleasant lives.

Her father cleared his throat. "How dreadful."

"It gets worse, Papa." She paused dramatically. "He has a knife in his back and another in an indelicate place. And he's on the bookshop floor."

Mamma sagged against him instantly. Mary stepped forward, holding back a curse, and helped him drag her to the bed.

"We don't have time for this," she hissed. "Jane is downstairs. I'm afraid of what she will do."

"Very well," her father said.

"Nooo," Mamma moaned predictably. "We'll be out on the street without his aid."

Her father's lips tightened, but Mary tugged him away, avoiding the warped board in the hall that everyone tripped over. Her heart sank with the certainty that he thought only of Shelley's lost money.

Down the stairs they went, not attempting to avoid the squeaky spots. Jane had not moved, uncharacteristically, though she was splayed flat across the lowest tread, one hand to her ear, the other to her chest.

"Such beauty that would make the gods weep," she said, her voice not so different than her mother's moaning. "A tragic end, cast up on the shores of immortality!"

"Compose yourself," her father ordered. "And remove yourself from the stair."

Jane slowly rose to a sitting position, her hands still in place.

"Very graceful," Mary said acidly and followed her father into the bookshop.

"Where?" he asked.

"In front of Defoe," she told him.

He took Jane's candle and walked through the aisles uncertainly. Unlike Fanny, Jane, and Mary herself, he didn't work as a shop assistant.

"On the left," Mary pointed out when he nearly went in the

wrong direction. He had no need to read the books here. As a collector, a habit he could ill afford, his upstairs library was stuffed with books.

He exhaled loudly as he came across the finely dressed figure sprawled out on the floor.

"It is Shelley, isn't it?" Mary's voice trembled as she stood at her father's side.

His chin tucked into his cravat as he took in both blades.

"That's very bad," Mary said softly, pointing at the one between his legs.

"They will have to go before I move him." Her father gave her the candle and bent over the body. He huffed a bit as he pulled out the blades.

Jane trotted up to Mary, but her eyes moved in their sockets as their father removed the second blade.

"Don't you dare faint," Mary ordered, then thrust the candle at her. She pulled out a handkerchief so she could take the knives. They were still wet, and not some blood-rusted old blades from a Gothic novel but fresh-forged and plain, like a cook might use.

"Jane," her father said, his voice measured. "Run upstairs and fetch a bedsheet. If I roll him over, he will stain the floor."

Jane made a gagging noise, then left, taking the candle with her.

"Can you see to open a shutter?" her father asked.

Mary complied. With him here, they had nothing to hide. She doubted the body could be seen from the street. Faint outlines could be seen in the shop now.

"You don't think the murderer is still here?" Mary glanced around, her pulse picking up.

"No. I have heard nothing but us."

"When was there time to do this?"

"There are several fundamental issues," he said after a pause. "Why did Shelley come back? How did he get in? The front hall contains the only door into the house. There are no secret entrances. We share two of our four walls with other build-ings."

Light floated along the wall as Jane reappeared, holding a sheet.

"Keep it away from the flame," Mary said sharply. "This house is a torch waiting to ignite."

Papa placed the sheet alongside the body, then walked around it, as if considering the mechanics. Mary's nerves screamed with horrified sensation. Finally, he went to his knees, using the wall for support, and slid his hands under the torso.

"Mary, take the legs," he said. "He is too awkward to lift alone."

She put the blades on the edge of the sheet, shuddering, then complied. Together, they flipped the surprising heaviness of the form. She wouldn't have thought someone who ate so lightly would weigh so much. Maybe it was because he was dead.

Jane gasped loudly. She'd moved to the head and held the candle high.

Mary saw what she did. "Faith, you were right! It isn't Shelley!"

Her father put his hand on her shoulder. "Then, who is it? I don't recognize him."

"No," Mary agreed. "I've never seen him."

"His hair is like Shelley's." Jane's fingers went to caress it. "I see why you mistook him."

"Don't touch," Mary said. "You might raise his ghost."

Jane's fingers twitched but didn't move closer.

"Don't talk nonsense," their father insisted.

"It stopped her," Mary whispered.

His lips tightened, that familiar look of disapproval. Jane might be considered ungovernable, but Mary had been sent away far more than her stepsister. She missed those days when she could do no wrong, when her father had been a widower and not a husband.

"Now what?" Mary turned her attention back to the corpse.

"I'll go for the watch. The two of you stay here and watch the house. Don't let anyone in the door unless they are with me." He hesitated, looking at the body again.

Mary stared down at the face. Eyes half-closed, teeth exposed by slack lips, the features relaxed in death. Not a bad face, though candlelight hid much. "He doesn't look any older than Shelley."

"The villain thought it was him?" Jane suggested, voice trembling. "You remember Shelley's letter to Papa said someone had tried to kill him once."

"True," their father agreed, "but it does not follow that this is connected to Shelley in any way. Someone tried to take his life in Wales, not London. The assailant is unlikely to have followed him."

Mary shivered. "Where is Shelley?"

Her father glanced around, as if the poet might yet be waiting in a dark corner to be discovered. "He left some time ago. We had a talk, and then I let him out." His fingers lifted. "I am sure I set the latch."

"You forget sometimes," Jane announced.

"It doesn't matter," Mary said, defensive for her father. "Death comes when it will."

Her father took one last look at the body, then sighed and set his gaze on her.

"We will stand guard here until you come," Mary said, taking the candle from Jane.

"I may not return with the watch," her father cautioned. "I want to look for Shelley, wherever he is. I know he is staying with a friend, so I will inquire at those rooms first."

When he stepped away, Jane caught his wrist as he tried to pass her. "Go quick and carefully, Papa. There is a murderer in the streets somewhere. You don't want to be next."

"Don't shriek, Jane." Their father pulled away and left.

Mary didn't hear the lift of the latch, just the door opening and closing. The door hadn't been locked. "Secure the door," she hissed at her sister, unwilling to leave her vigil for the dead body.

After Jane walked away, Mary examined the body as dispassionately as she could, doing her best to ignore the scent of death, a far more complex aroma than she might have expected. They would have a time scrubbing the blood from the floorboards. No doubt Jane would claim she had a music lesson while Mamma set Mary to the odious task.

But enough of her resentments. She pushed the thought of Mamma aside and scanned the body. The young man's linen was good, white and no more creased than from a day's wearing. The velvet coat had been tailored to his broad shoulders. Shelley tended to hunch, but his shoulders were about the same width as those of this duplicate. The coat wasn't blue, she now realized, but green.

She let the candle drift slowly down his body, not being too missish to avoid the sight of the mangled crotch. His breeches had been torn by the knife, but it wasn't as if anything had spilled out of the gash.

Down to the boots, which likely had been put on freshly polished that morning. A young man of some vanity and wealth?

When she heard heavy footsteps on the stairs, her head jerked up. She had put Mamma out of her mind, but she had forced her way back again with an appearance.

Jane spoke in a low voice at first, but then it steadily rose into the shriek her father had cautioned against. Her mother followed suit, pacing Jane across the floor until she, too, saw the body. Her screech filled the air. If they hadn't lived in a neighborhood of prisons, surely the watch would have come running at the hideous sound.

Mary held out her arms, blocking the corpse with her own body. "Don't come any closer," she begged. "Papa will bring the watch."

"That group of drunks?" Mamma snarled. "What good will they do?"

"I don't know," Mary said. "Call the coroner, I suppose? Look for suspicious people?" She sidestepped to block her stepmother from getting around her.

"Who is it?" she asked. "Not Shelley? We need his money."

Mary shook with fury. The handsome poet's life reduced to nothing but his father's assets? Despicable. "It is not Shelley, madam. Calm yourself."

Jane appeared at her mother's shoulder. "It really isn't, Mamma. He's a stranger."

Mary's slight form was no match for Mary Jane Godwin's bulk in a rage. The older woman grabbed her arm and pulled her out of the way. Mary gasped with pain as she stumbled.

"Bring me the candle, girl."

Jane took the candle from Mary's hand with an apologetic noise, then hurried to her mother. Mary rubbed her sore arm, which would show bruises in the morning, and thought darkly of how she might escape this tilting house, this rapacious woman, the stench of the slaughterhouses and prisons nearby.

"It's not Shelley," Mrs. Godwin announced.

"We know, Mamma," Jane soothed. "I never thought it was."

Chapter 3

Mary

A couple of minutes later, Mary, peering through the book-shop door, heard men's voices grow louder as they came up the street. A key scratched in the lock, and the front door opened. Her father entered first, followed by three men, scenting the interior with tobacco and gin fumes.

Two of the men hung back with Papa, but the third, holding a lantern, walked right past Mary and inserted himself between her stepmother and Jane.

"Who's this blade, then?" the man asked around his unlit cigar.

"I've never seen him before," Mamma said.

"Two knives, you said?" he called over his shoulder, heading toward the windows and the corpse. Mary followed him.

"Yes, the very same ones I showed you," Papa confirmed. "Very plain, no markings."

The watchman poked at the dead man's leg with his boot, then held his lantern over the face. "Who turned him over?"

"We did," Papa said calmly, coming to stand next to Mary. "We thought it was our dinner guest, returned to the building."

"Maybe 'e did the killing," the watchman suggested.

"No," Mary gasped. "He's a gentleman."

The watchman sniffed. "Damme, this isn't the work of a duel." He gestured the other two men forward. They roughly turned the body facedown. He handed the lantern to one, then crouched to inspect the two knife wounds. After making a variety of sniffing sounds, he got to his feet, wiping his hands on his breeches. "That's a wound no man wants to receive. A woman was involved, no doubt."

"You can't think a woman did this, sir. The very idea." Mamma clicked her tongue.

"I didn't say a woman done it," the watchman said. "But a woman is to blame. You don't slice into a man's bait and tackle without reason."

One of the subordinates giggled. The high-pitched sound bounced off the shelves eerily.

"Couldn't the friendship of two men turn equally deadly for a variety of reasons?" Mary asked.

The men ignored her. "We'll take a message to the coroner's house. 'E's not one to go about at night. Too dangerous. 'Is man will be 'ere in the morning to make arrangements for the inquest."

The lead watchman gestured to his men, and they walked between her stepmother and Jane.

"You can't mean to leave the body here," Mamma said. "Not on the floor of our livelihood. We have children to feed."

The lead watchman stopped and looked her up and down. "Looks like you feed yourself first, missus."

Her stepmother gasped. "How dare you, you—"

Her father cleared his throat. "Now, now, Mrs. Godwin. Beecham, isn't it? You can't leave the body here. It will spoil the books."

The watchman chomped on his cigar for the moment.

"We could bring down another sheet, if you please," Mary suggested. "To wrap him in."

"There is a warehouse next door," her father added. "Still on the premises, if you will, and not so bad for our business."

"That's not our job." The lead watchman swore, expressing his irritation.

Her father winced as he pulled three shillings from his pocket. He hated spending money. It simply added to his debt. Three shillings was a lot for the watchmen, though, and the lead watchman snatched the coins.

He chewed wetly on his cigar. "If you'll take one shoulder, I can take the other, and the boys can take the feet."

Her father nodded. Mary ran downstairs, where the sheets they had washed on Monday were waiting to be ironed. She found a stub of candle in a holder on the mantelpiece of the kitchen fireplace and lit it in the nearly banked flame, then took it into the scullery. It took a minute to decide which sheet was most worn and large enough to contain a young man's body. She chose a much-mended sheet from Jane's preferred bedding. It would serve her right for all the shrieking.

When she returned with it, Jane gave a cry of outrage, but a curt order from their father hushed her. The four men set the sheet on the floor next to the body, then rolled the corpse and the first sheet into it.

"The stains," her stepmother muttered. "Oh, why us?"

Mary watched as the lead watchman carelessly tossed one side of the sheet over the dead man's face. Would she ever see it again? And if so, what state would it be in by then?

Her father must have shared her thoughts, for he muttered, "The floor of the warehouse will be colder than this. Better for preservation."

"The coroner will be 'ere in the morning," the lead watchman assured him. "Won't be a more suspicious death than this in the night, and 'e looks like a gentleman, too. Someone will want to know what 'appened to 'im."

"I certainly do," her father muttered.

"Is there a door to the warehouse from here?" a watchman asked.

"No, we have to go into the street. That's the only door in," her father said. "Mrs. Godwin, please open the door. Girls, step out of the way."

The men gripped their assigned body parts firmly, then, at the lead watchman's instruction, lifted.

Mary stepped out of the way as they passed by with their awkward burden. Why hadn't one of them just tossed the body over his shoulder? "They'll need the warehouse key," she said to no one in particular.

Her stepmother growled. "I'll fetch the key from the office, and you can take it to them." She stomped out of the bookshop through a rear door that went to the office where she did the accounts.

A minute later, Mary followed the watchmen into the street. She didn't see any dark drops on the pavement. At least the sheet had contained the blood. She went next door, holding up her candle stub, the key in her other hand.

"Oh, very good," her father said when he saw her.

She unlocked the door, the sound of the metal loud in the recessed doorway.

"Put the key in my pocket," her father said, "and go back inside."

She tucked it away for him and obeyed, a little shiver going through her at the thought of being outdoors alone with a murderer lurking nearby.

Before she could return inside, she heard her father ask, "Did anyone pay you men tonight to act as a lookout at my house?"

"No, sir." She recognized Beecham's voice.

Her father continued. "Did anyone pay you to scout out a place to put a body in this neighborhood?"

"No, sir." Mary heard offense creep into the watchman's voice.

"How about after the fact? Did anyone other than me pay you tonight? To look the other way? Anything at all?"

"No, sir." The man cleared his throat. "A quiet night until this."

"Very well," her father said. A door shut, cutting off his voice.

Mary realized she was alone on the street. Could the killer see her now? She shivered in her thin silk evening dress. When she rubbed her bare arms, she felt gooseflesh. Even at this late hour, the throughfare remained distinctly unquiet. Tormented noises drifted up the street from Newgate Prison. In the distance she heard a horse and carriage moving over cobbles. Someone sang a ditty outside a nearby tavern.

If she were a heroine of a novel, she would probably see a coach, lanterns glowing like yellow eyes, appear suddenly out of the dark, ready to sweep her away in consequence of what she had witnessed that night. It came to her suddenly, the title page of a novel, called *Mary, the Doomed; or, The Apprentice Bookseller of Skinner Street.*

> *A Romance; in which is depicted the wonderful Adventures of Mary, daughter of Fame, who was diverted from the track of virtue by the untimely death of a young man, who fell in her bookshop the victim of deadly violence, and, after she left the safety of her humble home, was kidnapped by the dastardly villain so he could obtain the person of a most rare beauty; how she was discovered despite the dark by a young poet, who had been tormented by the same villain; and the particulars of the means by which the poet caused the body of Mary to be conveyed in a*

sleep to the perfectly dreadful rooms where he accomplished his wicked machinations on the innocent virgin, whom he then falls madly in love with, though attended by a dastardly servant, who afterward betrays him to his lordly father, in the madhouse of which he is confined, and suffers torture; and how, to escape from thence, he assigns over his soul and body to Mary, who is ever faithful to him, even unto her ignominious death, shortly followed by his own.

The fantasy kept her warm as she darted back to the house. Mary hugged herself as she stepped into the front hall. Jane and her mother sat on the staircase directly in front of her, looking nervous and unhappy. A hint of shame swept through Mary as she realized she'd been having fun tonight, despite the murder and the fears of her stepsister and Mamma.

"It—it will be all right," she stuttered. "The body is removed. We will be able to open the bookshop tomorrow as usual."

"What will we do about the bloodstain?" her stepmother hissed ghoulishly.

"Clean it," Mary said with a frown.

Jane released her mother. She began to rock back and forth. "I can't," she said, then repeated herself.

"Don't be a goose," her mother snapped. "Go upstairs, Jane."

Jane, knowing an escape when she heard it, ceased her rocking and jumped lithely to her feet, then raced up the stairs.

Mamma gave Mary a speculative look as she lurched upright. Mary knew what was coming.

"Clean up the mess," Mamma said predictably. "I will set a kettle over the fire to heat for you, but then I will need to check on the children."

"Children?" Mary inquired. "You mean my brother, who is old enough to help clean up the mess himself?"

Mamma's upper lip curled. "Just go into one of your

daydreams, Mary. You can be Cendrillon, forced to clean the bookshop of her wicked stepmother."

With that, she stepped majestically down the passage. She'd expect Mary to haul the heavy bucket of hot water upstairs.

Mary's jaw tightened. The only way to escape the cleaning would be to run away. To where? She didn't have the money for passage back to Scotland, and the mere thought of boarding a ship made her stomach gurgle. Nonetheless, she wouldn't allow Mary Jane Godwin's pettiness to ruin her one good evening dress. She went upstairs to change. Maybe if she made enough noise, their kitchen girl would wake and come into the kitchen to help.

Ten minutes later she passed Mamma on the stairs, having changed into an old dress that had been too short in the skirt even before she'd returned to Dundee.

"Give the water another five minutes," Mamma instructed. "It will wash up faster if the water is hot."

"The blood, you mean?" Mary said evenly.

Mamma's candle was just bright enough that Mary saw her stepmother's eyebrow twitch. Mary smirked as she went downstairs. She was made of sterner stuff than the older woman.

The sound of the front door opening made her jump, though, as she arrived in the front hall. She held up her own candle and saw her father, alone.

"The body is secure?" she asked.

"Really, Mary," her father chided.

"How else would I say it?" She struck a pose. "Are the mortal remains of the tragic dead safely interred in their temporary tomb?"

"Not much better," her father muttered. He removed his hat and hung it on its hook. "I went up the street. I didn't see Shelley anywhere nearby or at his friend's rooms."

"He must have been the intended victim."

"I hope he isn't the murderer," her father said in a sour tone.

"Never! Mamma wants me to clean up the blood," she said tentatively. While he would never help with such a domestic chore, he might demand Jane aid her. Two of them could carry a heavy bucket better than one.

"It is good of you to help," he said. "I am most appreciative of anything you do to reduce your mother's considerable burdens."

"Stepmother," Mary correctly sharply. "Do not deny my own mother's existence."

"Of course not," her father said. "The first Mrs. Godwin is often in my thoughts." He plucked the candleholder from Mary's hand and went up the stairs, leaving her in the darkness.

Mary ran for the door and threw the bolt, then turned the lock. Why was everyone in this household so impractical? She muttered to herself as she felt her way to the kitchen, then looked between the kettle and another candle. She could never manage a bucket and a light source at the same time.

But heroines could rescue themselves in real life, even if it rarely happened in books. She lit a candle and took it up to the top of the staircase, then went back to pour the steaming water into a bucket. After adding a bottle of vinegar to her burden, she hefted the bucket and slowly climbed the steps. Her candlelight danced dimly along the walls.

She left her supplies in front of the bookshop door and went back for the candle. How was she supposed to see the parameters of the bloodstain in the dark?

After she had retrieved the bucket and had herself positioned on hands and knees in the approximate place where blood had been spilled, she realized she hadn't needed to worry. The blood was sticky on the wood boards. The stain would have to be scoured out of the wood in daylight, but she could at least get up the mortal fluids of the stranger.

Starting with a rag dipped in the vinegar, she worked the sticky stuff back into a liquid form, imagining that the contents of the bucket were turning into a ghastly brew. Not so far from the truth.

Her mind wandered predictably, considering how the poet hero of her story might rescue poor Mary, the daughter of Fame. But what of the real poet Shelley? If she'd understood her father correctly, the man had not been at home. Where was he this dangerous evening? Could he be lying hurt somewhere, or was he another pretty corpse somewhere in London?

Chapter 4

Jane

Mamma threw a little fit in the morning when she went to open the door and saw the disarray in the bookshop. Mary, Fanny, and I had to go in and make sure all signs of last night's corpse had disappeared before we'd broken our fast.

Of course, they had not. It still looked as if a terrible fight had taken place near the bow windows. I could see Mary had tried to clean the area well, but given the darkness and the blood, all she had managed to do was remove anything on the wood. A lot of brownish mess had been smeared around and had stained the surface in the process. It made me feel ill, for many reasons. But I had no time to examine my private thoughts.

Mamma wrung her hands and then threw them up, lamenting the cost of the repair. Fanny ran upstairs and came back again with a little rag rug she had made and placed next to Mary's bed, but it was too small to cover the stain. Which led to another round of laments and Mamma shouting insults in

French. Fanny took the *"imbécile"* and *"stupide"* in composed silence, though her head flinched back at each stabbing word. Would she do better to scream back?

Mary's features had pulled into the center of her face, and she rubbed at her arm.

"There's a larger rug on the floor next to where we iron," I said in her ear. "Go get it before Mamma develops apoplexy."

Her expression didn't change. I knew she didn't like taking orders from me, since she was slightly older, but she skirted Mamma and left.

I thought it rather too long before she returned, she who had no guilty conscience, but the rug fit.

Mamma's posture relaxed. She glanced at the small rug, now crumpled next to the windows. "Take that to the wash pile," she ordered Fanny. "It's filthy now."

"It isn't," Mary said. "The stain was dry."

Mamma's eyes widened. I knew it was the sign of another explosion. I grabbed the rug and thrust it into Fanny's hands. Mamma stormed off behind her, no doubt to offer up more casual abuse.

I heard the church bells ring. "It's time to unlock the bookshop door."

Mary rubbed her arm and called out as she went to turn the key. "I had a lovely idea for a story last night. Do you want to hear it?"

"Not right now," I said, impatient. "Mamma may not return for three hours or might reappear in an instant."

Mary took up the place behind the counter. I pulled out the feather duster and began to tidy the books, keeping my ears open for Mary's conversations with customers. I dreaded who might arrive.

We had more than usual. Word of the violent murder was out. One man, who ran a school in Cripplegate, gossiped that the hunt for inquest jurors had begun. When I was halfway around the room, my apron already streaked with dust, Mary disappeared up the aisle toward the windows.

"Papa just left," she reported.

"A meeting?"

"He'll have to go to the inquest."

My fingers tightened on the duster. "They should ask for us. We found the body."

"I found him," Mary said after a pause. "I am not *we*."

"Only an instant before I came along," I pointed out. I wondered what choices I'd have made if I'd been first.

"Still," she said, "you can't take credit for my actions." Her head turned at the sound of the bookshop door opening. She went up the aisle.

I stayed behind. The rag rug, which had been constructed from old aprons over the winter, looked very out of place, a womanish design in a place of business. Though we did a trade in children's publications, this was no place of whimsy. That existed only between the pages of novels. Cold, hard money matters, that was at the heart of the bookshop. I'd learned that lesson well.

I shook out my apron and feathers in the street, then returned to dusting. I gave special attention to each and every book around where the body had lain. Who knew what I might find now that it was light? Spots of blood on guinea volumes? Could I sufficiently clean bloodstains from fine bookbinding leather?

In fact, we should have gone through the place with a fine-tooth comb this morning. All the intelligence that resided in this household had not come up with such a notion until I had. Happily, I was already on my knees to make the lower shelves tidy. I began to investigate with purpose along the full outer wall. I hoped to find nothing needing concealment.

While Mary sold one customer a copy of Papa's novel *Fleet-wood* and another a translation of *Aesop's Fables*, I dusted like I had never done before. Each book fairly sparkled with my attention, as if it had just come from the printer. I even had to take my duster out to the rain-streaked street and shake it a second time.

I blinked in the light after the relative gloom of the bookshop. The temperature outside felt the same as inside the bookshop, though wind lifted stray hairs from my temples as I walked to the side of the house, out of any possible view of my mother, to beat out the feathers. The street was busy with the business of the prisons and courts. I could hear the animals in the distance, being sold at the market, but before I could direct too much attention to their fate, a group of men coming from one of the legal buildings headed toward me.

Papa was one of them. They must be going to the warehouse to look at the body. I darted around the building and back inside, the feathers half-fluffed, not wanting him to see me and think I was malingering.

Inside, Mary gave me a curious look as I stomped toward the windows, but she was busy with a customer asking about our educational offerings for young ladies, so she couldn't ask me questions. I pushed the stain-covering rug a little forward; then I went to my knees. Judiciously, I applied my duster to every book on the top shelf underneath the window, peeking up every so often to see if the coroner, the jurors, and Papa were coming here.

When the books on the top shelf were clean, I applied myself to the bottom. Some Wollstonecraft titles were here, growing old. We all knew that Papa had destroyed his first wife's reputation with his scandalous biography of her. Though the biography was nearly as old as Mary, her mother had not returned to popularity, except in that peculiar set of young idealists like Shelley.

My feather duster skittered along a book, making a crackling sound. Had I torn a page? Disaster if my error was caught. I pulled the book out. It was a copy of *A Journey Made in the Summer of 1794* by Ann Radcliffe. The pages remained uncut, and the book looked undamaged. I exhaled my pent-up breath with relief. What had crackled? My stomach churned with nerves.

I pulled out more books, all travelogues. They were fine, but when I reached in again, I pulled out a scrap of paper. Examining it closely, I was relieved to see fine notepaper rather than something from one of the books.

The words on it were handwritten in a beautiful script, not typeset. I climbed to my feet and held the scrap to the window so I could read it. It said, *We Poets in our youth begin in gladness; But thereof come in the end despondency and madness.*

A rather sad quotation. Surely the likes of Percy Shelley and other young men that Papa nurtured would never end so sadly. And yet we'd found a young man dead on this floor only the night before.

I glanced to the floor and saw the stain winking at me. Quickly, I adjusted the rug and went to show Mary my clue after our next customer left, followed by the porter holding their wrapped purchases.

Mary frowned over the scrap. "It's Wordsworth. Was it in a poetry book?"

"No, behind a travelogue." I snatched it back. "Do you think it fell from the dead man's hand?"

Mary stood up from the desk and walked languorously to the front windows.

Impatient, I danced around her. "Look! Here's where the body was, and here is where the paper was."

"I don't think it's possible," she said. "The bookshop door must have been closed, or surely Papa would have heard something from his study. If the doors were all closed, there would be no breeze for papers to float about."

I couldn't quite bring myself to lie down on the rug. Surprisingly, though, Mary did just that. She tried various ways her hand could have fallen open and the paper could have floated out onto the shelf.

"Not likely," I agreed. "He was dead facedown."

"Could he have placed it there before he succumbed to his wounds?" Mary asked. "My issue is that it sounds more like a suicide note than something to do with a murder."

"Maybe a suicide pact? His partner in death stabbed him and then went off to quietly take poison?" I pulled out the book the note had been behind, probably because it had fallen from the top shelf when I dusted. *Memoirs in the Life and Travels of George Fraser* was the title.

"Military memories," Mary said. "But this man did not have a military look."

"No interesting scars?"

"Nothing in candlelight," she said thoughtfully. "If he didn't leave the scrap there, could it have been the murderer who did? When did you last dust the books?"

We glanced at each other, then giggled.

"I remember Fanny dusting a couple of weeks ago," I said.

"It probably has nothing to do with the murder, but we shall keep it in mind." Mary turned at the sound of the front door opening.

We went to the counter, ready for the next customer; however, the bookshop door didn't open. Through the glass I saw Papa.

"Back from the inquest," I said, darting for the bookshop door.

"What happened?" Mary asked behind me as I walked out to confront him.

Papa put his hat on its hook. "Don't you two have duties in the bookshop?"

"No customers right now," I said. "Really, Papa, don't keep us in suspense."

He regarded us both coldly. I could tell his mind was already half in his writings upstairs on his desk.

"Please, Papa," Mary said, touching his arm. "I did find him."

He nodded at her. "Very true. Well, there is little to report."

"Shelley?" Mary asked. "Was he found for the court?"

"Yes. He gave valuable testimony."

I clapped my hands. "Oh? Did he admit to the murder?"

"Come now." Papa gave me a disapproving look. "The coroner had no information or insight about who killed the man, but at least the corpse was identified."

"By Shelley?" Mary intuited.

Papa nodded. "The very same."

I saw two men on the street. I knew they were about to open the door. "Who was he?"

"Cecil Campbell, an old classmate of Shelley's from Oxford who was also a poet."

"That is very good," Mary said. "I thought he was a poet."

"So did I," I interjected. Aping Mary seemed wise.

"The body has been released. Shelley had an address for the late Mr. Campbell, so I assume we will have our warehouse back very soon."

The door opened, and the men came in. Papa greeted them after a warning look at Mary. She returned to the counter, and I went upstairs to tell Mother the news.

That evening, after all the lights were off downstairs and we sat around the fire after supper, we heard a banging on the front door. Mary, Fanny, and I glanced between one another, a bit nervous. Papa went downstairs. Mary and I went to the window to check the street. While it was too dark to see, the house rattled as Papa walked out.

"It must be someone to collect the body," Mary said. "Oh, I wonder if Shelley is downstairs."

"Papa might invite him up for punch after," I mused.

"We haven't the money to buy lemons," she scoffed. "Wine perhaps."

"They will probably just go to the tavern, to keep the talk of death away from tender ears."

"With Mr. Campbell's corpse between them?" Mary turned away from the window. "Where is the cart?"

"Oh, good point. They aren't going to carry a body through the streets."

Mary opened the window to lean out. The smell of cabbage-scented urine hit my nostrils. Someone had been using the bookshop window as a trough very recently. "It's too dark to see much."

"What is going on, girls?" came Mamma's voice. "It is time for Willy to go to bed."

"Just checking on Papa," Mary said.

"He can take care of himself," she said tartly. *"Vite, vite."*

When we were upstairs supervising Willy, Mary clicked her tongue against the back of her teeth. "I cannot stand that woman! We don't know who was at the door. We had a murderer here last night, after all. Is Papa safe?"

"The knock was quite aggressive," I offered.

"Come now," Fanny said gently. "Papa didn't cry out."

Willy only reluctantly went to bed that night. He had a habit of pulling at his buttons. All three of us repaired different spots on his shirt while taking turns singing to him.

When we finally went downstairs, it was to the happy sight of Papa coming up them.

Mary clattered down the steps ahead of us, holding a candle. "Who was it? Did Shelley come?"

"No, child. Mr. Campbell's sister's husband came," Papa explained.

"We didn't hear wheels or a horse," I added.

"I wonder that you should have, as you had better things to

do than listen," Papa said. "There was a horse and a cart waiting at the warehouse. Mr. McAndrew had to come to me for the key."

"Did he seem like a killer?" Mary asked.

"No, child. He seemed a respectable sort of person."

"Did you have to help him carry the body to the cart?" Mary's candle wavered. "Did Charles help?"

"No, McAndrew had the driver help him."

"Had it changed a great deal?" Fanny asked. "The body, I mean."

"That is a very ghoulish question," he chided.

"I'm sure Mary wants to know," I said. "For one of her stories."

"I'm sure she's seen a body dead a day before." He cleared his throat. "Now, if you will excuse me."

We obediently pressed ourselves to the walls so he could pass by.

When a door above us had opened and closed, Mary said, "Yes, I've seen a body dead a day, but never one so handsome!"

Fanny sighed. "I cannot believe we could have a man stabbed in the bookshop, and no idea who had done it or why. Was Mr. Campbell even a customer?"

"Excellent question," Mary said. "Let us consult the register."

I took the bookshop key from the drawer in a little table in the front hall and unlocked the door.

Fanny shifted from one foot to the other. "We should be going to bed."

"You don't have to come," Mary said impatiently, sweeping past me. She set her candleholder on the counter and began flipping through the register, her hair uncomfortably close to the flame.

I went to her and coiled her hair into a loose knot at the back of her head. "Do you see Cecil Campbell listed?"

"Hold the candle up," she ordered.

I obeyed, moving the light along with her finger. She turned a few pages. We spotted the name Campbell at the same time.

"John Campbell," she read.

"Too common a name," I said. "Might not be a relation, even."

She kept turning pages. Fanny had hovered in the doorway, but I heard her go back up the stairs.

"Such a wet blanket," Mary muttered, flipping back another page.

Just as my arm was starting to tire, she saw it. "Here we are. Cecil Campbell. Purchased Mother's *A Short Residence in Sweden, Norway, and Denmark* two months ago."

"You would have liked him, I expect," I said, patting her shoulder. I lowered the candle.

"Yes," she agreed and closed the register with a thud. "No one who buys work by Mary Wollstonecraft is unworthy."

Chapter 5

Mary

"Shelley is here!" Fanny came into the schoolroom on Monday morning, her eyes shining.

Mary leaned away from Willy's primer. "That doesn't really matter, does it?" she asked carelessly. "Really, Fanny, we're trying to work here."

Willy's Latin tutor gave an obstreperous little cough.

Fanny ignored the tutor and waved her hands at Mary. "Come downstairs. He's calling for you!"

Mary was on her feet before she realized it. "Me? But why?" She smoothed the skirt of her favorite tartan dress. It did not match fashion at all, but it made her look like an original.

"Because Papa is out. Shelley went right out of the bookshop and upstairs to the office. Oh, he was on a mad tear." Fanny stepped back and banged her leg against the little pulpit Willy used to give weekly lectures to the family.

"Maybe he's the friend for you." Mary raised her eyebrows.

Fanny blushed and shook out her skirts.

"Don't go," Willy whined. His tutor frowned at him.

"I must. Don't learn anything without me," Mary cautioned and followed her sister out of the room. "Where is Jane?"

"Working in the bookshop, but it can't be long until it's time for her music lesson. Then you're to be in the bookshop."

"You'll take my turn, won't you?" Mary asked, glad Jane was safely occupied. "I must go to Shelley." Not waiting for an answer, she edged around her sister.

Her slippers slapped on the rickety treads as she dashed to the lower floor. The familiar scents of ink, tobacco, and paper filled her nostrils as she peeked into the library.

Shelley was wreathed in daylight, looking like a celestial being or, even better, a fairy creature, with his sandy curls and elven features. He had a good, strong body, though. Altogether a most arresting sight, and better than any hero in a novel. Should she model Diego or Fernando on him going forward?

"Mary!" he cried. No one could have missed the delight in his tone.

What had she done to deserve such joy? She stood uncertainly in the passage. He came out from the room, then shut the door behind him.

Shocked by her own daring, she touched his arm. "I am so glad to find you living, sir. I was afraid the body I found was yours."

"I am glad it was not," he said gravely enough, though laughter created upturned corners in his lips. "Would you have grieved for me?"

"Yes," she said decisively. "You are Papa's favorite pupil, after all."

"I have a great deal to say on topics of interest to him." Shelley grinned. "What say you? What did you see that night?"

"I am sure you heard it all at the inquest."

He touched her hand. A spark of electricity jolted her flesh. She stepped back, shocked.

"Why, you are a Galvanist, sir."

"Do you need reanimating, Mary?" he teased.

"I have yet to be born," she said, turning serious. "I have been offered two births."

"You want neither choice?"

She shook her head. "I must find my way to something better. I feared for your life, you know."

He pressed her hand again. No shock came, but she noticed how very blue his eyes were.

"Do you know anything else? They did not call you to the inquest," he said, ignoring her concern.

She tried to think of something to say about the murder. "They mentioned the two knives and the placement of them in the body?"

He nodded. "A very personal crime, I would say. I don't wish to offend with plain speak."

"My eyes witnessed the horror. What power can words have?" she retorted.

"Anything else?" he asked.

"I cleaned up the blood, but the next day Jane dusted the area, and she found a scrap of paper behind a shelved book. It may not be related, but it was a Wordsworth quote." She repeated the words to him. "It is about a poet, but it more closely matches suicide, not murder."

He nodded. "I do agree. It may not be related. Did she find anything else?"

"No." Mary considered. "But she didn't keep looking."

"I think we should continue where she stopped," Shelley said.

"You want to crawl around on the bookshop floor?" Mary

asked, incredulous. His breeches were a bit ink-stained, to be sure, but his forest-green coat was immaculate.

"To find a clue? Definitely."

"Very well, then. Jane is leaving in just a few minutes, and then the bookshop will be all ours. Unless there are customers."

"Can I see the scrap she found? To fix it in my mind."

"Of course. I'll go up and fetch it. I'll meet you in the front hall?"

"By all means. I will join you there."

Mary ran to find the scrap of paper where Jane had placed it in a copy of *Evelina* next to her bed, but it was no longer there. She went downstairs, hugging the wall, not wanting to rouse her stepmother from wherever she lurked.

The front door opened and closed as she made the final turn, and there was Shelley, holding out his hand to her, as if waiting for her to enter a ballroom and be announced. What a proud thing it would be to be his wife at a fete! Of course, she had heard Mrs. Shelley acknowledged as a beauty, and no surprise, to match her fairy prince of a husband.

She took his fingers in her grasp, feeling that electric shock again. "Sir," she gasped.

"You feel it, too," he said, a look of bemusement on his face.

"You must be scraping your boots on the floor." She glanced down at them. They were a bit scuffed, another show of the poetic carelessness of his attire.

"I never do that, Miss Godwin." His blue eyes shone their truth at her. "It is the electricity of the heavens, sparking between us."

"La," she said, blushing. "I am unused to these London manners. I have been in rough Scotland for too long."

"Will you return?"

She'd been seriously considering it. Her would-be betrothed was too young to wed, but he was eager, and he was her friends Christy and Isabella's brother. She could remain in the family who had welcomed her. Papa would never force her to wed, but life as a young bride might be preferable to life as a shop assistant across the street from the gibbet. If there was not a third choice. But even Fanny hadn't managed to leave.

Still, London had its own charms. Her gaze went to Shelley's soft, full mouth. She tossed her curls. "I think not. I am not of a provincial mentality."

"Very good," he approved. "You should not be wasted in Dundee, you child of illustrious parents."

"I have long thought I am meant to have adventures," Mary ventured.

"Adventures of the body or of the mind?" he asked.

"Both," she replied promptly, leading the way through the bookshop door.

"I don't think Papa is returning before supper," Jane said pointedly as they walked in.

Shelley bowed over Jane's plump hand. "My dear Miss Clairmont, we thought to continue your very intelligent search of the area where the body was discovered."

"Did you see the note?" Jane demanded. "I found a note."

"Well, no, my sweet, but I heard the words."

"It wasn't in your room," said Mary, irritated.

Jane thrust her hand under the counter, and it came back with a piece of paper. "Here it is."

Shelley gave it a more thorough perusal than it deserved, given that Mary had already told him the text. "Good quality paper, torn at the top and bottom. I wonder where the rest is."

Mary shrugged. "It might not be here."

"Did you tear it out of a book when you found it?" Shelley asked.

Jane's usual high color heightened. "No. That was it. See, it is handwritten."

"Very good," he murmured. "Keep watch, dear miss, while we search." He wandered off toward the wrong part of the shop.

Mary took his arm and pulled him toward the windows facing toward the prison side. "That rug is covering the bloodstain."

Shelley pushed it aside with his boot. "A permanent reminder of that dastardly deed."

Mary nodded and pointed. "That lower bookshelf, behind the travelogue by George Fraser, is where she found it. Not tucked in."

He went lithely to his knees, contorted himself to see the volumes, then ran his hands along the books on the last shelf next to the travelogue.

Mary knelt next to him, then did the same with the books on the higher shelf. "Nothing here."

"No," he agreed. "But I am suspicious. A quote on a piece of paper with the top and bottom torn off it. What else was on that page?"

"More poetry?" she suggested.

"A salutation. A signature," he said, sliding down onto his belly sinuously.

"What are you doing?" Her voice squeaked.

His voice was compressed by his position. "There is space under the bookshelves."

"Just a couple of inches."

"Come. Your hands are smaller than mine."

She obliged, sliding to her belly next to him. So improper, but with him, it seemed a game. He peered into the darkness, thrusting his fingers in as far as he could. She managed to fit her entire hand in by keeping her wrist very straight.

"You're right," she gasped, feeling paper touch her fingers. She had trouble grasping it but finally slid it between her middle and forefinger and pulled back.

"Aha!" Shelley crowed, snatching it from her. "Faith, if it isn't the same paper!"

"What is it?" Mary asked.

Jane made her way toward them, gathering her skirts. "Did you find more?" Her voice quavered as she crouched down, too.

"It's a request for a meeting," Shelley reported as the girls pressed close, one at each of his shoulders. "Here at the bookshop."

"Meet me at Godwin's. Nine of the clock," Mary read out loud. "That's right about when we tuck Willy in for the night."

"Mr. Campbell was lured to the bookshop by someone, but was it for murder?" Shelley peered at the paper.

"Are you sure it is matched from the same note Jane found earlier?" Mary asked, thinking of other possibilities.

Shelley ran his finger across the top. "Torn on just the top. Same handwriting, which I don't recognize."

"Nor I," Jane said quickly. "Are you sure you didn't write it, Shelley?"

"Of course not," he said.

"But you knew Mr. Campbell," Mary clarified.

"Of course," Shelley said. "We atheist poets are a small circle."

"Why would someone lure Mr. Campbell to the bookshop after it was closed? How could they even think to enter?" Mary asked.

"They would have to have a key. The landlord, perhaps?" Shelley suggested.

"There really isn't one. The building is in dispute."

"Previous tenants?"

"We have been here for years," Mary said.

"Someone adept in picking locks, then," Shelley said, pocketing the note. "And why not? It might very well be another skill a murderer might possess. Though I wonder who might have wanted to kill Cecil Campbell. No one had yet shown interest in what he had to say. He hadn't the money to publish as much as I have."

"Still, an atheist," Mary said. "Such men have enemies, as you have learned. No matter how obscure."

"That is true," Shelley said. "It is ironic that our best readers are the government spies who watch us. The Prince Regent loves his spies."

Jane jumped up. Shelley looked startled, but Mary had heard the door open and close, too. The footsteps of multiple people sounded on the floor. They had customers. She tugged the rug back into place while Jane ran to the counter. Shelley undulated to his feet and cocked a knee against the bookshelf, patting his coat pocket.

"George Fraser?" he said loudly. "I have always wanted to read his memoir."

"Why so, sir?" Mary asked.

"He fought in Ireland. I don't know if Mr. Godwin told you my biographical details, but I spent some time there, encouraging the Irish."

"And Wales, too, I believe."

"Very true. I shall have to find a reason to visit Scotland next, to see what lure it has." He smiled at her.

"Oh, excellent, Miss Godwin," said a lady coming toward her, dressed in a white apron-front gown that was already stained with street dust. Mary recognized Caroline Barnard, who had been a contributor to *The Parent's Offering* with the Juvenile Library the year before. "I have an idea for something new."

"Very good," Mary said, inclining her head. "Papa is away just now, but I believe Mamma is in her office. I will take you to her."

She led the contributor to the inner door, past Jane, who was showing a bottle of ink to a gentleman customer.

Mary was occupied with Mrs. Barnard for quite some time. When her belly began to growl, she went to the dining room and found Jane and Shelley dining with Fanny and her father. Her father looked displeased to see her and sent her to tend the shop counter. She folded a slice of bread over a hunk of meat and departed in ill humor as Jane and Shelley chuckled animatedly behind her.

She unlocked the front door. Jane must have barred it to avoid customers coming in. Mamma would be angry if Papa reported Jane's misdeed, which he certainly would. He tolerated no behavior against his standards.

At the counter, she perched on the stool and ate her food. No one came in other than the porter, a short older man with a bulbous nose and a limited intellect. He could follow only one instruction at a time, but he managed very well with that. Mary handed him a package she had prepared for a school in Bloomsbury.

Everyone in their community who had heard about the murder must have appeared already. Disheartening, really, to see how little trade had resulted. Someone had purchased an *Aesop's* while she had been occupied, and a copy of one of the histories. One of her mother's books lay discarded on top of a bookshelf. She jumped off the stool and tucked it back into its proper place.

Skinner Street had never been her mother's home, but Mary liked to think some piece of her spirit lived on wherever her books dwelled. Feeling in need of comfort, she opened another of her mother's books to see the engraving there.

"Hullo?"

Mary turned, startled, the book slipping from her grasp.

An attractive man somewhat past youth, dressed in white

breeches and a brown coat, bent to pick up the book for her. He had very white teeth and black hair that curled wildly around his ears.

"Thank you," she said, taking the book from him and tucking it back into its place on the shelf. "Is there something specific I can help you find?"

"Are you a servant or one of the family?" he asked, his gaze running down her tartan dress and then returning to her face.

"I am Mary Godwin," she said, lifting her chin.

"Very good," he said, taking out a small notebook. "I understand you found Cecil Campbell's mortal remains?"

She took a step away from him. "Are you a reporter?"

"No, miss. The family has hired investigators from Bow Street to look into Mr. Campbell's death."

"You are a Runner?" She perused him slowly, fascinated. He had faint lines around his eyes, marking him as a man no longer young, though his face otherwise remained unlined. She suspected a boxer's body lay under the clothes, judging from how his coat fit.

"Yes, miss. Can you tell me what you saw last night?" he persisted.

"I really shouldn't do that without my father present." Mary transferred her weight from one foot to the other. If she took this man upstairs, she'd have to step away from the shop, which would anger her father. But she couldn't stay down here alone with him, either. "What is your name?"

"Abel, miss. Fitzwalter Abel."

She nodded and went to the table in the front hall. A bell rested on top of it, there for summoning, if anyone could hear it. Doubtful that it would raise anyone, since the dining room door had been closed, she used her entire arm to ring it loudly at the base of the steps.

When she didn't hear motion, she did it again. Eventually, a door opened, and soon after, Fanny appeared at the landing.

"Do you need assistance?" her sister asked.

"Jane," Mary said. "And Papa and Shelley. Tell them we have a Bow Street Runner here to interview us."

Fanny's mouth rounded. She disappeared back upstairs. Mary returned to the bookshop. Mr. Abel had his back to her and was thumbing through a book of Roman history.

"Why has it taken so long for Bow Street to become involved?" she asked. "Mr. Campbell was killed five days ago."

"I imagine the family had to gather funds."

"Mr. Campbell was a gentleman, I believe."

"You'd be surprised by the state of gentlemen's pockets sometimes," he said.

She gasped at his insouciant tone. "You think Mr. Campbell was poor?"

"I have only just now been assigned the case. I was following a smuggler into Cornwall last week and arrived back in London this morning." He pulled out a pencil and tapped his notebook with it.

"Oh. Perhaps Bow Street had no one available to take the case before?" Mary suggested.

Mr. Abel grunted, then asked, "How are sales?" before turning around.

"We get by," Mary said. "I was in Scotland this past year. I've been here for only a few weeks."

"Did you know the deceased?"

"No."

"What about the rest of your family?"

"He was known to the business. We found his name a couple of times in the records, but he doesn't seem to have made an impression."

"Is that usual?" he asked.

"If he wasn't a disciple of Papa, it is likely enough."

"A disciple?" he inquired.

Mary shifted. Where was Papa? "My father is very well known.

He's a philosopher. People who believe in his work often reach out to him."

"Hmmm," Mr. Abel said. "I'd never heard of him before today."

"He's an older man," Mary said defensively. "A generation older than you."

The shop door opened. Her father came in, followed by Jane. Mary heard the front door open and close. She walked calmly to the windows and looked out in both directions, only to see Shelley's forest-green coat disappearing up Skinner Street.

Why hadn't he stayed to be interviewed?

"Is something wrong, Miss Godwin—" Mr. Abel asked, coming up behind her.

"Who are you, sir?" her father interrupted.

The Runner turned and inclined his head. "Fitzwalter Abel, sir, from Bow Street. The Campbells have hired me. I'd like an account of last Thursday night's events, if you please."

"Do you have access to the coroner's report? I stated all I know," her father said, crossing his arms.

"I did read it, yes," Mr. Abel replied. "But your daughters were not called, nor was your wife, and I understand they were present. I like to be more thorough."

"I assure you that I offered all my family's impressions to the court. They also have the murder weapons. Why don't you trace their origins?"

"The knives, yes," Mr. Abel said. "No markings, nothing unusual about the shape or metal. Any blacksmith could make them. But your daughters might know something."

Jane stepped directly in front of Mary. "I found a note," she said, tossing her curls. When the Runner raised his brow, she smirked and continued. "Yes, a note that the dead man himself must have left."

"What?" her father asked, startled.

Jane simpered now that everyone's attention was upon her.

"There has simply been no time to tell you, Papa. The book-shop purely swarmed with people today."

Mr. Abel glanced around at the empty shop, then offered her a pointed stare.

She colored. "Earlier, I mean. In the morning. It has slowed since the rain began."

"I have found a second note since," Mary interjected. "It seems that we have two parts of the same note, in fact."

Jane angled her curves slightly in front of Mary. "I found my note while dusting the bookshelves."

"I found my scrap underneath the same bookshelf," Mary added.

The Runner held out his hand. Mary glanced at Jane, then pulled hers from her shop apron pocket. Jane produced hers; then they both handed them to him.

"A request for a meeting and a bit of Wordsworth," her father said after Mr. Abel read them aloud. "A meeting of poets?"

"A meeting of a murderer and his victim," the Runner said sardonically. "Do you often host meetings late in the evening?"

"Never," her father said. "I might have friends in the house upstairs, but not in the bookshop, and not without me present."

Mr. Abel nodded. "Thank you. I will make all suspects as we identify them duplicate the note so I can compare the hand-writing."

"That seems most sensible," said Mary, impressed by his cleverness. Such a man might be a valuable friend, but he had none of Shelley's geniality.

"Are you married?" Jane asked.

Their father spluttered, "Jane!"

The Runner smiled. "I am not, Miss, er, Godwin?"

"Clairmont," she said. "Mr. Godwin is my protector, er, stepfather."

Mary blinked at the bizarre wording. Her stepsister had almost made it sound as if she was their father's mistress! It must have been a clumsy attempt to get Mr. Abel thinking about such things. She shuddered with the horror of it.

"Mary? Have you taken a chill?" her father asked.

"I think so. I was crawling about on the floor, looking for more of the note."

"Go make yourself a cup of tea," he instructed.

She curtsied and left the bookshop, happy to escape. If only she dared go after Shelley. But she had no idea where his rooms were.

Chapter 6

Mary

"What do you think you are doing, miss?" Mamma screeched from the open doorway of Mary's room an hour later.

Mary set down her half-eaten slice of bread and butter next to her book. "I was shaky, so Papa sent me out of the bookshop to warm up."

"Warm up, not laze away the day reading novels." Mamma looked at the copy of *Pride and Prejudice* on the coverlet with disgust. "Wipe your mouth and return to the counter, please."

"I wasn't working at the counter," Mary protested. "Jane was."

"She has gone to her music lesson. Downstairs, miss, instantly." Mamma stomped out of the room. Her footsteps on the stairs sounded like a beer barrel rolling down the treads.

Mary made a face and stuffed her mouth with the toast remains, then wiped her greasy lips with her handkerchief. She rose from her bed, then walked sedately down the steps with the novel. Maybe she'd have time to read it—under the counter, of course—during the afternoon. If the bookshop had been busy, she'd have heard people coming in from her bedchamber window.

For better or worse, some traffic did appear. A tutor, pock-marked and smelling of onions, purchased some Juvenile Library titles for his charges. A vicar's wife, most disagreeable, came in to flip through some of the books, but not buy them, for signs of atheism. The lady finally left, chased off by the sight of two cigar-chomping young dandies, who were eager for copies of *Political Justice*.

One of them attempted to flirt with Mary, but when Mamma popped her head in, they left quickly, as well.

"Did they have money this time?" she asked acidly.

"They bought one copy between them," Mary said, putting the greasy coins in the cash box.

Mamma left, satisfied. A dozen minutes later, Fanny appeared with a cup of tea on a tray.

"What's this?" Mary asked.

"Mamma didn't want you to be chilled," Fanny said.

Mary rolled her eyes. "You mean she didn't want me to leave the bookshop."

"You mustn't always think the worst of her," Fanny chided. "She is the closest thing we have to a mother. You must admit she's the only mother you've ever known."

"Unlike you," Mary said mournfully. "Tell me something you remember about our real mother."

"She always had a book in her hands," Fanny said. "When you were great inside her, she balanced the book on her stomach. She would read me a few lines from *Original Stories from Real Life*."

Mary giggled at the image. At least they both had their mother's works, even the one Fanny had mentioned, which was written for "children in need of improving."

She turned her head when the front door opened. Maybe Papa had returned, and he would share another story, but instead, through the bookshop door came a young lady, very pretty and auburn haired, with a lovely pink-and-white complexion, and in a lemon-yellow dress and blue spencer. Behind her followed a man in his early twenties, with wild, curly reddish hair. He wore a yellow coat in a marigold hue, with a purple waistcoat underneath.

"Such fashionable people," Mary said to Fanny in a low voice.

Fanny's face lit up. "Mrs. Shelley! It has been an age since we greeted you here. Are you looking for reading material? Something for your daughter?"

Mrs. Shelley gave Fanny rather a pained smile. Mary did not like her for it, any more than she liked her for her elegant prettiness.

"Who is your companion?" Mary asked rather rudely.

The young man inclined his head. "John Hocke, miss. And you are?"

"Mary Godwin," she said coldly. Who else would she be in this place, with her own sister next to her?

"Ah, back from Scotland, I see," he remarked.

"We had dinner with your family one evening when you were returned before, I recall," Mrs. Shelley said.

"A couple of years ago, yes," Fanny said.

Mrs. Shelley looked down her nose at Mary. "I believe you'd had a fit of temper and refused to join us that night. I recall your Scottish friend, however. Delightful young lady. A Miss Baxter?"

"A fit of temper?" Mary repeated. "Illness, you mean. We'd just come off a boat, and I am forever dreadfully seasick."

Mrs. Shelley kept her little half smile. "That is not what your mother said."

"Stepmother," Mary corrected through tight lips. "She was thinking the worst of me."

"I find her a most congenial creature," Mrs. Shelley returned. "I am glad you are returned to mind the shop."

Mary wanted to claw the eyes out of that pretty face. How dare she? Why had Shelley wed such an insolent creature as she? Fanny, who could sense her most hidden moods, put her arm around Mary's waist to keep her in place.

Mr. Hocke twisted his ginger fringe into place, then resettled his hat. Mary's gorge rose in the presence of both of them.

"I believe I hear Willy calling from the schoolroom," she said, gently disengaging from Fanny. "Could you please watch the shop, Fanny dear?"

Mrs. Shelley took a step forward and blocked Mary. "I have just returned to town from Bath."

Mary gave her a sideways glance, unable to face the beauty full on. "Will you be joining your husband in his rooms?"

"My place is with my husband." Mrs. Shelley's tone was stiff.

Mary knew she'd scored a point against her, but wasn't sure why. She waited for the young woman to move, but she did not.

Mrs. Shelley put her hand over her abdomen. "I must speak to Mr. Godwin."

"He is not at home," Fanny said.

Mrs. Shelley glanced at Mary again. "What is my husband's exact address? I seem to have misplaced it."

Mary shook her head. "I do not know it."

The young woman licked her lips and moved her gaze to Fanny. "Miss, er, Godwin?"

Fanny's tone dulled with the slight. "I have never known it."

The front door opened and closed. Everyone paused, waiting. A moment later, the shop door squeaked, and Mary's father came in, two crumbling volumes in his hand.

"Papa," exclaimed Mary, relieved. "Here are Mrs. Shelley and Mr. Hocke to see you."

Mrs. Shelley's nerves had been strained past the point of social niceties. She beelined to Mary's father and put up her hands in a prayerful position. "Please, sir, reveal my husband's whereabouts to me."

"I do not know where Shelley is at the moment," he said, stepping around her and offering the books to Fanny. "Can you see what you can do to clean these up? They would be valuable if we can stop the mildew."

"Please, sir." Mrs. Shelley's voice cracked. "You must have visited his rooms."

"He wasn't there," Mary's father said.

"He was at the inquest. Who found him for that?" Fanny asked, taking the spotted volumes.

"The coroner," her father said dryly. "I am sorry I cannot help you, Mrs. Shelley. You know as well as I do that he moves around a great deal. I believe he stays with a friend now."

"When—when will you see him again?"

"I do not know." He turned to leave the bookshop.

Mrs. Shelley darted forward and touched his arm. "Please."

Without turning around, Mary's father said, "I will send Shelley a letter through friends of his, who are not so mobile. I assure you I don't know quite where the young poet is staying from night to night." He opened the door and stepped out before more could be said.

Mrs. Shelley turned around, and her gaze went to Fanny. "Is he telling the truth?"

John Hocke stepped forward, an angry expression in his eyes. "Yes, is he?"

"How dare you!" Mary said, her temper finally bubbling out. "How dare you imply my father is anything but truthful?"

Fanny gripped the edge of the counter. Mary could see the tremble in her shoulders.

"We simply need to know," Mrs. Shelley insisted.

Mary stepped directly in front of her, only inches from her perfectly pretty face. "You and y-your man-at-arms may feel free to leave the bookshop this instant. We will not be intimidated. Look at my poor sister! She is all of a tremble, and for what? Some girl who cannot keep her husband in line!"

Mrs. Shelley's eyes went wide.

Behind Mary, John Hocke said, "Well, I say!"

Mrs. Shelley looked down her nose. "I see that you do not have the priestly manners of your father. These Scotsmen you've been staying with must be rough and low class indeed."

She gestured to John Hocke and then took his arm. They had a bit of confusion at the doorway, as she clearly did not want to release him, yet they could not get through the narrow door abreast.

Mary laughed loudly and went to Fanny. She locked her arm around her older sister's waist as the pair struggled out of the door.

"Oh, what if they go upstairs after Papa?" Fanny asked when they were in the front hall. "He wouldn't like that."

"We must keep them apart," Mary agreed. "Papa may also have the desire to keep Mr. and Mrs. Shelley apart. Anyone can see from her gown that she has a most expensive taste in clothes, and Shelley has promised Papa the money he needs. What if she talks her husband out of it?"

"Go!" Fanny urged.

Mary let go and darted to the door, but then she heard the outer door open and close. No one made any noise on the stairs. It seemed the dreadful twosome had left. She resolved right then to make them villains in her book, the leaders of a robbers' den, perhaps.

Back in the bookshop, she went to the windows. Outside, a boy sold newspapers and two men with a heavy cart moved toward a warehouse, but Mrs. Shelley and Mr. Hocke were already out of sight.

She returned to the counter. "What do you think, Fanny? Mrs. Shelley said she had just come to town, but what about Mr. Hocke? I bet he knew Mr. Campbell."

Fanny shivered. "You think he is the murderer?"

"Perhaps," Mary said solemnly. "I don't trust either of them."

Chapter 7

Jane

I had my fingers in the heel of one black evening slipper just as the dinner bell rang. I quickly righted my slipper, grabbed a shawl, and went downstairs, unwilling to miss any of the gossip. Mary had been too busy to tell me much, but she'd given me reason to believe that exciting events had occurred in the bookshop while I was at my music lesson.

When I arrived at the dining room, Papa stood at the fireplace with Shelley, who looked even more carelessly put together than usual. He had no elegance of dress, despite the obvious expense of his garments, but I liked him better for it. Why should not the current fashion of wild hair for gentlemen be matched with wild garments?

Mary entered behind me. Though her steps were light, I heard her little cough. Shelley had not looked up at my entrance, but he turned away from Papa when he heard the cough. A broad smile crossed his face.

"Miss Godwin! Miss Clairmont!" he exclaimed, then inclined his head to each of us in turn.

We both curtsied, black silk flowing smoothly over our knees as we moved in tandem.

"I am surprised not to see your wife with you, sir," Mary said, a flush of indescribable emotion in her gaze. "Did she not find you?"

"My wife?" Shelley's smile faltered. "You must be mistaken."

"I admit I had not met her before, but Fanny was with me, and she recognized her. She had a companion, a Mr. John Hocke."

I swallowed hard at the sound of that name.

Shelley's expression darkened momentarily. "Perhaps I should speak to the elder Miss Godwin."

"I'm right here." Fanny's ever-blotchy face reddened in some places and paled in others as she came in. "Can I help you, sir?"

"My wife?" he queried.

"Why, yes, she came into the bookshop. We didn't know your current address." Fanny blushed at that. "And Papa was not at home."

Shelley nodded. "Where did she go? To her father's home?"

"She didn't tell us," Mary said. "But she was cradling her belly."

"Mary!" Mamma's face darkened with rage.

Mary stood her ground. "It's true, Mamma."

Shelley snatched his glass of wine off the mantelpiece and tossed it back in one long swallow. Mary seemed transfixed by the sight of him. After another look at Mamma's thunderous expression, I grabbed Mary's arm and pulled her to our chairs. I could see John Hocke was the least of our problems.

Mary shook me off as soon as we were seated.

Papa adopted a vaguely pleased expression. "Congratulations are in order to you, sir?"

"I—I," Shelley said. "Well, we are separated, sir."

"I believe you married again in March?" her father asked tersely.

"Yes, that was a formal marriage, to ensure our Scottish marriage from three years before was not questioned. We officially remarried because of some financial business."

"She hasn't been living in London," I said.

"No, she had just arrived," Mary assured me.

"Her sister?" Shelley queried.

"She only had the one companion," Mary said. "Her sister did not come with her."

"I should have inquired after her," Fanny said in a guilty tone.

"There is no need to be polite about that woman," Shelley said. "She is a most dreadful creature and has much to do with the failure of my marriage." He inclined his head. "Thank you for the news, ladies. I will track them down tomorrow, since they have failed to find me."

"If I can do anything to assist, please do let me know," Papa said.

No doubt he was anxious that the wife's reappearance did not affect his attempt to acquire funds from Shelley. I had listened at enough keyholes over the past months to know that ruin would soon befall the Juvenile Library, our publishing firm and shop, if more money was not found. I just wanted to help.

What would it be like to have a young, vigorous father rather than one who was past his best days? I had heard unkind things said about Papa in the street outside the bookshop after men left his study. How unlucky it was to grow old. Even Shelley had thought him long dead. He had said so in the first letter he wrote Papa, some years ago.

I looked over Shelley speculatively. Here was a young man. Already a novelist, a pamphleteer, and a poet. He, too, would be portly, lined, and losing hair someday, all but forgotten. But he had his fiery years ahead of him still, and many adventures yet to come. Mamma hadn't wanted such a creature as Shelley when she met Godwin. She'd had two children already and her own work. Security had been her hope. But I wanted adventure. A man to take me to Switzerland, so I could see the land of my ancestors.

Mary, though, I was afraid what she wanted was him. Shelley himself, and not the adventures such a man could lead, with all his flitting about from England to Wales to Ireland, even to Scotland. So much better than tending a dying bookshop.

I had never thought more that we were two halves of the same girl.

The next day, Tuesday, Mary, Fanny, and I were all in the bookshop. We had been ordered to dust every volume. We had assented with good grace only in the hopes that we might find some additional clue to the murder. Under another shelf? Behind another book? We had heard nothing from the Bow Street Runner who had come and taken away what little clues we had found.

"Anything?" Mary asked, looking cross and witchy, her hair flying around like candy floss, as she climbed to her feet.

"No," I said from the facing shelf.

"Fanny, we need the broom," Mary called. "I found a cache of dead flies in the corner bookshelf, gathered by a villainous spider."

Fanny came up from another aisle, tsking. "We must clean more often."

"We just did this six weeks ago," I groused.

Fanny swept up the spiderweb-entombed flies. "It must be done monthly. More even in the fall, when the mud comes in."

Mary shuddered. "I cannot abide this life."

"Then you can say yes to your Scottish suitor when he comes to ask Papa for your hand," Fanny said.

"And return to your precious Isabella, since we are not good enough for you," I snapped.

"Oh, Jane." Mary put her dirty arms around me.

"Stop that!" I pushed her away, then laughed when I saw the black fingerprints I had left on the straps of her apron.

"We're all going to need baths," Fanny said.

The three of us had been making so much noise we didn't hear Shelley enter until his voice announced him. "Who needs a bath?" he asked.

Mary blushed furiously. Fanny dropped the dustpan, spilling dead flies across the floor. I held my belly and laughed.

Shelley stared at the three of us. Fanny went to her knees and scraped up the flies with her fingers. I saw the moment his face blanched. He turned away in disgust. I reached for his arm, for I knew we could not turn off this wealthy future baronet, whose money Papa needed, and then I tugged him toward the front counter.

"Let my sisters deal with the mess," I urged. "We are all thumbs with embarrassment, sir."

"Where do all those flies come from?" he asked.

"Smithfield Market. They drive the animals down the road in front of our house every morning," I explained.

"Why did anyone think this a good place for a bookshop? Wasn't anything available in St. Paul's Churchyard?"

"I have no idea," I said. "This is the second site. It's much larger than what we had before."

"I promised my help to your father. How can I not, as his disciple?" Shelley said. "But there is much I do not like to see here. The daughters of Wollstonecraft on their knees in the dust?"

Did that mean he would not mind me on my knees in the dust, since I was Mary Jane Clairmont's daughter and not Mary Wollstonecraft's? I could not afford to ask. Instead, I simpered in the manner I'd seen at school.

"What brings you to the shop today?" I asked, touching his hand.

He moved his hand away, and rightly so. I was foolish to feign flirtation with this young man who had a wife hovering around town, looking for him. He shook his head.

"What is it?" I pressed.

Fanny walked by, holding the dustpan full of crumbling flies straight out in front of her, the broomstick in her other hand.

Mary opened the door for her, then closed it and came to the counter, laughing. "All she needs to do now is mount the thing and fly away."

"I do not like to see you two girls living in this filth," he said.

"I do not want a shopgirl's life," Mary said, giving him a sidelong glance. "I wish for a life of writing and study, like my parents had."

"Your wife is very pretty," I interjected. Shelley's attention had been on Mary for far too long.

"Yes, that is undeniable," he agreed. "But we are separated, you know. There is nothing left between us."

"Except the baby?" I asked.

"She has my daughter," he said.

"And another on the way," I pointed out.

"I do not know about that," he said, his voice going terse. "Listen, I do need to see John Hocke."

My pulse quickened. "To find out what your wife is up to?" I suggested.

"And to speak to him about Campbell's death."

"Oh," Mary exclaimed. "Were they friends? Fanny and I did wonder what Mr. Hocke might know."

"They were known to one another. It is a very small circle, trading ideas and scraps of poetry."

"Are all these young men followers of Papa?" Mary asked.

"*Political Justice* is our Bible," he said. "What do you say, girls? Will you come with me and meet some men of my acquaintance?"

The door had opened as he spoke. Fanny stepped in, her hands free of the domestic apparatus.

Shelley looked up. "You'll mind the shop, won't you, Miss Godwin? So that Mary and Jane can go with me on my call?"

Fanny pressed her lips together and bowed her head. "Of course, Shelley. Whatever you wish."

Shelley took Mary's upper arm with one hand and mine in the other and fairly towed us out of there. Mary pulled off her dirty apron. I followed suit, and we dropped them over the pegs. We exchanged our caps for bonnets and added cloaks over our dresses. I wished he had chosen Fanny for the call instead.

We walked out into the May sunshine, what we could claim of it. A golden glow peeped slightly through the clouds. A fly buzzed past my nose. I batted it as Mary lifted her face to the sun.

"Are your petals opening?" Shelley asked her.

"Indeed, sir," she said with a smile. "I much prefer to be out of doors."

"Nature is where I am happiest, as well," he agreed. "My thoughts trip their way out of my brain better when I am not enclosed. Where do you like to go when you can escape the bookshop?"

"St. Pancras Churchyard, where Mother is buried," she said promptly.

"It is a beautiful spot," I agreed. "There are willow trees around the gravesite."

"We will walk there some night after dinner," Shelley promised as we left a row of warehouses behind. "But for now, we will make our way to Cripplegate."

"That is where John Hocke resides?" I asked with an air of innocence.

"Yes. He has rooms in Jewin Street, above a furrier."

"Not very elegant," I said.

"He does not claim to have money. It's my wife who has the wealthy family."

"And you," I said artlessly.

"I am all but cut off, though," he said cheerily. "For my Satanic ways."

"Parents are a burden," I said, turning away from the sight of a cart horse making a noisy deposit in the road. "But it is terrible to deprive you of what should be yours."

"Luckily, the moneylenders see it your way, and not my father's. I will get by. When my grandfather dies, Papa will have to come to terms with me, for I will be the heir to the baronetcy then." He dropped my arm, which he had been holding, and lifted his hand. "Things will change soon enough."

"Do you like your grandfather?" Mary asked.

"Hardly know him," Shelley said. "I have been away from my family for a long time. I can sneak a visit with my mother and sisters sometimes, when Papa is away, but otherwise I am banned."

"That must be strangely freeing," Mary commented.

"Both strange and freeing," he agreed. "I am very fond of my sisters and am sorry not to see them more."

"You can have us for sisters," I said promptly.

His look changed then, but I wasn't sure what it meant. He and Mary exchanged an odd sort of smile but said nothing.

"What sort of a man is John Hocke?" I demanded, to change the mood.

Shelley tilted his head back to me. "He is very social and finds company easy to come by, for he has no discretion at all. Of course, you can never know if what he tells you is truth or mere gossip, but he is always a good place to start, even for rumors about oneself."

"I like that," Mary said with a giggle. "Why would you need to learn what is being said about yourself? You know who you are."

"Who you are in the eyes of others is even more important," Shelley said. "When you are trying to do business. Whispers can destroy a reputation. That matters even more for a woman."

"We don't care about such things." Mary tossed her head. "We are Godwin's daughters."

"Well said." Shelley nodded. "Very well said indeed."

"I wonder what it says about your wife that she is in this Mr. Hocke's company," Mary mused.

I poked her for her impertinence. Shelley, walking a step ahead, didn't see.

"She never likes to be alone," he said. "Being in the company of those who never stop speaking is a comfort to her."

Mary frowned. "Then how do you hear your own thoughts?"

"You don't," Shelley said.

Our conversation became lighter then. Before I knew it, we had turned onto a street of warehouses. I saw ostrich feathers in one window and heavy bolts of cloth in another.

"Do you feel the bones underneath?" Shelley asked.

"What do you mean?" my sister asked.

"They say there is an ancient Jewish cemetery below the street here," he said, stomping on the pavement for emphasis.

Mary glanced down at her shoes. "Surely no one would have built over a cemetery."

"Happens all the time," he said carelessly. "What does anyone care about a lot of old bones once the memories are gone?"

"It would be much worse if people were still alive to care about the graves," Mary agreed.

I glared at them both. "We are concerned only about new bones today. One Cecil Campbell?"

"We ought to be able to learn something of interest about

him from Hocke," Shelley said, leading us into a building. "I found him all flash and no pan, myself."

We went up two flights of stairs, passing a straw-hat business and a button dealer, before we found a floor of residential apartments.

He knocked sharply at the door. It opened momentarily, a man behind it, his disheveled red hair ever so stylish.

"Hocke," Shelley said, his voice unusually brusque, lower than his musical high tenor.

"Shelley," Hocke greeted, entirely cheerful. He didn't look at me.

Shelley had released us, so that we stood behind him, peeping out around his arms. Hocke inclined his head to us. We both bobbed.

"Is my wife with you?" Shelley asked.

"No, I have Peter Corn and Charles Burgess here, though," Hocke said. "If you want to see your wife, she is at her father's house."

"That is the best place for her," Shelley said.

Hocke stepped back and flourished his arm, inviting us in. I walked in behind Mary, amazed. We went all sorts of places, especially with Papa, but this seemed rather daring as a public outing. A gentleman's rooms in the middle of the day.

Inside, the place had the air of very temporary lodgings, with but one comfortable chair, along with a deal table covered with unbound pages of printed text, and a quartet of unmatched straight-backed chairs in front of a fireplace with no fire in the grate. At least the bed, if there was one, was in a different room.

Leaning against the cracked mantelpiece was another young buck. In buckskin breeches and a superfine dark blue coat, he offered a prosperous and attractive appearance. He had dark hair, straight and rather greasy, and held a sheath of papers.

"Corn," Shelley grated, still in that odd tone.

"Shelley," Mr. Corn said, glancing up.

Another man sat in an armchair in the corner, an empty cup in his hand. He snored gently, his chin on his chest.

"Burgess is a bit older than we are," Mr. Hocke said carelessly. "He can't hold his drink like he used to."

"Corn," Shelley said again as I noticed strands of gray in the snoring Mr. Burgess's hair. "What news?"

"That dreadful business about Campbell, of course. Could have been any one of us, I suppose." He shifted his weight.

"I thought it was Shelley at first," Mary said boldly.

Corn shoved his papers into his jacket pocket. "Why?"

Mary glanced away, gathering her thoughts. "The body was facedown, and Shelley had been a guest at our table only a couple of hours before."

"Anything else?" Corn asked.

"He appeared to be about the same size and wore a similar coat."

"Tell me," Shelley interjected, "is anyone in our circle making it a point to break into businesses to hold clandestine meetings?"

Hocke laughed as I stood paralyzed, then gestured Mary and me into chairs. He fussed with the shutters, though they added no light, thanks to the soot crusting the windowpanes, then lit some kindling and started the fire. Corn opened a bottle of wine and passed around the pair of goblets that had been on the mantelpiece, after pouring out a large measure into each.

"He is being serious," Mary said after passing up the wine. "We found two pieces of a ripped note indicating a poet's involvement and an assignation."

"The only assignation that Campbell might have been a part of was with your wife," Hocke said rather nastily.

Shelley's nostrils flared. "He was entangled with Harriet?"

"So she told me."

My hands stole to my belly. Mary caught my gesture. Her

eyes rounded. Shelley and his wife had only just repledged themselves. Was that pretty young woman playing him so false? Who would do such a thing? No wonder Shelley seemed so careless of the situation. Bitter, even.

"I had thought there were two separate issues," Shelley said. "My marital problem and Cecil Campbell's murder, which may or may not be tied to me in some fashion. But now you tell me even that may be connected?"

Hocke drank down half of the goblet. "It isn't as if anyone thought you cared. You told Corn not long ago that you saw Harriet as a sister."

"I married her to rescue her from that dreadful boarding school. But it wasn't long before her sister moved in with us and quite ruined any attempt of Harriet's or mine to turn her into a scholar. We gave up. There is nothing left other than brotherly fondness." Shelley glanced at Mary. "Not that I had expected her to behave so shamelessly. She has an infant to care for, after all, and her sister to chaperone."

I could see Mary drinking in every word with wide eyes.

"My sister thinks there is a baby," I said after a moment.

"That is the Harriet problem, is it not?" Hocke said with another careless laugh.

Shelley snorted. "My father's problem, that an heir to the Shelley name might not be a Shelley, after all, if she has a boy this time. But it hardly signifies."

I was used to rather outrageous talk, but all of it rested in my mother's generation, not my own. Here were young men, not much older than Mary and me, carrying the torch of drama.

"You do not mind? Really?" I asked.

"It is only money, and a title," Shelley said. "What has it to do with me?"

Mary patted his hand. I realized I had missed the sheen of tears in his eyes. He was upset.

Corn passed Shelley the wine bottle, and he drank deeply until it had run dry.

"Women will ever be faithless," Hocke philosophized. "You were gone from home too long."

"Cecil Campbell must have been in Bath with her," Mary said.

"And why not?" Hocke asked. "It is a common enough place to go."

Shelley sniffed and knuckled his eyes. His lips had firmed into a tight white line. I had never seen him with that expression before. He stood and set the bottle on the floor.

"I thank you, gentlemen, for your intelligence, but I hear the pitter-pattering on the windowpanes. The rain has found us, and I must take these ladies home."

"Very well," Hocke said, posing. "I am sorry to give you bad news."

"Nothing of the kind," Shelley said airily. "I expected nothing less of my false wife."

Chapter 8

Mary

Mary could see Jane's nervous glances at Shelley in Mr. Hocke's chambers. She was probably afraid Shelley had murdered Mr. Campbell over his wife's infidelity. But Shelley hadn't known about the pregnancy until today. Even more evidence in his favor, he struggled to contain his emotions over the dreadful confirmation of his wife's unfaithfulness.

Mary could not help but be surprised at his reaction. She did not like Mrs. Shelley in the least and could not assign any goodness to her character. Her prettiness sank no deeper than a pebble into a puddle. Her husband, on the other hand, had great sensibility. While in the depths of his despair, he thought of nothing but returning his charges safely home from their excursion.

They said their good-byes to the Jewin Street poets and returned to the pavement, the cheap wine heavy in their bellies. Shelley had his hands clasped behind his back, instead of escorting them by the arms like he had on their way here. They passed a knot of men with hard, callused hands from years of working with leather and fabric. They were circling a woman with a tray and handing her coins in exchange for some kind of savory roll. Mary could smell hot onions and potatoes wafting around the men.

Shelley didn't offer to buy them any, and Mary hadn't any coins. To distract herself, Mary asked, "Shelley, are you going to go to her father's house?"

"Not with you along," he said, his expression becoming stoic. "That is never a happy place for me."

"What is the story of your marriage?" she asked.

"Mrs. Shelley went to school with my sisters. Dreadful place. I wanted to free her from tyranny, so we eloped to Scotland."

"What about your sisters?" Jane asked.

Mary detested the look of childish interest on Jane's face. Did she think Shelley would offer up his sisters as friends to Jane? They were well aware that the Shelley family was estranged. Poor Shelley, to be forced to answer painful family questions.

Shelley did not seem to mind, however, and answered calmly. "I didn't want to leave them in chains, either, but I had not the coin to free them all."

"Were you happy once you had freed Mrs. Shelley?" Mary asked.

"Gloriously, until her family intervened. Her sister is some decade older than we are and cast a decided pall over our lives when she moved in."

Jane twitched. Mary saw her fingers flex outward, and her sister stopped under a tree.

"What is it, Miss Clairmont?" Shelley asked, ever solicitous.

He ignored the drops of rain cascading around his hat. Mary huddled under the fresh spring leaves with Jane.

"Come now, we will get soaked," Mary chided. She lifted

her chin to Shelley. "Do you think your wife might have killed Cecil Campbell?"

His gaze moved from Jane to Mary. His lips turned down, then curved up in merriment. "That delicate, pretty wife of mine? You cannot think so."

Jane's jaw trembled, and she threw her hands into the air. Her eyes were wide; her gaze was fixed on him. "Then I call you murderer!"

A cart rumbling by, full of strips of leather tied down with rope, drowned out the worst of her howl and Mary's shocked gasp. Men holding their rolls stared at them, half-chewed food evident in their mouths.

She grabbed Jane's arm and held her in an iron vise as she towed her across the street, far away from the men who might hear her. "Are you mad?" Mary demanded. "Saying something like that on the street?"

"Really, Jane," Shelley said disparagingly. "Do not be such a child."

"But—but . . . ," she spluttered.

"Shelley is not a violent person," Mary insisted.

"He might be under such trying circumstances." Jane's voice had been loud, but at Mary's glare she had lowered her tone. She shook free from Mary's arm and went to stand under the stone overhang of a boot manufacturer.

Shelley followed her. He stood nearly a head taller, and his hat loomed higher still, protecting her from the lash of the rain. Mary pressed under the overhang.

"Tell me about these trying circumstances you think I am facing," he urged.

Jane licked her lips. "I submit that you killed Mr. Campbell because you already knew about the baby."

"This is not some lecture we are giving to Papa to impress him with our reasoning," Mary snapped. Jane, six months younger than her, still acted like a child much of the time. "Do not give in to her bad humor, Shelley. Jane is a fool."

"She seems to have a good mind to me," Shelley said mildly. "Why do you think her wrong?"

Mary glanced between them, rather shocked. She straightened like Willy did as he stood behind their lecture stand. "Sir, I did not sense any falsehood in your earlier tears."

He inclined his head. "Go on."

Mary and Jane shared a look. Surely reason could return Jane to good sense. "And, well, surely the killer thought he had murdered you, not Cecil Campbell."

"You think so?" he asked.

"The coat," Mary suggested. "His size. The place."

"You thought that," Jane said in a small voice. "I did not."

"Of course, we had not seen the note yet," Mary continued, "but it could have been meant for Shelley. We don't know. We know nothing about the situation, only something of Shelley's character."

Shelley patted Jane's shoulder. "Do you believe in my good character, like your sister does?"

She nodded.

"Then can we be friends again, Miss Clairmont? And sort out this business together? I assure you on my mother's honor that I did not kill anyone."

Jane blinked, and her eyes lost the glossy sheen they had possessed. "I never said we were not friends. I would think it rather exciting to be friends with a killer."

"Jane," Mary chided.

Shelley chuckled. "Such an imagination this girl has." Suddenly, he spun in a circle. Raindrops flew off his hat, splattering both girls. Mary wiped her face and laughed, and then all three of them were happy again.

Shelley eventually stopped spinning and offered them his rather tatty handkerchief to wipe off the rain. By then the sky had cleared, and they walked back to Skinner Street in good humor.

Mary drank in the joy, so different from the stresses that continually pressed down on her. Mamma's unending demands, lies, and disapproval; Papa's detachment, necessary to get his own work done; and the needs of Willy, Fanny and, most of all, Jane. Charles was at home, as well, resulting in an almost exasperating number of people in the large, creaking house. No wonder Papa had to go away to think.

How lucky Mrs. Shelley had been to have a boy like Shelley understand her suffocation in a bad school and offer her a way to escape. Mary wondered if she had any way out, beyond an early marriage and a return to Dundee. Would that really be any better than Skinner Street? Her suitor was only a little older than she. What poverty would he cast her into, with his deficits of education and age? Could he even pay for a doctor if her lying-in went as fatally wrong as her own birth had? There she would be, dead at eighteen or twenty, all the promise of her name wasted.

"Where have the pair of you been?" Mamma demanded when they entered the bookshop.

Fanny was nowhere to be seen, and Mamma stood behind the counter alone in the otherwise empty shop. The angry expression on her doughy face vanished when she saw Shelley.

"Hello, sir. My husband is in his study if you came to call upon him," she simpered.

Jane pulled off her cloak and handed it to Mary as if she were the maid. "I am sorry, Mamma. Mr. Shelley wanted us to pay a call with him."

Mary couldn't hear what her stepmother muttered under her breath. "I will show you up to the study, sir," she told Shelley, not meeting Mamma's gaze.

She stepped rapidly out of the shop, feeling as if a target was on her back, then flung off her cloak. She hung hers on her peg and dropped Jane's on the floor.

Shelley laughed. "That sister of yours is quite a dramatic little thing."

"This entire household coarsens me," Mary said. "I positively cannot wait to be away again."

Shelley gave her a speculative look. She shook her head. What could he do?

"Let me hang your hat so it can dry out a bit," she told him.

He handed it to her; then she led the way upstairs to the room over the shop. He had been there many times, but at least it took her away from Mamma and Jane. She knocked on the door, and when she heard her father say, "Enter," she opened it.

She ushered Shelley in, then stepped in behind him. The curtains were open to the street, offering a view of dank prison walls across the way. Her father was at his desk, dressed in his usual sober black.

"I'd like a word with you," Shelley said in a very man-to-man sort of way, not in his usual tone of deference toward his mentor, which she had heard him use at dinner.

"Of course, Shelley," her father said, setting his book aside. "Mary, a pot of coffee if you please."

Mary walked out without a glance at either of them and shut the door behind her. She could spare a moment to listen at the keyhole and was not above it, given the goings-on.

"You look troubled, my boy. What is it?" her father asked.

His voice was almost too muffled to hear, though she knew her father's voice well. She crouched down to put her ear closer to the keyhole.

"I need to tell you never to speak to my wife again," Shelley said. "She is not to be welcome here."

"She often orders books from us," her father said mildly.

"No trade, no dinners, no conversation," Shelley said.

Papa's voice became clipped. "What is amiss? We like Mrs. Shelley in this house."

"If you continue to engage with her, I won't give you any further financial support, no matter how much I revere your philosophical work," Shelley pronounced in a voice so clear and cold that Mary scarcely recognized it.

"If I have offended you, I am sorry," her father said, modulating his tone. "But you have made me promises. The Juvenile Library depends on what you do, Shelley. My debts are enormous. It is the burden I undertake to help our society."

"Some things are sacred, Godwin. I cannot have you dealing with my wife."

"What has happened?" Mary heard a book drop before her father continued. "Is there something I must know?"

"Your daughters have found a corpse in your shop very recently. Is that not enough?" Shelley asked.

"You cannot think Mrs. Shelley was involved," her father said.

"I cannot know anything, and neither can you. Not at this juncture."

"I apologize. You are right, of course, and it is very good of you to think of my daughters. I am sure your wife is of the highest moral character and is a credit to you, but we will not have her to dinner or elsewhere at Skinner Street until all this unpleasantness is sorted. I understand Bow Street is involved in the business now."

"What about a guard?" Shelley asked. "A male servant, at the very least. While they do tend to bring their own issues, a stout pair of male hands might be just the thing for your household right now."

"If you care to pay for it," her father said. "I haven't the coin, frankly."

"My pockets are to let until the post-obit loan business is finished or my grandfather dies," Shelley said. "My father would rather support my faithless wife than me."

"How can you say that? You were just remarried a few weeks ago," her father said.

"And have been separated since," Shelley reminded him.

Mary heard her father's chair push back. She dashed downstairs, hugging the wall, before he could think to check the corridor. He was no fool and might have realized he hadn't heard the sounds of her going downstairs.

She went into the kitchen and made coffee, but by the time she had carried the heavy tray to the front hall, Shelley's hat was gone from the peg, leaving only a circle of rainwater behind on the floor.

Mamma poked her head out of the bookshop. "What are you doing with that?"

Mary transferred her attention away from that sad wet circle with difficulty. "Papa asked for coffee."

Mamma looked at the cups. "He has no visitor now, girl. Give me a cup."

Holding back a sigh, Mary walked into the bookshop and set the tray on the counter. Mamma took double her usual amount of cream, muttering about the obscene cost of coffee all the while.

"It isn't, though," Mary protested. They'd been using the treat sparingly enough to have it last. "I brought this back from Scotland. It's smuggler's brew."

Mamma rolled her eyes. "What did Shelley want?"

"I went to make the coffee," Mary said. Why would Mamma never give her any credit, any praise?

"Right, girl. As if you ain't too good to pay attention. What is happening around here? Dead bodies? My daughter on the streets with a married man?"

Mary couldn't help but feel like Mamma was playacting. What did she know?

"Did you know Cecil Campbell?" she asked.

"Penniless nobody, just like most of your father's disciples," Mamma said dismissively before taking a swallow of her coffee.

Mary considered. "Shelley is penniless, as well."

"For now, girl, only for now. That family is very rich."

Such talk was beneath the family. "Papa has raised us not to care about money or possessions."

"And all the happier you will be for it," Mamma snapped, slurping on her coffee again. "If only we had raised you not to think, either, we would have a much calmer household."

Behind a bookshelf, Jane popped up, then disappeared again, a hunted look in her eyes.

She pushed the issue of Jane aside. It would not be long before their households were separated from each other, by marriage or work. "Does not anyone in this house appreciate the value of Shelley's words? Why, you used to write me about the delicacy and sense of his letters."

"Your father likes to be fawned over. Read the letters if you want." Mamma shrugged and turned away. She tossed back the contents of her cup and pulled a ledger from under the counter, then went through the door to her office.

Mary picked up the tray and went upstairs, hoping the coffee was still warm enough for Papa's approval. She'd had the sense just now that Mamma didn't like Shelley, if that was even possible, given the charms of the man.

Did many ignore his poetic gifts and just want his money? What a problem to have, to worry about why people really liked you, because you possessed something so many desired. Still, though, murder.

Who would want to kill him? Did Shelley have a will? He had nothing to leave now, but if his grandfather or father died before he did, that would change in the loss of a heartbeat.

The family had a number of callers in the afternoon. Papa looked very pale after a while. Mary went to the window on the landing after he left the parlor, and saw him racing to the privy in the rear garden, holding his stomach.

"Is your father unwell?" asked Amelia Curran, the painter

and daughter of Papa's Irish barrister friend, when Mary returned to the parlor.

"He has unwell moments," Mary admitted. "I hope the coffee I brought back from Scotland did not upset his stomach."

Miss Curran nodded. "It is best to stick to tea, I believe. You have a busy house this afternoon."

"I think everyone wants an update on poor Cecil Campbell's murder," Mary explained. "But all we have learned is the most dreadful gossip."

"Nothing you can speak about?"

"Not in mixed company, certainly," Mary said, glancing at Mr. Constable, the publisher, Mr. Smith, and Mr. Gill, all chatting in a circle of chairs in front of the fireplace.

Jane darted around, probably wanting to sing for them.

"Your sister has a nervous sort of energy tonight," Miss Curran observed.

"She had one of her little fits this afternoon," Mary said. "It was not good for her to become mixed up in this. It makes her thoughts queer."

"And why not?" Miss Curran shuddered. "I didn't even see the poor body, and it's given me an unpleasant dream or two."

Mary had slept very well.

When her father returned, he sent Mary down to close up the shop and Jane to help Mamma in the dining room. Mary heard the footsteps of everyone departing half an hour later.

Dinner was a quiet affair, just the family, with Mamma complaining that someone had sliced a good bit of ham out of her stores. Mary saw Willy's eyes dart from side to side and suspected her little brother was the culprit. Growing fast and hungry for extra nourishment. She hoped Mamma didn't discover the truth, for she'd hate to see her brother beaten.

After dinner, she pulled him out of the dining room as quickly as she could, then brought him upstairs to play dice games and keep him away from Mamma.

Eventually, Fanny and Jane appeared. Jane seemed exhausted by her earlier dramatics, and Fanny was quiet, as well. They all went to bed rather early, leaving Mary on her own.

She decided to go downstairs and choose something from the bookshop. While she ought to be nervous about roaming around downstairs alone after what had happened the week before, her senses had become so acute about the movements of the house that she would know if anyone snuck in.

She went with an unlit candle in her hand, ready to strike a match as soon as she reached the floor. When she heard a scrape in the front hall just as she reached the landing above it, she stopped, her ears straining. The front door opened and closed. Mary's heart began to pound. Had someone come in for another clandestine meeting? Another murder?

She didn't dare light her candle, and she didn't have a weapon. Scarcely daring to breathe, she took a giant step across the landing and peered over the balustrade. A lantern burned dimly on the table. No, someone wasn't coming in but was going out. Mary heard the snick of the lock as someone turned a key from outside.

Mamma, from the looks of the shadow in the street. Mary tiptoed down the steps, hugging the wall, then darted to the pegs in the front hall. The trunk underneath gaped open. Mary pressed it closed. Yes, Mamma's cloak was gone. Where was she going at bedtime?

Mary's thoughts went to Shelley. What if Mamma planned some harm to the gentle poet? She couldn't stand the mere idea of it. What if Mamma was in cahoots with the dreadful Harriet Shelley?

Mary ran to the table and pulled another key from the drawer, then grabbed her cloak and followed Mamma into the street, still in her thin evening slippers. She locked the door, too, not wanting to invite any malfeasance into Skinner Street, and followed Mamma into the night.

Mamma walked with straight posture and fast feet, as if daring anyone to stop her. Mary stayed in the shadows but kept her in sight, checking every time light appeared to make sure Mamma was still in view. Smoke pressed down from all the chimney stacks above buildings, but just enough wind moved through the spaces between to keep the street clear. Mary's confusion deepened as Mamma pressed on; she never took strolls, and a respectable woman, which she had become—at least, upon her marriage—would not have gone out alone in any case. Still, Mamma kept moving, headed west and south, as if going toward the river.

She stopped before that, though, and turned into Covent Garden. Was she headed toward the theater? Mary had been to Drury Lane before. They had seen Shakespeare's *As You Like It* there shortly after her return to Skinner Street.

Toes cramping in her tight slippers, Mary fell back a bit, nursing her cold feet. The area, full of activity even at this time of night, was lighter than the streets they had first traversed.

Mamma did go to the theater. When she crossed the street, Mary stayed in the shadows of the building on the other side. Mamma didn't go inside, however, but hovered on the pavement between a stanchion and the decorative fence. Mary ran across the street, her feet squelching in the ever-present mud, and slid against the shadows along the wall. Her slippers would be ruined, and Mamma would find out, but curiosity won over good sense. She waited to see what would happen next.

Nothing happened, except the sounds of the performance. Mary enjoyed the music as it floated from the few windows. A couple of orange sellers came out of the building from the rear and had a short argument over a man, never seeing the girl tucked along the wall. A man descended the front steps and lit a cigar. The smoke tickled her nose, but she managed not to sneeze.

She held her breath as the man approached Mamma. He didn't

say anything but jerked his head toward the opposite side street. Mary bit back a laugh. Did he think Mamma was for sale? Mamma turned her head and ignored him. The man grabbed her arm, and Mamma shook him off.

A constable walked by in the street. The man gave up and let Mamma go. Mary realized she'd stepped onto the pavement, and slunk back before she came into view and possibly attracted the man's attention, as well.

Just as she'd reached the wall, shadows moved. A woman dressed in a dark pelisse and bonnet crossed to the theater. As soon as the constable turned the corner, the woman came alongside the building and stood next to Mamma.

Mary strained to see any identifying features, but the light was too poor. Why couldn't Mamma have kept her assignations to nights with a full moon? Mamma greeted the woman; then they started walking.

Mary waited a few beats, then followed, hoping they wouldn't turn. She'd be perfectly visible in front of the theater. The women crossed the street. Mary could see a potato seller there, with a lit lantern. She slid around the side of the theater and back into the shadows alongside, then put her hands into her bonnet behind her ears to listen as best she could. If no carriages came by, she might be able to hear.

"Thank you for seeing me, Miss Westbrook," Mamma said before haggling with the potato seller.

Westbrook? Mary tried to remember where she'd heard that name before.

"Of course, Mrs. Godwin," the woman said. She had a London accent, fairly refined, with nothing of the fake French flourishes Mamma gave her speech to advertise that she was a translator. "Has there been any news today?"

Mamma took her potato from the seller and kept the warm oval between her gloves. "Shelley paid a call."

Mary's hands tightened around her ears for a moment. Now

she remembered the name Westbrook. Harriet Shelley's father was the Mr. Westbrook who owned a coffee shop in Grosvenor Square, along with other, less luminous businesses. Wealthy enough to be a lord, but in trade. But the woman with Mamma was a lot older and didn't carry herself like a beauty.

Shelley had complained about a sister, however. She had moved in while he'd been traveling, and he'd been unable to dislodge her from his household since.

Miss Westbrook took Mamma's arm, and they left the potato seller. Mary followed as best she could, catching scraps of conversation.

"How much money does the family have?"

"What comes to Shelley upon his grandfather's death?"

"What does he waste in a year on his pamphlets?"

"Perish the thought," Mamma said when Miss Westbrook suggested she might not get her share, as agreed. "We Godwins are honest people."

"I've heard you are very bad with a coin," the other woman said.

"My husband's debts drag us down, not our expenses. But the post-obits will set us all to rights. Our business debt, your gambling chits. All will be well."

"How?" Miss Westbrook asked. "He cares for me not at all. Frankly, he has lost interest in my sister, and I once thought her beauty such that no man could."

"You sound almost as if you wish the relationship was intact," Mamma said.

"I do, certainly," Miss Westbrook agreed. "I helped them get away. How could Harriet possibly have married better than a baronet's heir? It was a brilliant match for her, but I had no idea what sort of man Shelley was at the time."

"Or that your father and his would cut off the pair of them after the wedding."

"It has not been as expected." Miss Westbrook stopped walking for a moment and turned slightly.

Mary pressed herself against a railing, holding her breath. After a pause, the woman turned again.

"What is your plan?" asked Miss Westbrook.

"I manage my husband's affairs. When I see the documents, I will ensure the post-obits are enough for us both to get what we need. I can change a few numbers if necessary."

"I understand the rates are ruinous."

"It doesn't matter to us. Not a penny goes to the lenders without a death, and what do the dead need with money?"

Mary found herself unable to move when the women crossed the next street. She had learned a sickening amount and was a couple of miles from home. The streets were not safe, unless she could keep out of sight. She turned lightly, increasing her pace, despite the clawing of rage in her stomach.

How could anyone, however jaded, treat the sensitive, beautiful poet like nothing more than a bag of money?

Chapter 9

Jane

I was in the bookshop, minding the counter, the day after our disturbing trip to Jewin Street with Shelley, when a customer entered. My heart sank at the sight of him.

Claude Barre, a French émigré, possessed the same number of years, more or less, as Papa. Instead of being stout and balding like our parent, he had become thin, with a vast quantity of gray hair, which he managed by smoothing back after licking his fingers. His eyes were ratty red, and he was just as curious as a rodent.

"Bonjour, Mademoiselle Clairmont." When he inclined his head, his hat slid forward on his greasy curls.

"Bonjour, monsieur." I slid the song sheet I'd been attempting to memorize under the counter. "What are you looking for today?"

He clapped his hands together. "I have been led to understand you have a special prize in the shop."

My jaw clenched instantly. Where had he heard that bit of

intelligence? I tilted my head and blinked flirtatiously. "What prize is that, other than great learning?"

"A Wordsworth book."

I nodded and touched my throat. A shard of acid worked its way down to my belly. *Oh, yes.* "There are rumblings of an incredible new collection coming by the end of summer. You could put in an order at Longman, or we can write you as soon as it arrives."

"No, my dear." He licked his fingers tremulously and smoothed his hair back. "I am looking for something rare, not unpublished."

"*Très bien. Dites-m'en plus,*" I invited, though the pulse in my wrist had begun to thrum against the sleeve of my gown. I enjoyed practicing my French around him. When we had lived at the Polygon, we were surrounded by those who had escaped their war-torn country, but here they were not so much in evidence.

He smiled and put his hands on the counter. "I want the original *Lyrical Ballads.*"

"I think we have only the second edition," I said, my attention narrowing to his hands. Were they capable of violence? "The authors did some rearranging of the poems."

"I want the first," he said emphatically.

"I believe Papa has it in his collection, in his library. I can see if he will sell it to you, but he is with Mr. Place today, working on the accounts. I will have him call on you when he returns?"

"I know the edition he has in his library. He has shown it to me. It is the version with 'The Nightingale.'" He leaned forward. "No, my dear, I want the special edition."

I took a step back, my pulse kicking up again. My hand went to my neck as the air seemed to tighten around it. What did he think he knew? "What special edition?"

"The very first one. With Coleridge's 'Lewti,' before the poem was switched out and the paging ordered incorrectly."

He wriggled his fingers. "I am told you have it, bound in green crushed Levant morocco."

"That is very specific," I said, fighting to keep a tremble from my voice. "I should call Mamma for you."

Mary came through the door, dressed in her loud tartan dress. She glanced between me and Mr. Barre. I took a step back from the counter, relieved, and widened my eyes.

"Monsieur Barre is looking for a specific volume, a rare early edition of *Lyrical Ballads*. Are you aware of such a special piece?"

"I am afraid not. May we show you something else?" Mary said.

He glanced from me to Mary and back again. "I have been a faithful customer, no? Why will you not sell it to me? I will pay you a good price."

Mary's brow wrinkled in confusion. "It is Mamma you should speak to, or Papa."

He stomped his foot. "That is not true. You are in possession of it."

"Who gave you this intelligence?" she asked. "I assure you, Jane and I have little in the way of our own possessions. I brought no books from Scotland at all."

"Green leather," he said. "Surely you are hiding it from me."

"You have me at a loss, sir. We will scour the shop for such a volume. I will start right now." Mary pulled her apron from behind the counter and tied it around her tiny waist, then went directly to the poetry section.

"They say she is an intelligent girl," the collector hissed at me, "but she does not understand."

I stared him down. "We have no secret rare volumes. I cannot state this any more clearly."

He bowed his head, seeming to calm for a moment, then stormed out of the shop, slamming both doors behind him. I ran to the window and watched him exit onto the pavement, slicking back his hair, then march off in the direction of the Saracen's Head. A good thing, for he clearly needed a strong restorative. I wished I could have the same.

Mary returned to the counter. "What was that?"

"Wordsworth again," I told her. Wordsworth, that cursed poet.

"Do you think we have a rare book–stealing ring operating after hours in the bookshop?" she asked.

"Right under our noses?" I scoffed uneasily. "How could we miss one?"

"I have no idea," she said. "Our bedrooms are floors up, but Papa's study is just over this room. He is not so deaf as that."

"If you will take a turn behind the counter," I said, frantic for a moment of peace. I needed to gather myself together, to restore my calm demeanor. "I believe I am gasping for a cup of tea."

She nodded. "Chilly day. Bring me one, too."

The rest of the morning remained quiet. My secrets stayed my own. When I came downstairs, back from taking a volume to Willy's tutor, I found Shelley in the bookshop, leaning against the wall. He and Mary weren't looking at each other and were several feet apart, yet I had the notion they were in a strange sort of close communication.

He bowed to me. "Miss Clairmont. I came to assure myself that you were well after yesterday's excursion."

I frowned. "Of course, sir, I am in the best of health."

"Jane never recognizes her fits," Mary said. "It is one of her stranger characteristics."

"Mary," I huffed, "I am not strange."

She looked sideways at me, her lips curving.

"I am glad to hear it," Shelley said, pulling himself off the wall. "I happen to think both of you are quite extraordinary."

Mary's expression grew even more sly. "How kind of you to say."

"Mary expects such praise," I said tartly. "Being her mother's child. But I am very glad to hear it on my own account."

"Jane had a quite extraordinary encounter with a customer this morning, to borrow your word," Mary announced.

Mary never liked to hear me being praised. I gritted my teeth as I had lost Shelley's attention entirely. And on my own account, no less.

"Did she?" His gaze remained intent on hers.

"We have a collector of books who was desperate for the very first edition of *Lyrical Ballads*."

"Is that unusual?"

I stepped out from the counter, directly in front of Mary. "He was certain we had it, as if we'd come in possession of it recently. And you know that quote I found on the paper scrap was by Wordsworth."

"Yes, but it doesn't signify. The quote wasn't from *Lyrical Ballads*," Shelley said.

"It was still perishingly odd," I retorted.

"It sounds like a second bit of oddness, rather than being tied to the first." Shelley screwed his features into the center of his face. "When we found the second piece of paper, we realized that the entirety was a note. Not torn from a book."

Mary put her hand on my shoulder, then pressed down as she stepped around me. "Do you have the 'Lewti' version of *Lyrical Ballads*? You've said you have an extensive collection of books."

"I do not. I consider the poet too religious for my taste," he said.

"That is because you are an atheist," I suggested.

"I do not understand why they sent you down from Oxford for it," Mary said. "Your pamphlet was most polite."

He smiled at her. "It contradicted what I had to claim to believe in order to study there in the first place."

"Do you really not believe in God?" I asked.

"I do not deny that some power, a mysterious one, lies behind the universe," he said.

Both Mary and I leaned in.

"But I cannot accept that the Spirit that pervades this infinite machine begat a son upon the body of a Jewish woman," he said. He fisted one hand into the other. "Why would any being make man as he is and them damn him for being that very thing?"

I nodded. "Exactly so." The grief on his face caught at me so palpably that I wanted to give him a hug, as if he were a boy, like Willy, in need of comfort.

"Then it is not a fashion," Mary said quietly. "These are truly your beliefs."

He inclined his head and dropped his hands to his sides. "Since I was seventeen. The God we learn about is as much a tyrant as my father. I cannot believe in either one."

Her lips curved. "Then we, who have a good father, find it easier to believe."

"I don't," I interjected, but neither of them responded, too busy staring into each other's eyes. Damn and blast! Why did Mary tug at his gaze so? Wasn't I as interesting?

The front door opened, followed quickly by the shop door. Mamma came in with Fanny. When she saw Shelley, she bobbed a curtsy. "What can we do for you today, sir? My husband is out paying calls."

"Have him write me," Shelley said in a more formal tone. "He knows the subject."

"Very well, sir. Have a meal, girls. Then return to the shop," Mamma ordered. "Fanny, you mind the shop for an hour."

"Mamma?" Mary asked. "Do you or Papa have the very first *Lyrical Ballads*, bound in green crushed Levant morocco? Mr. Barre seemed to think we possessed it."

She looked confused. "I do not believe so. Ask your father. We've never had it in inventory."

"Come," Shelley said to Mary and me. "It is a fine day. Let us promenade and slake our hunger with pies."

"There is good food here," Mamma said. "I cannot expect the girls to depend on your hospitality."

"It is no matter." Shelley jingled coins in his pocket. "My wife always manages to be in funds, even when I am not. I have some blunt off her."

Mary smiled triumphantly at Mamma and flounced behind Shelley. I put my head down and skittered along with them, feeling as if a target hung on my back. Mamma, though, said nothing more.

We grabbed our cloaks and bonnets at the front door and went out into the May sunshine. The smells and flies of Smithfield Market did not subtract much from the brilliant light.

"It is impossible not to believe in some vast power behind the world on a day like this," Mary said, lifting her arms and tossing back the sides of her cloak so that it became a cape.

"I never said there wasn't," Shelley said agreeably.

"Where shall we go? Mamma will be angry if we take too long. I'm sure she has work to do in the office," I said.

"I saw a pie seller in front of the St. Sepulchre watchhouse." Shelley stepped in between us and took our arms.

We all smiled widely as we walked down Snow Hill toward the church. Even the sight of the prison, so common to our eyes, could not dampen our sun-sourced mood. I skipped a little for the joy of it, and Shelley joined me, letting Mary go as she did not join in.

Instead, she went to the pie seller while we scampered around her. I had not seen the leather-skinned man in the stained cap and blue apron before, but then I never had money for pies. We had sufficient food in the house, it merely needed preparing, and I could not deny Mamma had taught us the skills of keeping a house around our education, despite the servants she insisted Papa employ.

"Shelley, those coins, please," Mary said.

He capered over to her and spun her around before bowing to the pie seller and handing him coins. The transaction left us in possession of two eel pies and one hot potato that had not yet been turned into mash. Shelley wouldn't eat eels. We took them into the courtyard of the church and leaned against the sooty yellow walls of the ancient building to eat our food.

I lifted my face to the sunshine, wishing I could rip off my bonnet to take full advantage of it. The ribbon I had tied under my chin to keep it on chafed, and I knew I would have a red mark under my jaw all afternoon.

I glanced at Shelley and Mary. They were too busy staring at each other to look at me. I threw caution to the wind and untied my bonnet, then set it, flat top up, on the ground.

"You said you saw your wife?" Mary asked in a very placid tone, which did not mean she felt placid at all.

"I had to, of course. She wouldn't come to London without wanting something."

"Did you talk to her about Cecil Campbell?"

Shelley's tone was derisive. "Silly girl that she is, all she did was cry when I asked about him."

"Well, if she is mourning her dead lover . . . ," Mary said.

My eyes widened. I couldn't believe she'd say such a coarse thing!

"Indeed," Shelley said. "But the girl is too soft to kill an unwanted kitten, much less a man she gave herself to."

"Did you see your daughter?" I asked, desperate to change the uncomfortable subject.

"Yes, I cuddled little Ianthe for the moment she was in the room. My wife's father can afford a nursemaid to manage her."

"Will they stay in London now?" I asked.

He shrugged. "It's an odd time of year. I'd rather be anywhere but London in the summer."

"It's only May," Mary said.

He looked down at her speculatively. "True, true."

I rolled my eyes. "What about the most important matter? Did she have any idea who might have killed Mr. Campbell?"

"I didn't think to ask," Shelley said. "Once she started to cry. I might have asked it of Eliza, if I had seen her."

"That is her sister, correct?" Mary asked.

"Yes," Shelley agreed. "She's ten years older than Harriet. Black hair, which she is obsessed with. Very ugly. It is amazing that two parents could have produced such different daughters."

I wasn't surprised. Of course, Mary and Fanny were only half sisters, but one was an ethereal beauty, and the other, a plain mouse. Not fair for either of them, really. Fanny had no suitors at all, and Mary, two Scottish suitors, and, well, even a married man was enchanted by her. Not that marriage mattered. Papa had made that clear to us, even though he and Mamma had married for the sake of a baby, who died right away, before Willy came. What would Mary do? For me, I could not imagine marriage. Mamma made it look like such drudgery, for all that she must have been eager for it to chase after Papa like I'd heard people say she had. Papa had not even been a prize, despite his fame. After Mary's mother died, he had proposed to multiple other women and had been rejected. So the gossip went.

"Sisters can be entirely different," I said.

"Especially such sisters who are not even blood kin," Mary added.

Shelley smirked. "You two are very alike."

Mary folded her arms across herself. "We look nothing alike."

I pointed to my dark hair and Mary's flyaway golden glory, which shone around her bonnet. Shelley tapped us on the crowns of our heads.

"Underneath, that is where you are the same. Children of inquiry, both of you. Adventuresses. Dreamers. Have I not heard both of you say you want to write? Are you not full of ideas? And the principles of Godwin and Wollstonecraft?"

"But Mary is reserved, and I am loud," I argued. "I sing and she writes."

"Differences of manner and talents only." He took us each by one arm and twirled us around.

Half of Mary's pie fell from her hand and dropped to the garden bed along the church wall. She just laughed and twirled again, holding Shelley's hand. I had finished mine, but it sat heavily in my belly. I let go of his hand and leaned against the wall.

"What—what is this desecration!" spluttered a grating male voice. A head poked out of a recess along the church wall, followed by the rest of the body. His loose clerical frock coat had buttons stretched in their buttonholes over a large, round belly. I felt for him, given the chafing that his cravat must have produced against his multiple chins.

Mary's eyes went wide. She followed his gaze down to the scattered remnants of eel pie. "Fertilizer for the roses," she said politely.

Spittle flew from the side of his mouth. "I know you, Miss Godwin. Pick it up!"

She pulled a handkerchief from her sleeve and scooped up the gelatinous mess.

"I know you," Shelley said slowly, looking at the clergyman's face. "You always did talk nonsense. Why spite the roses to make a point? The eel might as well go to some good use for the plants."

Mary smirked and dropped the eel bits, though she wrapped up the crust in her handkerchief.

"I know you, too, Shelley." The other man sneered, his pale face going blotchy. "Sent down for atheism, right? How dare you set foot on holy ground?"

"He merely asked for proof in his pamphlet, from men who might have it," Mary said. "A proof that God exists."

"How dare he!" the clergyman shouted. "Faith is what is required. Faith is demanded. Do you not remember Doubting Thomas? 'Jesus saith unto him, Thomas, because thou hast seen me, thou hast believed: blessed *are* they that have not seen, and *yet* have believed.'"

"But Jesus offered proof," Shelley said, a very intent look in his eyes. "'Then saith he to Thomas, Reach hither thy finger, and behold my hands; and reach hither thy hand, and thrust *it* into my side: and be not faithless, but believing.'"

"He was an apostle," shouted the man. "What are you but someone who liked to cry out in great shrieking fits late in the night and keep us all awake? Your father should have locked you away, not attempted to educate you."

"This is Bartholomew Doone," Shelley said to us conversationally. "We were at school together but were never friends."

"You will suffer eternal damnation for your beliefs," Doone said stubbornly.

"Please, let us continue the conversation," Shelley said. "I am fascinated, and the girls will no doubt find your words highly illuminating." He pulled a couple of pamphlets from his pockets and held them out. "Here. Some reading material on the subject."

"Unlike you, I have fulfilled my duties to the Church," Doone said, ignoring the offering. "I am an ordained priest."

"Aren't you meant to teach and to guide?" Mary asked guilelessly. "Surely debate would help."

Doone's eyelashes fluttered. "Get you back to that bookshop of your stepmother's and away from this house of God!"

Mary's hand tightened around her dripping handkerchief. In a moment, she made her decision. She let the fabric unfurl. The macerated contents plopped onto the dirt in front of the priest's shoe. "Those who will not debate can hardly claim to be civilized," she said with a sniff and marched away.

Shelley laughed and followed her. I averted my gaze from the priest and trotted after.

"What an odious creature," Mary said when we were back on the street. "All you wanted to do was have a discussion."

"There is no discussion with Doone," Shelley said. "No imagination whatsoever. Probably makes an excellent priest."

Mary giggled. "While you make an excellent poet."

"Exactly. We are each suited to our separate sphere."

I heard the church bells sound. "We need to return to the bookshop, or Mamma will be angry with us."

"Run along," Shelley said to me. "Mary will be right behind."

I nodded and ran up the street. At least one of us would be in Mamma's good graces.

Chapter 10

Jane

"Shelley said he might meet us for a walk before it gets dark, since we didn't have very much time together earlier," Mary said, scrubbing a plate.

We were in the scullery, washing the best dishes from Papa's dinner with Mr. Robinson. They wanted to have a private conversation, so Mamma had shooed us downstairs.

"Yes, I heard him," I said. "There are still a couple of hours of daylight left. What time did you think he meant?"

"I expect it would be after his own supper," Fanny suggested.

"Where did he dine?" I asked.

"Not with his wife at her father's house." Mary slapped a clean plate down on the table.

I picked up my rag to dry it. "Dreadful person. I wonder what Ianthe is like."

"All children are sweet," Mary said. "And she will be lovely, with parents like that."

I nodded. "Quite. Perhaps Shelley will bring her on a walk one night."

"Hardly," Mary scoffed. "Ianthe is little more than a baby, and no interest of ours."

"I'd like to see her," Fanny said. "Do you imagine children of your own someday?"

"Why not?" Mary tossed her head.

"So many men have died in the wars," Fanny said, a hint of doubt in her voice. "We rarely see young men. What a pity that a poet like Cecil Campbell had to die. If we ever marry, it will be to someone like that."

"Yet Mrs. Shelley had both him and her husband under her thumb," I said.

Fanny's eyes went wide, and I told her what we had heard.

"Poor Shelley, to be so betrayed," she gasped. "Oh, I quite feel for his pain. Think of all Mother suffered from Gilbert Imlay when she was trying to save their relationship."

"Your father, you mean?" I asked.

Fanny flushed.

"Mother wanted to die," Mary added. "I hope Shelley is not so transported."

"He does have great sensibility," Fanny said after taking a deep breath that momentarily filled out her bodice. "We must comfort him when he comes."

"He didn't invite you," Mary said. "Just Jane and me."

Fanny's lips pursed. "But I am his good friend. I am sure—"

"No," I said, with what little authority I could muster. "We have important things to discuss."

"That horrid priest," Mary said. "And the murder. No, Fanny, you are much too far behind in the story. We cannot possibly waste Shelley's time explaining it all to you."

"You didn't find the body. We did," I added.

Fanny's lips were now little but a thin line. "Go on then."

She made a shooing motion. "Shelley's conversation is delightful, and I'm sure you don't want to miss a second of it."

I admired Fanny for behaving as the eldest girl should. Mary tossed off her apron. It landed in a dim corner. I dropped mine on top of hers, and we ran up the stairs.

"Stay below the windows," Mary warned when we were outside. She hunched her shoulders and hugged the side of the building until we had reached the warehouses.

I scanned the street, which was still brightly lit, though smoke from chimneys obscured the tops of some buildings. The smell of livestock had died down with the end of the day but would be renewed in the early morning hours, as men drove their bounty to Smithfield Market.

"Did Shelley say where to meet him?" I asked.

"Let's walk up to Charterhouse Square," Mary said, not answering the question. "It's the nearest bit of green."

"As long as we aren't there a second after dark," I said. "You know if you're there after the sun goes down, you can hear the ghosts of plague victims screaming."

"Hmmm," Mary said. "I've never been there after dark. It sounds fascinating."

Before we could walk in that direction, we saw Shelley walking up the street. He waved his arms in the air when he spotted us. I saw he had a notebook in his hands.

" 'In honoured poverty thy voice did weave songs consecrate to truth and liberty. Deserting these, thou leavest me to grieve, thus having been, that thou shouldst cease to be,' " he cried.

"What is that?" Mary asked when he reached us.

He put his hands on his knees and panted theatrically before standing up straight again. "Our conversation stimulated me. I'm calling it 'To Wordsworth.'"

We both clapped.

He smiled and bowed, then held out his arms. "Let us walk."

"We thought to head up to the square," I ventured.

He ignored me and led us down Snow Hill.

"We aren't going back to that horrid church," I cried, resisting.

"No, no. Let us walk around the prison. Much more stimulating for the brain than the church," he said.

"Besides, Reverend Doone might set the watch on us," Mary added.

Shelley snorted. "He hasn't the coin. For all my purse tightening thanks to my father, he had nothing at all. Existed on the crumbs of other boys."

"It is hard to imagine him having friends," I said loyally.

I waited for him to gather my arm up, but he did not, taking hold only of Mary. We reached the edge of Newgate Prison quickly. I couldn't help quivering. While we had multiple prisons in the area, one didn't really think about mortality except when one walked by the spot where the public hangings took place. On those days, this entire area was stuffed with crowds. Mamma warned us not to go out with money, because the pickpockets the crowds attracted would get it.

"I was thinking about crime," Mary announced.

Shelley's chin tilted toward her. "Oh?"

"We must know who killed Cecil Campbell. There cannot be too many people in your circle."

"Yes, the suspect list is small," Shelley said. "Who are they, would you say?"

"We don't know who the killer really was after," I added. "Was it Campbell or you, Shelley? We have to create a list for each."

"Whoever overlaps is the most likely," Shelley opined, marching us briskly along the forbidding prison's stone wall.

I fancied I saw old blood between the cobblestones in the road, and shuddered, but Shelley didn't notice. I sighed and started counting the names on my fingers. "The suspects are Mrs. Shelley, Eliza Westbrook, Mamma, and . . ." I hesitated. "John Hocke."

"What a disturbing list," Mary said from Shelley's other side.

"We cannot forget the would-be assassin from Tan-yr-allt," Shelley said.

"From Tremadoc, Wales, last year?" Mary asked.

"That is why I do not care to walk alone," Shelley said. "Safety in numbers, and my companions might notice someone in the shadows. But please, do explain the reasoning behind each suspect, Jane."

My cheeks went hot. "You know why your wife is on the list."

"Very well," he said. "She wanted to hide the evidence of her attachment to Mr. Campbell by murdering him. Or was angry at him and murdered him."

"With two knives," Mary added.

"Yes," Shelley said after a pause. "An excellent point."

"Whoever the killer was, they were very, very angry." I shuddered.

We turned the corner and continued our grim march around the prison. I supposed it was fitting to discuss possible murderers in such a setting.

"On to Miss Westbrook?" Shelley said.

"You would know better than us," Mary said quickly, tucking her chin into her shoulders.

That seemed odd to me. What was she hiding?

"She thinks of herself and Harriet as one unit," Shelley said. "Anything Harriet might do, she would do for Harriet."

"Very interesting," I said. "Sort of a proxy murderer."

"Or she might do it to protect her sister," he suggested.

"Very well. Then Mamma."

"Could she have done it?" he asked. "You were in the house with her."

"Not in the same room," Mary said, speeding up to match

our longer legs. "It's possible that Papa was with her the entire time, but she wasn't with us. We were upstairs, putting Willy to bed."

"We should check on that." I looked at Shelley hopefully, but he wasn't doling out praise this evening. He had a troubled look on his face.

"What in her character might make her a killer? And why?" Shelley asked.

"We know from the note that someone had scheduled a meeting in the bookshop. Who is more likely to do so than someone who lives there?" I took a turn too sharply and banged my arm against a jutting stone.

"Then there is your father and Fanny and Willy and Charles," he said, frowning at my yelp.

I rubbed my arm. "Even you, who had been there that evening."

Shelley lifted his finger and pointed down the street. "I don't have a key. Given the neighborhood, you must keep the door secured."

"Plus, it is the only way into the house," Mary added. "It wasn't Fanny or Willy. They were with us."

Three youths came toward us, barefoot but jaunty, despite their obvious poverty. I had no money in my pockets for them to pick. I pushed Mary to Shelley's opposite side, so they couldn't get to his pockets. "And Godwin?"

"How could he have the strength to kill such a young man, and why would he stab him in that way?" Mary stopped on the pavement and stared at Shelley. "Charles could be a suspect, but I cannot think of why."

Shelley stared down the young villains. One winked at him defiantly, but they crossed the street. "If Campbell had dishonored one of you girls in some way, might either of them not become violent?"

"Papa is much too busy thinking to act," Mary said in a decisive tone, paying no attention to the world around her. "He is not capable of violence."

"Most men are. I might have killed Campbell."

Mary laughed. "With poetry and pamphlets? Shelley, you are a vegetarian. You wouldn't even kill a pig or chicken."

He grinned. "But I might kill if someone harmed Ianthe. What would you do if someone hurt young Willy?"

Mary tilted her head. "I'd like to think I could harm a villain, for such a reason."

"We know it wasn't any of the younger people in the house, then. We rule out Godwin due to character and lack of reason to do such a thing. Charles and Fanny have no connection to the poetry circle. And your mamma?"

"She is unrefined and dishonest," Mary said. "She has secrets. I am certain of that."

"She has absolutely no reason to wish me harm," Shelley said. "Moreover, she was not in Wales when that mysterious person fired at me. Does she have reason to harm Campbell?"

"We never met him," I said. Little did Mary know that my exasperating mamma wasn't the only member of the family with secrets. "But he had been in the shop. Fanny or Mamma might have known him, but Mamma had no more reason for violence than Fanny, which is to say, none at all."

"I think the note will solve the crime," Mary said. "Fitzwalter Abel will uncover the killer with a handwriting match. He just needs to talk to the right person."

Shelley snapped his fingers. "There you go, girls. We didn't recognize it. Doesn't that rule out Mrs. Godwin and my wife and even Eliza? You two know your mamma's handwriting, and I know the others."

"Disguise," I said. "The killer could have written with their left hand or be a practiced forger."

Mary put her hands on her hips and leaned forward. "But that means the note will not help at all. How dreadful."

Chapter 11

Mary

Mary set her dustrag on the shelf below, distracted by the sounds coming from upstairs. Papa, although he looked unwell, had quite a number of people to tea. Mamma was with him, in order to keep the conversation going if Papa was unable.

She couldn't be surprised about her father's ill health this week. This had been a terribly cold winter, and in addition to the stress they were under with Cecil Campbell's death, it had been hard to stay comfortable.

In February the rest of the family had attended a frost fair on the frozen Thames. Heavy snow had fallen through the winter, further aging the Skinner Street roof. April had been almost warmer than they could have expected, but this month had returned to the pattern set earlier.

She wished the sun didn't shine so brightly through the windows. She wouldn't have minded needing a candle for light and could have used it to warm her hands.

The doors opened and closed in rapid succession. Perhaps customers would bring in some warmth.

" 'Double, double toil and trouble; fire burn and cauldron bubble,' " said one of the two young gentlemen entering.

"What?" Mary asked, feeling dull and confused, though she recognized the pair.

"You were wringing your hands, Miss Godwin," said John Hocke, Mrs. Shelley's friend.

His entire costume was buff colored, with a wine tailcoat. His top hat had a tilted brim, which gave him a cheeky air. Mr. Corn wore a bright green tailcoat and inexpressibles tucked into tall black boots, which exposed the muscular outlines of his thighs and other interesting bulges.

"I am cold." Mary couldn't relax in the presence of either man. Mr. Hocke was on their possible murderer list. And what about his companion? They had forgotten about him when making their list last night. Perhaps she could learn more, and she liked the idea of doing so without Jane present. She reached under the counter and felt around but didn't feel any gloves, just an old handkerchief crumpled in the corner of the shelf.

Footsteps above made the ceiling rattle. The men glanced up.

"Papa has callers," she explained. "What can I find for you today?"

"Godwin is the reason we are here," Hocke said, tilting his chin down. "Now that we have made your acquaintance, we thought it time to finally peruse *Caleb Williams*."

"A fine novel about murder," Mary said.

"Is it?" Hocke said carelessly. "I hadn't realized it."

Ha. She didn't believe that for a second. "One copy or two?" Mary asked.

"Two, definitely, so we can read it together," Hocke said.

While Mary walked to the shelf to gather the copies, she thought about how to draw out the two men. Mr. Corn seemed to be the quiet member of the pair.

"Here you go," she announced after she pulled the volumes off the shelf. Her father would be happy to have two young poets buying his old novel. "The first line is particularly good. It starts 'My life has for several years been a theatre of calamity.' Do you ever feel like that?"

Mr. Hocke shook his head in a kind of fit, as if she had startled him with the notion. "You say this novel is about a murder. I say, I've never been mixed up in such a thing."

"'Pon rep, what a bag of moonshine," Mr. Corn said, striking a pose. "The book is about Godwin's anti-government notions. The girl is befogged."

Why had she ever wanted to make the young dandy speak at all? "Yes, it describes how peasants are made to suffer for the crimes of their betters, and how unfair that is. The murder illustrates my father's philosophical points. Have you read *Political Justice*?"

"Only the original, fiery version," Hocke said in his tossing manner. "He really has changed, you know."

"Time and experience change all men, I believe," she said. "What about you, Mr. Corn? Are you a follower of atheism, or are you more in concert with Wordsworth?"

"Wordsworth?" he cried. "I'm not dangling after him. When was the last time he was revolutionary?"

"Ah," Mary said in her wisest tone. "A revolutionary. I see. Have you traveled to foment such, like Shelley?"

"Shelley is doing it too much brown," Corn opined. "I am done to a cow's thumb at the mere thought of him."

"He is very energetic," Mary agreed. "His thoughts are so quick. I find it enervating."

"But one cannot live with the man," Hocke proclaimed. "He's always full of some new notion, always moving. It's no life for a woman."

Mary's ears pricked up. "You would know, being friendly

with Mrs. Shelley. I have not much acquaintance with her, or Miss Westbrook, who I assume is a comfort and counsel to her."

"She is considerably older," Hocke said conversationally. "But a surplus female, you know. And what can an unwed woman know about much of anything?"

Mary suddenly found she profoundly disliked both of them. Had they ever possessed an original thought? "Did Mr. Campbell think as you do? Was he a sort of revolutionary, as well?"

"Spent too much time ape-drunk and mooning about in calf-love," Corn said derisively.

"Ah, I see," Mary said. "Perhaps love is what killed him?"

"Couldn't have been the drink," Corn said, toying with his cravat, tied in the waterfall style. "As he was stabbed, not jug-bitten, to death."

Mary crossed her arms and clutched her shawl, sighing dramatically. "It is hard for me to comprehend that we were all upstairs that night. I was in my brother's room, reading him to sleep. Where were you gentlemen when the terrible deed transpired?"

"It has been a full week gone now," Hocke said, picking up the first volume of the novel. "How can one be expected to remember?"

Mary gently removed it from him and asked for the payment. "I recall another line from my father's novel. 'My story will, at least, appear to have that consistency which is seldom attendant but upon truth.'"

"La, miss, but my lack of recall is the sad truth," Hocke said. "There is your consistency for you, eh?"

"We were on the cut that night," Corn said. "I won't pitch the gammon with you. Hocke won't remember a thing."

"Oh, you were drinking somewhere?" Mary said. "Around here?"

Corn put his finger to his chin. "Fleet Street somewhere to begin." He giggled suddenly. "We may have ended up in an establishment that is not polite to mention in front of a young lady, even Godwin's daughter."

"What is that supposed to mean?" Mary asked. "My fame is spotless."

Corn giggled again. Hocke clutched the padded shoulder of Corn's tailcoat and broke into uproarious laughter.

"Not fit for innocent ears, our exploits," Hocke said. "Come now, Miss Godwin, pray do not ask for more details."

"If you were together all the early evening, that is all anyone needs to know."

He inclined his head, his eyes twinkling merriment at her. "Indeed."

She heard the Skinner Street front door opening. "I'll take the payment, please." She wanted the volumes to leave with them. The Godwins could use the money.

Hocke stopped laughing with a cough and reached into his pocket, then tossed a gold guinea onto the counter. "Enough?"

George III's face seemed to wink up at her. She covered the coin with her hand and deposited it into the money box. "You know it is not. Two more of those for my troubles, please."

He sighed theatrically and allowed George II to wink twice more at her. "Books are so very expensive."

"A truth, even if there have been no others." She bobbed a curtsy after she put the coins in the money box. "Thank you for your business, sirs."

She pushed the volumes toward Hocke. As he picked them up, the bookshop door opened. Mary recognized their returning visitor, Fitzwalter Abel of Bow Street.

"What news?" she said, feeling quite lighthearted at the secured payment for *Caleb Williams*. Would all the volumes sell out now, because of the murder? Perhaps the novel would go into another printing, netting her father a nice fee, which would ease his financial worries.

The Bow Street Runner, however, did not appear to be in a

similarly good mood. Unlike the first time she had seen him, he held his tipstaff in hand. "I've been looking for you all morning, Peter Corn," he said in the direction of the poet.

Another man, of intimidating height and girth, showed himself. He had a hard stare on his face and looked to be a much rougher character.

Mary clutched the counter edge. Should she dash out the door for her safety and leave these silly bucks to the pleasure of Bow Street? But Mamma would have a fit if she left her post and any books were destroyed. Would there be a fight? How she wished Papa were here.

Mr. Corn broke into his giggle again. John Hocke took one look at the man behind Mr. Abel and flinched. Did he recognize the Runner or merely his air of menace?

John Hocke took a step backward, hugging his side of the counter, which left Peter Corn standing in an open area. The young buck had a confused, genial expression on his handsome face.

"Why are you raising a breeze?" Corn asked Abel. "Come now, I don't want to plant a facer on you."

"Don't threaten him, man," Hocke said with a groan. "Don't you recognize the tipstaves? They are from Bow Street."

"Peter Corn, I arrest you in the name of the king," Abel said.

Mr. Corn giggled yet again. While he sounded like a fop, Mary could see by his well-muscled appearance that he probably boxed with the Pugilistic Club or somewhere similar. She pressed herself against the wall, ready to drop to the floor if a fight broke out.

The smell of the room had already changed from that of books and ink and dust to the musky scent of fear. Corn looked from one Runner to the other, then glanced back at Hocke.

Mrs. Shelley's friend lifted his hands, palms up.

Corn pulled out a snuffbox and opened it. "What is this flummery? I've done nothing to interest Bow Street." He put a pinch of snuff to his nose, sniffed, then sneezed.

"We've done our research on you, Mr. Corn," the other man, who had not identified himself, growled in a low baritone.

Abel noticed Mary just then. She realized she was shaking.

"Hold up, Fisher. Let's get the girl out of here."

She shook her head. "No. I deserve to hear what is happening. If this is about Cecil Campbell, I found his body, after all."

Abel slid his tongue over his lower lip. "Very well, you can stay, Miss Godwin."

Corn sauntered the couple of steps up the counter and leaned over it, then put his hand under his chin and stared Mary right in the eyes. "Don't worry, my bluestocking friend. They don't cut up my peace. I've done nothing."

"But you've plenty of reason to hate Percy Bysshe Shelley," Fisher said.

Mary gasped as Corn tucked away his snuffbox and turned his head. "Do I?"

"We've been to Eton, which you attended at the same time as Mr. Shelley. We've interviewed people about your school days."

"What of it?" Corn said in a careless tone. "Who is telling old gossip?"

"Only four years old," Fisher said. "Not so ancient at all, for a grudge."

"As I recall, Shelley was the bullied party, not me," Corn said, lifting his head. "What should I care about some silly trouble-maker like him?"

Fisher patted his tailcoat, then pulled out a bundle of letters. "Do these look familiar to you, sir?"

"What? Old letters?" Corn asked after a glance.

"Letters addressed to you, at Eton. We've spoken to a Mr. Hogg, who says you are aware that Mr. Shelley wrote them to you, under the pseudonym of Miss Mary Walker."

"What of it? Hogg is an intimate of Shelley's. I don't deny it."

Mary still smelled his fear, sharp and musky all at once.

"A series of five letters," Mr. Fisher continued. "Four of which allude to responses by you."

"Where did you even find the old things?" Corn asked.

Mary noticed that his mouth had firmed. Slowly, he stood up straight from his position hunched over the counter. She made sure not to meet his gaze, for fear that he might attack her.

"A Dr. Lind had them in his keeping at his chambers at Eton."

A lost look came into Corn's eyes. "There were seven letters. I didn't keep the first one or two. Miss Mary Walker, claiming to be a cousin of my mother. The questions asked were philosophical, upon the nature of love."

"Did you profess love to Miss Mary Walker?"

"I—I," he spluttered, spittle appearing at the corners of his mouth. "It was quite an exchange. It whetted my appetite."

"You were humiliated when the last letter appeared."

"No, not at all," Corn whispered. "I passed it around to the other students. I was to meet her. Then Shelley said he'd written them as an exercise in philosophy."

"How did that make you feel?"

"I hated him," Corn said in that same low tone, then raised his voice as he fisted his hands at his sides. "I hate him."

John Hocke stepped around his friend and looked Fisher in the eye bravely. "But it isn't Shelley who is dead. These are childish things from years ago. Cecil Campbell is dead."

"Shelley and Campbell wore nearly the same clothing, had the same hair, were the same size. Campbell was stabbed from behind, in a house Shelley had been known to visit, was in fact having dinner at only a couple of hours earlier," Abel said. "We think the murderer meant to attack Shelley, not Campbell. That man's death was a case of mistaken identity."

"Dr. Lind revealed my shame?" Corn asked, as if the previous exchange had not taken place.

"Dr. Lind died in eighteen twelve," Abel said. "The letters came into the possession of his successor, who doesn't know you."

"I see." All the bonhomie seemed to drain out of Peter Corn. "I did not kill Campbell, nor did I attempt to kill Shelley. In fact, we were just discussing alibis. I was with Hocke here all the night, on Fleet Street."

"Where?" Abel asked.

Corn glanced at Hocke, who tucked his hands behind his back. "We were at the convent above the tailor's shop from dusk on," Hocke said. "Inquire there. I assure you that I never left Corn's side before midnight."

Abel's lip curled. He glanced at Fisher.

"Don't leave the city," Fisher cautioned, shaking his tipstaff.

"No," Abel said, with an irritated glance at his companion. "We'll hold you at Bow Street until we can prove your unsavory alibi." He raised an eyebrow. Fisher grabbed Corn by the arm and hauled him out of the shop so quickly that Corn must have been too shocked to employ any of his evident strength.

Fitzwalter Abel marched out of the shop without another glance at anyone. Mary sagged against the wall, still shaking.

"I do apologize," Hocke said in her direction. "Please pay my compliments to your father."

"What are you going to do now?" Mary asked.

"I dare not do anything," Hocke said. "My father will cut me off without a second thought if I become involved in this. Good day." He walked out of the bookshop. Mary could hear pacing in the front hall for a minute, but her brain was too scrambled to comprehend what had just happened.

Hocke must have been waiting for the Bow Street Runners to get away, for the pacing paused a couple of minutes later, and then he left the house.

She moved to the counter then and methodically wrote up the purchases in the shop ledger, her thoughts in a whirl. At least Hocke hadn't asked for a refund.

Mary was able to get through the rest of the afternoon only by locking the arrest into a box in her mind, so that no emotion showed. It seemed incredible that customers came in that afternoon with no awareness of the visit from Bow Street. A tutor, a woman with her child in tow, an old friend of Papa, and a middle-aged Frenchman looking for one of Mamma's translations. Mary served them all with serenity, for she did not want to hear reports that she had behaved otherwise.

Shelley came into the house just as she locked the shop door. She pressed herself against it as Shelley smiled at her.

"I think we are alone," he said.

"Not really," she said faintly. "Everyone is just above us."

He considered her. "Paler than usual, Mary. You are half a ghost, though just as lovely as ever. What has happened?"

She described the events of the early afternoon. Instantly, his expression changed to solicitude.

"My poor girl," he cried. "What a frightening situation."

"It means the police think the murderer was after you. As I thought," she said. "Do you think Peter Corn is the killer?"

"It is possible," he said. "Why did they arrest Corn?"

"They said you wrote him letters, pretending to be a distressed spinster." She screwed up her face. "What does that mean?"

He laughed. "It was a habit of mine those last years at Eton. I would write authorities as an innocent, asking for clarifications on knotty theological or philosophical matters."

"What was Peter Corn an expert on?"

He still looked amused. "That was my practice run. You see, my idea was to learn what I could and then pounce, in letter form, of course, if I saw the flaw in their argument. I wrote Corn a letter asking about the nature of love. It never occurred to me that the silly boy would decide he loved the letter writer."

"You didn't mean to hurt him?"

"Not at all. I have no animosity toward Corn. That would be why he was so confused. He has no reason to kill me."

"No, he really doesn't. You were just a boy attempting to understand theology and philosophy," she agreed.

"Yes. It worked out in an unfortunate manner, but we've long since sorted it out."

His grin charmed her utterly, somewhere deep inside, but she was still the placid Mary of the afternoon, so she continued, aware that time alone was short.

She touched his arm. "I think handwriting is one of the methods we might use to unmask the killer, if we outwit the possible ways one could deceive with it."

"The writing from the note, you mean?"

She nodded. "Would you come into the shop and write for me?"

He glanced down at her fingers resting on his superfine green coat. "Of course, sweet Mary."

She unlocked the shop. They always had pen and ink on the counter, to write out receipts and update the ledger with the sales.

"What shall I write on?" he asked, picking up the sharpened quill.

"We use these for receipts," she said, pushing a rectangular scrap of paper toward him.

He looked into her eyes for a moment, then dipped the pen into the ink bottle. "To Miss Mary, one receipt."

"For what?"

He bent his head and scratched. She suddenly longed to run her hands through those runaway curls. Would they spring against her fingers or collapse into a warm puddle against his elegant skull?

He set the pen on its stand. "There you are."

She turned the paper to see what he'd written. "To Miss Mary, one receipt. My hand. Truth. Shelley."

She smiled involuntarily, losing control of her expression for the first time in hours. "Yes, this is your hand. You wrote it very naturally."

"I have nothing to hide from you, Mary Godwin," he said. "I hope we are friends."

"Always," she whispered, blinking hard.

"Do you have something in your eye?" he asked. "Here, blink against my finger. If it is an eyelash, I will fix it for you."

Mary ceased breathing as he set his finger against the tender skin under her eye. She could feel his breath against her cheek. Surely that was enough, one of them breathing? She blinked, breathing his warmth and life into her lungs.

The shop door banged open.

"I say, whatever are you doing?" Jane demanded. "You're wanted upstairs, Mary. Shop hours are over."

"Fixing her eyelashes," Shelley said, pulling his hand away. "Mary had something in her eye."

"What's this?" Jane grabbed the scrap of paper. "My hand? Truth? What does that mean?"

"It was a handwriting test, Jane. To show my handwriting doesn't match that of the ripped note."

"This is no good," she said artlessly. "You're supposed to write the note. Not random words."

"It is enough," Mary said, snatching the paper away and tucking it into her apron. "It's not the same handwriting."

"I suppose he could have written the note with his left hand, and this one with his right," Jane said.

"You want me to be guilty?" Shelley asked gaily.

"The note went to Mr. Campbell, not you."

"Or to the killer," Mary said. "We don't know."

"Where were you that night, Shelley?" Jane inquired.

"I was staying with a friend on Old Bond Street. We had words, and then I went to a tavern after, alone. My friend was in low mood, and I did not want to sink to the same depths. Shall I write the note with my left hand?"

"No," Jane said. "I expect not. We're wanted upstairs, re-member?"

"This was enough," Mary said. It was the truth, for her. She knew Shelley to be innocent of any wrongdoing. But if the Runners had arrested the wrong man, what might the real killer do to ensure that Peter Corn stayed in the embrace of the magistrates?

"Is there room at the Godwins' dining table for one more?" Shelley asked hopefully.

Mary smiled at him, but Jane shook her head. "I'm sorry, but Papa already has four for dinner, and he looks a bit pale."

"I wouldn't like to disturb him, then," Shelley said quickly. "Another time."

He took each of their hands and bowed over them like a proper French aristocrat. The girls giggled at the gallantry, then walked him to the front door. Mary relocked the shop door before she and Jane ran upstairs, performing a symphony of creaks and squeaks on the old wood.

Mary paused at the landing on the first floor, but Jane tugged her on.

"You need to change your dress," Jane said.

"It's clean under the apron," Mary told her. "Just one little ink stain on the sleeve."

Jane shook her head. "No, Sir and Lady Aldis are here, along with the Currans. You need to refresh yourself."

"Oh, very well," Mary said. "Such a bother."

"You are a hoyden," Jane said primly, dragging her up the next flight of stairs, quieter this time, so as not to disturb the guests.

Mary tidied herself in her room and caught Jane up on the events of the day. "Bow Street has decided Peter Corn killed Mr. Campbell due to mistaken identity, thinking he was Shelley!"

She helped Mary pull her stained dress over her head. "You think they are wrong? That's why you were testing Shelley's handwriting?"

"Of course not. Shelley is an angel. But we had meant to check everyone's handwriting."

Jane held up the evening dress and slipped it over Mary's

head. "That is the business done, I suppose. One murderer caught. We can go about our business without fear now."

"Shelley doesn't think Peter Corn had a reason to kill him."

"You can't think Bow Street has it wrong. They are the experts in crime." Jane pulled the drawstring taut around Mary's waist and tied it. "Although, do we know if Mr. Corn had a reason to kill Mr. Campbell?"

"I do not know what it could be. The only motive he had was a silly one." Mary explained about the distressed spinster letters.

"We need to call on someone who knows Mr. Campbell and can tell us about his relationship to Mr. Corn."

"Mr. Hocke is intimately involved," Mary said.

"There has to be someone else," Jane said. "Everyone has sisters and mothers and aunts and things."

"And lovers," Mary whispered. "The best motive at all is related to Mr. Campbell's affair with Mrs. Shelley."

"There may be another motive that is even stronger," Jane said. "Because if you are right, there is no better a suspect than Shelley."

"No," Mary declared.

"No one would expect it, two girls coming up with the solution," Jane said.

"We can tell Papa when we sort it out. Mr. Hocke seems to have no end of funds. What is the state of Mr. Campbell's purse? We need to learn something of his family."

They went downstairs, and Mary mimicked locking her lips as they reached the dining room door.

Jane nodded and opened it.

Her father did indeed look pale, worn out by a busy week interlaced with bouts of illness. What had he been eating outside the house to take so ill? Her stomach had been sound as a drum. Mamma overspent on good food because she enjoyed it so much herself. They had access to high-quality meat because the market was so close. It would be difficult to buy bad meat if you were willing to pay for good, so close to Smithfield. It was, perhaps, the only advantage of living here.

Mary asked Papa about Mr. Barre's desire for the green leather *Lyrical Ballads*, thinking they would need extra money for a doctor, but he said he'd never owned it, though he wished he had. Her question led to a spirited discussion about the foibles of collectors.

Chapter 12

Mary

Midmorning on Friday, Mary begged her stepmother to allow her to take a walk, because the shop was making her head pound.

Mamma acceded with surprisingly good grace, so Mary grabbed a shawl and hurried out. She met Jane, who had begged off similarly from Fanny in the parlor.

"I am not sure we are dressed to pay calls," Jane said, tugging at her serviceable gray dress.

"At least my shawl isn't bad," Mary said, stroking the silk that had been her mother's.

"My gloves are new." Jane adjusted her bonnet around her dark curls with a sigh. "My understanding is that Mr. Campbell was a late-in-life child. His only sibling is a much older sister, Mrs. McAndrew."

"I don't know that name," Mary mused over the noise of a cart piled high with imported fruit passing by. "Must not be a literary or fashionable family."

Jane batted a fly out of her eyes. "Well, Russell Square. It is a good address, but not a superlative one."

"I would be happy with it," Mary said, hooking her arm into Jane's.

They walked briskly through the streets, attempting to stay close to buildings in order to protect their skirts and shoes from the worst of the dust. A momentary escape into the Queen Square plantings allowed them respite under the shade of a tall tree. Once they had dotted the perspiration off their temples and upper lips, they walked the short distance to the south side of Russell Square, where the McAndrews home was.

"Wasn't that Mr. Barre?" Jane asked, distracted by a man walking around the corner.

"Who?"

Jane licked her lips. "Our customer? The thin Frenchman who licks his fingers before he touches his hair?"

Mary didn't understand why she cared, and changed the subject. "I didn't see him. Do you think Mrs. McAndrew will let us in?" she replied. "We don't have a calling card."

"It's the right time of day," Jane said. "And you are Mary Wollstonecraft Godwin, after all. The name is known."

True. Mary permitted herself a small smile. Jane's name was of no interest to anyone.

They knocked at the door of the four-story terraced house. The family had money, to be sure, though the cream stone and brown brick weren't the most pleasing combination to Mary's eye.

When a maid opened the door, Mary gave her full name and asked to see Mrs. McAndrew. The maid allowed them inside, then vanished upstairs.

A few minutes passed; then their things were taken and they were led upstairs to a reception room in the back of the house.

Mary's first impression was green. The wallpaper had a green and ocher ivy design, and large green-leaved plants were displayed on columns in every corner. A screen in front of the fireplace had been japanned with botanical drawings.

A frail woman lay across a chaise lounge at the far end of the room, underneath a large window that looked out to a very green back garden. She wore a long-sleeved green wool gown with a heavy shawl over it, and a cap pulled low over mousy brown hair, which peeped out untidily.

"This is Mrs. McAndrew," the maid said.

"Tea," ordered the lady of the house in a very subdued manner. The maid bobbed in her direction and left.

Had Mrs. McAndrew been doused with laudanum to deal with the stress of her brother's death? Her face seemed drawn into lines of near starvation, with sharp, jutting bones at every angle. Her illness must predate her family tragedy. A wave of guilt poured over Mary. They shouldn't be here, intruding on an ill woman's grief.

Then the corner moved. Jane shrieked and clutched Mary's arm.

A young woman dressed in black came out of the shadow created by the pulled-back curtain next to an enormous plant. She had black hair to match her mourning gown, pale skin, and bright blue eyes that fairly bulged from their sockets. Her inquiring look at the pair set the lady of the house into motion.

"I am Mrs. McAndrew," the ill woman said, struggling into a sitting position. "This is Sophia Campbell."

"Campbell?" Mary queried.

"My father's cousin," Mrs. McAndrew explained, her voice fading.

Mary cleared her throat, which was rather dry from the walk. "We wanted to pay a condolence call, you see. You are the only family we could find for poor Mr. Campbell. We are sorry to disturb you, Mrs. McAndrew."

"You knew him?" asked the bereaved.

"We found him," Jane said baldly.

Mary gave her an admonishing look. Miss Campbell's eyes bulged farther.

"Chairs." Mrs. McAndrew waved a hand, that looked like a leaf in the wind.

Miss Campbell slid around Mary and pulled two chairs with ivy-patterned cushions away from the wall. After she had arranged them to her satisfaction, Mary and Jane sat.

"Tea," Mrs. McAndrew said again.

"I'll see what is keeping the maid," Miss Campbell said, though it had been only two minutes, and made her departure.

"Tiresome," Mrs. McAndrew said, then covered her mouth with a skeletally thin hand while she yawned.

"I am afraid I did find your brother," Mary said, deciding to plow on so they could leave all the sooner. "I don't know if you are familiar with the bookshop my family has in Skinner Street. I went to fetch a book after dinner and found him there."

"Murder," said the lady of the house.

"Very clearly," Mary agreed, leaning forward. "Such a tragedy."

"Arrest," Mrs. McAndrew said.

"I was there again." Mary clasped her hands in her lap, her fingers sweaty under her gloves. "When the Bow Street Runners came to arrest Mr. Corn. He'd been shopping with Mr. Hocke."

Jane wiggled, irritated, on her chair as Mrs. McAndrew said, "Friend."

"Friend of your family or just of your brother?" Mary inquired.

"Family," the lady said decidedly. She tilted on the chaise cushion.

Mary leaned forward to help her up. The lady put one hand to her temple.

"Dreadful," she said. "Energy."

"Gone, I suppose," Jane suggested.

"Children, house." Mrs. McAndrew shook her head.

"No time to mourn properly?" Mary suggested.

"My family, deceased." The hand drifted to her lap, like a leaf in autumn.

"So very sad," Jane said, swiping at her cheek.

"I believe Mr. Hocke is also a friend of Mrs. Shelley," Mary said. "We first met him with her, then met Mr. Corn at his rooms initially, but it was only the second time I'd met him that the arrest occurred."

"Almost strangers," Mrs. McAndrew said.

"Exactly. They seemed to have alibis, though." Mary coughed. "Not the best alibis. Still, I couldn't be sure that Mr. Corn was arrested fairly."

"Both alibied?" Mrs. McAndrew inquired.

"By each other, you see. But they claimed to be around other people at specific places. I do wonder, with the length of time it has already been, if anyone would properly remember them."

"No one would know it was important at the time, whether they were there or not," Jane said.

"Dreadful," said the lady.

"I know it is terrible to ask what you thought. Would another poet want to do this to your brother?" Mary asked.

"But that's not the theory," Jane interjected. "They think Peter Corn killed Mr. Campbell, thinking he was Shelley."

"No motive to kill my brother," murmured the lady.

"For Mr. Corn?" asked Mary. "Or no motive for anyone?"

The door opened. The maid came in, carrying a rattling tray, followed by Miss Campbell, holding a bowl of porridge and a napkin. The companion rearranged tables so that the porridge was easy for Mrs. McAndrew to access.

"Pour," Mrs. McAndrew said, waving at Miss Campbell.

She poured tea to everyone's tastes, while Mary wished for lemonade, more suitable to the warm day, especially since a low fire still graced the fireplace in the room.

"I hate to go back to our conversation," Mary said after she had drunk her tea and Mrs. McAndrew had eaten one small bite of porridge. "But were you making the point that Mr. Corn had no specific motive to kill your brother or that no one did? The motive they have for Mr. Corn to kill Shelley seems very weak to me."

"No one would have wanted my brother dead." Mrs. McAndrew seemed to have gathered strength from her single bite. "He was like any young man, only better. High-minded, philosophical, no vices." She punctuated her remark by taking another bite.

Mary turned her gaze to the companion, whose tea was left forgotten on the table. She seemed to be holding back tears. "You were fond of your cousin?"

"Of course not," Miss Campbell snapped. She rose and trotted out of the room.

"Handkerchief," Mrs. McAndrew called behind her.

The door closed, rather loudly, behind the companion.

"Dreadful girl. So strange."

"She's very sad," Mary suggested.

"Yes," Mrs. McAndrew agreed before taking another small bite. "Poor Cecil."

Mary nodded. "Thank you for your insights. I believe you would say that the real target had been Shelley, and not your brother at all."

Jane harrumphed.

"You do not agree?"

"Did Bow Street tell you of the note Jane and I found—or two pieces of it, at any rate—which seemed to indicate Mr. Corn had been lured there to a meeting? Shelley had been to dinner and left again, and he received no note." Or at least Mary assumed so, since he hadn't mentioned it.

Mrs. McAndrew picked up her spoon and took one bite before setting it down again. "There, four bites. Tell Sophia."

"You could take twenty and still have more in the bowl," Jane suggested. "Why don't you have a fifth bite?"

Mrs. McAndrew shuddered slightly.

"I'm sure it must be hard," Jane said softly. "Perhaps some tea with milk?"

Distaste crossed the lady's features. "I liked champagne, when we could get it."

"The news from France is very good," Mary said. "I'm sure the, er, merchants will have it again soon."

The lady passed a hand over her face.

"You are fatigued," Jane said. "We will let you rest."

"Is there anything we can do to see to your comfort?" Mary asked, rising.

"Chilly," the lady said.

Mary went to the bellpull to ring for the maid while Jane stirred up the fire.

"I am very sorry about your brother," Mary said. "Do you know of any particular friends of his that we could speak to?"

"Mr. Hocke came often," Mrs. McAndrew said, then yawned.

The maid came in.

"We'll see ourselves out," Mary said, "so you can make Mrs. McAndrew comfortable."

She followed Jane out of the room, disappointed by the lack of information.

At the top of the staircase, Jane pointed at the window. "Look, that Miss Campbell has left the house."

"Why?" Mary said, seeing a young woman in a black dress vanish between passing carriages. "She left so suddenly."

"I'm suspicious," Jane said. "Shall we follow her?"

"Yes," Mary agreed. "She lives in the same house and might have more to offer about Mr. Campbell. Mrs. McAndrew has turned her brother into such an angel already that we will get nothing from her."

"He might have been an angelic sort of person," Jane suggested.

"A lover of Mrs. Shelley's?" Mary asked. "I think not."

"We think highly of Shelley, and he is married to the lady," Jane said as they clambered like hoydens down the staircase.

"She was our age when they married. People claim our characters are not yet formed. Could she have been any different?"

Downstairs, they reclaimed their outerwear, opened the front door, and emerged onto the pavement, blinking in the sunlight. The smell of a well-maintained house and fresh flowers vanished when the door closed, leaving them with all the various smells of horses on the breeze, along with the higher note of evergreen.

"Courting couples are often in each other's company very little until the wedding," Mary said. "A girl could deceive a man, I expect."

"Especially in the upper classes, so they say," Jane said. "And marriage is so deceitful, anyway."

"An appalling institution," Mary agreed. "Little more than slavery."

They scanned the street. A young woman with black hair and a cap was not up or down the road.

"Across," Jane said just as Mary spotted her. "She's gone into the park."

Mary had missed her because of the hedges blocking the park from the street. "Let's follow."

They waited for a rider to pass, then dashed into the road to cross to the substantial patch of green at the center of Russell Square. Glimpses of the white cap flashed as Miss Campbell weaved her way through holly oak and lime trees. As they followed her path, the city seemed to become green and hushed, the sounds of cabs and carriages and men receding. They could hear children, their small feet crunching the gravel.

"So lovely and cool here," Jane said. "Why don't we walk in this square more often?"

"I prefer to visit Mother," Mary said, thinking of the willow trees around her grave.

When they reached the center, they saw Miss Campbell. She wrung her hands together and paced back and forth behind a bench with quick, jerking steps. A bonneted mama pulled her young child away from the bench, leaving it empty.

"Miss Campbell," Mary called, stepping forward. "You seem to be in some distress."

Jane followed her, adding, "It must be difficult to see your cousin in such a state."

"She brings it on herself," Miss Campbell said calmly.

Did she know she had been followed? It seemed unlikely, since she had never turned around and they had hardly been the only people on the street.

"What troubles you, then?" Mary asked.

"It's not as if I like Cousin Emma being ill," Miss Campbell said, straightening her back. "It's just that I believe her illness is of the mind. She thinks her clothing is too tight, so she must not eat. It is a kind of mania."

"I thought her clothing fit her loosely," Mary said.

"It is much too warm for the season," Jane added.

Miss Campbell gestured. "She is always cold. Walking here would be a torment between the outdoor temperature and her weakness. I shouldn't speak so to strangers."

"It's not as if anyone thinks she killed her brother," Jane said.

"Jane!" Mary exclaimed. "Really."

"Emma has not the strength to do anything so dreadful as what happened to Cecil." Miss Campbell's lips twitched as she stopped speaking.

"She is only a danger to herself?" Mary suggested. That summed up the poor lady, though one could not know the true source of her illness. "Does she have other brothers and sisters?"

"None who outlived childhood. Rather a small family on

both sides. I see nothing wrong with marrying young and attempting to have a large family. It is not as if the family trusts on either side needed to be split many ways."

"Who are you to marry?" Jane asked.

Mary clutched Jane's upper arm. "She's saying she was to wed Cecil Campbell, Jane."

Jane's mouth went round.

"It was rather a secret engagement," Miss Campbell said almost apologetically. "The family is not supportive, since I don't have a dowry."

"Why not?" Jane asked. "You mentioned family trusts."

"Me, I'm just a poor relation to the Campbells. You see, Emma's mother married beneath her, so the trusts came through her mother. Emma married Mr. McAndrew, who has done very well for himself in banking and is therefore equal enough. But me, I'm the daughter of a family of music teachers. You can imagine the scandal when Emma's mother married the man who gave her voice lessons."

"Gretna Green?" Jane asked in a tone of great interest.

"Somewhere in Scotland to be sure," Miss Campbell said.

"Were you going to run off to Scotland, as well?" Mary asked.

"It might have come to that. We are, well, were, in Cecil's case, very young still. He did not have access to funds until he was twenty-five, but he thought me comfortable enough with his sister."

"If she lives another four years," Mary said gently.

Miss Campbell's lips trembled. "Yes, it is all rather dreadful, isn't it? No one wants a female music master. I am trying to learn other skills, to be a governess properly when she is gone, but I wish she would have a care for herself. She's only thirty."

"I am sorry for your troubles," Jane said earnestly. "It is rather a lot to bear."

"My reading is so much better, but I need to learn French and geography. I don't sew well, though I do try." Miss Campbell wiped her eyes. "Now we don't see anyone, so I would never hear about positions."

"You could apply to some sort of agency," Mary suggested. "Or what about a school?"

"I wanted a husband," Miss Campbell said. "But now I will not meet another young man."

The companion running off like she had had seemed suspicious to Mary. But she could see now that Miss Campbell had no reason to want Mr. Campbell dead. They could cross Emma McAndrew and Sophia Campbell off a suspect list, not that they had ever been there.

Mary glanced at Jane, who half closed one eyelid at her.

"Did you care that your beloved was in an intimate connection with a young married lady?" Jane blurted.

Mary stared at Miss Campbell, who had gone white instantly. She swayed in her unsuitable indoor slippers. Mary grabbed her around the waist and guided her onto the bench.

"You didn't know," she said, sitting next to her and patting her hand.

Jane dropped onto the bench on the other side of Miss Campbell, rocking it a little. "Yes, you see. We've been told he'd been up to some sort of nonsense with Mrs. Shelley, and now she's with child."

"What bad form," Miss Campbell said faintly. "Oh, my stars."

Jane looked at the other young lady's midsection. "Could you have the same issue?"

"We wouldn't judge," Mary said quickly. "We are Godwin's daughters."

Miss Campbell smiled faintly. "There is no privacy in the McAndrew home. I do not doubt they would cast me out if I got myself into a scrape."

"But then you'd be married," Jane said. "He'd have taken you to Scotland, wouldn't he?"

"Cecil was very young. Just twenty-one."

"Shelley is twenty-one and has been married for years," Mary pointed out.

"Cecil is still very attached," Miss Campbell started. "Was attached, I should say, to his sister. He did not have a boisterous or independent personality."

"What did Mr. Campbell write about?" Mary asked.

Miss Campbell hesitated. "He wrote a lovely long poem about the pet bird he'd had as a child. I loved his ode to rabbits. But I will say his circle had influence on his most recent work."

"Those in the circle were his friends?" Mary summed up.

Miss Campbell looked dubious. "Yes, I think that is true in the main. He loved to box. That is very fashionable now. He would ride out to matches with the others, but he didn't gamble. I don't know how he came across Mrs. Shelley, but as you say, marriage is not much respected in that circle."

"You believe in it," Mary stated. "I can see that you do."

"I am not of an independent mind. I want a husband. It is better than this," Miss Campbell said. She made a circle with her hands. "Do you know I never leave Russell Square? My cousin makes herself too ill to pay calls or shop."

"My stepmother wants me to work in our family bookshop, while Jane gets to go to school," Mary said. "I understand the restrictions of family life. I can understand why Mr. Campbell was so very important to you and why you would wait for him to sow his wild oats."

Miss Campbell's lips tightened. "John Hocke was a bad influence. I expect my Cecil would have been true otherwise without that devil whispering in his ear."

Mary raised her hands. "But it was Peter Corn who was arrested, not Mr. Hocke."

"Mr. Corn is a dandy," Miss Campbell said. "Perhaps a bit of a fool. Mr. Hocke is another matter."

"He has a motive to want Mr. Campbell dead?" Mary asked.

Miss Campbell pointed to her little finger on her left hand. "Cecil's body was missing a gold ring when it was returned for burial."

"You think Mr. Hocke wanted it?" Jane asked after a squeak of outrage.

"His pockets are always to let. Ruffians are searching for him." Mary's fingers went cold in her gloves. "Ruffians?"

"Moneylenders," Miss Campbell explained. "They send out men to break knees and heads and such, I believe, when loans are not repaid."

"I cannot imagine one small ring would be enough to hold off such men. One hears of fortunes being lost on betting. If they were aficionados of boxing and Mr. Hocke was in a habit of betting wrong?" Mary shook her head.

"I think the fact that I believe Mr. Hocke could kill for money says enough," Miss Campbell said. "What if there was a boxing match and Cecil won? He could have been killed for the contents of his pockets."

"A capital notion, except he was lured to the bookshop with a depressing poetical note," Jane mentioned.

"Exactly how one would lure Cecil somewhere," Miss Campbell said. "Whoever did this knew him well."

"We don't have the entire note," Mary added. "There could have been a line at the bottom asking him to bring his purse. We haven't found any more of it."

"They probably tore off the most incriminating part," Jane said, wriggling on the bench.

"Like their signature," Mary said archly. "We don't mean to make light of this tragedy, Miss Campbell. I myself will never forget what I saw."

"Nor will I," Jane insisted. "We will discover the truth of the matter and bring that person to justice."

"What was the poetical note?" Miss Campbell asked after a thoughtful pause.

Mary patted her hand. "It was a line from Wordsworth. 'We Poets in our youth begin in gladness; But thereof come in the end despondency and madness.'"

"It sounds like a threat," Miss Campbell said after mouthing the words silently. "Cecil was most certainly in his glad phase. He adored poetry. He spoke in couplets whenever possible."

"A threat," Mary said, turning the notion over in her mind. "We hadn't thought of that."

"What would have brought Mr. Campbell to despondency and madness?" Jane asked.

"Mrs. Shelley, most likely," Mary said. "I would not have known of her interesting condition from looking at her."

The three young women glanced between each other.

"You can't think Shelley's wife a murderer," Jane gasped.

"Mr. Hocke is her dear companion," Mary said. "Maybe she talked him into becoming her instrument."

"For a sizeable payment, perhaps," Miss Campbell said. "That could explain all! If Mr. Hocke lured Cecil to the bookshop and told him he was to be a father, Cecil would refuse to run off with Mrs. Shelley because of his love for me, and then Mr. Hocke would kill him because of Mrs. Shelley's outrage, for the coin she would pay him!"

"I suppose it could have happened like that," Mary said. "He did not act like a killer when Mr. Corn was arrested, though. We also don't know if Mrs. Shelley wanted to run away."

"What does a killer act like?" Jane asked. "The only killers we have seen were about to have a noose thrown around their necks outside Newgate Prison."

"It is easy for men to kill. So many men become soldiers, and those who do not are often fascinated with the business of war," Miss Campbell said. "If I was a poet, I would write about that, I suppose."

"I am not convinced Mr. Campbell was the target, and not

Shelley," Mary said. "But I appreciate you helping us to understand him."

"There is certainly a motive for Shelley to want him dead," Jane remarked. "For his sake, I am glad Mr. Corn was arrested."

Chapter 13

Jane

"Shoo," Mamma hissed at me when I walked up the stairs late the next morning, after finishing the breakfast dishes.

Mary clattered down the steps from the upper floors, holding our shawls. She had her street shoes on. "Mr. Hogan has called for Papa, with reinforcements," she whispered.

I followed Mary, not daring to take the time to gather my own things. There would be shouting. When we reached the front hall, I asked, "What about Willy? Is Charles here today?"

"Charles took Willy to Somers Town, to play in the fields near our old house. Come now, we should go."

"Fanny?" I asked. Of all of us, she would be the most sensitive to the argument that was sure to follow, for Papa would not have the money to pay his creditors.

"Paying a call. It's her birthday, you know."

In the street, a buzz seemed to hang in the air, with more people around the neighborhood than usual. When we walked across, we could see why. The portable gallows were being secured into place in front of the Debtors' Door, with loud hammering sounds adding a drumbeat to the neighborhood.

"A hanging tomorrow," Mary predicted.

"I hope Papa's creditors do not come again," I said. "We will not want to be forced outside during the hanging."

"No," Mary agreed. "Murder or not, I don't want to imagine someone we know hanging from the gallows."

"Do you think Mr. Corn will take his turn there someday?" I asked.

"Not if we can sort out what actually happened," she told me. "We must investigate Mr. Hocke. Did Mr. Corn have money that night?"

I winced. "We can be sure that Mr. Hocke needed it if he did."

"The problem is," Mary said as we walked past the Debtor's Door, "that Miss Campbell, by her own admittance, is very sheltered. She would know only what she was told, and we don't know whether her intended was a truth teller or not."

"Not is my vote," I said. "For he was making love to her while toying with Mrs. Shelley."

"According to Mr. Hocke," Mary said. "We have only words, not proof of anything."

"The proof is Mr. Campbell's poor dead body," I said.

We turned into Fleet Lane, which took us away from Newgate, though we were just walking along another forbidding prison wall.

"What can we do today to learn more?" Mary asked.

"My favorite people!" cried a familiar voice.

I glanced away from Mary and saw Shelley. Hatless as usual, but in a fine coat, though one of the buttons had a string hanging from it.

"You girls shouldn't be here. It is not a good area," he scolded, taking our arms. "Come, let us walk over to Lincoln's Inn Fields. We can sit under a tree."

"That is good, for we cannot be at home right now," Mary said, smiling at him.

"No? I thought to take tea with your father."

"His creditors press him, and Mamma shooed us onto the street," she explained.

"I do hope to ease his suffering soon, but there is a good deal of paperwork involved. They like to examine me, and hope desperately that I am in poor health, as well as the rest of my family, so that the funds may be claimed sooner rather than later." Shelley began to whistle, which made no difference in this part of town. No one looked at him. "What has been happening since I saw you last?"

"We talked for quite a while with Mr. Campbell's sister and intended," I said.

"What conclusions did you draw?" Shelley asked.

"That we know only supposition and not fact," Mary said. "His intended points her finger at Mr. Hocke, not Mr. Corn. She says Mr. Hocke has ruffians after him about a loan and that he would kill for money."

"Did Campbell have money?" Shelley asked.

"Don't you know?" Mary asked. "He was part of your circle."

"I don't notice money. He never seemed hungry, and his clothes were good."

"He had an intended," I dropped in.

Surprise flitted across Shelley's face. "I didn't know he planned to wed."

"It seems to have been a secret between them. But truly, who would kill Cecil Campbell over a secret engagement?" Mary asked.

Shelley tilted his head. "Another woman? Her family?"

"His sister is too ill," Mary said.

"We didn't meet her husband," I added.

"The other woman is your wife," Mary said. Even though she had said it softly, a man walking past them in a stained butcher's apron still gave them a curious look. She turned her head away and pretended not to notice.

Shelley sighed dramatically. "If Cecil Campbell is truly the father of Harriet's child, Miss Campbell herself could be the killer."

Mary shook her head. "It would be easy to believe that, but Miss Campbell seemed to be mourning Mr. Campbell."

"More than seemed," I added. "She really is. She is bereft without him. Her options are few now."

"People do things against their best interest," Mary said. "Then regret them later, as deeply as if they had not been at fault. But we interviewed this young lady at some length, and I did not believe her a killer."

How right my sister was. Regret felt like poison in my veins.

"I will ask around about the state of John Hocke's pockets," Shelley said.

We passed some men in wigs, and then we were in a green space, so foreign to the neighborhood around the prisons. Shelley collapsed under a tree, all knees and elbows. Mary composed herself and sat next to him, making sure her ankles were covered.

I sat across from them, in the shadow pattern of dancing leaves created by the tree branches overhead. "I wonder who the biggest liar in this business is." Other than myself.

Shelley smiled that sweet smile of his. "Me."

"You?" Mary asked.

"For I have pretended these people and this society are my world, and they are not, not any longer." He plucked a stalk of grass and made it dance with his fingers.

Mary smiled that secret smile of hers.

"I wish we could stay here all night, and tomorrow, too," I announced. "I do not want to be on Skinner Street with the hanging tomorrow."

"I will work on a story," Mary said. "It will be set somewhere far away from here."

"Will it have murder?" Shelley asked.

"Grievously so." She had a twinkle in her eye now. "La, sir, just you wait for my tale of woe."

"After that we shall hear Jane's," Shelley declared. "I'm sure she has the imagination for a tale."

"Of course," I agreed, pleased he had included me. "You will be too saddened by my tragic tale to sleep. Your pillow will be soaked with tears."

"That's the spirit," Shelley said with relish.

Mary looked daggers at me, but I could tell Shelley had as much interest in my tale as hers, and why not? I had just as much imagination.

We passed Sunday shut up in the house, as expected. The patterning of a dress upon pink and white jaconet muslin that Fanny had received for her birthday consumed our time, while Mary spun tales.

On Monday Mamma sent Mary and Fanny down to open the shop. Fanny brought her sewing basket, in the hopes that they could sew seams in between customers. I went to my lessons, then arrived at the bookshop at eleven.

A familiar customer entered after I had made one small sale to an older man I had not seen in the shop before. John Hocke, alone this time. I hoped that he had enjoyed *Caleb Williams* so much that he had returned for more of Papa's volumes rather than for another subject. I would enjoy placing the bright gold guineas in Mamma's greedy hands this evening.

"How did you like the book?" I prattled. "Falkland is such a devil. To think of being so consumed by pride and reputation."

"Is he?" Mr. Hocke said carelessly, giving me a wink. "I am not so far in the book as to reveal that."

"I think it is obvious pretty early, what with that business about the trunk," I said less certainly. "We will have a grand discussion about it when you are finished."

He inclined his head. "I look forward to it, Miss Clairmont.

I admit I am nowhere near done with even the first volume, though it is a very good story."

"La, sir," I prattled. "My father has written a number of very good books, so you have more to look forward to when you are finished with this one."

"I look forward to them," he said, nodding. "I do have other news, however."

"Oh?" I found it hard to swallow.

The color on his cheeks heightened. "I have to admit that I did not spend every moment that night with Corn. I blush to explain why."

"You were together for part of the evening."

"We were, indeed." He licked his lips. "Campbell was discovered about the hour to retire, I believe. Well, we must have separated about an hour before that. I had assumed Corn to have indulged in the same, ah, activities I was, but he went off to Covent Garden."

"Do the Bow Street Runners know that?"

"They have a witness who had seen him in the streets. Of course, they want to put him here, on Skinner Street, but Bow Street doesn't have that."

"Where was he seen?"

"Fleet Street. And now the person he was meeting has told me where he went."

"Oh?"

Hocke nodded. "He went to the Drury Lane theater and met—can you imagine?—Miss Westbrook there."

"Eliza Westbrook, Shelley's wife's sister?" I said cautiously.

"Yes, that lady."

The story had to be true, because Mary had said Mamma met Eliza Westbrook there, as well. The woman must take all her late-night meetings there, which was not a terrible idea, given the amount of traffic and light around the theater. "Why were they together at the time of the murder?"

"That is the question. They were a bit cagey on the subject. It won't have been romance. She must be thirty."

"I understand she is unattractive, as well," I said baldly.

"I thought perhaps she was passing some communication from her sister to Mr. Corn, though why it would be necessary, I do not know."

"You have said Mr. Campbell was Mrs. Shelley's particular friend. Could Mr. Corn have moved into the role?" I wondered aloud.

"It's havey-cavey business. But with the state of things between Shelley and his wife, I don't suppose she has to be secretive, and why would her sister be in the middle of it?"

"I have it on authority that she behaved as middleman in between Shelley and his future wife when they courted. That without her help, they never could have gone to Scotland to elope."

"Shelley has a family with money and title, a fair bit of mouse for the trap. I don't know what she would want with Mr. Corn. He has ambitions of being a proper Corinthian. He doesn't want a mistress. He's in the fancy. His ambition is to be invited to join Watier's."

"A gambling man?" I asked. "On boxing matches?"

"Likes to move with the game, as it was. No ties, just a good time. Not like Cecil Campbell at all. He had a romantic streak."

Mary ran into the room then, ending the casual conversation, which I knew was mere prelude to the real subject. "Can you close up the shop?" she asked, not seeing Mr. Hocke. "Mamma needs your help for an hour and said to close."

I pointed at Mr. Hocke.

Mary startled. "Oh, blast! I am so sorry. I did not see you there." Her eyes drifted to his hands.

It was then I remembered that Mr. Campbell had a missing ring. I investigated Mr. Hocke's hands, as well, but he wasn't wearing any rings. Of course, if the story about him was true, the ring would have gone to a pawnshop or directly into the hands of the ruffians who collected for his moneylender.

"There is plenty of work for a woman to do around a household, without running a shop, I would imagine," Mr. Hocke said easily. "My mother is forever exhausted."

"Indeed," Mary said. "But we are a literary family and must have time for our writing, as well."

"Oh? Do you have literary ambitions, Miss Godwin?" Mr. Hocke said.

I grew alarmed, for Mamma would expect us both behind the house to stir the washing.

"Oh yes. Right now, I'm trying to write a story about moneylenders and their enforcers," she said.

My mouth dropped open. I covered it with my hand before he could see it. Clever girl, my sister, to so easily have come up with a way to learn about his financial problems. I envied her that quick wit.

"Surely such men cannot be in your acquaintance or experience," Mr. Hocke said.

"They are not, sir," Mary said, artfully casting her eyes down. "I just need a few bits of detail. Have you ever heard any stories that might aid me?"

Mary in that moment had much in common with the Westbrook sisters, with her baited trap full of trembling girlhood.

"I might at that," he said, with no embarrassment whatsoever.

I supposed that if even Prinny had his moneylenders, why would any gentleman of the realm care if his pockets were to let?

"First of all, you can find such places around Ludgate Hill, maybe in a little court off Fleet Street, and up the stairs, in some upper office, you will find such men who style themselves as Messrs. John King and Company or Messrs. Paul Lever and Company. There will be a man who is of the Hebrew race in charge, sitting behind the desk, and there will be at least two hulking fellows near him, or more if there are valuables on the premises, and a large safe, as you can imagine."

"Excellent," Mary said, her forehead screwed up as she listened carefully.

"You go in and list your valuables or property. They keep it all nice and tidy in a ledger. Then coin appears from somewhere after the deal is done. If you're a gambling man, you might have walked in with the man you owe money to." He cleared his throat. "You never want to see those hulking fellows show up in your life. That's bad business."

"What happens?" Mary asked.

"If you've missed a payment, they will take it out of you in blood, not that this rewards you with a reduction in your debt. It's merely an incentive to find the blunt."

"Have you known anyone who has been so attacked?" I asked.

"Almost took a beating myself," he said cheerfully. "But I had the coins in my pocket, at least enough to satisfy them. I need to change my ways. The experience taught me that." I knew the path he had taken to change his finances. I wished he had never come to our bookshop.

"How does a gentleman find the money to repay these fellows?" Mary asked. "Is it a matter of waiting for your allowance?"

"If you have one," he said. "Mostly, you hit up any of your friends for their ready coin."

"And then you are in debt to them."

"But they don't have the hulking fellows," he pointed out. "It all becomes a bit of a muddle, until one inherits. I tell you, some families are simply too long lived."

I thought about Papa and his creditors and hoped he chose them more wisely than Mr. Hocke. He tended to do business with men who revered his work. That must help, for he seemed to withstand a great deal of shouting but no violence. The information explained why Mamma sent us away, however.

The shop door opened again. I turned, startled. But it was only Papa, and with the door open, I could hear Mamma's yelling even from the back of the house.

"I'm going to take over the shop," he said. "Go help with the laundry, girls."

I knew Mamma must be in an unusual fury for Papa to come here. He never troubled himself with the shop.

I pulled off my apron and set it under the counter, then nodded to Mr. Hocke and took Mary's hand.

As I pulled her out, we heard Papa say, "How are you liking *Caleb Williams*, sir? I understand you took possession of him recently."

Chapter 14

Jane

Papa did not last long behind the bookshop counter. Not two hours after we'd gone to work on the washing, he came outside to say he'd closed the shop because he needed to return to his study.

Mamma's eyelids slitted down. She said something rude, but Papa walked off as if he hadn't heard her. Sometimes, I wished we could do the same. Mary had already not been doing her share. She'd nicked her finger on a corner of the washtub, and tears ran down her face whenever the soap hit her cut.

"Open the shop," Mamma barked at Mary.

"I'm bleeding," Mary said, holding up her abused finger.

She turned to me. "Find your sister something to wrap her finger in, and then come back here."

"Yes, Mamma," I said and dragged Mary off, grateful for the break.

"Go open the shop," Mary said, giving me a little push. "I'll fix my own finger."

"Mamma wants me outside," I told her.

Mary looked directly into my eyes. "Papa knows how to escape her. Why can't we?"

I glanced around the hall, then back to Mary. Blood dripped down her finger. "Deal with that," I ordered. "Good heavens, Mary."

In the shop, I tied my shop apron around my waist and reached under the counter to pull out the first volume of *Zofloya; or, The Moor*. Mamma would not like to see me reading it, but it was gripping stuff. I tried to forget the interrupted conversation with Mr. Hocke.

The shop door opened some minutes later. I didn't put the book away, assuming Mary had finished with her finger. Instead, the book was plucked away from my hand.

"Ah, Rosa Matilda," Shelley cried. "Who is the Count Ardolph in our lives?"

"Your marriage wasn't happy before Cecil Campbell came along, from what you've said," I pointed out, pulling the book from his hand and hiding it away again. "It didn't need someone to come in and break it up."

"No, I suppose Eliza did the job well enough, without introducing the blanket hornpipe into the mix. Free love is something I believe in, sharing whole minds, whole bodies, not this desperate sneaking-about business."

"That led to a mere mooncalf dying," I added, blushing furiously at his crudity. "Leaving a desolate intended behind."

"Was the secret betrothed a follower of free love?" he asked.

"Miss Campbell seems very sheltered."

Mary entered. "Did you tell Shelley what Mr. Hocke said about Mr. Corn's alibi?"

"No," Shelley said, straightening.

"Mr. Hocke admitted they had separated for the evening and Mr. Corn was really with Eliza Westbrook," I said.

Shelley's face went very red. "I am incensed. How dare she

be so hypocritical? I declare her my enemy. Harriet is my wife, and I will always regard her with sisterly affection, but I am done with Eliza." He clutched his hair on either side, above his ears. "How is it that I have enemies all around me?"

Mary moved close and put her hand on his arm before I could even stir from the counter. "There now, Shelley, that is not true. Look here. At this very moment, you are among the best of friends."

He sniffed. I could see the shine of tears in his eyes. "Will you betray me, too, Mary?"

"Never," she whispered in the same tone she used to soothe Willy. "I am your good friend."

"So am I," I added, but they didn't even turn in my direction. I had the sinking feeling that something was happening between them that I was being excluded from.

Shelley lifted her hand from his arm to his eyes. "What is this? A bandage? Surely an incomparable like yourself cannot have a wound?"

"I cut my finger on the washing tub," Mary said much more prosaically.

He kissed her finger right there in the middle of the shop. I was pleasantly scandalized, then irritated, as the moment seemed to go on.

I untied my apron and threw it on the counter. "There, I am going for a walk, Mary. You are in charge."

I stormed out of the shop, a dark whirlwind of frustrated energy. I didn't care, I didn't. Mary would leave when her Dundee suitor came. Would Shelley come around anymore once the vultures had torn his money from him and Mary was gone? Perhaps none of us could hold his interest.

I grabbed my cloak and went into the street. The very air still seemed to hold the stench of expectation and bloodlust from the hanging yesterday. Scraps of paper littered the ground, newsprint that people had wrapped around oysters or shaved ham, bits of pamphlets and broadsheets announcing the hanged man's career.

I knew I should go around to the back gate and help with the washing, but my thoughts were all in a muddle. Tears dripped down my nose. I wiped them angrily away. How could I help my family when everything I did went wrong?

My feet started north without me really deciding my path. I wanted as far away from the prisons as I could manage, this perilous, stinking, death-dealing neighborhood. How could Mamma have brought us here, tied our fates so completely to the Godwins and Skinner Street? Was our life before them really so bad? I scarcely remembered a time before Mary, but I wished I could. Something separate, something mine. She had Shelley's regard; I could see it. What did I have?

"I am me," I said, my own little war cry. I would follow my own drum. Even if it had to take me down paths all by myself.

Before I knew it, I found myself in Jewin Street, at John Hocke's address.

I considered Mr. Hocke while I rapped on the door of his chambers. His dandy ways made him seem as if he must have some sort of private income, but he borrowed money from the low sort of moneylender, and he frequented convenients, which meant he couldn't afford a mistress. Not to mention what else I knew of him. But it was safer to forget now that a man was dead. I must know who had done it. Had I exposed my household to more death, or was it a mere coincidence?

Mr. Hocke opened the door. His cravat looped around his neck but wasn't tied, and he didn't wear his coat.

"Miss Clairmont," he said, with an expression of pleasure, which I found very gratifying. "Is Shelley in the lane?"

I kept irritation from my voice. "No. I am paying a call alone."

"Ah, I am flattered indeed. Come in." He stepped back.

I stepped in, feeling both very grown and very foolish. Inside smelled of fires gone out and puddles of spirits grown sticky on surfaces.

"I do apologize," he said, hastily stoppering a wine bottle and taking a crumb-laden plate off a small table in front of a chair.

I wished to threaten him but could not, under the circumstances. "Do you have family, Mr. Hocke?" I inquired.

"Doesn't everyone?" he said.

"Do you have a wife somewhere?" I asked.

His eyes widened. "Why? Are you looking for a husband?"

I laughed. "Sir, I am Godwin's daughter. I asked because I wondered what was to be done about Harriet Shelley."

He frowned. "She's a married lady who wants nothing more than her husband back under her roof."

"Does she? Given Mr. Campbell?" I asked.

"He had other plans for himself. And Mrs. Shelley has her child to think of. If her next lying-in results in a son, then the future of the Shelley name rests in that child."

"But it isn't Shelley's?" I queried.

"I think you will find he knows differently," Mr. Hocke said with confidence.

"Free love," I said softly.

"Yes, and I don't know what he has to be so upset about. He has his own entanglements. But the child is his. Mrs. Shelley is quite certain."

"Women aren't as knowledgeable on this subject as men might believe, my mother always says," I said, wondering about the entanglements he had mentioned.

"It doesn't matter, for they are married. Married twice in fact. I am sure this is just a little spat."

"What are Shelley's entanglements?" I said sharply.

"That lovely young creature Cornelia Boinville."

I turned that notion over in my head. "I have heard the name. My father knows them. I believe Mrs. Boinville takes a motherly interest in Shelley, and her daughter teaches him Italian. He has hopes of visiting Italy."

He raised his eyebrows but said nothing.

I prattled on. "I believe travel is most freeing. I hope to see Switzerland myself. I have a connection to the place through my father's family."

He continued to say nothing.

"La, sir, I intended to interview you, not the other way around." I threw up my hand. He had never offered me a seat. I did not feel welcome. "I suppose I wanted to understand more about Harriet Shelley."

"To what purpose? You think she killed Mr. Campbell in order to quell talk about the father of her child?"

I put my finger under my chin. "La, he is dead in either case."

"I will say that I believe Mrs. Shelley made a grave error in marrying Shelley. When you do not believe in God, you are cast on your own morality, and he seems to be flailing in his."

"You do not believe in free love, then?" Was he suggesting that Shelley had killed the dead man?

He opened his mouth as if to give me a quick answer, then hesitated. "I am part of the same atheist circle. But I do think when one chooses to marry for whatever complicated set of reasons, that is the person a spouse is most entwined with, and getting involved from the outside will never end well."

"Then you believe in marriage?" I asked.

"I do not believe in God or marriage. What do you think about that?"

He could not challenge a daughter of Godwin in this.

"Some things are necessary due to society," I said. "Marriage can be required to protect women and children, given the current legal state of affairs. But I think as long as one has some family protection, life will go on well enough whether married or not. Having no attachments at all seems frightening to me."

"We do not want you frightened, Miss Clairmont," he said. "A beautiful little morsel like yourself, with such uncomfortable secrets."

He put his arms around me. I stiffened, not being used to such an embrace.

"La, sir," I said, my guilty conscience thumping along with each beat of my heart. "Such a fuss. I am not frightened."

He stared into my eyes; then his gaze descended to my mouth. "You are a liar. I can feel you trembling. Shall we make a sort of bargain, you and I?"

I put my hands on his wrists, then tightened my fingernails against his flesh. He let me push him away. "I wanted to see what you were going to do about Mrs. Shelley," I said stiffly. "That is all."

"She is not your problem or mine," he said. "I did not kill Cecil Campbell, and neither did she. You can take your mean suspicions elsewhere, Miss Clairmont."

"I meant to leave as friends," I said.

"I cannot imagine how." He turned away from me.

I took the opportunity to go out the door, my heart and nerves fluttering. But when I reached the street, I giggled. I had investigated by myself and cleared two murder suspects! I'd like to see Mary accomplish as much on her own. However foolishly, I'd been trying to save us all.

When I arrived at the bookshop, I found Mary still there. "Where have you been?" she demanded.

"I went to have a conversation with Mr. Hocke," I said loftily. "Oddly enough, given his circle of companions, he does not believe in free love."

"I do not think that is information of any value," she said with a sniff. "Cecil Campbell believed in marriage. It did not stop him from his lovemaking with Mrs. Shelley."

"La, that Mr. Hocke is a scoundrel, I believe," I said. "But I do not think him a killer. There is something in this business of an atheist circle, however. Who else is a part of it?"

"Reverend Doone at St. Sepulchre might know. He hates the atheists, according to Shelley."

"Why don't we ask him?" One such as me did not belong in a sacred place, but the clergyman did not strike me as a very holy man.

She considered me, then glanced out of the bow windows. "We might be able to catch him at tea. I expect he puts on quite a display."

I still wore my cloak, so I locked up the shop while Mary made herself ready.

Clouds had come in while I was inside, darkening the sky. It matched the scene around Newgate as we marched past on the way to the church.

Neither of us was entirely certain where the vicarage lay, but eventually, we found it. Delicious scents wafted around the woman who opened the door, and I knew we were right to come at tea.

"We are seeking spiritual guidance," Mary said piously. "Is Reverend Doone available?"

"Stay here," she ordered. "I will be back in a moment." She walked down the passage along the staircase, then knocked on the first door.

I strained my ears to hear what was being said, but she had a rather quiet voice, and I could hear nothing. I took Mary's hand in my own. What sort of nonsense were we in for?

A moment later, the woman returned, breathing heavily. "Reverend Doone will see you."

As suspected, all the comforts were available. A fire had been lit against the growing storm, and lamps glowed around each corner of the room. Reverend Doone sat at a round table, with a full complement of tea things: a fat-bellied pot of the congenial beverage, a tray of ham sandwiches, one of scones, and one of fruitcake with white frosting. He was a man after Mamma's heart.

He saw us appear and wiped the edges of his mouth with a white napkin, then stood, using the table for support.

"Come to apologize, I suppose. Shelley with you?" He lifted his chin.

"No, sir," Mary said with a curtsy. "Of course, we do owe you an apology for our behavior."

"Stay away from the likes of Shelley," he advised in a paternal tone, losing his posture of belligerence. "Nothing but trouble from that lunatic."

"Lunatic?" I asked. When his eyes narrowed at me, I bobbed a curtsy. "Very sorry for our behavior."

"Hmm." He coughed into his napkin, then balled it in his hand and returned to his chair. He waved his hand at us.

"You'll have to find cups in the cabinet. Then have a seat."

Mary followed his finger to a delicate rosewood cabinet, one of a set, that stood on tiny round legs against the wall. She opened the cabinet door and rattled around until she came out with a pair of cups and saucers that had a lovely green and pink floral vine pattern.

"Very pretty," I said when she set them on the table and dusted them off with a napkin.

"The vicar inherited the set from his grandmother," the man of God said. "If you break them, I will never be forgiven."

He smiled at me, and I recognized that his fire had gone out in the presence of two pretty girls and no Shelley. We could have quite a companionable time, and I meant to. The plates rattled as we distributed food, ignoring the ham in favor of scones with marmalade and some of the cake, thick with candied orange peel and lemon.

"We have a very good table at Skinner Street," I said after I took the first bite. "But nothing quite this delicious has graced it before."

"It takes a few months to make the cake properly," he said. "And not an inconsiderable amount of certain spirits that one cannot obtain legally right now."

I giggled. "France is open again, is it not?"

"Certainly, if you want to go there," he said. "But it will not be the France of our parents' day, before all these years of war."

"My mother survived the Revolution," Mary said.

"At great cost," he pointed out. "I've read your father's memoir of her. There is no doubt she suffered. Let that be a lesson to you both that excess in learning is a detriment to women's health."

I saw the fists Mary made when her hands dropped to her skirts. I did not blame her, though I envied her for the way her face could remain serene when she was all boiling kettle underneath.

"We are here to ask you about these atheists," I said, quickly changing the subject. "You have known Shelley for years. What do you know about his circle of poets?"

"I do not believe Shelley stays in place long enough to have a circle of anyone," he said with malicious glee. "He spends a great deal of money printing his ridiculous poetry and tracts, most of which are burned as soon as the printers read the contents."

Under the table, I reached for Mary's hand and squeezed it. Icy cold.

"Shelley is a dangerous man. He was a crazed boy, a real bedlamite. Screaming all hours of the night, disturbing everyone with his questions about the Bible. Disordered dress." The priest fingered his well-brushed black coat and shook his head mournfully.

"Lord Byron dresses so," I said, remembering the handsome poet from a party we'd attended with Papa. "It is one of the current styles."

"Poets are never good role models," he said. "No, you girls

should find men of faith to marry. Don't throw your lives away pining for men like Shelley. Shelley's own family hates him so he is never in funds. For all we know, Shelley might have killed the man found in your bookshop himself."

So Hocke had suggested.

"You would prefer Shelley be the target but would accept that he might have been the weapon?" Mary asked.

"He is mad enough." The priest sliced off another hunk of cake and set it on his plate, then reached for the butter dish.

"Shelley will not eat flesh," Mary said. "I cannot believe he would kill a person if he will not eat an animal."

"You are too young to know what marriage is," he said. "The terrible anger that exists in possession of a beautiful creature you cannot hold. Even a man who would not eat flesh might feel rage upon coming across his wife's friend."

"He would not lure," Mary said. "Whatever happened, we know Mr. Campbell came because of a note."

"Shelley might have wanted to have the business out," Reverend Donne said. "A poetic duel, as it were."

Mary's hand pulsed in mine as our host stuffed a large bit of cake into his mouth, and left his lips glistening with butter as he chewed. We sisters rose as one. Reverend Doone stood a beat after, crumbs still on his mouth. "Thank you," she said. "We will see ourselves out."

"Can you imagine being married to a man like that?" Mary asked, holding her sides and stopping along the side of the church. "I would die every day. All our education wasted in favor of watching one man stuff himself with cake."

"Very good cake," I added, then giggled.

She rolled her eyes at me. "I begin to think these atheists no bad thing."

"Then you do not think anyone in the atheist line killed Cecil Campbell?"

"No, but a man of God might."

"Come now," I chided. "Reverend Doone had nothing to do with any of this."

"He hates Shelley," she pointed out. "He lives in the neighborhood."

"I had not thought of that," I admitted, leaning my head against the cold stone wall. "We really have no idea who the murderer is, do we?"

"Reverend Doone misunderstands Shelley," Mary said. "And we, in turn, are not understanding something fundamental about Mr. Campbell's death."

I knew she was right, even though I knew more than she did.

Chapter 15

Mary

The next morning, Mamma sent Mary to Smithfield to pick up the household's weekly order from her favorite butcher shop. Mary agreed without protest, feeling dull after a night dreaming of bloody knives and faceless people in arguments with one another.

When she went up the street, she noted that the chill had kept down the stink and the flies, but the weather wouldn't last. How would she survive a summer in this neighborhood? No doubt the implied violence of living here between the prisons and the slaughterhouses made sweet dreams impossible. She'd been lucky not to dream of actual murder.

How could she flee this unwholesome environment? She lifted her hands and stared at them. On her left hand, she traced an escape back to Scotland and marriage. On the right, a shopgirl life in her father's house. Rain misted her fingers as she traced the lines.

"You all right, miss?" A man pushing a cart of oranges stopped in the street and looked at her inquiringly.

She dropped her hands. "Very well, yes. Thinking with my hands."

"Be careful, or you'll lose your purse." He nodded to a pair of boys, with too-short trousers and too-long jackets, approaching her on the street. "They'll lighten it in a moment if you pay no mind."

"Mamma wouldn't like that. Thank you." She set her back against a warehouse wall and waited for them to pass, her arms crossed over her chest, covering her reticule. Her thoughts immediately seized back on her topic.

Many would caution against an engagement to Robert Baxter. He was kind and sweet, but very young, only a year older than her. Thankfully, she had no desire for training in how to pursue financial advancement, so the fact that he was not yet established in life did not trouble her. The Baxter family believed in community property, not individual gain, just like her father.

However, while Mary was no atheist, she hesitated to return to a household upended by religion. Jane had argued against even considering such a marriage because of the drama caused in their community by Isabella Baxter recently marrying her older sister's widower, David Booth.

When the boys had passed, she forged on to the butcher shop. The noise of the shoppers grew as she reached the market area. She imagined herself staring out at the cloud-reflecting blue waters of the Firth of Tay, instead of trudging down a dusty road in an area of London devoid of nature.

"Mary!"

She glanced up, losing that image of serene water, and saw an even more beautiful sight.

"Shelley!" Her cheeks warmed as he came up to her and leaned slightly, as if she was his center of gravity.

His coat was the standard gentleman's blue, but it enhanced

the color of his eyes, and his breeches were tightly molded to his rounded thighs. She wanted to leave her body and mingle her essence with his, to dance in a poetic wonderland of pure intellectual stimulation. Funny that the path to his mind led through his handsome face.

How could she think of spending her days with a Robert Baxter when men like Shelley existed? If only he had brothers like himself but unwed.

"How are you this fine spring day?" he inquired with a bow.

She laughed and wiped the moisture of constant drizzling rain from her cheeks.

"You are here to weaken your spirits?" he asked, pointing to the row of dead fowl on hooks lining the window.

"Mamma sent me to pick up her order for the week."

"Must you do everything yourselves?" He pulled a mournful face, making her laugh.

"The servants are overwhelmed, so they say. It is a big household with three unmarried daughters and two sons."

He kept his frown. "Your family's goal is to work you to death in an insalubrious neighborhood as a shopgirl?"

"I have another hope." She straightened proudly. "I will write. I know I can do it. My father will help me find publishers."

Shelley tilted his head, birdlike. "I will freely admit your father made a great deal of money in publishing some twenty years ago. But he does not enjoy the same level of success now, and his contacts are aging."

"Do not speak as if you do not revere him," Mary warned.

"We are talking of your business." He took one of her hands. "You plan to support yourself on the fruits of your yet untried skills as a writer."

"At least I am honest about my plans, or my thoughts of them." Her pulse was leaping in her throat from the glory of having her hand in his.

A man walked out of the shop, jostling Shelley. He stayed calm, instead of bristling with anger like many men would, and just stepped out of the way, dropping her hand in the process. The man ignored him and marched down the street, holding packages of meat stained with blood.

"Revolting, isn't it?" Shelley asked.

"Yes," Mary agreed, the sight reminding her of Mr. Campbell's corpse. "Every thought I have seems to turn back to what happened in the bookshop. It is as if I am having one conversation, but underneath the thoughts of the murder run on. Why can people not be open about their affairs? Secrets breed danger and death."

"Marriage makes for secrets, for no two people can share everything about themselves."

A pair of boys walked past them. One of them glanced at her speculatively. She recognized them as the pickpockets the orange seller had warned her about earlier. They must have a circuit.

"Cecil Campbell was not married."

He started to speak, but she held up her hand.

"A moment, Shelley. I must get the meat, or Mamma will be cross. Will you walk back to Skinner Street with me?"

He bowed. "It would be my pleasure."

She went into the shop and was grateful to surrender her purse to the butcher so she would not have to worry about the boys anymore. When she exited, Shelley immediately took the packages from her.

"You'll get blood on your hands," she warned. "That is why I'm not wearing gloves."

"Ah, well, there is undoubtedly blood on my name." He chuckled darkly. "Or will be. I wouldn't be surprised if my own father wanted to kill me."

"I'm sure he didn't come into London, mistake Cecil Campbell for you, and stab him twice," Mary said.

"No, he would never think to write a note containing poetry," Shelley said, inclining his head to move her away from the shop. "But he'd be happy if I died."

"You are his only heir," Mary protested. "Your sisters need you, as does your mother."

"I have a young brother and an uncle," Shelley said. "Well, a half uncle, properly, from Sir Bysshe's second marriage. I'm sure he would see to the womenfolk. At any rate, I have considered the matter. What about Eliza? Harriet's sister would love for me to be dead."

Mary would not mind that being true, but still. "She has alibied Peter Corn, and if we believe that, then she has an alibi, as well."

Shelley shook his head. "I believe nothing out of that woman's mouth."

It was time to confess. "I know it is true that she meets people at Drury Lane. I saw her there myself with Mamma one night."

He stopped in the middle of the street. "You did? But how?"

She pulled him out of the way of a horse he hadn't noticed coming toward them, then pushed him against a building.

"You are very strong, Mary," he remarked.

"You could have died," she retorted. "I am not a lady of leisure in any case. I work in the household, some of it very heavy work, and move around all the books."

"Books are very heavy," he agreed with a twinkle in his eye. "Oh, Mary, you are a picture."

She smiled, though she couldn't look him right in the eye, not exactly. How was she to react to such a compliment? He leaned forward, his face coming very close to hers, despite the packages of chops between them.

She licked her lips, knowing from her experience with Robert what his expression meant, his position. His gaze dropped to her mouth. They stayed there for a moment, breathing in each other.

He straightened. "No, no, my sweet. You are too pure for me."

She tilted her head up to catch that honeyed breath again.

His mouth tightened into a flat line for a moment. "Now, you must distract me. What is this of a meeting between Harriet's sister and Mrs. Godwin?"

Mary clutched one hand into another and felt the bite of her nails in her palm. She felt trembly and hoped words would fasten her back to earth. "Mamma went for a walk at night—very unlike her—so I followed. I did not like how they spoke about you."

"I expect it of Eliza, but Mrs. Godwin?"

"They want your money," Mary said flatly, digging in her nails again. "Still, though, they cannot possess it if you are dead."

"True. Eliza might kill me in a fit of rage, but she would not plan anything."

"Exactly. Eliza's alibi for Peter Corn could be false, of course, but she is not the killer of Mr. Campbell. At least not if the death was meant for you."

"Maybe she wanted to kill him for my wife's sake," Shelley said, leaning his head against the brick of the building behind him.

"That knife through the private regions is very telling, I think," Mary mused. "It is a very intimate wound."

"Who was that intimate with Campbell?"

"Your wife and Sophia Campbell." She considered. "Eliza, living so intimately with your wife, might take her part."

"She might. She has before." He rubbed the side of his nose, leaving a streak of brown blood along it from the packages. "My wife cannot have an alibi. We know Eliza wasn't with her."

Mary was shocked to silence for a moment. Mrs. Shelley had no alibi. "When does Mrs. McAndrew go to bed?" she said, moving through her mental list of subjects. "If she goes to sleep early, it is possible Miss Campbell does not have one, either."

"We should learn more of her," Shelley said.

She waved a fly out of her face. "We should, but first, I must get those chops to Mamma."

"Dreadful things," Shelley said.

"You can compose an ode after you've washed your hands and face," she said, grabbing his arm to tug him along.

At the house door, he handed the packages back to her. "I think I will see my wife today," he said. "Not that I think Harriet a killer. She is like a sister to me now, and I would never suspect a sister of murder."

"Then Sophia Campbell is our target," Mary said, humoring him, though she felt differently. "I will see her if I can."

"Very good. Please offer my compliments to Mrs. Godwin. And see if I can be invited to dinner? I will stop by later."

"I will," Mary said, wanting to touch him again, but her hands were full.

Shelley went down the street, whistling cheerfully. She shook her head and went inside, then ran to the kitchen to divest herself of the meat. Her night of bad dreams had left her.

"What are you so cheerful about?" Jane snarled, narrowly missing her thumb as she chopped turnips.

Mary set the chop packages on the wooden table across from Jane. Thérèse, the cook, grabbed for them, then walked away. "I met Shelley on the way to the butcher shop. By the way, mind your purse outside. There are pickpockets working nearby."

"Did you lose the coins?"

"No, because an orange seller warned me. But, anyway, Shelley and I think we need to learn where Sophia Campbell was the night of the murder. Maybe she inflicted that intimate horror upon Mr. Campbell. Shelley thinks—"

"Pishposh," Jane interrupted rudely. "Shelley knows nothing."

"You aren't wrong, Jane," Mary admitted, pouring water from the kitchen can into a bowl and washing her hands. "What do you think? Will you pay a call on Mrs. McAndrew with me?"

"Yes, because I want to make a new friend, not because I suspect Miss Campbell of killing her betrothed." Jane slammed the knife into a turnip, breaking it in two.

"You are strong," Mary observed.

"Humph," Jane responded.

After lunch Mamma gave them leave to take a short walk in the rain. When they left the house, Jane protested that a short walk didn't mean Russell Square.

Mary pulled her along. "If we don't get to a garden, I will simply die. You cannot imagine the flies at the market. I have spent these past hours feeling them crawl over me."

"Sounds like something out of a book," Jane said. "I am surprised you do not want to spend the afternoon writing."

"I am afraid the horrors would return," Mary said, trotting across a street arm in arm with Jane. "Walk faster. If we do that, we cannot possibly feel guilty."

"I wish there was some sort of garden closer to home," Jane whined.

"Think of Miss Campbell's congenial face happy to see you," Mary urged, moving her shoulder away from Jane's dripping bonnet.

They made good time and, as such, were within the parameters of the correct time to make calls. Mary rang the bell at the McAndrew home.

When the maid answered, she smiled politely in recognition.

"Is Mrs. McAndrew at home?" Mary asked.

"She is, miss," the maid said, allowing them in.

The lady of the house had felt well enough to come down-stairs. After Mary and Jane left their cloaks with the maid, they went into the receiving parlor and found Mrs. McAndrew with a lady whose half-white hair gave her away as a generation older, along with a lady young enough to be her granddaughter.

Mary and Jane were introduced to Mrs. Smith and Mrs. Quest. Then Miss Campbell poured tea for them, as Mrs. McAndrew pronounced herself to be too unsteady to lift the pot.

"Very kind of you girls to visit," Mrs. Smith said approvingly. "It does Mrs. McAndrew good to have a spot of company, I'm sure."

Mary noticed that she smelled of tobacco. She must be fond of the pipe. "We met Mrs. McAndrew just recently," she said.

"They found Cecil," Mrs. McAndrew said wearily. "You understand, after he died."

Mrs. Quest, voluminous curls bouncing on her cheeks, slid to the edge of the settee where Jane had been gestured to sit, as if murder were catching.

Mary smiled at that thought. She hoped it was not.

"We don't want to tire Mrs. McAndrew," Jane said very rapidly. "Perhaps, since you already have company, we could take Miss Campbell for a walk?"

Miss Campbell froze over the teapot. A stray drop of the dark brew slipped from the spout and splashed onto her black muslin.

"Oh, she cannot leave when there are calls being paid, dear," Mrs. Smith said with a throaty chuckle.

"Duties," Mrs. McAndrew said, with a languid flap of her hand. "Tea, Sophia. More of those little fluffy cakes."

Jane took a cup and saucer from the companion's hand. Mary mouthed, "Sorry," to her when she took hers. Miss Campbell pretended not to notice.

Mary had no idea if a companion ever had an afternoon off,

but this would not be it. While it seemed like she performed easy work, a companion could not call her time her own. It would be difficult for her to find another man to marry. She hoped very much that Miss Campbell hadn't ended her betrothed's life in a fit of rage over his behavior with Harriet Shelley. That seemed terribly self-defeating.

Chapter 16

Mary

Shelley popped his head through the bookshop door a few minutes before the church bells would announce closing time. Mary straightened from a tower of copybooks.

"Mr. Shelley," she said formally, fighting against the tingles of awareness that raced down her spine, "how are you this afternoon?"

"Very well, thank you. I have been to Mr. Westbrook's house and seen Eliza, who is a perfect villain."

"I am sorry to hear it." She poked a couple of bottles of ink into place.

He took the rag from her hand and swiped at the bottle tops. "Yes. Harriet was not at home. She was walking in Mayfair with someone. I don't know who."

"Who takes care of your daughter?" Mary asked.

"There is a nursery at the Westbrook home." He smiled. "I played with Ianthe for an hour. She was not in the best mood, for she has a tooth coming in, but she chewed on a cold towel, and that seemed to help."

"Poor little thing. It was sweet of you to sit with her." Mary heard the St. Sepulchre bells ring. She immediately went into the front hall, untied her apron, and tossed it on the peg, then went to lock the front door.

Her father came downstairs before she could return to the bookshop, a copy of *Common Sense* in his hand.

"Looking for fundamental truths?" Shelley asked, coming out of the bookshop.

"Good afternoon, Shelley. I did not know you were here. We had a hanging at Newgate a couple of days ago. I was refreshing my mind on the causes of tyranny."

"What catches your attention?" Shelley asked.

From memory, her father quoted, " 'To say that the constitution of England is a union of three powers reciprocally checking each other, is farcical; either the words have no meaning or they are flat contradictions.' "

"Absolute power," Mary said aloud to herself.

"What?" her father asked.

"I was simply thinking that someone who kills is taking absolute power for themselves. They become like a king in that moment."

"An absurd and worthless person to be sure," said Shelley, who clearly knew his Paine.

"Yes, and like a king, they don't know all the facts," she added.

"Like whether they were killing Shelley or Campbell," her father said.

"That note seems to have been a deliberate lure," Shelley said. "But why did they want Campbell dead? And can we really know what goes on in the mind of a king?"

"Only by asking him. The killer isn't a stranger," Mary argued. "It's someone who knows how to get into the bookshop after hours."

Her father nodded. "Well reasoned, Mary. The house was

not broken into by a thief. The street door is locked at five. They needed to know how to get past two doors, and quietly."

"A customer," Shelley said. "To be sure."

"A follower of poetry, which indicates a certain class of person," Mary added. "The key is the same for both doors, however. Only one is needed."

Her father patted his stomach. "Come upstairs, Shelley. Mary, lock up the shop and go help Mamma."

She nodded and went back to her duties. It took her half an hour to sweep the shop and sort out the pencils some little hand had thrown into disarray. The shop was primarily set up with teaching supplies. Everything else was tucked away since it wasn't supposed to be known that the famous radical William Godwin owned the shop. His juvenile books were written under an assumed name.

Her hand hovered over a broken pencil lead at that thought. How many people knew this was Godwin's shop and knew about the contents of the bottom shelves in the back of it? Likely, an even smaller number than the sum total of poets in London.

She smiled. If only her father had a subscription list of anarchist poets. He did not, but he did keep a diary, which would show his correspondence.

"I bet the killer's name is in Papa's diary," she said aloud.

"Why?" Fanny asked.

Mary turned, putting her hand to her fichu. "I didn't hear you come in."

"Mamma wanted you to finish up here. She thought you might be reading."

"No, I was gathering pencils to sharpen. A child broke a half dozen leads." Mary displayed the broken pieces.

"You have to keep an eye out," Fanny chided gently.

"The parents were blocking me in at the counter, talking about whether Greek myths were really suitable for children.

As if Papa's *The Pantheon* hasn't been a bestseller for years. Do they want their children ignorant of what other children know?" Mary replied.

"They are merely concerned," Fanny said. "I heard Shelley's voice. Is he dining with us tonight?"

"If Papa asks him to, I'm sure he will."

"I do wonder what sort of person Mrs. Shelley has become," Fanny said, "that things between them have come to this."

"She wasn't at home when Shelley called today," Mary said.

Fanny's cheeks flared pink, and her chest bloomed, as well. "Went to see her lover, I suppose."

"It hardly signifies," Mary said. "Do you think she is wicked? I wonder what Mother might have thought."

"Shelley is no tyrant," Fanny said, "to torture a wife."

"No, but his beliefs are not compatible with marriage."

"Neither were Papa's, but look at him and Mamma," Fanny said. "It has worked out well enough, as long as the household is set up to his satisfaction. If Mrs. Shelley was a different sort of woman, I'm sure she could have come to the same accommodation with her husband."

"Meanwhile, there is no one to feed or take care of Shelley," Mary declared.

No one else had come to dine that evening, so dinner was simple, a stew made from the chop trimmings. Shelley ate a potato and a prodigious quantity of honey cakes.

"Do you think we can apply anything from *Caleb Williams* to the mystery at hand?" Mary asked as they were finishing the cakes. "It starts as a mystery about who killed a local tyrant, after all, and the murder drives the rest of the novel."

"'Man ought to be able, wherever placed, to find for himself the means of existence,'" Mamma quoted, with a significant glance at Shelley.

"'The actual means of existence are the property of all,'" her father said, continuing the quotation. " 'What should hinder me from taking that of which I was really in want, when in taking it, I risked no vengeance and perpetrated no violence?' "

Mary gritted her teeth. "Yes, I know that the book is a framework for the philosophy of *Political Justice*, Papa. But you must have done research on the subject of covering up murder, since that is what Falkland does."

"It did him no good," Shelley interjected. "He saves himself by pinning the murder on lower members of society."

"Ones with good motive," Mary added.

"That is the problem, isn't it," Shelley said. "The Hawkinses have as good a motive as Falkland to kill Tyrrel."

"Throughout the book, men with money and station are given credibility, and those without are not," Mary said. "Who do we not look at with suspicion because they have a higher rank?"

"Me," Shelley said with a laugh. "I don't have much of an alibi. I could have written that note and enticed Campbell here to revenge myself on him for his actions with my wife."

"You detest Wordsworth." Fanny smiled sweetly at Shelley.

"That may be the most important angle of all," Shelley said with mock thoughtfulness. "Who would quote Wordsworth?"

Her father leaned back in his chair and began a discourse on exactly the wrong parts of his first novel. He took for his topic a discussion of Caleb Williams's attempt to make an honest living, an attempt in which he is continually thwarted.

Shelley pointed out that Caleb would have been just as thwarted if he had decided to throw in with the band of thieves, since he had to run away from them after the old woman who lived with them attempted to kill him.

They went round and round until Mary's head spun. "I think I will take a walk," she said quietly. "Jane?"

"You cannot go alone," Shelley protested, ignoring his own argued point. "You must allow me to escort you."

"There is mending to do," Mamma protested.

Mary put a hand to her temple. Her father noticed. "The fresh air will do the girls good," he pronounced. "Fanny can help you."

Shelley jumped up and helped Mary and Jane with their chairs. Mary went out without a backward glance. Really, Fanny had brought it on herself with a lack of creativity.

They went out to the street without checking the weather, but fortune favored them with a clear night. Mary pushed her bonnet back so she could see better.

"Where should we go?" Jane asked.

"Let's walk up to the Charterhouse Gardens. We can walk in the old monk burial ground," Shelley said. "Come." He pulled them across to Cow Lane.

Mary kept an eye out for the pickpockets as they skirted the market. Plenty of people were around, but more the sort who clerked in London and had long walks in and out of the city on either end of the day. They passed a number of food sellers doing brisk business in pies, sausages, and other portable foods the clerks could bring home for their evening meals.

The air seemed to change around them as they entered the monastery ruins. The gardens remained. Fragments of old gravestones dotted the grassy area. Mary took a deep breath of new grass and wildflowers, old trees and fresh leaves. Sometimes it was hard even to smell spring on Skinner Street, but here it seemed they were far away from the gray stone and dirt of civilized life. No wonder her mother, Wordsworth, and others of their generation had experienced so much pleasure and sublime feeling in natural landscapes. Even this facsimile of one made her heart sing.

"I crave wildness," she said to no one in particular.

Jane, in response, spun around with her arms wide. Shelley laughed and imitated her. They kept spinning.

"I'm glad no one is here to watch you two sprites," Mary

said but then realized she was wrong. A woman was seated on a sturdy branch that had grown parallel to the ground.

"I'm fluff in the wind!" Jane said with a giggle.

"Damn and blast," Mary muttered. "Of all the people to meet in a burying ground." She went to Shelley and touched his arm.

He grabbed her arm and spun her around. "Come, Mary, have some fun!"

She wrenched her arm away and hissed at him. "Your wife is over there."

He stared at her. Slowly, his eyelids closed over his brilliant blue eyes. When he renewed his gaze, the laughter had gone from his face. He stilled, looking over Mary's shoulder at the tree, then walked in that direction.

"How very odd to see you in this part of town and alone, Mrs. Shelley," Shelley said.

Jane stopped mid-giggle and clutched Mary around the waist. Mary lifted her chin, and they went to stand next to Shelley.

"I was with a friend and decided I needed fresh air," Mrs. Shelley said.

"It is not safe," Shelley said. "This is London, not Bath. You are a mother and should not take such risks."

Mrs. Shelley pursed her lips. "Why do we not leave for Wales, as you promised? You said you would take rooms there in June for us."

Before Shelley could speak, she continued. "We could leave tomorrow. I could borrow money from Papa to hire a private conveyance for the five of us."

"Five?" Shelley asked coldly.

"You, me, Eliza, Ianthe, and a nursemaid. I cannot be expected to do everything in my condition." She touched her stomach.

"Firstly," Shelley said, "I will not support Eliza any longer."

"She is my companion and dearest friend!"

"She is a troublemaker. Why is she wandering about London

late at night, in Covent Garden no less, plotting against me?" Shelley asked. "People will think her Haymarket ware."

"She is going about her business," Mrs. Shelley sniffed. "It is none of my affair."

"It is when Eliza provides an alibi for the man Bow Street arrested for the murder of your lover," Shelley snarled. "What is she trying to do? Close the net around me?"

Mrs. Shelley bit her lip. Mary thought she did so to suppress a smile.

"Are you expecting a child?" he demanded. "Are you certain?"

"Of course. It is my second. I know the signs." Her voice was almost serene, not appropriate to the spittle-flying accusations her estranged husband made.

A cruel smile danced on Shelley's beautifully molded lips. "Who is the father, then?"

"You, of course. We may talk about free love, but the child is yours."

"In law," he said.

"In truth." She bit lower, her teeth passing her lip and sinking into the flesh below. The pretty color of her skin reddened.

"I don't believe you," Shelley said, his cheeks going very red. "Get up."

"Why?"

"I must take you home."

"That's very gallant," Jane said snidely, while Mary stood frozen at the horrible notion of these two beautiful people having coupled, and recently.

In reality, the child would be Shelley's responsibility regardless of who fathered it, just like his wife. She could see how much it pained Shelley to listen to her lies. Shouldn't free love be freeing? Why were they so upset? This was the natural conclusion of the life they led.

Mary stayed silent as Shelley pulled his wife off the tree

branch and marched her between the Tudor ruins and out to the street.

"Well, I never," Jane huffed when they were alone. "To leave us alone like this."

"It is really not dangerous here, not on a May evening," Mary said. "What else could he do? We do not want to walk with them and listen to the argument."

"You would not want to listen, for fear that Mrs. Shelley might not be right about something," Jane suggested.

"I think she might be mad," Mary said, sounding as nasty as she felt.

They walked out of the garden themselves. The city smells quickly overtook the air in the green garden, matching Mary's dark mood.

"Does it matter if she is?" Jane asked.

"It is bad for her children," Mary said. "And it makes sense that Shelley would not want to live with her."

The stream of clerks had largely vanished, replaced by lower-class courting couples out walking and men on their way to evening amusements. An older man rode by on horseback, a medical bag strapped to the saddle. A baby cried above them in one of the buildings.

"You don't think Shelley will give all the money he promised to Papa to his wife?" Jane ventured.

"More likely, it will get split between Mamma and Eliza Westbrook," Mary said. "Either way, it leaves us with nothing. You and I, we shall have to make our own way in life."

"Better than marriage." Jane shuddered. "I do not like the looks of it."

Chapter 17

Jane

"Mamma, I must have some fresh air. I'm expiring!" I cried after the twentieth or thirtieth customer left late the next morning. "I can scarcely speak for the dust."

"You speak very well for someone who is dying," Mamma said, pulling off her apron. "Neither of you has been in the bookshop nearly enough for my tastes recently."

We'd been in the bookshop more than enough for my tastes, but I kept my mouth closed.

"I am not your servant," Mary said severely. "I am my father's daughter. If you work us half to death, you'll only have to send us to Ramsgate again or north."

"You'd like that, wouldn't you, miss?" Mamma fixed Mary with her beady eyes.

I had a bad feeling about what would come out of Mamma's mouth next. She didn't look upset.

"You were sent from Dundee for making love to a young son of the house. It was one thing not to marry that David

Booth, but you cannot think to entice a seventeen-year-old boy into marriage. Who would pay your bills? You will not be going back there, and working in the shop is better than being sent to Ireland and your aunts." Mamma's lips twitched, and she moved toward the door.

"He'll be eighteen in the fall—" Mary began.

I coughed, interrupting her. My throat really was irritated.

"She needs water, Mrs. Godwin," Mary said mockingly. "Surely you would not deny your singing treasure some water?"

Mamma threw up her hands, straining the shoulder seams of her dress. "She is only a daughter."

"Mamma!" I said, shocked, and coughed again.

"Mr. Edward Pilcher comes today, and I must have everything settled in the kitchen," Mamma said.

"Uncle Edward is coming?" Mary said with dismay.

He was really my uncle, being married to Mamma's sister, but none of us liked him. A cut above us, was what he thought, and he liked to take little digs at Mamma's disrespectable ways before she married Papa.

Mamma turned back with a sigh. "Mary, mind the shop. Jane, go fetch both of you some water, but if I see a drop of it in the shop, I-I'll cane you both." She flounced out of the shop.

I widened my eyes at Mary, secure in the knowledge that we were much too old to be caned, then darted out myself. Thankfully we had a lull in customers. I had no idea why we were so popular today.

When I came back with glasses of water, Mary was leaning over the counter, reading a newspaper.

"You'll get ink on your hands," I warned.

She clamped her fingers around the glass I had handed her and drank deeply, leaving sooty fingerprints all around. "I suspect this is why we had all the trade today." She pointed to an article.

"Oh?" I glanced at it. The article was about Peter Corn and his arrest. I winced. "He won't do well in Newgate."

"No. I hope someone can pay for special privileges for him."

I heard the front door open without pleasure. It seemed that our break was over. After quickly draining my glass, I popped it under the counter and wiped my damp hands on my apron. Mary giggled, and I realized I'd made wet, dark streaks down the fabric, since I'd transferred newsprint ink onto my own hands. She'd managed to daintily wipe off her stained fingers on a dusting rag.

The shop door opened. A man of mature years—a dozen or so years older than Shelley—stepped in. When he saw us, he smiled pleasantly. "Good day."

He said it in a very singsongy way, which told me he wasn't local to London.

"How can we help you?" Mary asked. "Are you looking for books or for schoolroom supplies?"

"Neither," he said, pulling off his hat and scratching above his ear. "I'm looking for Mr. Godwin."

"He doesn't work at the bookshop," Mary said, with a hint of suspicion in her voice.

He turned up his lips at her. It wasn't exactly a smile. "No, but he lives in this house."

He was a moneyman; I could feel it. We'd seen far too many of them lately. I should be happy about busy days at the shop, and not irritated, for we needed the trade.

Mary and I glanced at each other. I patted the counter. One of us needed to hide the money box from this man.

"I'll see if he is available," Mary said, nodding with recognition at my gesture. "He had calls to pay, and I don't know if he has returned."

She pulled off her apron, for it irritated Papa to see it on her outside the shop, and went out.

"What is your name?" I asked.

"I am John Williams."

"You aren't English," I said.

"Welsh."

"Ah," I exclaimed. "I could not pinpoint your accent."

"Now that you've heard it once, you'll recognize it again."

I expected that he'd exaggerated it. He'd dropped his *y*'s, but I listened carefully. Being musical, I had an ear for such things. "Our friends the Shelleys were in Wales," I said. "Do you know them?"

"I do, and Miss Westbrook, Mrs. Shelley's sister," he returned.

"Did Mr. Shelley give you a letter of introduction to my father?" I didn't say he was in town, for I did not know his relationship to this man.

"He did not. Pleasant weather?" His gaze drifted down to my stained apron, then up again.

"It's been a dreadful May, really," I said, glad to turn the conversation to pleasantries. "Though it managed not to rain the day of the execution."

"Execution?" he asked, startled.

"Newgate Prison is just down the way. This is quite a notorious area. We had a hanging only a few days ago. It's a good thing you didn't come then, but the pickpockets are still in the neighborhood, so mind your purse," I said cheerfully.

Mr. Williams crossed his arms and turned away from me. "Nice amount of stock you have here."

I was distracted from his money-counting calculations of the products in the shop by two florid women in flower-bestrewn straw bonnets.

"Good day," the taller of the two said. "Do you happen to have a copy of *Aesop's Fables*?"

"Oh yes, we have a really excellent edition." I calculated how to keep my gaze on the counter at all times while I led them to the shelf. "It's called *Fables, Ancient and Modern*, by

Edward Baldwin." I put my back to the shelf and pointed to a handsome leather-bound volume. "Translated less than a decade ago and beautifully done, too."

The shorter woman crouched down to take it from the shelf. "Illustrated?"

"Yes, madam."

The other lady craned her neck and looked around the shop, her gaze sliding past Mr. Williams. "My faith," she cried, as if just thinking of something.

Liar.

"A young man was found dead here not that long ago, was he not?"

"Yes, madam," I repeated. "Were you wanting to make a purchase? We have some very nice copybooks. They can be used for household accounts if you do not have children in the schoolroom."

Mr. Williams smirked at my pointed attempt to get a sale out of the woman. The other lady clutched the volume of fables. I did think she might buy it. I returned to the counter and held out my hand. "That will be one guinea, please."

"Oh," the taller woman said with a shiver. "How can we know that the books do not have bloodstains on them? From the murder, you know."

"He died under the bow windows," I said.

"A stabbing, was it not?" she asked. "They can be very bloody indeed."

"There was a rug underneath him," I lied. "Really, it did not affect the stock at all." Would the price of the books increase if they had bloodstains?

She clasped her hands to her bosom. "Could you show me?"

The other woman came to her, holding the fables.

The Welshman seemed transfixed by the women's cheerful nattering on about Mr. Campbell's demise. He didn't move from his position next to a tower of pencil boxes.

I didn't like to leave the money box, but I figured that Mr. Williams was after more than a few coins, so I walked the ladies through the murder scene, then managed to persuade them to take into their hands both the fables and a book of Greek myths, as well as a travel memoir, though not Mary Wollstonecraft's.

"Scandalous," the taller of them said when I offered it to her.

I quickly put Mary Wollstonecraft's small volume back on the bottom shelf.

"Mr. Earl would never allow it in the house," the other woman agreed.

Cheeks flaming, I quickly took their guineas and showed them the door. I loved to sell Mary's mother's books, but I had to judge the customers properly. Apparently, those after the thrill of murder did not like to read about women who refused to live their lives in narrow confinement. At least I had sold Papa's fables, written under a pseudonym.

I heard Papa's voice in the hallway as the women left. He greeted them pleasantly; then he and Mary came into the book-shop.

"This is Mr. Williams from Wales, Papa," I said. "He knows the Shelleys."

"Yes, I am familiar with the name. How are you, Mr. Williams?" Papa looked very vicarish in his dark clothing, but his expression was tense.

"I would like to speak to you about Mr. Shelley, in fact, and your dealings with him."

"Very well. We can go up to my study." Papa held out a hand, guiding Mr. Williams to the door.

Mary and I listened as they went up the staircase. We heard the study door open and close above us.

"You mind the counter. I'm going to listen," I said, throwing off my apron.

She nodded and handed me one of the water glasses. If we

were caught listening at doors, we could claim we were going for water, but really, the glass served as an aid to hear through doors.

I crept upstairs, hugging the walls to lessen the creaking, wishing I knew where Mamma was to reduce the risk of being caught. When I reached the upper floor, I crouched by the door, ready to spring up if I heard anyone on the steps, and leaned my ear toward the keyhole on the study door.

"I must tell you, Mr. Godwin, that I've had a letter from Miss Westbrook," said Mr. Williams, the accent making his voice unmistakable.

"I was not aware that you were in contact with any member of that household," Papa said pleasantly enough.

"Yes, she had some concern about Mr. Shelley's post-obit loans," Mr. Williams said.

"I see." I heard Papa's chair squeak as he settled into the leather.

"Yes, I understand he has been very reckless with amounts. You must know, Mr. Shelley has a previous financial commitment in Wales. I will make it clear that any of the money you believe is coming to you out of the loans belongs to William Madocks for back rent and pledges to the Tremadoc community campaign."

"I understand that Tremadoc was the scene of some violence," Papa said. "I have no notion what your master claims to be owed, but Mr. Shelley assures me that he worked off his rent in supporting the community by writing letters and helping the poor members."

"We do not see it that way," Mr. Williams said.

"Then take it up with your men of business and do not trouble me," Papa said.

"You are mixed up in his rather chaotic exertions," Mr. Williams responded.

" 'What should hinder me from taking that of which I was

really in want, when in taking it, I risked no vengeance and per-petuated no violence?'"

I understood Papa was quoting his own work.

"Documents were signed." Mr. Williams's voice had gone hard.

"Shots were fired," Papa returned. "The family fled, and here I see you pursuing them all the way to London. Any group of sensible men would consider the debt nullified. To charge rent on a domicile one could not stay in for fear of murder? Young women, babies, servants, all at risk of their lives? No, sir, I do not accept your so-called debt as one of honor. Be gone from my house, sir."

I slid from my perch beside the door and quietly descended the steps. I made it almost to the bottom before Papa's study door opened. Turning swiftly, I pretended I had just started to walk up.

"Good afternoon, Mr. Williams," I said cheerfully as I passed him on the stairs.

He pulled the brim of his hat over his eyes and said nothing. I paused and waited until I heard the front door close, then ran down to the bookshop to tell Mary what had happened.

Papa retold the story to Shelley at dinner, full of righteous indignation, as if orating the tale from a pulpit. Mary had man-aged to seat herself next to the poet and grabbed his arm to hold him steady when he went pale and seemed to swoon in his chair. Mamma pulled away his plate of vegetables and his wine-glass. Fanny clutched me, tears in her eyes.

"The sheer effrontery," she whispered.

"Indeed," Shelley said, blinking rapidly. "Mrs. G., my glass?"

Mamma pushed it toward him again somewhat reluctantly. He drained it. Fanny rushed to the sideboard to fetch the bottle and filled it again.

Color reentered Shelley's face.

"How can they think you owe anything after the dreadful end to the arrangement?" Mary asked.

"What was that circumstance exactly?" I added.

At Fanny's cry, I amended, "If it will not pain you to relive it."

Mary patted his arm. "Sir, it is we who are most keenly interested in your progress and must understand what forces align against you. Particularly if they are the sort that will arrive here on Skinner Street."

"Demanding money," Mamma added.

"Or sending notes that lure poets to their deaths," Mary said. "What if this is at the heart of Mr. Campbell's murder? Here we have clear proof that Shelley's enemy knew he had friends here."

"Why would Mr. Williams come to demand money if he had killed Mr. Campbell?" Fanny asked. "Surely he'd have run back to Wales for fear of being discovered."

"It has been some time now," Mary pointed out. "Someone else has been arrested. Perhaps he feels safe in his perfidy."

"He did not have the look of a killer," I said thoughtfully. "Just a regular sort of man of business."

"He was not after coin in any case," Papa said. "He wanted to warn me not to take any, as it belongs in Wales."

"That is utter calumny," Shelley said after draining his glass again. "I gave my name and my hands to their cause, and this is how I was repaid."

"Yes, tell us," Fanny urged with flushed cheeks.

"Late February of last year," he said, "we had gone to Tremadoc in Wales with the most altruistic principles. The idea was an embankment, to reclaim land and build an ideal village. The construction was faulty, and it took a great deal to keep the embankment intact. I had some concerns, due to the owner's debts, that the workers were not being treated well. Liberty and concern for our fellow men ever being in my breast, I was not against them fighting for their rights. Of course, the moneymen saw things very differently.

"When my former servant returned from his detestable stint in prison due to passing seditious material, I knew matters were coming to a head. The moneymen wanted my money, but not me, to support the community, which is, of course, always my aim."

"Hear! Hear!" Papa said. "But you must be more circumspect, Shelley. Look at the fate of the Hunt brothers. Organizing into associations, publishing seditious information . . . It is the path to jail, not progress."

"It is an abomination, is what it is. Are we not free men?" Shelley asked.

"Are we?" Papa asked rhetorically.

"*I* am."

I smiled at Shelley's emphasis. I did believe him free, freer than most men, despite his dependents.

"On February twenty-sixth, I armed myself before going to bed. It seemed wise due to rumblings in the village, reported by the local girls who worked in the house. We retired well before midnight, but not half an hour had passed before I heard a noise in a room downstairs," Shelley reported.

"One of the servants, I hope," Mary said.

"No." His mouth turned down. "I heard footsteps moving, so I went into the billiard room and kept following them into a little office. There is a window there, opening to some shrubbery, and I saw it open. A man was climbing out."

I put my hands to my chest in the attempt to keep my heart from beating clean out. "No phantom."

"No phantom at all, but a villain with a pistol." Shelley's voice rose. "He fired at me! I fired back, of course. I'd been carrying my pistols. But my gun misfired, and the man left the window and ran at me."

I panted as he paused and took a deep draught of wine before continuing.

"He knocked me down. We fought on the floor." He wind-milled his arms wildly. The dregs of wine in his glass arced into the air as he made punching gestures.

Mamma leapt up and grabbed the glass from his hand before he could break it. Fanny sponged wine from the tablecloth with her napkin, then knelt on the floor to scrub at the dots.

Shelley stared at the wall, transfixed by the scene in his head, not noticing the frantic action around him. Or perhaps he did, because he began to speak again as soon as Mamma set the wineglass on the sideboard and Fanny dropped her stained handkerchief into the chamber pot hidden in the sideboard.

"I still had one loaded pistol in my hand, so I fired it. The villain shrieked. Did I wound him? I thought. Even with the single candle flame, blood darkened his garment in the area of his shoulder."

I tore away my fichu and dabbed my forehead with it, strug-gling to keep my composure. "Shelley," I gasped.

Mary glanced at me, expressionless, then leaned toward Shelley. "You poor man. Do go on, and you will never have to share this story again, sir."

"Poor darling," Fanny whispered. Her chest went splotchy when Mamma shot a suspicious gaze in her direction.

"He rose to full demonic height, despite his wound," Shelley continued. "He cried out, 'By God, I will be revenged! I will murder your wife. I will ravish your sister. By God, I will be revenged!'"

"Madness," Papa said. "They knew your house well, to be so specific."

"He was some tool of the moneymen, of that I am sure," Shelley agreed. "He fled then. One of the servants peeked in and found me on the floor. She went to get my wife, who brought Eliza, and we all stayed downstairs in the parlor for a couple of hours."

"Did anything happen after that?" Mary asked.

Shelley pulled a pencil from his pocket and drew a dreadful demonic figure on the tablecloth, ignoring Mamma's look of horror. "I advised all to retire in the end, thinking it impossible a wounded man would revisit the house that night. I had some notion he had, however temporarily, lost the use of his arm."

"He had a gun, not a knife," Mary said. "Unlike Mr. Campbell's killer."

I laced my fingers together over my heaving chest. "How likely is it that there are two murderers in Shelley's life, Mary? I ask you. This was last year. Surely the man could have obtained knives by now." Regardless of my own poor choices that might have brought other villains into the house.

"Dan Healy, my returned servant, and I sat up, while the women retired. After some time had passed, with us waiting in the dark, I sent him to see what o'clock it was, and then I heard a noise at the window."

"Oh, no." Fanny put her hands over her face, as if her instruments of hearing resided in her eye sockets and nostrils.

Shelley nodded. "A man thrust his arm right through the windowpane, breaking the glass, and fired at me! I was wearing my dressing gown, and the hole in it was as big as my fist, but it wounded only the fabric, not me. I fired, but again, it misfired. A bad pistol, I would guess. An old saber decorated the room, over the doorway. I tore it down and aimed a blow at the miscreant." Shelley chuckled darkly. "I will give him credit for animal courage. Instead of running, he grabbed the old blade and attempted to wrest it away from me."

"As if he knew the house well enough to know the sword was dull," Mary suggested.

"He had the strength of ten men," Shelley reported. "I was at my last gasp, losing my grip, when Dan returned. The villain broke through the rest of the glass and disappeared into the blackest of nights."

"Truly the blackest?" Fanny asked carefully.

"The wind was as loud as thunder." Shelley waved his arm. "The rain came down in torrents. I was not sure what to do, but I heard the next day that lies were being told about us in the village, that I would run away without paying my bills."

"They could not kill you, so they attempted to ruin your character," Fanny said.

"Yes," Shelley agreed. "I could not stay in Tremadoc, with the women to protect, so we departed on that Saturday. It is not my fault that I could not settle my accounts. We were in danger."

"You cannot think you owe them a penny after all that," Mamma said agreeably.

Mary frowned. "Why would Mr. Williams come now to warn Papa?"

"He wants to blacken my name," Shelley said.

Mary rubbed her lips together. I noticed how Shelley stared at them.

"What I mean is, nearly two weeks ago, Mr. Campbell was killed. Mr. Williams didn't show up until today. It doesn't seem like the two situations are related," Mary said.

Shelley nodded. "That is a good point, but Mr. Williams works for Mr. Madocks, not Mr. Leeson, the moneyman who is the largest employer in the area. He owns the quarry. It was reported to me that Leeson has claimed he will force me to flee the country."

"Maybe he had Mr. Campbell killed in order to scare you," Fanny said. "As he is in your circle."

"Yes," Mary said, visibly warming to the theme. "Mr. Leeson doesn't want you dead, but terrified. He probably hopes you will clear your debts and pledge even more, in hopes of removing this terror from your life."

"How wise you are," Shelley said. "Mr. Leeson's men could be poking about my life. They probably knew Campbell was friendly with my wife, and killed him as a warning to me." He slammed one hand into his other, making a fist. "He had no money of his own. They are after mine."

None of us could eat after this troubling declaration. Could one of us be next?

"They threatened your wife that night," I said tentatively. "What guard does she have?"

"Her family home," he said. "They have plenty of money, many servants." He looked around his place at the table. "Might I trouble you for another glass of wine?"

"I am sorry, sir, but no more has been decanted," Mamma said quickly.

"Why don't we leave the ladies and go into my study?" Papa tilted his head.

Shelley's expression became a bit less morose. I knew Papa kept a bottle of gin in there. They placed their napkins on their plates and departed, leaving us to clear the table.

After the door closed, Mamma walked around the dining room, muttering under her breath in irritated tones about the wine damage to the rug and the pencil and wine marks on the tablecloth. She wanted Shelley's money to pay off business debts and run the household, but it seemed she would have to work for it.

"Mary and I will clear the table," Fanny said gently. "Why don't you put Willy to bed, Mamma? You rarely have the time to spend with him."

I pressed my lips together to hold back my smile. Mamma didn't like putting Willy to bed. She liked to sit in the dining room with her feet up and a slice of cake in her hand after we'd all gone to his bedroom. Tonight, though, she pasted a sickly smile on her face.

"What a sweet idea, Fanny." She put her hand on Willy's shoulder. "It is time to retire, Willy."

He slowly slid off his chair, then pointed at the pencil drawing Shelley had made on the tablecloth. "Is it a real monster?"

"No, Willy, just a man," Mary said. "Shelley's terror makes it far worse than it was, but it was long ago."

"And far away," I added. "We have nothing to fear."

Mamma and Willy walked out. I shut the door behind them, then went back to study the drawing. Fanny cleared away utensils and dishes, while Mary breathed over my shoulder.

The head leaned to the side, with a saturnine leer across its lower face. The arms ended in sticks rather than fingers, and the legs were muscular. Unclothed, the body had a sort of neck and torso, with no further definition.

"I do not know how this could possibly be used to identify a soul," Mary said. "What is that at the top of his head? Horns?"

"It could simply be hair mussed by the wind. Terrible weather that night." I touched one of the massive calves. "A quarryman?"

"I don't think there is anything here we can build upon for a proper description." Mary shook her head. "It's a poet's conception of a human turned monster, is all."

"It's not John Hocke, at any rate." I tapped the thick thigh. "He's built upon slimmer lines."

"Pay attention, Jane," Fanny admonished. "The sketch is of a man in Wales, not here."

"We'd have noticed if anyone looking like this came to Skinner Street." I stared at the demonic drawing, trying to discern what the real man might look like from these hints.

"Fisher, the Bow Street Runner who came with Mr. Abel to make the arrest that day?" Mary shuddered. "He was a nightmare figure."

Later, I could not forget that dreadful image of the man Shelley had sketched on the tablecloth. Those bushy brows, the forehead wrinkles, the long column of nose. I could not wipe the idea that the features were specific from my mind.

Mary helped me out of my dress. A pin had been sticking me under my arm, which had not helped my mood. I rubbed at the spot and quickly pulled off the rest of my clothes, then slipped into my nightgown.

"When did you develop those hips?" Mary asked. "You did not have them when I left for Dundee last time."

I hugged myself. "For all the good they will do from behind the bookshop counter."

Mary laughed. "You are pretty enough. You will manage."

"Will I?"

"You sing very well."

"Where does that take me? Up on stage? You know our parents would not like that."

"It is your life," Mary said. "It might not be a very genteel one, but what does it matter? You don't have a family name to live up to."

"It is good not to live under the burden of money," I said. "But women have so few opportunities."

"I will make my living with my pen, like my mother, and yours, as well," Mary declared. "Good night."

I thought about what she'd said when she was gone. I had ideas, didn't I? Why couldn't I be a writer? Papa had earned thousands of pounds as one, regardless of what had happened with his finances more recently.

I wouldn't be forced into any assignations I didn't want, like a singer might be. Why, they were little better than prostitutes. They said men of the upper classes used stages like brothel drawing rooms, picking and choosing the women they wanted.

If I had a lover, I'd want to choose him myself.

I slid under the covers and moved my feet around, trying to warm up the sheets. When I tried to calm myself, that terrifying drawing of Shelley's rose from my memory to transport me.

I sat up in my bed with a shriek. I thrashed, unable to get the thought of that drawing come to life out of my head. My fingers went to my face. I bit back a loud cry, my body shuddering. Recent events tormented me.

I vaguely heard the door open, and a slight, warm form got under the sheets next to me.

"Stop," I cried, afraid it was the beast from Shelley's drawing. "Leave me."

"Shh. It's only me, your Mary," said a soft voice. A hand went to my hair and began to stroke it.

I broke into great racking sobs, unable to stop them. "Where shall I find comfort?" I cried. "Where is my sweet rest?"

Chapter 18

Mary

Mary pushed herself against the headboard. Her arm that had been stretched around Jane had gone to pins and needles. She flexed her fingers, wincing, until the feeling had passed, then climbed out of bed and went to the street-facing window. The lock had broken long ago, and the wood squeaked against itself when she raised the sash. She could see stars, but the new moon provided no illumination. As her gaze moved down to the street, bright yellow light flashed, then a redder light. Someone was lighting a cigar outside the bookshop.

What if someone was breaking in again? Gritting her teeth, Mary pulled Jane's dressing gown on and stole out of the bed-room, taking her unlit candle with her. Quietly, she padded down the stairs, then went into Papa's study.

He'd gone to bed, but she lit her candle in the remains of his fire and went to the window, one floor over the bookshop. The windows were kept very clean here, and she could see down to the street.

Two watchmen walked from the direction of Newgate, their staffs clapping lightly against the cobbles. They stopped in front of the shop.

Mary watched as they conferred with the cigar-holding figure. One of them lifted his lantern, and she recognized the man. Why was Bow Street watching the bookshop? Had Mr. Abel been warned of further mischief here?

The watchmen departed, leaving Abel alone. Mary darted down the last flight of stairs, then shoved her feet into shoes. She unlocked the front door and went out with her candle, holding it below her chin so Abel could see who it was.

The cigar moved in her direction. "What are you doing out, Miss Godwin? The watchmen called one o'clock a few minutes ago."

"I saw a figure from the window," she said. "I was afraid it was someone trying to get into the house again."

"Again?"

"You know, like the night Mr. Campbell was murdered."

"Someone with a key, you mean."

"The killer doesn't belong to our household."

"How can you be sure?"

She drew herself up. "Surely you cannot be suggesting that anyone who lives here might have been responsible."

"Why not? It is as good of an explanation as any. The watch walks their beat starting at nine p.m., and they saw no one in the street."

Mary tightened one arm around the folds of Jane's dressing gown. "Mr. Campbell had to have come in, certainly."

"That is true. They missed him, though he could have been in the building earlier."

"I don't understand." Her candle wavered as she started to lift her arm. "You took Mr. Corn to the magistrates. Why are you still watching the house?"

"Because of his alibi."

"Mr. Hocke gave him one for one part of the evening. I

know Eliza Westbrook gave him one for another. But I sincerely doubt Miss Westbrook met Mr. Corn outside a brothel," Mary argued. "Therefore," she said, speaking more slowly, "he is not completely alibied for the night."

He chuckled. "You don't want him to be freed?"

"I want the killer to be arrested, whoever he is. My father and Mamma had no reason to lure a poet to the bookshop and kill him."

"I do not know about that. What if he was interfering with one of their daughters?"

"From the sounds of things, he was much too busy interfering with Mrs. Shelley," Mary said. "Do you have some new information?"

"Do you?" he countered.

"Mamma is a schemer," Mary said. "But Papa is a perfect darling. Neither of them is a killer."

"What about Shelley? He is under watch by the Home Office."

"He'd probably be proud of that fact, if it were true."

"Oh, it is. He has incited violence against the government before. You cannot deny that he's a dangerous man."

"A fascinating one, certainly." She realized how her words sounded. "To the Home Office, I mean."

"A married man," Abel said softly. "Take care."

She drew herself up. "I'm Godwin's daughter," she said. "We are at least as dangerous as Shelley."

"Your father is a thinker, not a doer," the Runner said. "I think your mother took more action in her short life than he ever has. Shelley is the one who went to Ireland to foment unrest. He is the one who angered the business owners in Wales, passing around seditious pamphlets and upsetting the workers. Do you know what his work was there? It was supposed to be demanding money from the farmers and other smallholders. He's a supporter of the Hunt brothers."

"They have much support in the literary community," she

returned, pulling her dressing gown more tightly around herself. "You do not understand. In my world, all the things Shelley does seem quite normal. We are not conforming sort of people."

"I see that you are not, but I will have someone hang for Mr. Campbell's murder." He tapped his cigar. Ash fell.

"I merely want you to hang the right man," Mary said. "What about the note fragments we found? They are a very good clue."

"I haven't found a match," he admitted, "but perhaps someone disguised their handwriting."

"There must be something more you can do."

He puffed smoke. "Perhaps someone will pay me to investigate your Mr. Shelley further."

Mary's lips trembled. "He has not caused any trouble in London."

"This is where most of the printers are," Abel said. "He does his best seditious work here."

"Don't you think there is room for voices, for philosophy, for change?" Mary asked.

"Do you think it is right to remove God?" he retorted.

"Shelley is not an out-and-out atheist, whatever he may say to stimulate conversation. He is inquiring for proof. That is his point. There is no proof of God."

"I disagree."

"You may, but to threaten him is unfair. He is a poet."

"Kill all the poets, I say." Abel took one last drag on his cigar and dropped it in the street. It took only three steps for him to disappear into the night. The new moon hid much.

She cupped her candle flame and went back inside, internally arguing with the Runner. Instead of wasting time with that, she went into action.

In Papa's study, she wrote a note to Shelley, then stole a coin from the purse in her father's drawer to pay for the delivery. It took only a few minutes to run to the prison and find a ragged street urchin to take the note to his lodgings.

After her brief adventure outside, she went to bed but found it hard to fall asleep. With every beat, her heart expanded and contracted with fear for Shelley.

Eventually, dawn broke. Mary took a moment to wash her face and hands, then tiptoed downstairs and went out again, covered well in her shawl and cloak.

It was raining. Puddles filled every cavity and turned the streets to mud as she went northwest, angling toward what used to be home, a much more pleasant area on the outskirts of London. Would Shelley have received the message? Would he come?

On feet sped by fear, she made her way to St. Pancras and the churchyard where her mother's bones lay. After she spread her shawl in a square next to the monument, she sat, receiving slight shelter from the cornice top of the fine Portland stone monument.

She knew the inscription by heart, had traced the stone carvings of letters and numbers from her earliest memory. It came to life under her fingers, as it had so many times before.

MARY WOLLSTONECRAFT
GODWIN
AUTHOR OF
A VINDICATION
OF THE RIGHTS OF WOMAN
BORN 27TH APRIL 1759
DIED 10TH SEPTEMBER 1797

The death date, so painfully close to her birth date of 30 August 1797, never ceased to create a painful pang.

Her stomach rumbled. When she glanced around her, she

saw a dandelion head and clover in the grass and nibbled a bit of both. Bitter and sweet in turn, the wild herbs gave her something to do while she waited.

The rain stopped, and the sun moved into view from behind a cloud. She pulled out her notebook and a bit of pencil. Knowing she couldn't stay long, was there some way to leave a note for Shelley here, in case he came later?

"Mary!" came a loud whisper.

She glanced up. Her heart skipped a beat as she saw Shelley, unshaven and all the more glorious for it, coming toward her, wearing boots stained with mud from his morning walk.

"Shelley!" She scrambled to her feet, tucking her notebook away. Her cloak, and even her skirts underneath, felt damp despite the protection of the shawl over the grave.

"What a beautiful spot," he said, stopping a mere foot away from her. "Your dear mother must rest peacefully here."

"As peacefully as she can, with her place usurped and her daughter turned into a shopgirl," Mary said tartly.

"You didn't want your father to marry again? He had two little girls to care for."

"By marrying Mrs. Godwin, he very suddenly had four children," she said sourly. "Then Willy was born."

"I do not deny the extreme strain on his finances," Shelley said. "But a man must have children. Turning you into a shopgirl, however, is unacceptable."

"What about Fanny?"

"She does not seem to mind so much, but I see how you strain under the burden." He put his hand to his chest. "It hurts me to see any creature in pain, but most particularly one with the potential you have for thought and study. We must change your fate."

"How?" Mary asked. "No one seems to have any suggestions. I guess I had better accept that Scottish marriage when it comes."

Shelley bit his lip and turned away. "You may not find your-self with such a congenial husband as me."

"Robert is a nice boy. I think he will be a nice man. It is just—"

"What?"

"Such a dull life. At least my mother can be said to have had adventures. A woman must remain alone or marry the right sort of man to have adventures."

He put his hand on her shoulder and stared into her eyes. "Never say that Mary Godwin became dull."

They smiled at each other. "I am so glad you came," Mary said. "I have important news to relate."

He nodded and glanced around. "What is the news?"

She told him what she had learned and concluded. "If the magistrates let Peter Corn go, I think you will be arrested next."

He struck his head lightly with his fist. "Honesty and truth are never welcome. The world is all about money."

"I know, Shelley. Please, stay out of sight."

Shelley nodded. "Do you think me guilty of anything terri-ble, Mary?"

"Of course not. My father does not always agree with your methods, but that is because he has grown old and tired."

Shelley stilled suddenly.

"What?" Mary asked.

"Someone is approaching."

"It is a burial ground," Mary said.

"You might have been followed." He looked into her eyes. "We will leave separately. I will be in touch. Thank you for the warning."

She nodded, but before she could take so much as a step, he grabbed her hand and kissed the palm of her glove, then ran around the willows and disappeared in the opposite direction of the two women coming their way.

Her hand sent tingles of heat all the way to her neck. She could feel her pulse beating frantically there. A kiss on her palm. Why, she'd never heard of such a thing before. So romantic. She closed her fingers around the kiss.

The shop had a lot of customers that morning. Mary felt cross and unsettled by her early morning tryst with Shelley but didn't know what she should tell Jane. Her sister's bedroom did look down over the street, however, and she supposed Jane could just have easily seen Fitzwalter Abel.

As a governess pulled her charges away from Jane, who had just returned from school in a playful mood, Mary gazed at her speculatively. At sixteen, Jane attracted many a wandering eye, but the pair of them were quite young to be wed. Fanny, though, was twenty now. Might the Bow Street Runner have been wandering around outside in the hopes of seeing one of the girls in the household?

Just then, Fanny made an appearance. "Jane, I didn't know you were home."

"I just came in. My French mistress has a cold, and she ended class early."

"You can take over the counter for a little while, can't you, Fanny dearest?" Mary asked. "I have such a headache." She shook the money box. "We have had a busy morning."

"Can't Jane watch the counter? I'm supposed to pick up the sausages Mamma ordered," Fanny said.

Jane put her hand to her forehead melodramatically. "My head aches so. I need the fresh air."

Fanny smiled gently and took her apron from under the counter. "Go, girls."

"We'll pick up the sausages," Mary assured her, heading for the front hall. She grabbed her cloak and went into the street, pulling up her hood.

Jane shivered next to her. "I didn't warm up at all. What is wrong with the weather?"

"It is a lot worse compared to this morning."

Jane pressed herself against the door as a cart went by, splattering mud nearly to their shoes. "You went out?"

"To see Shelley. I made an assignation with him after the events of last night."

"His description of his Welsh night of terror was so dreadful I nearly swooned," Jane agreed.

"No, what you did was keep me up half the night." She relayed her conversation with the Bow Street Runner.

"How very disturbing," Jane exclaimed. "How can we protect Shelley from Bow Street?"

"He needs people on his side," Mary said. "People who will speak up for him, like Eliza Westbrook did for Peter Corn. Shelley needs to be in a position where no one involved in this business would consider him a suspect."

Jane nodded. "What is your plan?"

"Cecil Campbell's sister. I think we should try that family again," Mary said, turning resolutely in the direction of Russell Square. "If she is on Shelley's side, surely that will do the trick."

It took an age to reach Russell Square, but the maid answered the door quickly and let them in. They were allowed into Mrs. McAndrew's private receiving room and were so grateful to see the fire that they went straight for it.

"I hope no one appears until we are dry," Jane said, shaking out her skirts.

"And the maid brings tea," Mary added, pulling off her gloves to warm her hands.

While the timing did not work out in their favor, the maid came in with a tray just behind Mrs. McAndrew, who walked in leaning heavily on Sophia Campbell.

"This is very cozy," Mrs. McAndrew said laconically after they were seated. "Are we to enjoy your company frequently now?"

"I am sorry to disturb you," Mary said. "We've come on a mission of some urgency."

"What is that?" Miss Campbell asked, handing Jane a steaming cup.

"I've spoken to the Bow Street Runner," Mary explained. "He indicated an intense animosity toward Mr. Shelley. I am afraid they are going to frame him for your poor brother's death."

"I have heard nothing to indicate he is innocent," the lady said. "Does he have an alibi, like Mr. Corn?"

Mary struggled to remain calm. "La, no, he says he was at a tavern alone," she said merrily. "A gentler creature you will never meet."

"He does not like Wordsworth," Jane said.

When the lady's features turned in her direction, Jane added, "He would not quote Wordsworth in a note."

"That is hardly evidence," Miss Campbell scolded.

"I don't think Shelley's tavern alibi is any good," Mrs. McAndrew said.

"Shelley is not claiming he was in anyone's sights all evening," Mary said. "In and of itself, isn't that a sign of innocence?"

Mrs. McAndrew's eyebrows rose. "If it wasn't him, then who?"

The door opened, and the maid came back in. She took a silver plate to her mistress, who removed the card that had been placed on it.

"Mr. Hocke?"

Mary straightened. "John Hocke?"

"He wants to pay his respects, if you please." The maid bobbed.

"Send him in," Mrs. McAndrew said with a decided lack of interest.

"There is a curate at St. Sepulchre who doesn't like that circle," Jane suggested, her gaze darting from one person to another. "He went to school with Shelley."

Miss Campbell gasped. "Surely a curate wouldn't kill."

Mr. Hocke entered the room. He walked straight to the sofa and bowed to Mrs. McAndrew before taking a seat. "What is this about murderous curates?" he asked.

"Murderous curates are unlikely outside of fiction," Mary said.

Miss Campbell continued. "Perhaps some other violent anarchist in their poetical circles was jealous of Cousin Cecil?"

"Violent anarchist?" Mary asked. "My father's circle is not violent. He believes in individual study to develop reason. If that happens, he thinks government would fall away without violence, as it hampers reason."

"Mr. Campbell was not a pure Godwinian," Miss Campbell said. "If I might be excused?"

Mrs. McAndrew waved her hand. Miss Campbell rose and went to a tall, thin-legged display cabinet that had drawers in its bowed lower compartment. She pulled out a notebook and brought it back to the sofa.

"It may have been unseemly of me, but I liberated Mr. Campbell's last notebook from his room and brought it out here for study," Miss Campbell said with a blush.

"Do you think a clue is in his writings?" Jane asked eagerly.

"I hoped to find something," Miss Campbell said. "But so far, I have not. However, the work does show how he leans away from Mr. Godwin's writings."

"How did you come to know Mr. Godwin's work?" Mr. Hocke asked curiously.

"Mr. Campbell often read to us in the evenings," Miss Campbell said.

"Read us something," Jane urged.

"I do not think you will find it comforting." The companion took a breath and read from the page. "O Man! Fearlessly fight on! We waste not our powers, we howl not at the uncaring moon, when we gather together in defense of Liberty. From the dark English shores to the wild, secluded hills, we bring our minds to the contemplation of immortality. Under the banner of our bodies and souls, no tyrant to guide us, but indeed, to vanquish them, grind the clerics and death itself under our boots . . ." She paused. "The fragment ends there. These must be his last writings."

"That is very different from Shelley's *Queen Mab*," Jane said.

"Oh?" Mrs. McAndrew said. "I do not have much of a head for poetry."

"I love it," Mary said. "Here are a few fine lines, instructive of Shelley's thoughts." She recited the lines:

> *The consciousness of good, which neither gold,*
> *Nor sordid fame, nor hope of heavenly bliss,*
> *Can purchase; but a life of resolute good,*
> *Unalterable will, quenchless desire*
> *Of universal happiness, the heart*
> *That beats with it in unison, the brain*
> *Whose ever wakeful wisdom toils to change*
> *Reason's rich stores for its eternal weal.*
>
> *This commerce of sincerest virtue needs*
> *No meditative signs of selfishness,*
> *No jealous intercourse of wretched gain,*
> *No balancings of prudence, cold and long;*
> *In just and equal measure all is weighed,*
> *One scale contains the sum of human weal,*
> *And one, the good man's heart.*

"There's no talk of revolution," Miss Campbell said.

"No," Mary agreed. "No violence, except on behalf of the government. They are both certainly anticlerical."

"I don't understand why anyone would murder another over poetry," Jane said.

"I do not think this is about poetry," Miss Campbell said. "The government throws men of intellect in prison, to be sure, but they do not burn them or stab them."

Mary thought back to the position of the knives and shuddered. "No one would mistake Mr. Campbell and Mr. Shelley for the same person in their words, only in their similar size and wardrobe. Truly, this crime seems so personal to me. The murderer had to have been so close. He could not have mistaken one man for another."

Jane put her head in her hands. "We need to check Shelley's alibi."

"You can't go to a tavern," Miss Campbell said, shocked.

"Maybe Mr. Hocke would go with us," Mary said. "What do you think, Mr. Hocke? If we can prove the alibi, it is something to take to Mr. Abel."

"Peter Corn is still in prison," he said. "Why are you concerned about Shelley's alibi?"

Mary explained the night's events.

"I can understand better your concern for Shelley now," Mr. Hocke said. "I want nothing more than truth, so I would be happy to go with you."

Mary considered him. "I appreciate your amiability."

He nodded. "The tavern in question is near Skinner Street."

"Please do what you can to find justice for my poor brother," Mrs. McAndrew implored, lifting her gaze as Mr. Hocke rose.

"I will do what I can, dear lady." He inclined his head respectfully.

Mary and Jane followed upon Mr. Hocke's heels as he went downstairs.

"I didn't know that Mr. Campbell was so extreme," Mary said when they were on the pavement. "Did he want bayonets in the street?"

"He believed in equality for all and didn't see any way to have that under the present government system," Mr. Hocke explained as he led them across the street in the direction of Skinner Street.

"Who is Mr. Shelley's friend at Old Bond Street?" Mary asked. "I have forgotten to ever ask his name."

"It does not signify, for Bow Street will know the name already. They must think the friend is someone who will lie for Shelley."

I would. Mary startled herself with the thought. Truth mattered little to those in authority.

"Will it do any good for us to find more witnesses?" she asked.

"They couldn't have two men locked up for the same crime, right?" Jane asked.

"They could say the two men worked together," he said. "Come, let us make haste. The clouds are very dark, and I do not want my clothing ruined."

Mary bit back a smile. He had indeed dressed very nicely for his visit to the McAndrew home. They turned into Fleet Street and walked to the Rose and Crown. Two large windows displayed a dim interior.

"It looks about empty," Mr. Hocke said. "Let us try for the owner."

Jane clutched Mary's arm as they walked in. This was not the sort of place young ladies went. The interior was one large room, with a massive fireplace, unlit, at one end and a few large, square tables with mismatched chairs. Unadorned wood, with slivers peeling up from the surface, comprised the floor.

"My good man," Mr. Hocke said, going up to the counter that ran along an interior wall. "Are you the owner of this establishment?"

Mary and Jane stayed behind their companion as he spoke, addressing the counterman as Mr. John. He appeared to be about Papa's age, with gray hair spiking out from above his ears. His linen seemed yellowed behind his apron.

"We're here about that nasty business of my friend Cecil Campbell's murder," Mr. Hocke said. "Someone involved claims to have been here that night. A man named Shelley. Perhaps with a companion?"

"A Runner did come by to ask that question," Mr. John agreed. "I'll tell you what I told him. I never remember anyone who isn't a regular. This Shelley means nothing to me other than he hasn't spent many coins here."

"Did he spend any here that night?" Jane peeped up boldly.

Mr. John ignored her. "I can't help you, or him. I'm busy with the regulars in the evening. They keep this here establishment going in good weather and foul."

"Thank you," Mr. Hocke said and walked out, trailed by the girls.

"Shouldn't you have offered him money to talk?" Jane asked.

"Don't have any," he said.

"Mr. John has rather cultured speech for a tavern owner," Mary suggested.

"It can be a prosperous line of business," Mr. Hocke said. "Never look down on a tavern owner. It's promising work. A shilling or two might make a barkeep talk, but not the owner."

"Should we go back in the evening?" Jane asked.

"Stay away from low places at night, miss. I suspect Mr. John will instruct his people to stay well out of this mess. You aren't going to keep Shelley safe with his alibi."

Mary put the heels of her palms against her eyes to ward off tears. How could they keep him from being arrested?

Chapter 19

Jane

"Thank you for escorting us home, Mr. Hocke," I said as we reached the corner of Skinner Street.

"Please do not walk us to the front door," Mary said. "Unless you are finished with *Caleb Williams* and need another book."

He waggled his finger at us. "Were the pair of you out without your father's permission?"

Mary laughed. "You can see how important our business was."

"Yes, listening to the bad poetry of a dead man is most important," Mr. Hocke said sarcastically. "I do admit I miss it, though. Our circle of friends is much reduced by the recent tragic events."

"Why?" I asked, uneasy at the thought of the poet's circle separated, each with different goals, distrusting one another because of what had happened. "Shouldn't you be together all the more, drawing together in sorrow?"

"And comforting Mrs. Shelley," Mary added, with an innocent smile, which I didn't believe for a moment.

"Sadly, it seems to have broken us apart. Suspicion, you see. It has to have been one of us. Peter is arrested, Shelley is on the wind, and of course, Cecil is dead."

"Who is left?" I asked.

His gaze swept over me as he spread his hands. "Just me, I suppose, and Burgess. The larger anarchist circle gathers around the Surrey County Jail, where, you know, Leigh Hunt is imprisoned."

"A dreadful business," Mary murmured.

"I find myself wanting to visit with Miss Campbell," he said, "as a relic of poor Cecil, I suppose, but you cannot separate her from Mrs. McAndrew."

"I have tried," I said. "And failed, for the most part." It must be as hard for someone like her as it was for someone like me to make friends.

Willy came around the corner and waved his thin arms at us. "You need to come inside. Mamma is looking for you both."

"Did she see us?" I asked.

"No. I saw you from the window. Come."

"Thank you, sir," Mary said to Mr. Hocke.

We gathered our skirts as he touched his fingers to his hat brim in a salute, and then we dashed to the house behind our brother. While we took off our cloaks in the front hall, we agreed we were grateful that no parents were there waiting for us.

"We should relieve Fanny," I said, glad to be away from Mr. Hocke and his dreary problems. "She will have other chores to get back to."

However, when we walked into the bookshop, we found Mamma gritting her teeth behind the front counter. She put her finger to her mouth in an imperious gesture. A child dashed to the counter, holding a pencil. A governess, obvious from her drab dress, followed with a copybook and a copy of *Tales from Shakespeare* by the Lamb siblings. Mamma took the offered money with a sickly smile, and then Mary opened the door to let them out.

"Where were you?" Mamma demanded as soon as the customers were safely out of the house. The porter cowered in the corner with a ball of string and a pile of copybooks.

"Fanny was watching the bookshop," Mary said innocently. "We went for a walk. The air is dreadful today."

"Dreadful, is it?" Mamma snarled. "We all have to breathe it, Miss Pretention. A walk won't make it any better. Fanny has more to do than your work—"

Papa came in, holding a pencil with a snapped-off lead. "Have you seen my penknife? I seem to have mislaid it somewhere."

"No, Mr. Godwin," Mamma said. "But you had better have a talk with your younger daughters. They have left Fanny to do their work yet again."

Papa turned to us, going stern. Mary, already very pale, went whiter, with spots of color high on her cheeks.

"Jane is trying to make a friend in Russell Square," she said. "We keep trying to see her, but her mistress blocks the connection."

"Mistress?" Mamma's eyes narrowed. "You are attempting to make a friend with a servant?"

"No, my dear," Papa said. "All are equal."

"Not a servant," I said. Mamma had become less and less a Godwin follower over the years. "A companion. She is in the home of her cousin, who is ill but very selfish. Poor Miss Campbell can scarcely leave the house."

"That is not your concern," Mamma said.

Papa's gaze sharpened. "Miss Campbell? Is she some connection to the young man who died here?"

"His betrothed," I said. "A distant relative of his."

"Jane." His voice went stern. "What if she killed him, or someone who did not like the engagement did so? I will not have you running about town, possibly tangling yourself up with a murderer."

My hands shook with thwarted intention. "She's just a girl, Papa. Not much older than us, and very sad."

"I forbid it," Papa said.

I bristled. How could he deny me a friend, when Mary did whatever she liked right under his nose? "At least I'm not having trysts in graveyards."

Mamma's eyes bulged in their sockets. "What?"

The color drained completely from Mary's face. I knew I should feel bad, but I wanted the focus off me. I did not want any more restrictions on me than there already were, for good reason.

The door opened. We all turned, fearful that a customer had heard us, but it was only Fanny.

"She met Shelley early in the morning," I said, the words starting to drag. "I bet she is in love, with a married man, no less."

"Why should that matter?" Fanny asked. "We are no believers in unhappy marriage, and Shelley says he and his wife are separated."

"I am not in love with him," Mary said, finding her voice. "Maybe Fanny is, though, to defend him like this."

Our parents stared at each of us in turn.

"Why would you meet him early in the morning?" Papa asked patiently.

"To warn him to stay away from here," Mary said simply. "I saw Fitzwalter Abel outside, and he made threats. Shelley is a friend of the family, Papa. It is my duty to warn him against a corrupt governmental force."

"I cannot deny that," Papa said. "But you should have allowed me to write him. We will talk more in private."

Mary inclined her head and mumbled, "I acted as quickly as my thoughts."

"Fanny?" Mamma said.

We all looked at her.

"Yes, Mamma?" Fanny asked very steadily.

"Has anyone from Bow Street been bothering you?"

"No," she said. "I haven't been mixed up in any of that." She sent Mary a resentful sideways glance.

"I cannot help but notice you spend quite a bit of time staring at Shelley when he comes to dine," Mamma said. "More than is appropriate."

"Ha!" I chortled. "She loves him!"

Fanny's plain face went pink and red in blotches. "I do not deny it."

"What?" Papa demanded, his normal placidity ruffled.

Her cheeks reddened further. "He is attracted to me. I thought I liked his wife well enough when we met her two years ago, but she has played him false."

"*Attracted to me?*" Mamma thundered.

"No, no, we will not have any of that." Papa shook his head. "Fanny, how could you be so silly? He is no more than courteous to any of you."

Fanny drew herself up. "I think he likes me very much indeed. He needs someone quiet and helpful after years with a decorative butterfly as his wife, and her sister is enough to drive him mad."

"What do you mean to do about it?" Mamma asked slowly.

Fanny almost looked pretty with the flush under her skin. "I don't know. I will see what he says now. You well know that I am the only member of this family he invited to live in his household last July. He offered to bring me to Lynmouth with Miss Hitchener."

I thought that very passive. If I claimed to be in love with someone, or someone with me, I would do more than wait for them to speak. What a milk-and-water miss Fanny was.

"Madness." Mamma snorted. "We hadn't even met him in person at the time."

"Still," Fanny said, "he may well invite me again when he returns to Wales this summer." She placed her hand on the ring of keys at her waist.

"He will not say anything of the sort," Papa said. "We need you here. Fanny, take Willy upstairs. Jane, you stay here with your mother and manage the shop. Mary, I will see you in my study."

He stomped out of the room and rattled the house as he went up the stairs. Blank faced, Mary took a spare penknife from under the counter and went out behind him. Fanny, holding herself so still that even her fingers didn't twitch, strode out with Willy without a protest.

"I need a chamber pot," I gasped and ran out after her.

Once I reached the base of the steps, I paused, waiting for Papa and Mary to go behind the closed study door. Then I crept up the stairs and went to listen at the study door. Why was Papa focused on disciplining Mary when Fanny had just declared her love for Shelley?

I couldn't hear anything yet, so I crept an inch or two closer. Papa would have better luck disciplining Fanny. She was such a mouse, but one never knew when one of her rare outbursts might occur. Then her Wollstonecraft blood showed. Would she declare herself to Shelley, or even to his wife? What if she tried to join that household? But which one would that be? Shelley claimed not to live with his wife. My thoughts were so jumbled. I had to admit that Shelley appeared to like me rather well himself. He had cast a spell on all three of us. I had perhaps fancied that he liked rescuing girls from school. He had swooped in and taken Harriet Westbrook from her school, with her sister's help. He had considered plotting to rescue his two sisters, as well, but hadn't the money to support them properly. Besides, he would not have the help of my sisters to take me out of school, and it was hardly onerous to go some mornings to a day school, which was unlike the sort of residential place that Harriet Westbrook and the Shelley girls had attended, as that was more like a convent than a school.

I heard a drawer shut. Finally, Papa began to speak.

"Mary, you will lose a father's love if you become involved with Shelley."

"Why?" she retorted. "Because you and Mamma are after his money?"

"I will not tolerate you speaking so about me or your mother in such a tone." Grit laced his monotone.

"She is not my mother." I heard rustling. "That lady there on the wall, who died because of my birth, is my mother. I will not have you call Mrs. Godwin such."

"Mary, I cannot send you away again. You are too old to be fostered upon another family, and we cannot afford boarding school. You must learn to conform your interests to the bookshop."

"I was not raised to be a common shopgirl."

"Given how few opportunities there are for women to earn their livings, working in a shop is an excellent opportunity."

"Perhaps I will marry Robert Baxter when he comes," Mary said with the hauteur of a queen.

"He will come only to ask me to hold you in amber, to make you wait. He's seventeen, Mary. Who knows if he will still want to wed you when he comes of age? I will not agree to hold you for him."

"He's old enough to travel all the way here to ask for my hand."

"That is romance, not reality. I will not risk you to a child."

"Do you expect me to wait forever, then, growing old like Fanny under Mrs. Godwin's thumb?"

Papa grunted. "Fanny is twenty. She has her future spread out before her."

"Mamma treats her like a servant," Mary retorted.

"She is a member of this household. Perhaps I have erred in

letting you leave for so long, but I assure you, you are not a guest here and do have duties. Duties that do not involve running off at dawn to warn murder suspects."

"He deserved the warning," Mary cried. "How could I not offer it when I knew his danger?"

"Tell me," Papa urged. "It is my duty to deal with it, not yours."

"You do not love him for himself. You love only his money. I've heard Mamma scheming with that Westbrook witch."

I heard a foot stamp and more movements across the floor, away from the door, thankfully.

"Do not tell me you love this very young married man with a pregnant wife."

"The child is not his."

"You cannot know this," Papa said. "You cannot know what goes on in a marriage."

"I do not care," Mary cried. "Fanny may delude herself that he loves her, but he and I have an intellectual understanding. I know his truths as he knows mine."

"Of all of us, you know Shelley the least," Papa said. "You met him only a few weeks ago. This is all fantasy. He is charming and desperate. I have seen a strange mood creep over him these past weeks. I sincerely hope this is a time of change for him, to take him off the path of an active revolutionary. After all, he could have been murdered that night in Wales."

"Yes," Mary said. "That only deepens my affection for him. The strength of his beliefs is compelling."

"He is a married man with dependents," her father said. "He cannot afford more strain upon his very limited prospects."

"Because he has debts? Because he has offered so much to you?" Mary spat.

"I will not see any of my daughters become the toy of a confused young man," Papa said. "This is not good sense. This is nothing more than an excess of sensibility. The very fact that your own sister has professed her affections for him, her fantasy that this is returned, should give you caution, Mary. You have a good mind, and you know better than to indulge in such fantasy, whether the matter is Shelley or the Baxter boy."

There was a pause. I strained, for fear I had missed something. But then Mary spoke.

"Why did you turn down David Booth for me? I was a better choice for him than Isabella. Marrying his dead wife's sister is forbidden in his community."

"I made inquiries. I was not convinced he was a good choice of a husband."

"Why not?" she asked.

"You are innocent yet, Mary, whatever you think about yourself." I heard a pause. "The truth is that not all men are . . . kind to their wives."

"You do not think Mr. Booth was kind? His wife was an invalid."

"Sometimes women do not desire to recover."

I put my hand to my mouth to hold back my gasp of horror.

Mary's tone matched my thoughts. "Are you saying she wanted to die? Like my mother did when Mr. Imlay was cruel to her?"

"It is possible, yes. My suspicion was great enough to deny him your hand in marriage."

"I see." I heard a windy sound, as if Mary blew out a breath. "Then I feel sorry for poor Isabella. You cannot feel the same way about Shelley. Mrs. Shelley is nothing if not blooming."

"Going around town claiming her unborn child is not his . . ." Papa's voice died off. "I do not like speaking so about men to you, Mary, but if you or Fanny become mixed up in his troubled affairs, it will not go well for any of us."

"I believe him pure in his intentions."

"In one moment, he might be. But there will be another moment, and he will feel differently. Trust me, there are things I know, people I know, that you do not."

"I give my love freely, as does Fanny." Mary's voice rang with conviction. "You cannot prevent that."

"Do not think that philosophy can overcome the difficulties of Shelley's situation or the ever-seeking nature he embodies. You cannot hold him."

"That is not the point," Mary said. "That is exactly not the point."

"I have spoken." I imagined him wagging his finger at her. "Use caution in your dealings with him. As I believe in your good sense, I will keep you here, but I have decisions to make about Fanny's well-being. It may be that, like you did, she needs to go away for a time."

"Where will you send her?" Mary asked. "I cannot fail to notice that harsher duty will fall upon me with her gone."

My eyes widened. Mary wasn't wrong. It could be dreadful to have Fanny gone, all the duties of the house and Mamma's dramatics and lies focused upon the two of us. I closed my eyes and my fists, hoping Papa wouldn't take such a drastic action.

"I have a deep correspondence. I shall find somewhere in my letters a believer in my principles who has offered any of my household shelter, just like the Baxters did you."

Like the Shelleys had.

"She is a woman grown," Mary said. "You cannot send her away for an education."

"Is she?" Papa asked. "I wonder if her character is quite formed yet. In any case, go and help Mamma, and later on we shall have a treat and go to the theater for *Othello*."

I darted up the stairs to make my claim to my mother good. I saw Mary when I was coming back out of my room.

"Are you in very much trouble?" I asked.

"No thanks to you, little sneak that you are," she said in that deadening, calm voice, which I had long since learned held rage cupped underneath. "But it is Fanny who played the fool, and she will pay for it."

"Being sent away could be an excellent thing," I said, not

pretending I hadn't heard the conversation. "After all, she is completely wrong about Shelley. He doesn't care a fig for her. It's as if she was born an old maid, elderly but with a coin in her pocket, always assuming men are after her."

"Very apt," Mary said. "But once she is gone, the noose is around our necks. Beware."

"The noose being Mamma?" I shuddered. I could not disagree.

She nodded. "I'm going to the kitchen. We will have a cold supper before the theater."

"Mamma wants me in the bookshop. But what are we going to do about the rest of it?"

"I have an idea. But I don't want to talk to you about it." She shouldered past and beat me to the stairs.

The next morning, just before we were to open the shop, I found Mary pacing in her bedroom, waving a feather not yet cut into a pen back and forth.

"What is wrong with you?" I demanded. "The bells are about to ring."

She stopped in front of me and stamped her slipper-shod foot. "Who, I pray, is our Iago?"

"I do not know who the villain of our piece is," I said, exasperated. *Othello* was just a play, and this was real life. "But I do not want him to be an Iago. I want there to be a full and perfect reason for the murderer's villainy. Otherwise, what is the point of justice?"

"What if we never know at all?" she asked.

"I find that unacceptable, but if we don't sort out the matter before Fanny is sent away, we will never be able to."

"She was dreadful last night." Mary set her feather down on the small desk in her room, which had been liberated from the schoolroom. "With such a temper, one might have thought her a third of her age."

"I expect your mother behaved like that," I suggested.

"What is that supposed to mean?" Mary demanded.

"Don't you remember the story of how Papa and your mother met the first time? How they argued and disliked each other thoroughly and had to let life grind down their sharp edges before they could meet again and fall in love?"

"Don't speak of my mother so," she snapped. "You didn't know her."

"I feel that I do, through her books. That's the only way you really know her. Her books and Papa's stories about her. And really, their time together was so much shorter than his with Mamma's."

"What would he say to memorialize Mamma, I wonder?"

Mary's arch tone made me giggle, but I stopped in mid-laugh. "There are the bells. We must fly."

Fanny came in, red-eyed and mulish, some hours later to relieve us for a meal. Mary went immediately to the front hall and grabbed her cloak.

"Your dress is very nice," I said to Fanny. "Where did you find the lace to finish it off?" I'd been waiting for her to debut her birthday present, but she'd needed more material to decorate the top of the bottom ruffle, a part she could easily replace when it was damaged by the elements.

She grunted at me and turned away, so I went out, shut the door, and confronted Mary.

"Where are you going?" I asked. "It will take only a few minutes to eat, and then I'm sure Fanny will want us back. She's probably wearing her new dress to pay a call."

"I am going to the Westbrook house," she said, pulling on her bonnet. "I must see Harriet Shelley."

"Are you mad?" I demanded. "She is none of your affair. Papa doesn't even invite her to dinner anymore."

"She holds the answers. I'm sure of it."

"Her sister will be guarding her like a dragon over its treasure hoard," I protested.

Mary tied her bonnet ribbon under her chin. "Are you coming or not?"

"They do not live close by."

"All the more reason to go now, then. Before we have quite exhausted polite visiting hours." She handed me my bonnet and cloak; then we went into the street. At least she had invited me along.

It would have taken us as much as forty minutes to reach Mayfair, but we were able to get a ride from a cart departing the orange warehouse next door, halving the journey. I felt much less guilty as we bounced along in the back, smelling the sweet scent of oranges emanating from the crates.

"If only one would conveniently pop out," I said. "I could quite do with an orange right now."

"Hmmm," Mary said, her expression content.

"Are you composing something?" I asked. "How will you remember it?"

"By thinking about it, instead of replying to your insolent questions," she snarled.

"You're probably writing a love note to Shelley," I teased. "Too bad Fanny has already beaten you to it."

I expected Mary to laugh, but instead, she said, "Fanny has no talent for composition, in the literary sense."

"No, but she does have a keen eye for dressmaking," I said. "Her new dress is lovely."

"I like looking nice as much as the next girl, but it cannot be one's only attainment," she said airily.

"You don't like looking nice. You like standing out. That ridiculous tartan dress you brought home from Dundee . . . I cannot abide it." I sniffed. "It does get you noticed, however, which is what I am sure you intended."

The cart rattled to a stop only a five-minute or so walk to the Westbrooks' coffeehouse. We jumped down and thanked the driver.

"Your height and overabundance of hair get you noticed," Mary said. "Why cannot I have a dress?"

"Please, you are the most ethereal beauty, like a fairy queen." I was irritated to concede that much. "You should take better care of your complexion, or it will not stay so milky white."

She tugged her bonnet forward.

I laughed. "Ha! Vanity, thy name is Mary Godwin."

She stomped away, nearly colliding with a nanny holding the hand of a sticky-faced young boy. I trotted in her wake down the street.

We found the coffeehouse, which was the landmark we needed to locate the Westbrook home about a mile away in Chapel Street. They lived in considerably more splendor than we did. A pert young maid with a clean white apron and cap opened the door of the newish house. We asked to see Mrs. Shelley, and the maid opened the door to a parlor that had a small fire crackling in the grate. She took our cloaks and bonnets and left. The room was feminine, with delicate figurines on low tables and gold cushions on the chairs.

"A different sort of life, no?" I asked. "I can't imagine Shelley here."

"He wouldn't notice," Mary replied, smoothing her hair. "He could live in grandeur or squalor. I do not think it would matter."

"I hadn't really thought of him in a place like this." I picked up a china shepherdess. She had a serenely silly expression. Looking at her made me feel stupid.

Mary put her hands out to the fire. "Mrs. Shelley went to school with his sisters. They were bound to be the same sorts of people, not like us."

"It makes me feel silly, thinking he was one of us," I admitted.

I had the sudden urge to knock over the pouting shepherd boy posing on the spindly table next to the coal hod.

The door opened, and the same maid came in, carrying a tea tray with beverages. Directly behind her was a black-haired woman, much older than us, and after her, Harriet Shelley, looking less tidy than when I had seen her last.

I let my gaze slide to her abdomen and back up again. While there was no sign of a child yet, her frizzy hair had not been properly styled, and she had a yellow stain on the shoulder of her white dress.

"We hoped to meet with you in private," Mary said, looking as uncomfortable as I had ever seen her in my life.

Miss Westbrook took her sister's arm and looked down her hook of a nose at us. "I am my sister's protector in all things."

"Protector?" I asked. "What danger are we to Mrs. Shelley?"

Miss Westbrook turned her dark-circled eyes to me. "Your father is trying to get money out of Mr. Shelley."

Mary laughed. "You are conspiring with Mrs. Godwin to ensure you benefit from those loans. And they are from the estate, not from Mr. Shelley's pockets."

"Conspiring?" Mrs. Shelley asked, with an adorable frown.

Miss Westbrook shook her head like an annoying bug had lodged there. "Ignore the words of these ill-bred girls. They should not even be received in this house."

"Your father owns a tavern," I snapped. "Don't give yourself airs."

"I'm to have a title one day," Mrs. Shelley said in a snooty little voice, which I didn't recall from previous interactions.

"Shelley doesn't care about such things," Mary said. "I am sorry to understand that his wife does."

Mrs. Shelley's chin pressed into her neck, giving her a double chin.

"I'm sure you have very little notion of what my sister's husband thinks." Miss Westbrook's forehead crinkled.

Mary's tone went sweet, sweet like a viper about to strike. "Do you always let your sister speak for you, Mrs. Shelley? Does she arrange the assignations with your lovers, as well?"

"How dare you!" Miss Westbrook cried.

Mrs. Shelley, though, took a step toward Mary, then another, until they stood nearly nose to nose. An interesting pair they made, with Mary's hair in a glowing nimbus around her cheeks, no matter how she tried to pin it back, and the other woman, a little older, a riper goddess, frowning back.

"You are very attractive," Mrs. Shelley said. "My husband will ever dawdle with such creatures. But he married me, and there is no way to escape the parson's noose."

"We were not raised to believe in marriage," Mary said in a low, dangerous tone. "And your husband has come to that conclusion, as well. You do not even live together."

"Next month my husband is taking a lease in Wales for us again," Mrs. Shelley said with a toss of her head. "Any married lady might visit her family."

"And her lover?" Mary inquired. "Are you acquainted with Miss Campbell? She is heartbroken at her betrothed's loss, though I see you cannot be bothered to wear mourning for the poor young man."

"Why would I wear mourning for Cecil Campbell?" she asked.

"Because he was your lover," I said impatiently. "Let us at least be frank about that."

She licked her lips. "My husband allowed his friend Hogg to fall in love with me, but I don't like him. Shelley didn't like Mr. Campbell. Foolish, he called him."

"You claim you would take only lovers your husband approved?" Mary asked, twisting her fingers together.

Mrs. Shelley's expression went serene. "I don't think you can understand. You are too young to understand how theory becomes practice."

"Who is the father of your child?" Mary asked.

She batted her lashes. "My husband, of course."

"On paper, he will be, thanks to damnable marriage, but who is truly the father?" Mary demanded.

Miss Westbrook put her hand on her sister's shoulder. "How dare you! Take your uncouth notions out of this house at once."

"It is fine," Mrs. Shelley said. "My husband will imagine such things to suit him. He is forever confiding in some female or other to gain their support, their love, if you will."

I startled when she began to laugh. She put her hands over her belly.

"Oh, you cannot believe the drama we had with a school-teacher who fell in love with Mr. Shelley," she said gaily. "She offered herself on the altar of true philosophy, an ugly, middle-aged spinster. Well, I must say you are a more tempting morsel than her, but you are not even the only such girl to throw herself at him this season."

"It is a nice trick to change the subject," Mary said. "You have perhaps more intelligence than I credited you for. Shelley's temporary loves are not the issue here, but the father of the child you carry. Would you say that Mr. Campbell desired you?"

"Of course." Her lashes fluttered again.

"Did he make himself a pest?"

She pursed her lips. "Frequently."

Mary licked her lips in unconscious mimicry. "Who was angered by this?"

"I was," Miss Westbrook interjected. "He upset my sister."

"But you did not kill him. You were with Mr. Corn," Mary said. "Straight from a brothel."

Miss Westbrook's sallow cheeks went pink. "I did not know that until much later."

"Why were you with Mr. Corn?" asked Mrs. Shelley, turning to her sister.

"Let us keep to the topic," Mary said. "Who else was angry with Mr. Campbell?"

"Mr. Hocke," Mrs. Shelley said. "He did not like how Mr. Campbell's violent poetry upset me."

"He considers himself your protector?"

"Yes, I suppose so."

"He is a close friend of Shelley?" Mary continued inexorably.

"No, we met him in Bath. He is a young man of fashion."

"What does he have to do with your circle?"

"He says he is engaged in a course of study and must be satisfied before he sets pen to paper on his own behalf." Mrs. Shelley smiled tentatively. "He writes beautiful letters, and he binds his friends' work into notebooks for them. He is good with his hands."

"Does he make love to you in these letters?"

"Don't answer that," Miss Westbrook said. "Send them away."

Mary's lips curved into one of her secretive smiles. I could see she felt she had a victory.

I was not convinced. But it didn't really matter. Cecil Campbell was dead, and understanding he might not be the baby's father was only one piece of information, not the key to the puzzle. I still knew more than Mary did.

Chapter 20

Mary

Mary and Jane had to walk home from the Westbrooks' because no carts would allow them a ride. They bowed their heads against the rain and trudged through the damp streets.

Mary watched water flow down the side of the roads, churning up the muck never-endingly created by horses. What caused the weather to be so foul? Was there truly a God so omnipotent that he would change the weather to suit chasing after a murderer of one insignificant anarchist poet? She saw a dull sheen on the edge of the street and pulled a penny from the muck.

Jane squeaked when she saw it. "Let's share a penny bun!"

"I have to believe Mrs. Shelley about Cecil Campbell," Mary said as they left the bakery. "I don't think she loved him."

"No, he has only Sophia Campbell to mourn him," Jane said, taking her half of the warm yeasty treat. "I don't even think his sister cares, not really."

"Too wrapped up in her own concerns, and perhaps soon to

join him in the grave," Mary agreed. "Do we think Mr. Hocke killed him?"

"In order to get him to stop pestering Mrs. Shelley? Seems a ridiculous motive to plan a murder. There must be more than that." Jane dodged a sodden mass of decaying cabbage, grabbing Mary's arm for support.

"You may have a point. A crime of passion is one thing, but we know this was planned, because of the note. We are still missing the motive. It is not an illicit pregnancy or a secret engagement."

"It is rather a lot for one young man to be mixed up in," Jane said tentatively, then stuffed her half bun in her mouth.

"Not in this circle. Look at Shelley. Look at my mother's life. All those years of quiet, and then everything changed, and she decided to have adventures." Mary stared at the iced bread in her hand.

Jane spoke through her mouthful. "I want to have adventures. Do you?"

"We'll never have them under Mamma's thumb." Mary handed the other half of the bun to Jane. Her chest tightened, the same as it did every time she knew she'd have to leave Papa again. How she loved seeing him every day. But that path was not hers, that of the dutiful daughter. Fanny already had that role.

"You didn't answer me." Jane pulled Mary against the window of a hat shop, chewing again.

"What?" Mary pressed her hands together, feeling the collected moisture from the rain squelch between her palms.

Jane swallowed. A bit of icing glistened on her upper lip. "Do you want adventures?"

"Of course, we both do. I do not see how it can be otherwise. We were not raised to know our place."

Jane laughed as Mary gestured. They needed to return home. "Our place is to do what Mamma tells us."

"But she always says we were given far too much education." Mary considered as they walked. "I know I do not have the spirit of compliance."

"Fanny does, and she was raised the same way."

"I disagree." Mary kicked a stone back into the road. They were nearing home now. She couldn't wait to get out of the rain. "Look at her claiming Shelley was interested in her, when she is the most boring girl alive. She wouldn't have said it if she wanted to fall in with every little scheme of Mamma's. Can you imagine if she had Shelley's baby?"

"It would ruin everything for all of us," Jane said.

"Our prospects, you mean?" Mary laughed. "What prospects are those? To marry some other penniless poet who hasn't been foolish enough to marry a young girl early?"

"We're the same age Mrs. Shelley was when she ran away."

"Look at her life now. Back at her father's house, with a baby and an older sister always there to sponge off her." Mary wiped Jane's lip. She was such a child. "She's much worse than Fanny."

"At least their father is wealthy."

"We were not raised to want wealth," Mary chided. "Or things, for the sake of them. Do you really think it matters?"

"If not, what does?" Jane asked.

Mary opened the Skinner Street door. "Warmth and a hot cup of tea at the end of a walk." She pulled off her cloak and bonnet and put them on their pegs.

Jane followed suit as Mary went to the table in the hall. "What is it?"

A thrill went through Mary as she picked up the letter there. "A note for me."

"From who?"

Mary recognized the handwriting, but she wasn't about to tell Jane after her earlier betrayal of a meeting with Shelley. She ignored the question. "I'm going to the kitchen for that hot cup of tea."

She trotted down the hall to the back stairs, hearing the shop door opening behind her. For a moment, she heard the start of Mamma's harangue at Jane; then she closed the door to the basement steps, and the noise faded away.

Mary woke just before dawn the next morning, as the watch called the hour. She hurried into her clothing, a simple old dress not much better for anything than washing day, but she dressed it up with a pretty lace fichu and took care with her hair. After a few minutes with her brush and pins, she chided herself for being silly, since her bonnet would cover nearly all of it. It wasn't as if she could make it curl fetchingly around her cheeks. She was lucky to have it lay flat for an hour.

After she tiptoed downstairs, she slid into her shoes and pulled on her cloak. She recoiled, discovering it was still wet from the walk home yesterday. Jane's was no better, but Fanny's was dry, so she put it on and pulled a warm winter bonnet from the trunk under the pegs. After a moment's consideration, she pulled out wool gloves, as well.

As she stepped into the street, a wave of animal scents swept over her. Men were driving cattle down the road toward the market. If Shelley were here, he'd berate the men for the condition of the cows. They did not look fit to be turned into meat, between their bony flanks and the flies that swarmed them.

Mary went the opposite direction. The note from Shelley said to meet him at her mother's grave half an hour after dawn, and Jane didn't know, so there would be no consequences this time.

Amazing, really, that her brain had behaved, and she'd woken with the watchman's call, when she normally slept right through it. But she'd wanted to rise, and sleep had left her at the right moment.

It made her feel quite powerful. She would have skipped down the road if it had not been so childish. Her plans were anything but, however. Going to meet a young man, and at the most sacred place in her life. Such an occasion demanded a certain mature demeanor that was well within her power to summon.

As the sky brightened, rain held off, despite ominous clouds that looked like they had sucked up all the coal smoke rising from chimneys. She reached the burial ground and darted through the graves, breathing in the sweet scent of grass still heavily dotted with dew. A figure leaned against the side of her mother's monument, looking down at a small book in his hand.

She forgot everything she might say and just stopped and looked at him. Where was his hat? Why was his hair so tousled and wild, yet glowing and alive with good health? How could his nose be slanted so perfectly and his lips be so full? How could he not be hers?

Between her feet and his, buttercups formed a circle in the grass in the path between the graves. A fairy ring, creating a barrier between her and Shelley. If she passed through, could she ever go back to the mortal world?

Her breath caught audibly, and he looked up. As he grinned at her, she forgot the fairy ring and ran to him. He took her hand in his and kissed it, then tucked his book away.

"Miss Mary Wollstonecraft Godwin, out of bed at this impossible hour."

"The watch woke me," she said breathlessly. "Are you staying out of sight as you must?"

He held out his wrists to her. "No shackles yet."

"Whatever are we going to do to protect you?" She doubted this ethereal creature could survive prison. Sturdy fictional Caleb Williams could survive the insult to limb and mind and keep a fire in his belly, but Shelley? She knew all too well the grinding horror of prisons, living so close to them. He needed fresh air and freedom like any cat born to the world.

"Cultivate friends," he said. "Friends to hide me and keep me. I might walk to Field Place. Papa is away sometimes, and Mother will take me in."

"You must not. They would think to look for you there. It's your ancestral home."

He spread his arms wide. "Then I need a new ancestral home."

"With Mrs. Shelley as the queen of the house?" Mary's mouth turned down. Her mother had loved a married man and had exiled herself to Paris during the Revolution because of it. Yet that hadn't been when she tried to kill herself. That had happened when an available man had rejected her and Fanny, his own daughter.

"We are separated," he said.

Mary hugged herself. "Yet she denied very convincingly that her child is Cecil Campbell's. What would happen if you were convinced your wife was faithful to you? Would you return to her? She said you are going to Wales in June."

"I will never go to Wales," he said. "I have an assassin waiting for me there. Even now, I watch the shadows on the buildings as I walk by, making sure none of them are following me."

"Sweet Shelley, that is sense," Mary said. "But your wife says differently. You were just wed again recently."

"That is to protect Ianthe. You must understand. Harriet, guided by Eliza, left me." He placed his hand on the top of her mother's grave. "I cannot vow on the Bible, but I will vow on your mother that the baby cannot be my child. No. I have known no woman for months. If you are convinced the babe in her womb is not Campbell's, that is what I believe, as well, but the conception is the mystery to me."

Mary put her hand to her lips. He was celibate? A creature made for love like him? All the insinuations made at the Westbrook home, and even those that had dropped from Mamma, fell away. Elation filled her veins. She could have risen from the ground and hovered above it and not been surprised, as well. He was free of the Westbrooks! She was certain of it now.

"What is that smile dancing on your lips?" he asked.

I do not see why you cannot be mine. She laughed. "I am happy, is all. Let us talk strategy, sir. Walk me back to Skinner Street. Surely it is safe at this early hour."

He held out his arm to her, and she took it. When they stepped between the graves, she glanced back, feeling like she'd forgotten something important, and saw the buttercup heads of the fairy circle had been trampled into the grass.

Chapter 21

Jane

I ran to help a seamstress struggling with a large parcel as she came out of the dress shop down the street from my school. "Tabby, are you going in to London?"

Tabby shifted her weight, trying to keep the package aloft. "Yes. I 'ave to deliver these dresses for a party tonight in Mayfair."

I gently lifted up one corner of the wrapping and saw heavily embroidered silk. "I'll help you carry it if I can ride with you." I hefted the bottom of the enormous parcel into the cart.

"Can you take her?" the seamstress asked the driver.

He nodded and took a sip from his flask. We both climbed in and arranged our skirts on top of the clean straw that had been laid in over the bare boards of the cart.

"Watch the parcel," the seamstress warned. "I'll get a thrashing if anything gets damaged."

It wouldn't do to have the paper covering rubbing apart on the boards. The delicate fabric would be ruined. "I'll take one side, and you can take the other," I promised. "How many dresses?"

"Ten, can you imagine? Four young ladies and their mother. We'd been making them and 'olding them until they paid something on account."

"Why did they pay finally?"

"It is the eldest daughter's coming-out ball. They couldn't wait for the dresses any longer." The seamstress giggled, exposing a gap in her teeth. "You can't snag a good 'usband in last year's fashion in Mayfair."

The conversation about aristocrats and the activities of the ladies distracted me enough that I paid no attention to the path the cart took into London. Tabby told one amusing tale after another of sibling rivalry, tiny dogs that hid under skirts, and ladies so addicted to sugar that they destroyed all their fine fabrics with jam stains.

When I glanced away to wipe the tears of laughter from my eyes, I recognized the square where the Westbrooks lived. "I had not realized we have come so far," I gasped as the cart stopped to let a sweeper clear the road of dung. "Can I get down, please?"

"Jump down," the driver said and held the reins taut.

"Thank you, Tabby," I said. "You are so amusing I forgot I needed to go home." I climbed inelegantly over the back of the cart and dropped into the road. I'd be terribly late getting home, having gone so far into London. Mamma would scold me for woolgathering.

In orienting myself for my walk to Skinner Street, I noticed the door to the Westbrooks' had opened. Harriet Shelley stepped out. She wore an embroidered green pelisse, the waistline fitted tightly to her still small waist.

I pushed myself into the ivy covering the corner of the house I had stopped at as she passed by, not wanting to talk to her. An irresistible urge to follow her struck me. If I discovered some new information, Mary would forgive me in a moment.

I hugged myself, forgetting that Mamma would be angry even if Mary appreciated my Bow Street Runner tendencies.

Mrs. Shelley turned up the road, her reticule dangling at her side. I'd be more mindful of pickpockets if I were her.

I waited until she was to the edge of the square before I followed. She walked quickly, as if she had an assignation to attend. After a few minutes, we passed the Westbrooks' coffeehouse. She didn't hesitate but, shortly thereafter, turned into a court down the street from the Grosvenor Square location.

I saw a familiar face behind the window of a newsagent's shop. Why was Mrs. Shelley meeting John Hocke? What mischief was he up to now? She disappeared behind the door. I hoped he wasn't bringing the willful wife into any of my affairs.

I counted to ten in my head and walked to the door with my head down. Adjusting my bonnet to block my face as much as possible, I read the hand-painted sign next to the door, which advertised news, stationery, and even a circulating library, along with a brand of patent medicine. I opened the door and went in.

Newspapers and other forms of reading filled the space inside. Brown bottles with white labels waited on a shelf behind the counter, ready to conquer illness like a row of tin soldiers prepared for battle. Mrs. Shelley and Mr. Hocke stood next to each other in front of a bookshelf, not looking at each other.

I went directly to the shelf on the other side of the door and stared very hard at the Minerva Press offerings there, trusting in my bonnet to protect my identity.

"What am I to do?" I heard Mrs. Shelley say.

"About him?" asked Mr. Hocke.

A man entered the shop and went directly to the counter. I picked up a copy of *The Nocturnal Minstrel* and pretended to consider it, but I'd missed a few rounds of the conversation I was desperate to hear.

"He can't know." Mrs. Shelley paused. "Does he know?"

"Do you want us both to be killed? Say nothing," Mr. Hocke urged.

"He's not a violent man," she said.

"He shot his pistol in Wales. He could have killed someone."

"Someone shot at him first," she protested.

"This gravely wounds his dignity. He must think the child is his," Mr. Hocke insisted.

My eyes grew wide. They were talking about the pregnancy! Here was proof that Shelley really wasn't the father of Harriet Shelley's baby. La, such a foul liar his wife was!

I set down the book and picked up another, *The Houses of Osma and Almeria*, and pretended to read. If I tried to leave, they might notice me. I needed them to leave first.

"He will." Her tone was confident. "I have made sure of that. Whatever he might suspect, he cannot rule out the possibility."

"Miss, are you a member of the circulating library?" The shopkeeper must have come out from a back room without me noticing. Another man passed by me and went out the door; it was the gentleman who had just entered and gone to the counter.

"Ah, no," I stammered, my heart hammering in my chest. "Are these books not for sale?"

"No." He listed off membership prices and attempted to sell a membership to me.

I listened patiently. "I will ask my father."

Escaping him, I opened the door and went out. Somehow, Mrs. Shelley and Mr. Hocke had left without me even noticing. The sales attempt by the shopkeeper had gone on for quite some time.

Ahead of me, at the mouth of the court, the illicit pair separated. Needing to go home, I followed Mr. Hocke but stayed well behind him and took an alternative route to Holborn as soon as I could. My head buzzed with the conversation I had heard.

If Harriet Shelley had convinced herself that Shelley wouldn't know he wasn't the father of her baby, then how could she herself be sure? Was her ploy to convince John Hocke that he was? But why? Regardless, Shelley would be listed as the father. A male child would even be the heir to old Sir Bysshe. At least what I had heard had absolutely destroyed any concern I had for Harriet Shelley. An unfaithful and deceitful wife, she was exactly why people like my father had railed so against marriage. Being forced to stay wed to support such a wife was insupportable. Had she been the mistress of both Mr. Campbell and Mr. Hocke? La, this free love was complex.

I walked quickly, unsure of what to do. Mamma would be having fits, but being this late, what would another hour matter? I decided to find Shelley.

When I popped into the tavern I knew he frequented sometimes, I found him in a corner, writing in a notebook. After a quick wave to catch his attention, I returned to the door. I didn't want any men in the space thinking I was available for their coin.

Shelley's head popped out of the open door a few seconds later, smiling genially, followed by the rest of him. "My dear Miss Clairmont, what an unexpected pleasure! I will walk you home. I know this is your neighborhood, but this isn't the safest of streets."

"I am well aware of it," I said, pleased that he would consider my safety. "But I am concerned about you. Mary told you to stay out of sight. What if a Runner passed through this tavern? You could be arrested."

"Everyone does not know my habits as well as you." He winked at me.

"I saw your wife today," I told him, cheeks heating, as we strode up the street.

He pressed me close to a building as three large laborers walked by, smelling strongly of ale. I took his arm and pushed back when the men were gone.

"Go on," he said, not shaking me off.

"She met that villainous Mr. Hocke at a newsagent's shop. They are attempting to deceive you, Shelley, without remorse." I didn't want anyone I knew trusting Mr. Hocke.

"I am not surprised. Poor Harriet does not have your emotional resources."

I shook his arm. "How can you be so calm? Mr. Hocke must have murdered Mr. Campbell, thinking he was you. Mary was right all along. You were the intended target."

"We shall have to see about that," Shelley said. Instead of crossing at the next intersection, he compressed my arm against his so that I could not pull away and continued walking north.

"Where are we going?"

"To Hocke's rooms, of course," he said. "We cannot delay, don't you think?"

"I—I don't know if he will be there," I said uncertainly. "They were near Grosvenor Square when I left them."

"Harriet will need to be home before Eliza frets," he explained. "Hocke will not want to walk all the way to his rooms, so he will find a hackney."

"Is he lazy?"

"It is lazy to steal someone's wife when any unattached female will do. It's not as if Harriet told me she wanted a separation. Quite the opposite. She has begged me to stay. It does not seem to cross her mind that it is her dishonesty that has ruined our lives together."

"She does not have a lick of truthfulness in her body," I said. "She and her sister both."

"I had such hopes when we married," he said, his mouth turning down. "But so much of the plot was dreamed up by Eliza. Money and position, not learning and philosophy, was their goal, and I was fool enough to fall into their machinations. Eliza is an old schemer and quite outwitted me."

I shook his arm. "Come now, Shelley. You were very young then. It is done. You have friends who love and esteem you now."

"And enemies who want to kill me," he said in a raspy voice, very unlike himself. "Will I live to see twenty-two? My father will be happy that I am dead and have ceased blackening the family name." He stopped in the middle of the road and raised his hands to the sky, ignoring the cart that bore down on him.

I shrieked and pushed him, but he had a solid form, despite his eating habits. After running around him, I reached for his arms and pulled him out of the way of the cart.

"There are other heirs," he declaimed. "Perhaps Hocke's child will win all in the end. It won't matter to me. I shall be dead."

"Or Campbell's child," I agreed. "But do take a care for yourself. Do not let them win by getting killed in the road."

He laughed, then kept laughing, until he was bent over, his hands on his knees. I leaned against a wall and watched him. He seemed to be having a minor fit, but I was too unnerved to join him in it.

Eventually, he straightened. "I am blessed to have friends like you and the rest of your family. Come, let us go see Hocke."

A half hour later, we were knocking on Mr. Hocke's door. Shelley had predicted correctly, for the man opened the door himself, though he'd come in so recently that he still wore his hat.

"Shelley? Miss Clairmont?" He looked confused as he glanced at me.

I stood my ground. I had surely concealed myself well enough in Mayfair. Even my bonnet was too drab to be memorable.

"We have come to accuse you," Shelley said dramatically, with a pointing finger.

"Then you must come in and have a drink. Saturday evening, right? Day of rest tomorrow?"

"From creditors, yes," Shelley agreed, entering. I followed.

"A blessed day, whether your creed is money, God, or the pleasures of the flesh."

Mr. Hocke chuckled, but the sound fell away as he caught the queer sort of taunting expression on Shelley's face. He glared at me. I kept my expression blank. Our host pulled a deal table from against the wall and set it in the center of the room. He took a set of loose papers from the table and tossed them in a chest, then lifted the small book press from the table and put it in the chest, as well. Then he poured red wine into glasses for the three of us.

"It is odd to see you alone," I observed, pushing one glass toward Shelley and taking my own. "I always imagined your rooms as a sort of moving party."

Mr. Hocke shrugged and drained his glass. "It is quiet now without Campbell and Corn. Everyone is so suspicious of each other since the news about that note you found was publicized."

"Did your circle have a habit of breaking into bookshops?" Shelley asked, cocking a hip against the table.

Mr. Hocke smirked.

Shelley set down his glass, untouched. "You shouldn't break into bookshops. Godwin has enough troubles without that."

"No harm is done," Hocke said, looking at me. "Read a line or two by candlelight, commune with our muses while we write our own words."

"No harm is done?" I dashed my glass to the floor. Oddly, the vessel did not break, but wine spread over the floor, dipping through the spaces between the floorboards. "Your little game became deadly!"

Shelley picked up my glass and set it on the mantelpiece. "Who participated?"

Mr. Hocke snorted. "Are you going to pretend you and your friend Hogg were not part of it?"

I put my hand to my mouth. This was news to me.

Shelley shook his head. "We came once, by invitation. I had no idea the game was a regular one. I told you this was not kind to Godwin and left."

"It doesn't matter," the other man said. "I was not there that night. I have an alibi."

"You do not. You were not at the brothel long enough," I said. "Your alibi disappeared."

Mr. Hocke's features changed into something more saturnine. "I went from the brothel to the arms of your wife, Shelley. She did not seem to mind it any."

My friend, in a sudden violence of motion, swept his arm down the mantelpiece, sliding all the ornaments to the floor.

The cacophony of breaking glass nearly drowned out the sound of a knock on the door. Mr. Hocke glanced at the mess in disgust and went toward the door.

"Shelley, there is no point in this. The next thing you know, you'll be asking the man to choose his second," I scolded. "Come, this does not match your principles. You do not care about your wife."

"She is a sister to me." His face had contorted with emotion. "The mother of my child."

"You do not care who your father's heir is," I soothed. "You do not care about chastity or faithfulness."

Mr. Hocke returned to the fireplace with his friend Charles Burgess in tow. He presented a more alert appearance than the first time I had seen him, though given the skinny bones of his wrists, which poked from his coat sleeves, I wondered that he had the energy to stay awake.

"What is this mess?" Mr. Burgess inquired. "Does no one have the will to clean it?"

"Shelley having one of his little fits again," Mr. Hocke said with a sneer.

"Found out you were trifling with his wife, eh?" Mr. Burgess made his way to the armchair in the corner, sat, and pulled a newspaper from his pocket. He covered his face with it.

"What do you know about this?" Shelley asked, approaching him and snatching the newspaper away.

"I know he has no need for brothels when your wife is willing to go to an inn with him," Mr. Burgess said, pulling out a different newspaper from another pocket and laying it over his eyes.

Shelley moved to snatch the second newspaper, but I darted forward and pressed it to Mr. Burgess's lazy face.

"What say you? An inn?" I demanded.

"They were at an inn together the night Campbell met his end," Burgess said through my hand. "I wouldn't feel safe coming here if I thought Hocke a killer."

"Can you prove it?" Shelley demanded.

A snicker rose from under the newsprint. "Ask your wife."

Shelley turned to Mr. Hocke, fury contorting his face. "She is not here, and you are." He pointed an accusing finger at the dandy.

Mr. Hocke straightened his cravat. "I was with Harriet. It presents a difficult alibi for the night Campbell died. Easier to pay a whore to lie for me, but then we had that business with Eliza Westbrook. It never occurred to me that Corn would be arrested. Dreadful business."

"You weren't with Corn at all?" I asked.

"Obviously not, but there is no reason for Miss Westbrook to lie. I believe her."

"I do not believe any Westbrooks," Shelley said haughtily. "Where were you with Harriet? Can you prove it?"

"We were at the Bull and Mouth. You know the place? Past St. Paul's."

"Did you sign a guest book?" Shelley asked.

"They did have one. We signed as Mr. and Mrs. Hocke, I believe." His lips shifted, his expression changing to merriment.

"Of course," Shelley said, with acid dripping from his words.

"Oh," Mr. Hocke said, turning. "I meant to tell you. I paid off my debt with a loan from my brother."

"Back to a life of all fun and no desperation, then?" I asked.

His grin crinkled his eyes. "My brother will not take the debt out of my kneecaps, I can tell you that much."

A snore came from the corner. Mr. Burgess had become so bored by the conversation that he had fallen asleep. Shelley, on the other hand, vibrated with anger. I sincerely hoped I would never see these men again and left the chamber behind Shelley.

We returned to Skinner Street in silence. I tried to ask him a question about the bookbinding equipment I'd seen, but he held up his hand to halt me. Shelley bent into the wind as if something pressed him forward. I walked half a step behind to give him privacy.

A night at an inn a couple of weeks ago would not produce a pregnancy to cause all this anguish. Mr. Hocke had presumably met Mrs. Shelley at other times previous to this. Or Mr. Campbell. Or both. Where had Mr. Hocke found the money for inns before his brother had given him funds? Had he borrowed from the moneylenders to pursue his illicit temptations? What were the economics of lust?

When we arrived at the bookshop, we found Mary there alone.

Shelley straightened, a gentle smile calming his face. Mary went to him immediately and patted his arm. "What has been happening?" she asked.

He glanced around the room to make sure we were alone, and told Mary all. She remained silent through the telling.

As I put on my apron, Shelley said, "Will you go to the Bull and Mouth with me tomorrow? I want to check the inn's guest book myself."

"Of course," she said in her most soothing voice.

My hands dropped from the apron ties. "Shall I go with you?"

"No, that's quite all right," Shelley said. "You've been upset enough."

"I only spilled wine," I said, shocked by how he overlooked his own messy act of violence. It was all very well for men of fashion to pretend their actions did not exist, but the rest of us had to deal with the consequences of their behavior as well as our own.

"Come, let us fetch you a cup of tea," Mary said. "I'll take you upstairs, then fill a pot with my own two hands."

They walked out as if I wasn't even there, leaving me to mind the bookshop.

Chapter 22

Mary

"You're sending me to Wales?" Fanny asked tearfully.

They were about ready to sit down to a Sunday luncheon of cold meats. Mary looked at all the brown-gray slices of flesh with disfavor, but not much else was on offer.

"It is for the best, Fanny," Papa said. "You have not been as helpful to your mamma as you ought recently."

"We can afford to have only one of the three of you gone at a time, and it is your turn," Mamma added, taking her seat.

"I will do better, I promise," Fanny said, twisting the fabric of her sleeve in one hand.

"I am very disappointed at your dramatics," Papa continued, pulling back his chair. "Pining over a married man and giving yourself airs. Think of the lessons presented by the first Mrs. Godwin. It will do you no good to think of Shelley. Go away, like your mother did to France, and find something inside yourself."

"I am not a philosopher, like you and Mother," Fanny said in a quiet voice, her face blotchy with incipient tears.

"You can still be thoughtful and kind," Papa said. "And useful."

"In Wales?" Fanny said in dubious tones.

"It is a very small settlement, I believe, but you will have room and board. There are children there you can teach lessons to." Papa cleared his throat. "We will gift you with a few of the Juvenile Library titles. You know them well."

"I'm—I'm to be an unpaid governess?" Fanny collapsed into her chair.

"A guest," he said. "But I know you will want to make yourself helpful."

Fanny glanced around the table. Jane looked away, but Mary caught her gaze and kept it.

"I went away," she said as she pushed Jane into her chair and took her own. "It was quite the best thing for me." Though Mary had been much younger and was not meant to be an unpaid servant. How could Mamma do this to Fanny? Though she had brought it on herself, in the main.

Fanny's lips trembled. She put her napkin to her eyes.

"Shelley went to Wales," Mary soothed. "You might very well find a different poet there. The scenery is dramatic enough to attract them in droves."

Fanny laughed or coughed—Mary wasn't sure which—then bowed her head. "Thank you for thinking of me, Papa. I only wish to be a help."

"Good," he said, then turned his head to dismiss the subject. "Mrs. Godwin, please pass the roast and a couple of those small potatoes."

The infamous inn being only a few blocks away, Mary had no trouble meeting Shelley in the afternoon, after lunch. Papa and Mamma had disappeared upstairs, probably to nap, and Jane had, very nicely, offered to help Fanny pack.

"Can I go with you?" Willy asked as Mary tied her bonnet.

"No." Mary ruffled his hair. "We are going on a delicate mission, and it is always a risk being with Shelley because of Bow Street's interest in him."

"It's Sunday," Willy said. "They can't arrest him."

"Not over debts, but if they decide he is a murderer, I doubt the day of the week matters. No, we will go quickly. Practice the speech I wrote for you. You can give it at dinner tonight, so that Fanny can hear it before she leaves." She buttoned her pelisse over her church dress and went into the street.

She and Shelley had agreed to meet in the yard at Barts, the venerable hospital not far away. Light rain fell as she made her way through the streets, which were gloomier than usual because it was Sunday.

Her heart lightened considerably when she saw Shelley peering at a statue in the courtyard. A few feet away, uniformed men settled a patient with bloody bandages covering his leg on a stretcher and took him through a door. The cart that had brought him rattled away, leaving a dark stain in the dirt.

Shelley smiled at her as she came over. Her heart skipped a beat as she stared up at him. A more beautiful man . . . No, a more beautiful soul had never existed. Why did the world torment him so? She wanted to gather him close and keep his dear heart safe from the foibles of the world.

Eventually, they both had to blink. He chuckled and plucked a stray hair off her pelisse.

"Will we ever be dry again?" he said ruefully as the hair refused to drop from his damp fingers.

"I understand why it wants to cling to you," Mary said. "You are a force of attraction."

He inclined his head, then rubbed the hair until it fell away. "You flatter me, sweet Mary. But today is not for sweet."

"No, we seek bitter fruit." She swallowed hard. "Shall we go to the Bull and Mouth?"

He offered his arm. They walked out of the courtyard as another cart came in, holding a rotund man clutching his chest.

The yard at the Bull and Mouth presented a considerable

contrast to the hospital. Instead of a stern stone edifice of deep age, the inn had a rickety, slapdash air. Boxes, crates, and traveling cases littered the yard. A loggia on each of the three upper floors was protected by decorative screens, but everything was yellowed and darkened from coal damage. People moved purposefully from entrance to exit, coach to yard. The chimneys puffed smoke into the air, and the rain pushed it down again. Mary hadn't heard coughing in the hospital yard, but she heard it here. Boys, coughing as they went, some with cloths over their lower faces, moved purposefully with shovels, trying to stay ahead of the horse muck, which coated the cobbles.

"A spot of tremendous romance," she said darkly.

Shelley chuckled in her ear. She hadn't realized he was quite so close, but then he tugged her out of the way of a carriage coming in quickly, the driver already shouting for ostlers.

"You are a good friend to me, sweet Mary," he said. "I appreciate you standing by me in my troubles."

She pressed herself against a railing. "Of course. We all do at Skinner Street, some more than others."

"Some jealousy?" he teased.

"I am concerned about Fanny," Mary admitted. She told him about Wales. "She seems to have some fantasy that you will rescue her from her household duties, but she is Papa's favorite, and to send her away will be painful for him."

"Papa's favorite? You are the one he speaks of the most."

Mary smiled at him. "Yet he asks Fanny, not me, to do any manner of small tasks for him, and he did not send her away before."

"Your health," Shelley protested. "We all worry about that, especially when you have so much conflict with Mrs. Godwin. I am very sorry to hear there is any thought of sending Fanny away, as she manages your stepmamma so well."

"Fanny leaves tomorrow," Mary said. "She is quiet and sad. Only she remembers our mother, and the housekeeper who took care of us the first couple of years, then left, and then all the dramas with Mamma. She is Papa's rock, while Jane and I come and go."

Shelley frowned. "I hope he has some scheme to make her useful, so that she does not focus on her own sadness too much. She does not write like we do."

"Or read, not really," Mary agreed. "She just likes to be busy. She spends her time learning about schools. She must hope to open a school someday, or at least to help our aunts with their school."

Shelley sighed. "Fanny is the buffer between the parents and the children in Skinner Street. She should not go."

"Perhaps it is not too late to stop her," Mary suggested. "You could speak to Papa."

Shelley shook his head. "He is the paterfamilias, and I will not interfere in a decision already made."

Mary sighed. "I know you cannot. I suppose we had better finish our business here."

Shelley looked at her very intently, his large blue eyes catching the light. The sun had peeked from the clouds momentarily, and he seemed to glow in its rays. How could any of them not be susceptible to such a celestial being as he? He even smelled like some sort of rich fruit, rather than the usual scents of sweat and leather.

"Maybe she should go to Wales," Mary said. If Fanny stayed, she would continue to pine over Shelley. How could she not? The answer was Wales, as her wise father had decreed.

Shelley stepped away from the railing, losing his sunny spot, and stalked across the yard, his nose intent on the main entrance of the Bull and Mouth. He disappeared behind a crowd of travelers who had just stepped down from a private coach. Mary raced to follow, holding her skirts above the cobbles.

When she reached the interior, she went temporarily blind. The overhang of the loggia overhead made the main hall of the inn exceedingly dark. Lamps burned on the walls, but the smoke decreased their illumination. Shelley spoke to the maid at the counter.

"I cannot show you the guest book, sir," she protested. "You are not a guest."

Shelley winked at her. "I'm looking for my wife."

The maid glanced at Mary. "She's right next to you, sir."

Mary's mouth opened. She blushed very hard. "Oh, I'm not—"

"She's not," Shelley said at the same time. Their eyes met as they laughed.

Mary's palms went itchy under her gloves. She grabbed the turned-wood edge of the counter. "We need to see if she's arrived yet, you see. Mrs. Hocke? Is she in the guest book?"

The maid nodded and opened the thick leather cover of the book centered on the counter. She ran her finger down the page. "What day do you think she came?"

"I think you have us for May fifth, correct?" Shelley asked. "Then we left on the sixth, and then she ought to have returned alone last night."

"Since he is already here, as you can see," Mary babbled.

The maid turned pages. "Yes, that's your signature on the fifth."

"If I may?" Shelley swiftly turned the book before she could protest. His mouth went taut before he forced a smile. "Yes, I recognize Harriet's handwriting." He tapped the page, and Mary saw Mr. Hocke and Mrs. Hocke signed separately, in two different scripts.

Shelley turned the pages. "But she does not appear again. What has happened?"

Mary clapped her hands. "I know. She is at the Saracen's Head this time."

"Ah." Shelley tilted his head. "Of course. How silly of me. Thank you." He dropped a coin onto the guest book and pushed it toward the maid, then took Mary's arm and tugged her out of the smoky room and back into the yard.

They dodged a dogcart and a boy leading a horse. Shelley did not speak. Mary kept an anxious eye on him. Jane had recounted the broken glass at Mr. Hocke's the day before. He was laboring under intense personal pressure.

"I would kill for a drink, but I cannot take you anywhere," Shelley muttered.

"There is the public room here."

"It is too close to home," he said, putting his fist to his forehead.

Mary keenly felt his distress. "It appears that your wife and Mr. Hocke both have alibis for the night Mr. Campbell died. What if Eliza Westbrook was not with Mr. Corn?"

"I am sure she was with Peter Corn, since the Bow Street Runner did the investigation."

"Do you not want to dig deeper? You must hate her," Mary said.

"I am of a philanthropic temperament, and the Westbrook women are welcome to my money," he declared. "However underhanded their methods. Come, we must get you home so that you can spend some little time with Fanny before she departs."

Chapter 23

Jane

Papa had left with Fanny and her trunk for a coaching inn quite early. Mamma, locked in her office, worked on tradesmen's bills. Mary and I stood behind the counter at the bookshop. She hadn't spoken to me all morning, had just scribbled away in her notebook. I had no idea what her thoughts were, or mine, really. A curious sort of numbness had descended upon Skinner Street. We hadn't seen a single customer, though the porter had taken some packages with him to mail.

"I'm going to take a walk," I announced. "You do not need me here."

"You should be at school, anyway," Mary said, taking out a penknife to sharpen her pencil.

"Not today, nor this entire week. Classes were canceled." I smiled brightly. "But you are right. No one will even notice I am gone."

I fled the bookshop before she could protest and clapped my bonnet on my head. In the street, I fastened my cloak and the strings of my bonnet against the wind. Clouds were visible in the distance, predicting a coming storm.

I needed green space to counteract my bleak mood. I did not have the heart to go past Jewin Street or into any space that held graves, so I decided to return to Russell Square. I had given up hope of being friends with Sophia Campbell, but the garden there appealed to me.

As I walked up the street, past the McAndrew house, a slight, tall figure darted across to the gardens. Miss Campbell must have found herself at leisure. I followed her up the path. When she paused to adjust her shoe, I stopped next to her and feigned shock. She tilted her head and blinked at me.

"Why, if it isn't Miss Campbell! I had decided to walk here myself but expected you were busy with Mrs. McAndrew."

"She is staying in bed today, and her maid can tend her," Miss Campbell explained in a cool tone. "I do enjoy days like this."

Wind rattled against her bonnet. She grabbed it. I helped her secure the strings better, then retied my own.

"Dreadful spring we are having," I remarked.

"For many reasons," Miss Campbell said, pulling a face. Then she smiled. "I am happy to see a friendly face, though. You don't need to be at the bookshop?"

I hadn't been sure she recognized me at first. Gratified, I linked my arm with hers, and we walked up the path to the center. "Very little foot traffic today, so I left Mary there alone."

"Have you heard anything more about poor Cecil's death?"

She said it casually, without dabbing her eyes and without a catch in her voice. Had she mourned him and moved on in the space of less than three weeks? A man her entire hopes should have been fixed upon? I wondered at her demeanor, but what did I know of love? I had never been in that state myself. They said it had made a fool of Papa and had killed Mary's mother, so I had learned it was a danger more than a blessing.

"Peter Corn continues to stay in custody, but my sister saw the Bow Street Runner, who appears to be keeping a close eye on poor Shelley."

"Does anyone know where he was that night?"

I bristled at the question. Must we speak of that night again? It was for the best that Miss Campbell had little free time, for I did not think I wanted to be friends with her. I walked around the center of the garden, ignoring all the humanity there—children playing, nannies gossiping—and continued to the next path. Miss Campbell had to trot to keep up with me.

"He was lingering in a tavern, like many young men his age," I said after a long enough pause to ensure she knew I'd taken offense.

"Who else is left?" Miss Campbell asked.

"Shelley uncovered a solid alibi for Mr. Hocke and Mrs. Shelley," I said with a shrug. "Mary and Fanny and I were upstairs with our brother Willy. Where were you?"

"Here, I suppose, in Russell Square."

I heard a shout, then the sound of running feet. Miss Campbell grabbed my arm in a fierce grip. I looked in all directions, but I could not tell where the sounds were coming from until a tree branch cracked to our right. More shouts came from that direction; then a man sped into view through the trees. When he arrived in our vicinity, I realized he was really just a half-grown boy, a little older than Willy. He tripped on a tree root bulging on the edge of the footpath and sprawled not ten feet from us.

Two men followed closely behind, holding tipstaves.

"Bow Street," I whispered. "What has this child done?"

The more hulking of the Runners grabbed the lad by the back of his collar and hauled him up. Was the man Fisher, the one who had been in the bookshop to arrest Peter Corn in front of Mary?

When the second Runner stopped, breathing heavily, I knew

my theory was correct, for this man was Fitzwalter Abel, the Runner I had met. I clutched Miss Campbell's arm with both my hands.

"Well, well, if it isn't Ragged Jack Hornigold," Mr. Abel said with a sneer. He lifted his hat and wiped sweat from under his floppy black hair.

"Never 'eard of 'im," the boy said with a pant between each word.

Mr. Fisher grabbed one of the boy's hands and pushed his sleeve up his skinny arm. "Birthmark that looks like an octopus. Yep, that's him."

Young Hornigold attempted to pull away, but Fisher just laughed and gripped him tighter.

I released Miss Campbell and went toward them. "Don't hurt him. He's not much more than a child."

"He's a vicious criminal is what he is, miss," said the Runner.

"What could he possibly have done? Been forced into a life of crime by some older man?"

"Hush now, Miss Clairmont," said Mr. Abel. "This is not your concern."

"You know her?" Mr. Fisher asked.

"She's one of the girls who found Campbell's body a few weeks back. Lives by the prisons," Mr. Abel explained. "And this young miss, I believe, is a relation of Mr. Campbell."

Miss Campbell bobbed very slightly, blushing, as she said her name.

Mr. Fisher grunted. "This miscreant will get his neck stretched because of his thieving ways."

I was surprised the Runner could find such eloquence in his crudely formed head. "Must thieves die? I am sure he was taking only what he needed, perhaps for a widowed mother and younger siblings? My father teaches us—"

"It's the rule of the land," Mr. Abel said. "Come now, Miss Clairmont. Your stepfather's philosophy is very out of style.

Hornigold's early taste for figging law has turned to life as a ding cove and he floors his victims, to make it even worse."

"He doesn't look large enough to beat anyone," I protested.

"That's for the magistrates to decide, not the likes of you or me," Mr. Abel said. "We've been paid to hunt him, and we have."

"Well done of us," Mr. Fisher added with a snort, turning his back on us.

"I want to go home now," Miss Campbell whispered, pulling meekly on my sleeve.

"I will escort you," I told her.

I noticed that Mr. Abel stared very intently at her, not in the way of men who desired a woman, but more like a cat having a staring contest with a mouse before pouncing. Maybe he knew she hadn't much of an alibi. Without saying anything more, I turned away and led Miss Campbell toward where the children played.

It didn't take long for us to be back along the street.

"Will that poor boy ever see the sun again?" I said with a shiver as we waited to cross.

"Magistrates are usually lenient with stealing," Miss Campbell said. "But if he's really been beating his victims, he probably will hang."

"I wonder if he killed anyone." I had already mostly forgotten the features of his young face.

"No," Miss Campbell said. "The Runners would have said so, I think."

"Have you met them before?"

"No." She took my arm and led me between two carriages, the second moving much more slowly than the first.

"Mr. Abel seemed to know who you were."

She unlocked the front door and led me in. "He knew you, of course, and must have assumed who I was given the neighborhood."

"As you say," I said, doubting it very much. Now that we knew Mr. Hocke and Mrs. Shelley were innocent, should I look at Miss Campbell as her lover's murderer? But why, when all her hopes were bound up in him? I did not like her demeanor now, however. Had she been pulled into the poets' game?

I was handing my things to a maid when Miss Campbell surprised me with an offer to take tea with her. When we reached the parlor upstairs, though, she stopped so suddenly that I bumped into her. I looked over her shoulder and saw Mrs. McAndrew, looking peevish on her sofa.

"Where have you been?" she demanded.

The companion rushed forward and straightened the blanket over Mrs. McAndrew's legs. "You must be feeling better. Usually, when you lie down in the afternoon, you are asleep longer than this."

"Worse, rather than better, miss," Mrs. McAndrew returned. "And Miss Clairmont, returned yet again, I see."

Was she as ill as she claimed? "We met by accident," I explained. "I like the paths in the garden here."

"Is the day fine?" the lady inquired.

"It was until we saw a boy arrested by two Bow Street Runners." I braided my fingers together. "I was surprised to see the Runners in such an elevated neighborhood."

"Which ones?" she asked.

"Fitzwalter Abel and Mr. Fisher," I said. "We have seen them at Skinner Street."

"I don't know this Mr. Fisher," Mrs. McAndrew said. "But Mr. Abel is related to a coachman who serves a local family, and lives above a coach house nearby."

"That explains why he seemed to know Miss Campbell, then," I said.

"He did not," Miss Campbell returned. "Can I ring for tea, cousin?"

Mrs. McAndrew closed her eyes. "No. I think I will rest here. Escort your friend out and return to me."

Miss Campbell stood very still for a moment, then tilted her head to me and walked out. I followed, feeling pity for the girl. Between Fanny, Mary, and me, we had plenty of opportunity to abandon our duties for a time here and there. But in this house, Miss Campbell had little recourse for escape.

Now, with Fanny gone, would Mary and I find ourselves in similar straits? It seemed intolerable to live like this.

"I'll fetch your things," Miss Campbell said when we reached the front hall.

I held out my hand to her. "I don't know you well, but you do not seem to have the same demeanor as before. What is going on? You do not seem to be mourning any longer, now that the shock has passed."

Miss Campbell hung her head. "I didn't love Cecil."

My mouth dropped open. Her whisper seemed to bounce off the walls, hit the door, then resound into my ears again. "No?"

"I had a previous engagement, before I ever came here, to a blacksmith in the village where I was born," she admitted.

"You wanted a more elevated life?" I asked.

"A better place within the family, financial security," she explained.

"Blacksmiths do very well," I said. "It is skilled work."

"But dirty." She wiped an imaginary speck off her black skirt. "Not like the life of a gentleman. I did not want to be a blacksmith's wife."

"I suppose not," I said slowly. I understood what she meant. I was raised in the world of thinkers, after all, men who made their money with their pen. I had made desperate choices in an attempt to shore up that life. Who was I to judge her?

"He came to London after me, to find another way of life." She looked sheepish. "I thought to leave him behind, but then he appeared here. Such a contrast to poor Cecil."

"Foppery versus a man with muscles?" I suggested. I knew any number of girls at school who sighed over the man who chopped wood for the vicarage instead of over the rail-thin curate, though he would have a better living.

"It is worse," she said suddenly. "Cecil was a fool. I could not abide his dreadful poetry and silly friends."

I blinked. What a revelation of my new friend's character. I had to put her in the same category as Harriet Shelley now, a false lover. At least Mary was a calm, reliable sort, maybe the only one in my life. This hunt for new friends seemed hopeless. Perhaps I had better cleave to my stepsister, forming myself to her tastes, and give up the desire for new acquaintances.

I arrived at Skinner Street with much to think about. Instead of shirking duties, I went to the bookshop and helped Mary dust. Some pencils were broken, as they habitually were, so I was sharpening them when Mamma came inside.

"You don't both need to be in here," she said grumpily. "We have company for dinner. Jane, go help Thérèse."

Lazy Thérèse. What was the value in insisting on servants as Mamma did? If we had to do half her work, why go to the expense of her? "Why don't you tell her that her services are no longer required?" I said tentatively. "Fanny is a better cook than she is, and Mary is returned now to help. You could sack Thérèse and bring back Fanny."

"Pray don't tell me how to run my own household, miss," Mamma snapped, breathing heavily, as she passed a shelving unit. "I thought so!" she cried triumphantly.

I heard a cry of pain from my sister. Rushing over, I saw Mamma had grabbed her by her arm. I sighed. Why had Mary not been sensible enough to drop her notebook and return to dusting as soon as Mamma arrived? Mamma held all the power, and we were merely her underlings.

Biting my lip, I went to the kitchen to do Thérèse's work.

Mamma valued the status of saying she had a French cook more than the benefit of one. She was really quite hopeless with the management of servants.

"Bonjour," I called when I walked in. Thérèse sat on a stool, crying into her apron. I didn't bother to understand why. She had once been a petted younger daughter of a low-ranking French nobleman, but her family had been guillotined after spending most of their fortune helping their youngest children escape execution. This one had never recovered from the strain of having to make her own way in the world.

I picked up a knife and began to peel potatoes.

An hour later I discovered why Mamma had been eager to set a nice table. Shelley had arrived at some point for the meal. Papa also had another guest, a man who was some decade younger than he and who had written utopian philosophy.

"You must try these," Mamma said, passing the potatoes, which I had covered with milk and cheese, to Shelley. "My Jane is such a good cook."

Papa glanced at me. "No school today?"

I shook my head. "No, Papa."

The philosopher dumped a solid third of my potato dish onto his plate as soon as Shelley took an abstemious amount. I did not like the man enough to remember his name.

"Mr. Townsend is such a genius," Mamma said. "But, alas, he has no funds to support his great work."

Shelley passed his glass to Mary so that she could pour him more wine. "How do you think Fanny is getting along in her travels?" he inquired. "Is she staying with friends along the way or at inns?"

"We have friends near the canal," Papa said. "She is staying with them tonight, outside Swindon."

"You would be interested to read Mr. Townsend's work, I am sure," Mother said. "His image of a utopian society would fit alongside your *Queen Mab*, I think, Shelley."

"Do you have copies of his work in the bookshop, ma'am?" Shelley asked, falling into her trap.

"Alas, he has not the money to pay for publication," she said.

"Why not publish it yourself?" Shelley asked after taking a bite of potato. "Jane, did you really make this and not your cook? It is delicious."

"Thérèse was having one of her sad days," I said sourly.

Mary smirked. "Her family died in France, you see."

Shelley made a chopping motion with the side of his hand against his neck. He and Mary both giggled. I leaned forward, readying myself to gain the upper hand in the conversation about my own potatoes.

"You know we cannot do that," Papa said. "The Juvenile Library is not for philosophy but for children."

"I thought to raise a subscription," Mr. Townsend said. "Twenty pounds would go a long way, sir. I could write letters to other like-minded men."

I wrapped my fingers tightly around my napkin under the table. How dare Mamma be so coarse when Shelley was already in such financial distress?

Papa cleared his throat, an uncomfortable expression on his face. I knew he would not think it wise to put Shelley's money, or even his promise of money, in any other pockets than his own.

"It does not take twenty pounds to write letters," Shelley said in a hard tone that I did not recognize, though Papa did not seem to notice.

"I h-have some debts," Mr. Townsend stuttered. He reached out his hand and fluttered his fingers at Mary for the wine bottle.

Mary passed him the bottle without comment. After hesitating for a moment, the philosopher emptied the bottle into his glass, filling it until just an inch under the lip.

No one could be surprised why the man had debts. He was decidedly not starved in appearance, and his personality was unlikely to win him fame, unlike, say, that delicious Lord Byron.

Shelley stood suddenly, though at least he had finished his potatoes. He walked around the table, and I saw some sort of sleight of hand with Mary before he turned back to Papa.

"Thank you for your hospitality, but I am afraid I have an appointment."

"Shelley, you must consider our table as your own," Papa said.

Shelley inclined his head. "I do thank you and will return."

After dinner, when we were putting Willy to bed, I demanded to know what Shelley had done in that final moment in the dining room.

"It was a note," Mary admitted.

"Are we to meet Shelley?"

She sighed. "At the churchyard at dawn."

"Good," I said happily. I didn't like being left out. I had too much at stake.

I shivered all the way to St. Pancras the next morning. We had both bundled up in flannel petticoats and scarves, to the point where I found it difficult to breathe. Anytime I moved the wool from my lips, I could see my breath coalesce in the air.

"May twenty-fourth," Mary muttered. "May twenty-fourth! Are we living in the artic wastes?" Her breath puffed a ghost of white in front of her.

"Shelley should have asked us to meet somewhere closer," I said.

"This is our place," Mary said implacably. "How could he choose anywhere else?"

"We could be watched," I said, damning her sentiment.

Mary stopped dead in her tracks. "You may be right. I hadn't thought of that. For such a child, you say intelligent things sometimes."

I stuck out my tongue at her.

She laughed, then grew thoughtful. "I wonder why Shelley never laughs. I suppose a fairy knight such as he has already seen the world and finds nothing funny about it."

"He is seeking transcendence, not humor." The church came into sight. I bowed my head under the rain. "Here we are. Maybe we can stand under those willow trees."

We found Shelley had already thought of that. He did not have a notebook out but paced back and forth under the branches, his head in a thoughtful pose.

Mary dashed under to him, knocking a branch, so that a waterfall prevented me from entering directly behind her. She did not notice. I had to wait for it to subside.

"What is the news?" she asked.

"So eager for pain, sweet Mary?" he asked.

Finally, I pushed the branch aside, soaking my glove, and slid under the rest until I was protected from the rain, if not the cold.

"Shelley," I announced, demanding attention, "I think—at least, I am afraid—that Sophia Campbell killed Cecil Campbell."

"Tell that to Bow Street," he said with a snort. "They will laugh you off. She has no motive. Quite the opposite."

"But she didn't love him," I protested.

"You need to think more logically," Mary said. "What is love when there is position at stake for a girl with nothing?"

I pressed my lips together and decided not to tell them about the rest of my walk in Russell Square yesterday. I turned away and stamped my foot.

"Why don't you take a little walk to soothe your nerves?" Shelley suggested. "I will converse some few minutes with your sister, and then you can return home before the house wakes."

"That is difficult to do," Mary said. "Mamma will have to rise early, now that Fanny is gone."

"Then go," Shelley said to me, with a shooing motion.

I wrung out my dripping glove over Mary's shoe, then flounced out from under their willow and found one of my own. I wouldn't be surprised if I froze to death before they were done. Maybe I should just go home, but I didn't like either of us being alone or seen with Shelley right now. Mostly, I didn't want to be alone for my own sake.

That afternoon, I had a music lesson in Covent Garden, not far from Bow Street. I spent the morning in the bookshop; then Mary came in to take over so I could leave.

I stuck my nose in the air and refused to speak to her before I went upstairs to grab my shabby old cloak to replace the one in the front hall, which was still soaked from our dawn adventures. I bundled up, still lamenting how I had been treated that morning, so I decided to point out that I was no fool.

I went into Mary's bedroom and opened her journal, then started a fresh page. I wrote, "I am taking care of everything for dear Shelley's sake. I will see Mr. Abel today and tell him to arrest Sophia Campbell so that Shelley doesn't need to hide from him anymore." I wanted the business finished for my sake.

Two hours later I left the respectable rooms above a gin shop where I occasionally took lessons from an older lady who often performed in the provinces, and walked up Bow Street. No women were about this part of the street, and curious looks were upon me. I screwed up my courage and went inside the headquarters of the Runners to speak to the man in charge there.

I found a man at a desk in an antechamber to the magistrates' court. All sorts of men in the middle age of life walked around with cigars lit in their hands or leaned against the walls or went in and came out of the next room.

"Is Fitzwalter Abel in attendance today?" I asked the clerk, or whatever he was.

"Why?" he asked, looking down his stubby nose at me.

I hesitated. "I thought he might be here."

He scratched his chin. "His doxy, are you?"

"No," I said, startled. "This is in connection to a case. He lives above a coach house, but I do not know the number."

"What do you want to tell him?"

"I want to tell him who killed Cecil Campbell," I explained.

The noise in the room dimmed for an instant, as if I had the spotlight. I glanced around, wondering if Mr. Abel might appear, after all. Instead, Mr. Fisher walked through the doorway toward me. Behind him, a man entered information into a book behind a desk.

"Looking for Abel?" he asked me.

I nodded, my knees quaking. He was fearsome in appearance, and his face seemed carved from primordial clay. "Is he at home today?"

"He was up half the night on business," Fisher said after spitting into a corner. "Might be rising now."

"What is the address?" I didn't want to tell him anything, especially since my courage was failing in front of the eyes of all these men.

He regarded me closely. "I can take you there, or if you don't want to spare the time, just tell me what you know."

I didn't want anything to do with Mr. Fisher. I turned my head away. "It's for Mr. Abel's ears only."

He smirked and told me the address. "Good luck to you, miss."

I didn't look him in the eye or speak to anyone else, but took myself out of there as fast as I could. Outside the building, I leaned against the wall, taking deep breaths until the taste of tobacco left my mouth. I knew I should simply go home, but Shelley had made fun of me, and Mary had called me a child. I had to prove them wrong. Also, if they ruled out Shelley, Mr. Hocke might come under renewed suspicion next. He could reveal more than I liked.

The wind swept down the road, lifting every portable scrap of anything. Soon I would be able to see my breath again. Only the time of year kept the lamps from being lit because the clouds were so low. I could not stand here any longer.

I shivered and walked toward Russell Square and Mr. Abel's coach house, wishing my thicker cloak had been dry.

When I reached the address in a mews a block behind the square, I found the doors open. A young man, his cap pulled low, knelt by a carriage wheel, making some sort of repair with a metal tool. I glanced around but did not discern how to reach the upper story. There were no smaller doors or staircases.

"Good afternoon," I called, staying a little outside the space. I could feel the welcome, brazier-made warmth radiating at me even from here. "Is Mr. Abel upstairs?"

"Just stepped in, miss," said the man, in a not unfriendly manner, with a quick glance up.

"I'm here on Bow Street business," I said. "Could he be rung for?"

The man leaned forward and laughed while wiping his hand on his apron. "No airs here. You just run up those stairs and give him the message." He pointed behind him into the gloom.

"Thank you." I moved into the coach house. After skirting the carriage and the man, I found the stairs more by touch than by sight.

After climbing the staircase, which was open to the room below, I found that part of the top floor held hay and the other side had been boarded off, with a door cut into the boards. A rickety affair. I knocked. The clicks of my knuckles resounded hollowly.

I waited. The scent of hay tickled my nose and offered a summertime ambiance that did not exist in the wintery outside. The door opened very narrowly, but I recognized Mr. Abel's handsome, rather wild features.

"I am Jane Clairmont," I said. "I bring you a suspect."

The space between his brows creased, but the door opened wider. He stood with his sleeves rolled up and his coat gone. I could see droplets of water on his hands.

"I see you, but you are alone," he said.

"The word of one," I amended. "I have news on the murder of Cecil Campbell."

He stepped back and let me in. I hesitated for a moment. I could stand here at the top of the stairs and tell him, but it wouldn't be private. Did I owe a murder suspect that?

"Come, come, girl," he said impatiently.

I stepped in. He shut the door behind me. The room didn't look as bad as the makeshift wall indicated. The wood had been painted, and the exterior window was clean. A large iron bedstead hung with curtains on three sides took up the middle of the room, probably to capture the heat from below and not the cold emanating from the outside walls.

"It must be cold here in the winter," I said, observing the lack of a fireplace.

"It's cold here now," he said, wiping his fingers on a cloth. He tossed it over his wash bowl.

"Well," I said, "I am happy to find you here. I want you to arrest Sophia Campbell."

"Why?" he said, without any reaction.

"She is not mourning Cecil Campbell. We thought her exempt from suspicion because she needed him, but she told me she had another lover from her home village and that she despised her poor cousin. I think she killed him because she could not stand to be around him anymore." I took a breath and stormed on, warming to my topic. "He was soon to be her only tie here, with Mrs. McAndrew dying and—"

A burst of pain came almost before Mr. Abel's arm moved. My gaze bounced from one wall to the other as my head rattled from the punch. My vision darkened; my neck and cheek fired up with pain.

"How dare you insult a fine lady?" he said, his voice hard.

"She's not a fine lady," I said, confused, raising my hand. "She's just a companion from the less fortunate side of the family."

Another blow caught me in the same spot. My body half turned. I lifted my hand to my cheek, uncomprehending; then a solid shape slammed into me. My ribs hit the black metal of the ironwork at the foot of the bed, then slid off. He grabbed my arm and twisted it behind me, then pushed me against one curtain before I could gather my thoughts to scream. All was pain.

I fell face-first into the curtain. The fabric ripped as he forced me down. I gagged on the dusty stuff, some elderly velvet from a finer home than this. "What?" I tried to say. Then his other hand picked up my skirts. I tried to scream then. The fabric took the sound from me. Cold air licked my thigh above my garter. Struggling did no good. His hand holding my arm at a painfully awkward angle kept me in his control. My other hand was trapped under my body, and he knew how to press hard enough to make movement impossible.

I thought franticly. I was a prisoner, helpless, splayed underneath him. The taste of vomit and blood filled my mouth. I did not want to lose my innocence like this.

I heard pounding. The door burst open, bounced off the wall. A man shouted. The joint-breaking pressure on my arm eased. Abel shouted and let me go. I fought the curtain, my only assailant now, and attempted to stand. My balance failed as I sneezed, and I half fell onto the bed, tearing the curtain completely from the rod.

When I had it clawed away from my eyes, which were streaming from the dust, I saw Shelley grappling with Mr. Abel. They moved around the room in a macabre imitation of a dance while I spit dust, blood, and bile on the old velvet. Shelley, taller, and pressed to Mr. Abel's back, had one arm around the Runner's neck and the other around his waist. The Runner grabbed his water jug from the table and slammed it against Shelley's arm. My protector lost his grip around Mr. Abel's neck.

I winced, sneezing, and struggled off the bed. The chill of my backside eased as my skirts fell into place. Mr. Abel lifted the jug again. Shelley needed me; I ran at the Runner headfirst and butted him from the side. He rammed into the wall next to the window, which rattled in its frame.

Shelley pulled me behind him, then put his arms up in a boxing stance.

Abel, with blood running down from a cut over his eye, from where he'd struck the window frame, laughed darkly and pulled a knife from inside his waistcoat. It still had a sheath on it.

I wrapped my arms around Shelley's waist and pulled him toward the door. He didn't resist. I heard footsteps coming up the stairs, but I didn't turn to look until we reached the exit.

Then I looked, for fear it was Mr. Fisher, but it was only the young man from downstairs, coming to see what the noise was about.

"Let us depart," I begged him. "I have been grievously attacked."

"By who?" he asked, looking at Shelley.

"This man saved me." I wiped dust from my eyes. My voice was thick with the ancient stuff. "Please, stand aside."

He did so, looking confused. I pulled Shelley down the stairs with my jelly strength, then left the warmth of the coach house for the cold street. Only then did I feel how hard I was shaking. I vomited in the street. No matter what I had done, I did not deserve this.

Chapter 24

Mary

Mary brought a basin of water and a soft cloth to Jane's bed. She wiped her stepsister's tear- and dust-streaked face while Shelley clucked over the blooming bruise on her wrist. Jane had been crying so long, she had the hiccups. When she was clean, Mary tended the lightly bleeding cut on Shelley's face. Even when he winced, he didn't separate his arm from Jane's shoulders.

"You will be fine," he said soothingly each time she shuddered with another rush of tears. He sang her a little song and, when that didn't calm her, recited a poem:

> *Lovely gems of radiance meek*
> *Trembling down my Laura's cheek,*
> *As the streamlets silent glide*
> *Thro' the Mead's enamell'd pride,*
> *Pledges sweet of pious woe,*
> *Tears which Friendship taught to flow,*

Sparkling in yon humid light
Love embathes his pinions bright:
There amid the glitt'ring show'r
Smiling sits th' insidious Power;
As some wingéd Warbler oft
When Spring-clouds shed their treasures soft
Joyous tricks his plumes anew,
And flutters in the fost'ring dew.

Jane smiled a little bit. "Coleridge makes crying sound so pretty." She sniffled and wiped at her eyes, but the tears seemed to have departed.

Mary sighed at the exacting kindness of Shelley as she poured wine for all three of them. She could imagine him wiping away his tiny child's tear with similar sweetness. How she wished she could be the mother of such an elevated being's children, a man kind instead of ever rational. As much as she loved her father, sometimes she wished for a sweet hug. Reason was not the only answer to the world. Sensibility was important, too.

"He has his uses," Shelley agreed before draining his glass.

"How did you know?" Jane asked, then winced when the rich liquid hit her bruised mouth. "How did you know what was going to happen?"

"I followed you." Shelley coughed. They must have walked quickly through the streets; they were both damp and flushed from the rain and their exertion.

"Were you keeping an eye on us here?" Mary asked. "You are supposed to be hiding from Bow Street."

"I still must be somewhere," Shelley explained, "and there are plenty of nooks to perch in around in Covent Garden. I saw Jane outside her music lesson. When she left there with such a sense of purpose, I knew I must follow."

"You could have simply walked with me," Jane said. "I would not mind the company."

He tapped his forehead. "But that would not have been me hiding." He pointed to the floppy tricorne hat on the floor. "I was wearing that for a disguise."

"It looks decayed, like a long dead thing," Mary said with disfavor. "Much like the mummy Diego is going to summon from Egypt in my story."

"Do tell," said Jane, sinking back into the mattress. "I do not want to think anymore about what happened right now."

Mary prattled along, making up elements of *Isabella, the Penitent* that she had not fully formed, until Jane fell asleep, heavy with pain and wine. Mary gently placed the wash bowl back on the stand and set the dirty towel underneath.

Shelley eased off the bed and covered Jane with a blanket, then gestured Mary out of the room.

"I will speak to Godwin," he said in the hall, all the lightness gone from his eyes. He looked like what he was, a nobleman with responsibilities. "He must know what has transpired. I do not think Mr. Abel's actions should go unnoticed by his supervisors."

"You cannot tell Father tonight," Mary cautioned. "Mr. Hogan is here dining. That is why Mamma has not been looking for us."

Shelley made a face. "No, I don't want to be in the middle of that until we can sort out the post-obit loans. Well, Jane is safe enough tonight. No matter who you see in the street after dark, stay indoors. I will call on your father in the morning, and we will go to Bow Street."

Mary clutched his arm. "You were very brave."

Shelley shook his head. "Your sister was very foolhardy, more like. Bow Street is not to be trifled with. Those men are not softhearted poets."

He smiled at her, then went downstairs. Mary tiptoed through the house to find Charles and tell him what had happened.

*   *   *

The next day, Mamma sent the porter to manage the book-shop counter so that Jane could rest under Mary's supervision. They shut themselves into the parlor across the hall from the bookshop, a collection of periodicals scattered around them. Mamma came in an hour later with the post and collapsed into her favorite rocking chair with a grunt.

"Not returned from Bow Street?" she asked, breathing heavily.

"I've seen no sign of Papa," Mary said. "But he hasn't been gone long at all."

"Where is Shelley keeping himself these nights?" Mamma asked.

"Last we heard, he'd moved to Fleet Street." Mary shrugged.

"I found him there a couple of days ago," Jane said, then closed her eyes again.

"You went to his rooms, as well?" Mamma demanded, horror on her ruddy features.

"No, I saw him in a tavern," Jane said, eyelids drooping.

"You'll be the death of me yet," Mamma muttered.

Mary returned to her copy of the *Edinburgh Review* and attempted to read a review about a book by Sir Humphry Davy, which normally would have interested her. It failed to capture her attention, possibly due to the distracting wheezes of Mamma.

"You have a letter from Mrs. McAndrew, Jane," Mamma said after flipping through the folded sheets.

"Odd," Jane said, half dozing on the hearthrug.

Mary took it from Mamma and sliced it open. After she perused it, Mary went over it again more carefully. "Jane, this is interesting."

"What?" She yawned.

"Sophia Campbell has gone missing," Mary reported. "Mrs. McAndrew is asking us to call on her."

Mamma frowned. "Who?"

"Mrs. McAndrew's companion. She was secretly betrothed to Cecil Campbell," Mary explained.

Jane finally sat up when the parlor door opened. She stirred the fire as Papa entered, bringing in the scent of damp wool.

"What is the news, Papa?" Mamma asked.

"We made our report regarding yesterday's experience with Mr. Abel," he said. "Is there tea?"

"No, Papa," Mary said, rising. "Shall I fetch you some?"

"Just bring me a glass of port," he said, pointing to a cabinet.

Mary went to comply as her father continued. "Mr. Abel had not checked in at Bow Street today."

"He's missing, then, just like Sophia Campbell," Jane said.

"What?" Papa exclaimed.

"Jane just had a letter from Mrs. McAndrew. The girls have been asked to call at Russell Square." As Mamma spoke, Mary tipped a little of the port into a glass and drank it down. The warmth flowed into her belly.

"Mr. Abel lives near there. I don't like it," Papa said.

"Was Mr. Abel supposed to be at Bow Street today?" Mary asked. "Or is it normal for him to be gone?"

"I had the distinct impression they felt he was missing," her father said.

Mary wiped out the glass, then filled it and brought it to Papa. "Why didn't Shelley come back with you?"

"He went with that Fisher fellow to Abel's coach house to see if he can be retrieved."

"Very brave of him," Mary said, licking her lips to get the heavy, sweet taste of the port off them. "I told him to stay out of sight."

"He is a gentleman, and he will do as he must," Papa said, then drained his glass. "I need to get back to my reading. Keep the house quiet." He left the room.

Mamma shivered. "Stoke the fire, Jane. Then you and Mary may go to Russell Square."

"Can we take Charles with us?" Jane asked as she added another lump of coal. "I want a man along."

"I'll leave the porter in charge of the bookshop, God save us."

"Thank you, Mamma." Jane reached for Mary's arm. They went into the front hall and poked through the hanging garments for something warm.

Mary put on Fanny's fur-lined pelisse. She hadn't taken it with her to Wales. Jane enfolded herself into Mamma's massive wool cloak. They had less luck with the shoes, but after a few minutes they were as warmly dressed as possible. Then they went to the printshop to attempt to talk Charles away from his work.

It wasn't hard, since he didn't like working for the Juvenile Library. As they walked to Russell Square, he regaled them with his experiences in Edinburgh and his hopes to find a new life in Europe if he could ever be free of the detestable family business.

"Mamma will feel sorely betrayed," Jane warned. "Papa and she spent a great amount of coin having you trained."

He shrugged. "It was not my decision. They did it to feather their nests, not mine. I do not even like Mamma."

"That is hardly the point," Jane argued. "You owe a duty to her."

"They will ruin all of us with their spending," Mary predicted.

"I would not expect Papa to stay out of debtor's prison," Charles said predictably. "I will do my best with the Juvenile Library until I see the end coming, but I will flee then, mark my words."

Mary tuned out his boasting and focused on the music of her own thoughts instead. She puzzled over the nature of a girl such as Sophia Campbell. The girl possessed a positive mastery of secret engagements. How had she managed it twice? Mary had not even known David Booth had wanted to replace his dead wife with her before he had spoken to Papa in January, and young Robert had paid such obvious compliments to her that she'd been sent home from Scotland.

"What are we going to say to Mrs. McAndrew?" Mary asked when the thought struck her. "She doesn't care about what is going on. She just wants someone to fetch and carry for her."

Jane stopped dead in the street, almost crashing into a lady who was walking in the opposite direction, holding a small dog. "My apologies," she said to the lady, then turned to Mary. "You don't think she's asked us to call to offer one of us the position?"

Charles laughed. "What would she want with either of you lazybones?"

Mary folded her arms across her chest. "I would never agree to such servitude."

"Me either," said Jane. "We must find Miss Campbell and return her to her mistress."

"You haven't found Mr. Campbell's killer yet," Charles said. "What makes you think either of you two fluff-brains can find a missing companion?"

"We are more likely to understand the mind of a woman than a man is," Mary said, ignoring her stepbrother. Though it irked her that he was placed above Fanny in the household, despite being a year younger, she scarcely knew him, given their mutual long absences. She preferred for that to remain so. He was Jane's brother, not hers. "Where would she go?"

"The park in the center of the square, to clear her thoughts," Jane said.

"Did she remove from her employer's home entirely?" Mary asked. "If she took her possessions, she wouldn't have gone to the park. She'd need a place to rest her head. I hope Mrs. McAndrew has written her family, wherever they live."

"We don't know," Jane said. "But the park is not so large.

Let us look around. I expect the lady wrote Miss Campbell's family at the same time she wrote us."

They reached Russell Square, which seemed quiet, with no activity at the McAndrew house. Whoever the lady had written, they were the first to come.

"This is very nice," Charles said as they crossed into the garden. "How long has it been here?"

"Less than ten years," Mary said. "You can see the trees are not very tall."

Charles took the path into the center and charged forward. Mary took Jane's arm and marched her along the outside.

"You don't really think she is here, do you?" Mary asked.

"She could be Mr. Campbell's killer, and we can be the ones to go to Bow Street," Jane pointed out. "Is there a reward?"

Mary pulled her down the next path toward the center. "You had a very dreadful experience just yesterday. Think more clearly, Jane. You must grow up a little."

"What do *you* think is going on, with your lofty months more of life than mine?" Jane's tone was acid.

"I find it suspicious that both of them have gone missing. Why not together?"

Jane chewed on her lip for a moment, then stopped on a path. Ahead of them, Charles circled the minders of the playing children, looking for a face he wouldn't recognize, anyway, since he'd never met Sophia Campbell. "Do you think he's hurt her, like he attempted to do to me?"

"I think that Mr. Abel must have been Miss Campbell's first intended husband, to behave like he did," Mary exclaimed with a burst of insight.

"Oh." Jane's mouth hung open. "Was he the blacksmith?"

Mary frowned at her. "You said he was strong."

Jane nodded. "I thought he boxed or something like that, but yes, he could have been a blacksmith."

"What would be their purpose in disappearing now?" Mary tapped her chin in thought. "Did she leave willingly?"

"Did he kidnap her and take her to Scotland?" Jane countered.

"To be married?"

"Yes. Shelley and his wife married in Scotland," Jane said.

Mary winced at the information. It gave her a pang in the belly that he could go to such trouble and be so betrayed. "Well, if it is true, Miss Campbell will find herself married to a very dreadful specimen."

"Yes, but she likely killed Cecil Campbell so she could be free to marry Mr. Abel."

"Or he killed Mr. Campbell to make Miss Campbell marry him," Mary said. "We do not know the scenario."

"She is a deceiver," Jane declared. "Her entire demeanor had changed when I saw her last."

"I know enough to fear Mr. Abel, for Shelley's sake." They had reached the center of the square. "We must relay our suspicions to Mrs. McAndrew. Perhaps someone in the house will know if Miss Campbell knew Mr. Abel, or if we are merely pulling at straws."

"Charles!" Jane called and waved. He had just started down the far path, but he heard her and came back.

Mary glanced over the benches and the people there to the trees beyond. Why was it that brains seemed to work better in nature? She supposed her mother would say that new scenes created new impressions. Nature was ever changing.

The three of them returned to the street and rang the bell at the McAndrew home. The maid recognized them and led them upstairs to the private parlor. Mrs. McAndrew sat upright on the sofa, her skin white other than high spots of feverish color on her cheeks. An older woman, who had the overly curled and ironed appearance of a lady's maid, held her hand soothingly.

In the chair across from the sofa, Mary saw the unexpected sight of Reverend Doone.

His chins quivered as he rose and dipped them in acknowledgment. Jane ignored him and rushed to Mrs. McAndrew's other side to take her free hand in sympathy and sit beside her.

"It's the most dreadful thing," Mrs. McAndrew quavered. "To be so betrayed."

"Are her things gone?" Mary asked bluntly. "We were not sure from the letter."

"The betrayal is complete," the man of God said heavily, patting his belly. He glanced around the room, as if looking for the tea tray, which was not in evidence.

"The household must be in an uproar," Mary said.

"It is indeed," he said. "I imagine Mrs. Godwin never would allow such a thing? She seems a comfortable woman."

"She does put effort into her comfort, yes," Mary said. "We never go hungry on Skinner Street."

He smiled beatifically. "Perhaps I could call on you someday? You can share with me the bounty of your own beautiful hands?"

Mary stiffened. How dare he attempt to make love to her at such a difficult time, even if Jane was taking up all Mrs. McAndrew's attention with her prattling? "How flattering, Reverend, but my father wouldn't like it. He's a confirmed atheist, you know."

Charles cleared his throat. He shook his head slightly. The reverend pinked and looked away.

"Whatever will we do?" Mrs. McAndrew said, her voice rising. "It was my duty to keep her safe, you know."

"Were you aware she had some sort of arrangement with a blacksmith from her village?" Mary asked.

"Mr. Abel, you mean?" Mrs. McAndrew applied her handkerchief. "I thought I told you about him already."

"You said he lived nearby. I didn't know he and Miss Campbell had a prior acquaintance."

"Yes, the family wanted her taken away from the neighborhood before she married beneath her. We thought bringing her here would give her some social polish."

"He followed, though."

Mrs. McAndrew shuddered. Jane and the maid rocked slightly along with her. "Yes, to become a Runner, of all things. He's intelligent, I'll give him that."

"You've met him?"

"My housekeeper has found him in the servants' dining room a couple of times, entertaining the girls with tales. I forbid Sophia from venturing into that part of the house. He was allowed entrance here once, to report my brother's demise."

Mary allowed a pause to recognize grief before she continued. "You don't think they were in contact since she's been in London?"

"She'd been forbidden contact with him before she ever came here," Mrs. McAndrew wheezed. "There had been no attempt to send letters."

She had been allowed to leave the house alone, however. They had seen her outside. There were plenty of ways Miss Campbell could have met Mr. Abel, particularly with him living nearby.

What sort of future was Miss Campbell meant to have between the floors of the house, not really fitting in anywhere? And what of basic human desire, for all that Mr. Abel was a brute? They might have grown up together, and she'd known him at a tenderer age.

"You don't think Miss Campbell had any reason to hate your brother?" Mary asked carefully.

Mrs. McAndrew sniffed. "No reason."

"His poetry was very violent," Jane said.

The lady's color rose. "He believed in revolution, as do many men when they are young," the lady said. "Sending them off to soldier removes the notion."

"Mr. Campbell did not take a commission, I believe?" Mary asked.

"No. He had a weak chest. Scarlet fever when he was young. It made him all the more martial, to see the reports about the war and not be able to do anything himself."

"Were they close, Mr. and Miss Campbell?"

"No closer than any two cousins." Mrs. McAndrew's gaze went flinty. "Why, do you think something untoward occurred?"

"Miss Campbell told me she and Mr. Campbell were pledged to one another," Jane said.

A squeak escaped from Mrs. McAndrew. The maid shrieked and pulled away but was gripped too tightly by her mistress to escape. Jane slid a couple of inches to the other side.

"It cannot be," Mrs. McAndrew said with a gasp. "The shame of it. She was a blacksmith's doxy."

Mary's eyes widened. Had things gone so far with Mr. Abel that the family had discovered it? No wonder the bond had proved impossible to break.

"I do hope they can be found," Mary said. "One of them could be your brother's killer."

"Surely not." Mrs. McAndrew dabbed at her eyes with an embroidered handkerchief. "Some tinker or a servant."

The maid edged a scant inch away.

"There is no sign of any other connection?" Mary asked. "That you are aware of? His poetic circle has not yielded any suspect without an alibi."

"He loved his family and his poetry," his sister said. "I know of nothing more."

"Thank you for seeing us," Jane said politely. "I am sorry we could not help."

Mary, Charles, and Jane left the room and went downstairs.

Charles glanced around the front hall. Ancestor portraits glared from the walls.

"It's very different than Mr. Abel's cold room above a stable," Jane said. "But it's its own sort of prison."

"If Mr. Abel were a worthy man, I could see wanting to escape." Mary stared at the front door. "But he isn't."

"She doesn't know that," Jane said. "And she is no better than he."

"Jane," Mary reproved.

She flushed. "I don't mean that she shared intimacies with her beloved, choosing him when her family did not. I mean that she lied to Mr. Campbell. She didn't love him but accepted his proposal."

"I wonder what she would have done at the moment Mr. Campbell was ready to announce it to his family or take her to Scotland," Mary mused.

Charles went still. "If he told his sister, she'd have killed Miss Campbell herself. Poison in her tea wouldn't take any effort. She'd have made a servant do it."

"That isn't the situation here," Mary reminded him. "It's her beloved brother who died."

"But if Mrs. McAndrew knew her brother had betrayed them with the girl, she might have been angry enough in a moment to order him killed."

Mary imagined the ill lady upstairs like a spider in a web, tugging strands to give orders of evil intent. "It's too complex, I think. She's hardly Lucrezia Borgia."

"Let's go home," Jane whined. "I don't like this house."

"This isn't where the murder happened," Charles said.

"I don't like our house, either," Jane added, then flounced to the door and opened it.

They walked home at a slow pace. Would interviewing Mr. Fisher bear any fruit? He had to know what Mr. Abel was doing most of the time. Was Shelley safe from him? They didn't even know if Miss Campbell and Mr. Abel were together. What if she was floating in a river somewhere, drowned, like her mother had almost been?

When the threesome arrived at Skinner Street, the porter came out of the bookshop and handed Mary a note, then returned to the counter.

Mamma came out of the parlor. She didn't like to leave him alone to work, since he couldn't count properly. "Jane, you had better take over the counter." She went upstairs.

"Who is the note from?" Jane said, not moving.

"Shelley," Mary said. She opened it.

Charles frowned. "Why is he writing you?"

"Because I told him to stay out of sight, since Mr. Abel had suggested Shelley killed Mr. Campbell."

"Campbell came here due to a note with a scrap of poetry on it," Charles said. "That's the sort of ruse a girl might make." He went to put his coat on its peg. It slid right off onto the floor, but Charles went upstairs, anyway, leaving it there.

Jane sniffed and righted the garment. "Does Shelley want a meeting?"

"At Mother's tomb at dawn."

"I'm coming with you," Jane said, puffing herself up.

"Fine," Mary said, knowing that Jane would leave them alone if asked as long as she was included in the first place.

That night, after they had tucked Willy in and done a few things around the house that were normally Fanny's responsibility, Mary and Jane sat on the bottom stair, in front of the Skinner Street door.

"Would you sleep with me tonight?" Jane asked. "I'm afraid I'll have more nightmares."

"Maybe I will. It will be easier to sneak out from one bedroom to meet Shelley." Mary hugged herself. "Who is left to have killed Cecil Campbell?"

"Other than Mr. Abel and Miss Campbell?" Jane asked.

"Mr. Abel told me he was in Cornwall the week Mr. Campbell was killed. I remember thinking it odd that Bow Street had not appeared before. I would have thought Mrs. McAndrew would have hired them straight away."

"Miss Campbell could have sent Mr. Campbell the note," Jane suggested.

"She'd have to disguise her handwriting," Mary said. "He would have known it."

"That is child's play," Jane said impatiently, rubbing at her eyes. "Who else?"

"Mamma," Mary said. "She could easily have sent the note to Mr. Campbell. She might have found out about the poets breaking into the bookshop and wanted to put a stop to it."

"My mother a killer?" Jane hugged her knees. "She seemed quite affected by the body that night."

"She's a woman of mystery," Mary said. "She could have been playacting or, having killed the man, been shocked by the sight of his murdered corpse later."

"You've known her since before you can remember," Jane retorted. "She's not mysterious and . . . and, well, I don't know what else."

Mary shivered. "I don't like living under this roof with her, I'll tell you that."

"It's not as if we have anywhere else to go. They can't afford to send me back as a boarder to school, and you aren't welcome in Dundee unless that marriage proposal comes."

Mary sighed. "I have aunts. Even you have relations. Surely someone would take us."

"Only if we are prepared to earn our own bread. We are too young to be teachers or governesses."

"Or writers," Mary said. "I want to make my living by my pen, like Mother did, but Mamma is sure to prevent that, with her scheme for making us endlessly toil in the shop."

"What do we do tonight?" Jane asked plaintively.

"I'll stay with you. We'll bolt the door."

Mary snatched up the candleholder. They went upstairs, and she bolted the door as soon as Jane sat on her bed.

"Do you have anything that can be used as a weapon?" Mary asked. "A penknife?"

Jane sniffed. "No. I'm so sleepy." Her head dropped to the pillow. She slid into slumber like a young child.

Mary stared at her, still holding the candle aloft. They needed to wake just before dawn to meet Shelley. She supposed she ought to try to sleep.

After she blew out the candle, she settled down next to Jane, sharing her pillow, and let the soft noises of her stepsister's breathing lull her into sleep.

Chapter 25

Jane

Mary and I shivered in our heaviest cloaks, our shoes picking up dew, as we squelched through the St. Pancras burying ground the next morning.

Shelley's face lit with a smile as he saw us approach the Wollstonecraft memorial. He leapt up from a thick tree branch nearby, tucking away a notebook.

"What are you writing about?" I asked impertinently.

He pulled his book out again and opened a page to show me. A sketch of water, with a boat. "I hope to own one someday soon."

"It sounds delightful," Mary said with an air of impatience. "But it has been three weeks since Mr. Campbell died, and now Miss Campbell is missing, as well."

"That is troubling," he said, beginning to pace along the grave.

"Mary thinks my mother killed Mr. Campbell, in order to scare away the poets breaking in to meet in the shop," I said.

"I do remember her complaining about a wine stain on one of the books," Mary announced, making me wince. I had not been aware of the stain before now. "She must have suspected some mischief."

"Come now," Shelley chided.

I was pleased by his tone. I didn't want anyone thinking too hard about unusual book damage in the shop.

"I don't think your mother is the killer. She wants money from me, remember?"

"It doesn't matter that she doesn't want you dead," I said. "We uncovered a motive for Mamma to want Mr. Campbell dead." It made me feel ill.

"I suspect Mrs. McAndrew," he fired back. "She might have wanted to get the family fortune away from Campbell's line because he'd have spent it on printing poetic works. I've done some investigating."

"Does he have a fortune?" I asked.

"He, like me, had some expectations. I have learned that a recent unexpected death changed his prospects, just months before the murder."

"Then why did he not set up his own establishment?" I asked. "Why live with an ill sister?"

"That is no doubt precisely why," Shelley said. "Assuming he even had time to consider leaving. I would imagine he wanted to support her in her illness."

I could see Mary hung on his every word. I was afraid they would start another flirtation and leave the subject of poor Mr. Campbell aside. "I will not be able to sleep ever again if we do not solve the murder today!" I announced.

"Shh," Mary scolded. "Listen to Shelley. He has so much insight into the matter."

"And he's so funny," I mocked. "And so handsome. Come now, we need to find out if Mrs. McAndrew has an alibi."

"I worry that she could have harmed Miss Campbell or set

her on the path to ruin in Scotland by abetting her," Shelley said, frowning at me. "Whether she killed her companion or not, I do not think Mr. Abel a safe partner, even if he intends to marry the girl."

I shivered in memory of what he had attempted to do to me. Shelley reached for my hand and pulled me close. "It is well, Jane. You are safe."

"None of us are safe," Mary said, tugging me out of Shelley's arms. "Until we unmask the killer and remove them from the streets. Do you know we haven't even changed the lock on the Skinner Street door?"

"I can find the money to pay for it," Shelley said.

"You do too much already," Mary cooed.

I glanced between the two of them, then decided to walk briskly to keep myself warm until Mary could be persuaded to leave. Out of earshot as much as possible.

Shelley walked us to the edge of the burial ground half an hour later, after I had complained of hunger.

"There is a bakeshop nearby," Shelley said. He escorted us through the slowly warming streets, then dashed in and bought a few buns for us to share.

"Where should we go now?" Mary asked him as I pushed half a bun into my mouth.

"I want to know what Bow Street has uncovered about Mr. Abel's investigation," Shelley said. "Why don't we go there? Someone is on duty at all times."

"Are we sure he didn't kill Mr. Campbell?" I asked hesitantly.

"He told me he'd been in Cornwall the week Mr. Campbell died," Mary said. "We should check that now, I suppose. I never thought Mr. Abel could have murdered Mr. Campbell, but—"

"But we did not know he was an abuser of women or Sophia Campbell's previous intended," I interrupted.

"We should definitely check that," Shelley said, then angrily stuffed an entire bun into his mouth.

We walked to Covent Garden and entered the headquarters of the Runners. An older man was on duty behind a desk.

"Good morning. I'm Percy Shelley," our friend said, as if we hadn't been afraid only days ago that he'd be arrested at any moment. I supposed that fear was gone with Mr. Abel missing.

"Yes? Mr. Shelley?" asked the man deferentially, despite his gray chin whiskers.

I was impressed by how easily Shelley showed dominance. Every line of his dress and body was superior to the clerk.

"You probably know that Fitzwalter Abel has not appeared here in a day or two," Shelley said.

"Very aware," the man said, opening a ledger in front of him and running his finger down the page. "He is not assigned out of town at the moment."

"Was he in Cornwall three weeks ago on assignment?" Mary asked.

The clerk flipped back. "Yes, he and Fisher were sent there to look for a runaway groom who had stolen an expensive watch."

"Did he keep any kind of notes here?" Shelley asked. "We are particularly interested in knowing what he'd learned about the McAndrew family in the matter of the Campbell murder on Skinner Street."

"If a Runner keeps notes, they are all in his rooms unless a matter goes to court. I don't believe they caught the groom, so nothing has been updated here," the clerk said.

"And no killer has been caught in the Campbell murder?"

"Chances are that Abel kept it all in his head like," the clerk said. "Besides . . ." He pulled out another ledger from behind the desk. "Mr. McAndrew was paying for the investigation into the Campbell murder. Why would Mr. Abel have wasted his money investigating the paymaster's family?"

Shelley sighed. "I shall have to find the funds to deepen the investigation myself, then."

"Is there any chance you could send word to Skinner Street if Mr. Abel comes in?" Mary asked. "You could send a boy. We would pay him for delivering the message."

"If I'm on duty," the clerk agreed. "Believe me, we want to know what Mr. Abel is up to, as well. He's one of the best, you know."

Shelley thanked the man, and we departed, disappointed not to have learned anything useful.

"What are we going to do now?" I asked.

"I'll raise some funds today," Shelley promised. "We can pay for another Runner to track down Abel and Miss Campbell. I should be able to get the money tomorrow. Has he decided she is the killer, and is he trying to force a confession from her?"

Mary shuddered at the brutality that implied. "What about a Runner to investigate the McAndrews?"

"I'll do my best," he promised. "It will take some time, but there are a few sympathetic people who would like to see Campbell's killer caught. It is unfortunate that most of them have no money at all." He smiled.

"Poetry is a poorly paid profession," I said.

"Unless you are Byron, and he practically donates his work to the nation," Shelley said. "But we do not do it for money."

"Write to Lord Byron," I suggested. "You never know. He might donate to the cause."

"It is possible." Shelley looked thoughtful. "We do have some slight connection through Leigh Hunt."

"Remain hidden," Mary urged. "I cannot forget that Mr. Abel threatened you. Therefore, you must consider yourself still in danger."

"He seems to have lost interest in me," Shelley said.

"We may be able to relax on your account," I declared, "but not on Mamma's. We must return indoors before she rises."

I heard Shelley's voice outside the bookshop some hours later, but he did not come in. Papa already had one caller up in his study, and soon all three men departed.

I tried to relax my shoulders and stay calm. London still had a killer on the loose. What if Mrs. McAndrew had been fibbing all along about her health? What if her husband had wanted her brother dead?

I could even imagine that indolent Mr. Burgess had faked his exhaustion at Mr. Hocke's in my presence. Really, who was left? Mr. Hocke? Mamma? How could my sins remain hidden in the uncovering of the murderer?

I jumped as the door opened. Mary came in.

"You can take a quick stroll," my stepsister said. "The rain has stopped. I'll stay here."

The porter finished wrapping a selection of schoolbooks for some baronet's children. "I'll deliver these to Cavendish Square, and that's me done for the night."

"Thank you," I said.

Mary wrapped her arms around herself, pulling her shawl close. "I wish we could lock the outer door."

"That would keep the customers out," I said.

"I suppose it wouldn't protect us against the killer. If it is Mamma, she's already inside." Mary laughed, but it had a hollow ring to it. "Go for your walk, Jane."

I shook my head. "I don't want to be alone. I'd take Fanny's little sobs to that today. Usually, I mind having the porter here, with his scent of gin and spoiled shellfish, but today he was a comfort."

"I like him being gone because it means we're selling books," Mary said. "If he's here, that means he has nothing to do."

My gaze went to the door. "You don't suppose he—"

"Killed Mr. Campbell?" Mary shook her head. "Whatever for? Besides, he doesn't have the key to the door. Mamma thought he would steal the wine if he had easy access to the house. He has only a key to the warehouse next door."

"I'm not surprised." I giggled. "I've seen him sleeping behind a barrel inside."

"It's quite a dull job," Mary agreed. "But necessary."

Mary put on an apron while I paced back and forth in front of the counter. Before I could formulate any thoughts, however, the owner of a small boarding school came in, and then someone from my own school, to purchase some works of a historical nature.

Shelley returned with Papa for dinner. He dined on turnips and butter, while the rest of us ate mackerel and pickled carrots, followed by venison.

I watched Shelley closely, but he seemed distracted and didn't pass any hidden notes to Mary. She kept searching his face, and though he smiled sweetly at her, Father kept the conversation focused on a translation he was reading about a shepherd. It was in French, so Mamma kept jumping in to helpfully translate words.

"Papa," I broke in during the briefest of pauses in his monologue.

"Yes, Jane?" he asked, his expression stern. While we were invited to contribute to the discourse, he did not like interruptions.

"Is it too great an expense to fit a new lock to the front door?" I asked. "We do not know who might have the key after recent events."

"The murderer had one," Mary offered, demurely keeping her eyes on her plate of stewed apple in pastry.

I winced.

"I will consider the matter," Papa said, then returned to his French.

Eventually, Mamma sent Mary and me to put Willy to bed. I had the sad realization that with Fanny gone, everything, simply everything, would fall on our shoulders without respite. Thankfully, Mary was here to share the burden. I could not imagine how I would cope in this house with only me for Mamma to order around.

"What's wrong?" Mary asked me as she walked past with the trousers that Willy had managed to cover with mud, despite the sun being out today.

I shrugged. "Just the horrors."

She rolled her eyes and went out with the clothes. When she returned, I sang a French lullaby, and Mary told Willy the story of the oak and the reed from Aesop. Willy's eyes were closed before the story was finished. We tiptoed out of the room.

"Will you sleep with me again tonight? I don't feel safe," I whispered in the passage.

She drew me to my room and sat on my bed with me. "What are you afraid of tonight? I'd rather rest without you breathing up my nose."

"You can make me turn over," I pointed out.

"What are you afraid of?" she asked again. "The porter?"

"Of course not. I am afraid I will have nightmares about keys."

"You should have spoken to Papa in his study at the proscribed hour rather than at dinner," Mary said. "He might have been more receptive."

"I wish we had a way to make money. We could change the lock ourselves," I said peevishly. All this had come about because of the lack of money. I wished we had something to show for our work at the bookshop.

"We could ask Shelley for it, but he's attempting to raise funds to track the runaways. We can cut his money up only so many ways."

"And Mamma and Eliza Westbrook hope it is only cut in half," I said.

"Yes," she said. "And Papa would prefer it all go to him. I will stay with you. I do not like this idea of keys, either. Now we will both have nightmares."

She didn't leave my room again, just borrowed my second nightgown, which covered her feet and puddled a little on the floor.

"When did you grow so tall?" she asked, climbing into bed. "You were shorter than me when I went to Scotland."

I blew out the candle and rested my head on her shoulder. "Time passes and people change."

"I don't think everyone does," she said. "Some are constant. Mamma, for instance."

We both laughed. "And Papa," I added.

"And Fanny, thought one could not match her now with the baby in Mother's books," Mary said.

"I hope she comes home soon. We are quite doomed without her to take on some of Mamma's demands."

"She is better at coping than we are," Mary said. "She always wants to please, and I never do. It is vexing." She yawned and rolled over.

I shifted so that only my hip bumped hers, and waited for the sheets to warm so that I could fall asleep.

"Why did you light the candle?" I asked sleepily sometime later. "Fanny, go away. I don't want to get up."

"Get up, Miss Clairmont." A female voice said the words, but I didn't recognize it as my sisters' or my mother's. Why would any of them call me Miss Clairmont?

I blinked and struggled up. Mary sat up with me, woken by my motion. She startled and pressed herself against the headboard when she recognized what was going on a beat sooner than me.

"Who—who is there?" I quavered.

The flame moved under a chin. Dark hair was illuminated with a sheen of blue, and protuberant eyes. *Sophia Campbell.*

"You ran away from Mrs. McAndrew," I said stupidly. "What are you doing here?"

"She isn't alone."

The candle moved, and Fitzwater Abel came into view. In the dim light, with his dark hair also picking up blue, they could have been twins, equally tall and slim.

I felt faint. Mary and I both gasped. She wrapped her arms around me. I wanted to jump up and run, but we were locked into my own bedroom. The window over the back garden was open.

"How did you get in? We are floors aboveground," Mary demanded.

"I saw a ladder in one of the warehouses when I investigated the area last week," Mr. Abel said. "Now look, girls, I need you to do some things for us."

"I'm not going to do anything for you," I said indignantly, remembering the ill fate Shelley had rescued me from in Abel's room.

Mary gripped me tighter. Not having the same horrid memories that I did, she remained calmer.

"La, sir," she said, rising to her knees.

A knife flashed in front of the candle.

"Miss Campbell," I squeaked.

A fumbling noise sounded on my table, and then my stub of candle flared in Miss Campbell's hand. I saw her air of triumph and realized the truth. "You aren't a victim, but Mr. Abel's accomplice!" I shrieked.

"Shh," she hissed, all demureness lost. "You'll wake the house."

"Only Willy is on this floor," Mary said. "He will sleep through the Second Coming. What do you want from us? Tell us, we'll do it, and then you can go."

Miss Campbell sneered.

"Do you have a key to the bookshop?" Mary demanded.

"Cecil had access," Miss Campbell admitted. "I wrote the note that brought Cecil to the bookshop that fateful night."

"I had a note, too," I said in a small voice.

"Why?" Mary asked.

"They paid me to go into the bookshop after hours," I admitted. "That went well enough, so I thought of another way to make a few coins. I paid for some of my music lessons myself when Mamma asked me to cancel them. It is such a good escape from Skinner Street."

"What was the other way?" Mary asked in a hard voice.

"To make books look like collector's editions," I admitted.

"That is why Mr. Barre thought we had that first edition?"

"Someone put out the word to collectors, and he went to the bookshop instead of Russell Square, where Cecil had it," Miss Campbell said. "We were making money to pay Hocke's debts and for us to set up a household. It was a partnership."

"Shelley said Mr. Campbell had inherited money earlier this year," I said, angry at the betrayal. Who in the gang had told Mr. Barre that I had the book? I was supposed to be a silent partner to this business.

"Just property," she explained. "A dilapidated property in Wiltshire that needed funds in order to produce again."

"You stole our books for your own purposes? Jane, how could you?"

"I wanted to earn us more money," I answered, temporizing.

Mary gasped. "Oh, Jane."

"I hadn't thought it through," I said, my voice sounding broken. "Mr. Hocke made it sound like such an easy way to make money. I only wanted him to take the books that never sold. He said he could turn them into something that would."

Mary put her hand over my mouth. "Say no more," she cautioned low in my ear. "We don't need any information," she said a hair louder. "You don't need to tell us anything except what you want from us now."

I could feel her reedlike body shaking against me. Slowly, I pulled the covers up higher, though I knew fear, and not warmth, was my problem.

"I need you two to stand as witness after I bring in my suspect," Mr. Abel said, taking a step toward us. His shadow grew even larger, dancing in macabre glee along the wall.

"You want us to frame your betrothed?" I asked, then squeaked when Mary pinched me. My mouth couldn't stop moving, though. "Why would Miss Campbell have wanted Mr. Campbell dead?"

"I didn't," the companion said, her voice losing some of its self-satisfaction. "Fitz had the idea of frightening him into giving me the money he had made from the book, and then we were going to run away. I did not kill him."

"I did." I sensed rather than saw Mr. Abel's sneer. "Let that be a warning to you. I killed Cecil to punish Sophia for betraying me, and I will throttle you both if you do not obey me."

"But you weren't in town," I cried. "How could you have killed him?"

"A fast horse," the Runner said with a sneer. "Enough of this."

"We will obey you," Mary said in the voice of reason I knew was patently deceptive. It cut under Miss Campbell's squeak of outrage. "Tell us what you want us to do."

Miss Campbell stomped her foot. "I *did* obey you."

"Shush," Mr. Abel said. "I am not speaking to you."

"Stop punishing me," she cried. "I made love to Cecil for us, to get his money. We were so close. Only one more elderly great-uncle had to die, and Cecil would have had two thousand a year!"

"For us?" Mr. Abel's voice had gone low and dangerous.

The candle moved, and she gripped his arm. "For you, my love. Why should the McAndrews be the only ones with nice clothing and a nice house? I stole Cecil's watch for you, remember? And three of his cravats."

The candle was snuffed at the same moment the Runner's fist flashed toward Miss Campbell's face. She cried out as he roared, "I want no leavings. How dare you offer me secondhand?"

"Fitz, Fitz," she sobbed. "The cravats were new."

He pushed his open hand over her face. Her knees buckled as she moaned, "You're hurting me."

He applied his strength until her head was only inches above the floorboards. She scrambled on the floor.

Mary took advantage of their moment of distraction by letting go of me and darting toward the open window. When she pushed the curtains aside, the half-moon provided additional illumination in my room. I could think of nothing to help us, shadowed as the room was even now, but she, foolhardy or crazed with fear, leaned out.

Was she looking for the ladder? Did she think to escape in nothing but an overlong nightgown?

I held out my arms. "Don't leave me, Mary!"

Mr. Abel's attention snapped back to me and away from the crying companion on the floor.

Chapter 26

Mary

Mary pushed the curtains to one side. She needed moonlight. Their lives were in danger, and she couldn't see what was going on.

Miss Campbell had gone to the floor after Mr. Abel had hit her. Just when Mary reached for her, the companion slowly rose to her feet. Miss Campbell's teeth flashed. One of her hands went up, while Mr. Abel stood over Jane, his finger lifted to her face. The candlestick Miss Campbell held connected audibly with the side of his head. His hat flew off as the second blow landed.

He pushed her away from him, still full of strength. She bounced off the foot of the bed. Jane shrieked again.

Miss Campbell made a feral noise. Her eyes bulged more than ever. Her thin lips pulled away from her teeth to form a mummy-like rictus.

Mary glanced wildly around the room for a weapon. Why hadn't they thought to keep stout sticks in the room after a murder had occurred in this very house? *Merde!* She cursed their lack of forethought.

Miss Campbell slipped and had to take a couple of quick steps to stay upright. Mr. Abel staggered a little, his arms going wide. Miss Campbell regained her balance and struck him again, over the eye this time. He put his arm up to his face and pushed her, driving her past the bed. Mary saw the blood dripping down the side of his face. She swallowed hard and reached for the ladder. It didn't quite reach the windowsill. It would be hard to get to it safely in the dark. What if she went to her knees and crawled under the bed, then reached Jane's door? Would Jane leap for escape, as well, or was she in a paralyzed huddle on the bed? She was still screaming.

Miss Campbell lifted her candlestick again. It shone bronze in the moonlight. Before she could strike, Mr. Abel grabbed her arm and tried to force it down. She stepped back but slipped again. He pushed her. She bounced off the wall and changed trajectory, heading toward the window.

Or so he must have thought. Instead, he attempted to propel her against the wall. Mary put her hands over her mouth to stop her own scream as Miss Campbell overbalanced against the windowsill, rocked, then fell backward through the opening. The motion made the house rattle. The open sash crashed down like a guillotine into the frame.

Despite the now-closed window, Mary heard a thud, then the sound of the ladder crashing across the rear yard. It made a massive cracking sound, probably from breaking over the metal washtub. As much as she wanted to look, she stayed huddled against the wall next to the curtains, trying to be invisible.

Mr. Abel pressed himself against the opposite side of the window and called down in a low voice, "Sophia? Sophia?"

Jane's voice quavered from the bed, "She's dead. You killed your true love, your wicked partner."

The Runner's boots squelched solidly across the length of the window. He grabbed for Mary. Her blood went cold when he made contact. His hand grasped her arm very firmly, despite the blood dripping down his face. It didn't even have the courtesy to impede his vision, but ran neatly along the side of his jaw. She felt as helpless as a field rabbit in the jaws of a fox.

Even worse, Miss Campbell had fallen with her heavy candlestick. Mary had no recourse, no weapon.

"I hope she killed you," she said in a low voice, "and you just haven't quite lost your animation yet."

"You aren't a very nice chit, are you, Miss Godwin?" Mr. Abel observed, squeezing her arm harder. Mary squeaked in pain.

Jane rustled in her covers. Mary hoped she was gearing up to run for the door. In an attempt to distract him, she said, her voice shaky, "Let go of my arm. I cannot feel my hand."

"Tragic," he murmured, pressing his body against hers. She could smell tobacco and gin on him, with an underlying scent of horse.

"Let go." She tried to pull away, but his grip remained firm. How much strength did he have left?

"Do something for me, and you will survive the night," he said.

"Unlike your beloved?" she taunted.

He let go of her arm. Blood returned painfully to her extremities. She hissed against the pain as his fingers moved to her chin and squeezed into the tender flesh.

"Listen to me. I need Mrs. McAndrew to be framed as her brother's killer."

Mary fought against the pain and desperation. Was he going to break her jaw? She couldn't speak. He noticed her lips working and relaxed his fingers slightly. She opened and closed her mouth a couple of times like a fish.

"We're girls," Jane said. "No one listens to girls."

Run, Jane, Mary begged internally. Why wasn't her sister running?

"You are enough in this case," the Runner said. "This room

runs along the full length of the house. I know you can see the street from the opposite side."

"It gets very drafty when the wind blows across my room," Jane agreed.

Hellfire! Why had Jane not had the sense to run? She'd simply been sitting in the bed, listening and doing nothing! Mary despaired of her. Didn't she realize they were both going to die?

"I want you both to testify in front of the magistrate at Bow Street this very night that you saw Mrs. McAndrew in the street outside the bookshop the night Cecil Campbell died."

"Why?" Mary asked thickly, trying to pry his fingers from her jaw.

"Jane knows why."

"What?" Mary asked. "I don't understand. What could Jane possibly know?"

He didn't release any pressure. "She knows she would want Mrs. McAndrew to be hung for the crime."

"You can't think to parade us through the dark hours of the night," Jane said with a gasp.

He smirked, tightening his grip on Mary. "I'll say I found you outside."

"In the dark? By the prisons?" Jane scoffed. "No one will believe it, sir."

"My sister is right," Mary said, pronouncing the words with difficulty. Her body, in an act of betrayal, or perhaps from sheer exhaustion, began a fine tremor. "We should send for the watch. That is more believable."

"Fine." His fingers released a fraction of their hold. "Write a note, which one of the servants can take to the watchhouse in front of the church, and they can escort you to Bow Street."

"Jane isn't allowed pen and ink for letters in her room," Mary claimed as his fingers gave way. "It's too messy. We'll have to go down to the schoolroom." Would her father hear them going down the steps and rescue them?

"I don't know the schoolroom," he said slowly. "I will take

you down to the bookshop. I know you have ink there. Then you can kick a kitchen girl awake."

He seized Mary's left arm. She used her right to massage her jaw while she tiptoed across the floor barefoot. Mr. Abel hauled Jane out of bed, still possessing an alarming amount of strength, despite his freely bleeding head. Jane gasped painfully as the cold floorboards made contact with her bare feet, but at least the Runner allowed her to tear the sheet away from the bed along with her.

They went down the steps. Mary made sure to step on every squeaky board, hoping someone would wake and hear them. Anyone but Willy, who would surely sleep through all, she prayed.

They made it to the front hall without a sound from anyone, except mice running along the interior of the wall.

"Light the lantern," he instructed. "But keep it at waist level. Don't think I will hesitate to strike if you lift it."

Jane gave an uneasy squeak as she went to comply. It took her a ridiculous number of tries to successfully light the tinder. The first splint went out before she could light the lantern, but as Mr. Abel growled, the second splint made successful contact.

He dragged Mary to the bookshop door, then sent Jane for the key when he discovered the lock. Despite the pain and blood loss, she could see he still kept his measure of caution.

Jane unlocked the door, and they went in. He went to the counter after grabbing the lantern from Mary.

"Where is the inkstand?" he said.

Mary went behind the clean, bare counter. "Mamma must have taken it up to trim the quill and refill it. She keeps her office locked."

He gritted his teeth, looking like a pirate of yore with that ferocious expression and blood freely running down the side of his face and pooling in his neckcloth. How could she have ever thought him handsome?

"I'll take you back up," he said.

"No." Mary started to shake her head, then stopped. The pain from her jaw radiated to her cheeks. She didn't want Mr. Abel going back to where the bedrooms were, where her family lay defenseless in sleep. Then she remembered. "My writing desk is hidden in the stacks in the corner where I like to perch and write."

"Get it," he snarled.

When she stepped by, she could see Jane's pale face in the lantern light. The Runner was digging through the shelf behind the counter. He pulled out a dustrag and dabbed at his wound.

Mary mouthed, "Run!" to Jane as she moved toward the windows. At least one of them could live to tell the tale. She debated if she was strong enough to break one of the windows. Mamma and Papa would be furious, but surely they would want her to live. Shelley would borrow the money to restore it.

When Mary reached the first shelf, where the copybooks were, Jane took her chance, breaking into a sprint. The sheet billowed after her. Mary watched, open mouthed, as her sister, hair falling out of her braid, ran, the white sheet streaming like a fast-moving storm cloud. Would she live long enough to include such a scene in *Isabella, the Penitent*?

The Runner dropped the rag and tore through the open door after Jane. Mary grabbed at everything on the shelf. Inkpots, pencils, copybooks, instruction manuals hit the ceiling as she threw them. Surely her father or the watch would hear the commotion?

Jane screamed in the front hall. Mary grabbed an armful of books and ran toward the bookshop door, then took a stance and hurled the books over her head at the ceiling.

Jane's cry cut off. Mary grabbed the lantern and saw Mr. Abel had his hands around Jane's throat!

Above them, the house rattled as a window opened. Mamma screamed out the window for the watch.

Mary swung the lantern at the backs of Mr. Abel's knees, hoping to set him on fire. The whole house could burn if it meant saving Jane. The Runner snarled and loosed one hand from Jane's neck to swat at the lantern.

The candle went out as Mary swung again. Darkness descended. She flailed wildly, not connecting. Then light appeared on the stairs. She recognized the stocky shape of her father and, behind him, Charles running down the stairs. Charles careened past her father and leapt down the last three steps, his arms out. He crashed into the Runner and set him flying away from Jane.

She fell to the floor, gasping, her hands around her throat. Mary went to her, dropped to her knees, and wrapped her arms around her shuddering sister.

"Unlock the door," Jane whispered between wheezes. "Go!"

Mary jumped up and complied, dancing around the men. Her father had Mr. Abel's greatcoat in his fists and was attempting to wrap the villain's arms up in it, while Charles punched him.

Mary turned the key in the lock and threw open the door. In the distance, she saw lanterns. Men ran in their direction as Mamma continued to call for help upstairs.

"Housebreaker?" came an elderly voice echoing in from the street. Not many people lived normal lives in this neighborhood of prisons and warehouses, but they did have a few neighbors.

"Murder!" Mary screamed. "There is a body in our back garden! Betrayal! Perfidy! Treachery!" She ran out of words as her throat seized.

Three watchmen came through the door, holding lanterns high. Coughs doubled her over, rocking her back against the wall. They broke up the trio of Papa, Charles, and Mr. Abel, each taking an arm. The elderly neighbor was right behind a watchman, with a nephew who'd been staying in his house.

"Very good, gentlemen," Mr. Abel said, a smile playing on his mouth as he straightened his coat. "This excellent family has been most distressed by events this evening."

"Wot did you find, Abel?" one of the watchmen asked.

Mary waved her arms. No! They were getting it wrong.

"I 'ear Bow Street's been looking for you for days," another said.

The neighbors came to stand next to Charles.

Jane pointed a shaking finger at Mr. Abel and stared, wide-eyed, at the youngest watchman. "He tried to choke me to death."

Mr. Abel shook his head and chuckled.

"He wants us to frame Mrs. McAndrew for her brother's murder," Mary added. "But we didn't see her here that night. Mr. Abel killed Cecil Campbell."

"Did you see him die?" the third watchmen said suspiciously.

"No, but Mr. Abel confessed to it. Right before he pushed Miss Campbell out my bedroom window," Jane rasped indignantly.

"There has never been an eviler person," Mary said. "In history. Not ever."

Her father, panting, put his hand on Mary's shoulder. "Mr. Abel has no business in my house so late."

Mary stopped speaking. She didn't want Jane to be arrested, too. Jane lacked the maturity to have considered the stupidity of her actions. She didn't deserve a prisoner's fate.

"Come, gentlemen," Mr. Abel protested. "I was chasing a killer."

"*He* is the killer," Mary insisted. "Check the back garden."

"Let's take him over to the governor's house at Newgate," the first watchman said to the second. "He can send someone to Bow Street to sort this all out."

"Come now," Mr. Abel said with a light laugh. "This is all the product of overwrought girls' imaginations."

"There's no body in the back garden, then, sir?" the first watchman inquired acidly. Though he was at least sixty, Mary could see he'd been a fine figure of a man once, perhaps a soldier.

"She fell," Mr. Abel said. He staggered slightly. The blood loss must finally be getting to him.

"The dead girl was stealing from the bookshop," Mary added. "There was an entire conspiracy underway."

"There was?" Papa asked, his fingers tightening on Mary's shoulder.

The first watchman gestured to the other two, and they both took Mr. Abel's arms. "You can explain it to the governor."

"I don't want to go to Newgate," Mr. Abel said emphatically, then fainted against one of the watchmen, who fell against the wall. He managed to keep himself and the Runner upright.

The three watchmen, Charles, and the neighbor's nephew each took a part of Mr. Abel, and they carried him to the prison, with Papa and the neighbor directing.

People came into the street, passersby and their scant neighbors. Mary and Jane clutched at each other, but it was much too cold outside for them to go in their nightdresses with the men. Mamma came downstairs in her wrapper and led them both upstairs, where she tucked them into bed, muttering that she missed Fanny, before going downstairs to rouse the kitchen girl to make them a hot drink. Jane pushed out a few words about stolen books and Mr. Barre before falling asleep.

When Mary was certain everyone would leave them alone, she shook Jane awake, then held her candlestick so she could take a good look at her stepsister. "Why didn't you run?"

Jane's lips trembled.

"Speak to me," Mary insisted. "What was going on tonight? We could have died. You owe me the truth."

Jane's fingers went to her thick braid. She toyed with the tuft at the end.

"The truth," Mary said. "I know I am missing something."

Her stepsister dropped her chin to her chest. She muttered something.

"What?" Mary demanded.

"It was Mr. Barre's fault," she said, her voice raspy from the attack.

"The collector?" Mary asked, bewildered. "Why?"

"He is so greedy. I thought we could make some money from him. I know he has it." Jane's cheeks moved in and out as she lubricated her throat. "Like I said before, Mamma was going to take me out of singing lessons forever soon, and school. We can't afford my education. I thought to make money of my own."

"What did you do?"

"I met Mr. Hocke at the bookshop. I let the poets in to meet here a few times over the winter, before you came home. I knew he was dishonest, and I told him about Mr. Barre. We made a plan to sell him rare editions. Of course, we didn't have them."

"Then what?"

"We had to make them." Jane put her fists to her eyes. "Mr. Hocke has the bookbinding skills required. I didn't know anyone would die because of this. I never meant any of it to happen."

"Of course not. But dishonesty breeds violence, Jane."

"I just wanted what we deserve. Why should we suffer so? Papa is a respected man of letters. He should have more."

"Five children are a lot to support. Mamma's extravagances have not helped."

"I see that. I am not a child. I wanted to help."

"Oh, Jane." Mary pulled the girl toward her.

"Are you going to tell? They will put me in prison." Fat tears slid from Jane's eyes.

Mary cradled Jane's head against her shoulder and felt her

skin dampen. "No. But you must promise not to be dishonest again. Look at the sort of people you drew to Skinner Street. The consequences were terrible. Two deaths."

"I never wanted any of it. Just the money."

"Which you didn't receive." Mary sighed. "We don't need much. Modest desires are best."

Jane slid her face from side to side against Mary's throat. "I'm afraid Mr. Barre suspects I was involved."

"You're just a silly girl. He can't possibly believe it."

Mary closed her eyes. Jane relaxed against her and slowly slid back into sleep. How could they stay here at this desperate house, in this failing business? Would Jane be able to resist the next temptation?

When Mary heard commotion in the back garden sometime later, she climbed out of bed, leaving Jane slumbering. At the rear window, she saw a half dozen men with lanterns talking over the crumpled remains of Sophia Campbell. Her heart skipped a beat when she thought she recognized Shelley for a moment, but it wasn't him. She yawned, her vision swimming. A man pointed to the sky as a light rain began to fall. Eventually, three of the men threw a tarp over the body, and they carried Miss Campbell off, probably to the same warehouse where her betrothed's corpse had lain.

This time, Mary did not follow. Mamma arrived with a pot of chocolate. Mary drank it dutifully while Jane slept on, and fell asleep next to her right after Mamma took the cups away.

The next day, Mamma took Mary and Jane to Russell Square by hackney coach. When Mamma presented her card, the parlormaid looked doubtful but took it upstairs.

An older lady came to fetch them a few minutes later and told them she was the housekeeper. Mary stored away her appearance, the waves of pure white hair braided into the crown, and the dull sheen of the bombazine silk and wool dress she wore in the color of mourning.

When they entered Mrs. McAndrew's parlor, they found her seated with a very thin man her age, dabbing at her eyes with a handkerchief. He stood when they reached the sofa.

"I am John McAndrew," said the balding man in the fine suit. "You must be the Godwin family."

They curtsied to him, and a maid showed them where to sit. They were not offered tea, however, though Mary could see Mamma looking inquiringly around for it, since the McAndrew couple had cups on a table next to the sofa.

"Please, tell us what happened to my wife's companion in your own words," the man of the house invited.

Mamma started speaking at the same time as Mary and spoke louder until Mary subsided and let her tell the tale she had had almost no part in. At least Jane remained quiet, due to the pain in her throat and the secrets in her heart. At the right moment, however, she pulled the fichu from around her throat to expose the bruises from Mr. Abel's hands. Mary untied her bonnet to show the bruising around her chin. Mrs. McAndrew gasped in horror, but her husband seemed unmoved.

Finally, Mamma wrapped up her embellished, innocent Jane–centric tale with the information that the coroner would hold his court that afternoon.

"I am very sorry to hear that my brother and his friends had been breaking into your bookshop," Mrs. McAndrew said.

"And stealing books," Mary added brazenly as Jane looked down. "Guineas' and guineas' worth, I expect."

Her husband cleared his throat. "We will pay for the locks to be replaced."

Mamma raised her eyebrows and settled her gloved hands very firmly in her lap, looking like an oversize bird of prey. Mary knew she was too canny to leave without the offered payment.

"I'm sure we shall leave you to rest and make arrangements as soon as the matter is taken care of," Mamma said.

A muscle twitched in Mr. McAndrew's cheek, but he rose and left the room.

"Such a handsome husband you have, Mrs. McAndrew," Mamma said. "And such a pity you have been left with no further comfort. What will you do now that your cousin has died?"

Mrs. McAndrew smiled faintly. "Mr. McAndrew is going to take me into the country. Wiltshire. We have a small estate. A relative is a vicar there, and I believe he has a trio of daughters. I expect one will do for me."

"I see." Mamma could not hide the look of disappointment on her face, but Mary could not see Jane or herself being content to fetch and carry even in Russell Square. Even to escape Skinner Street.

Mr. McAndrew returned with a handful of guineas. They took their leave after Mamma made a pointed comment about being parched and offered no refreshment. "This will not be the end," she warned.

"We are closing the house tomorrow," Mr. McAndrew said. "Good afternoon."

Mary descended to the street behind Mamma with a sigh, feeling a pang of sympathy for Jane. She had hoped to make a friend here, and it had gone terribly, desperately wrong. Taking Jane's arm, she squeezed it with more affection than usual.

When they left the hackney in front of Skinner Street, Shelley was there to help them down. Mary took in the tall young man in his deep blue coat and well-fitted breeches. His boots were freshly shined. Had he made such an effort for her, or did he have other calls to make today?

"Are you invited to dine, Shelley?" Mamma asked.

"Peter Corn is released," he told her. "I thought I might take the girls to retrieve him."

"I don't want them at the prison," Mamma said, aghast.

"It is only down the street, and I will keep the hackney, if that makes you feel better."

"Very well," Mamma said with a sigh and went into the house without paying the driver, holding her reticule with the guineas tightly in her fist.

Shelley handed the girls back in and told the driver to take them to the prison, silly, really, with it being so close.

"I don't know what Corn's condition will be," Shelley confided, explaining himself. "We will want the coach for Jewin Street."

"Mr. Hocke owes us restitution, as well," Mary said. She had to bury the truth of Jane's involvement as if she'd never known it. "For the stolen books."

"Hmmm," Shelley said.

Mary and Jane stayed in the coach while Shelley went to acquire his friend. Jane dozed against Mary's shoulder while Mary thought through the events of the night before. Would Peter Corn be in as bad a shape as Caleb Williams when he escaped prison in Papa's novel?

Mary was shocked when he appeared with Shelley. Jane's expression showed despair. Mr. Corn's two weeks' imprisonment seemed to have destroyed his wardrobe. The once beautiful green coat had a burn on one sleeve, and the shoulder on the other side looked like it had been chewed.

He blinked hard as he climbed into the carriage. "I find myself quite befogged by the sun."

"Didn't they let you go outside?" Mary asked.

"I was attacked the first day for my boots," he said sadly. "Very nice pair they were."

Mary noticed his current boots were cracked and unpolished. "You didn't win the battle, I take it?"

"No. Lost my boots and a couple of teeth," he said, patting the side of his face. "Happy to be alive. Cannot wait to have a bottle of wine in my hand and my friends around me."

"Some friends," Mary muttered.

Jane showed her throat to Mr. Corn as the coach rattled to Jewin Street. They commiserated over their injuries.

When Mr. Hocke opened the door, his expression was radiant. "I am in alt!" he declared. "Corn, you old darling! And the heroines of the hour! If only Mary Wollstonecraft could see you now."

"How could you steal from her family?" Mary demanded.

"What?"

"*Lyrical Ballads*, and what else?"

"Oh, just that one," he assured her, with a confused glance in Jane's direction. "The scheme had scarcely begun when Campbell turned up dead. Scared us off." He handed Mary two guineas. "I have learned the error of our ways."

Mary discovered she liked Mr. Hocke rather more than she had previously, at least after a drink or two. No wonder Jane had attempted to bring him into her schemes. He'd been a gentleman to keep her name out of the official explanations. Mr. Burgess, Mr. Hocke, and Shelley poured sherry for Mary and Jane. The poetry circle was reunited with two other exceedingly young men, down from Harrow by horseback for the occasion.

Shelley sat next to Mary on a chaise lounge, holding a tankard half-full of wine. "Jane tells me you managed to raise the house and rescue you both."

"I threw everything I could find in the shop at the ceiling," Mary said. "Mamma managed to get some money out of the McAndrews, but I don't think she realized how much else was damaged overnight."

"A small price to pay to have both of you safe," Shelley said. "Jane could have suffocated very quickly, you know."

Mary's lips trembled. "I was so frightened, Shelley. I was

afraid for anyone to come and help us, but in the end, we couldn't save ourselves alone."

He patted her arm. "You'd have thought of something, or Abel would have passed out from blood loss. That's what your father said."

She forced a smile. "As long as you regard me highly. I think that is enough to make me happy for perhaps the first time in my life."

He grinned and passed her the tankard. Their fingers bumped. She set down her sherry and took a sip of the greatly superior red wine. Across from them, Jane clutched her throat as Mr. Hocke made up an ode to her on the spot. Mr. Burgess held Mr. Corn's hand, showing the first emotion she had ever seen from him. The other two men sang a jaunty air.

Mary tried to imagine where poor, deluded, unlucky-in-love Cecil Campbell would have been seated in this circle of poets, but for once, her imagination failed her. Perhaps it was for the best.

Shelley bent his mouth to her ear. "Shall we take a walk?"

She shivered as his breath tickled her soft skin. "Tonight, after dinner. Let's finish our wine and speak in poetry for a little while longer."

Jane squeaked a little laugh, and Mr. Corn raised his glass in her honor. Shelley leapt up to offer a sonnet of his own in praise of the ladies of Skinner Street. Mary watched and drank, more at peace than at any moment since she'd returned from Scotland less than three months before. Isabella the Penitent would have to wait her turn in the spotlight.

She thought, though, that she would keep John Hocke's guineas for her own purposes. Mamma could fend for herself.

Chapter 27

Jane

"Our adventures have been quite enough to make me want to hide in bed and do nothing but read until summer finally comes." Mary sat in bed next to me that night, huddled in a shawl, with a copy of *Elements of Chemical Philosophy* on her lap.

The candles gave me just enough light to see the title of Part I. "On the Laws of Chemical Changes: On Decompounded Bodies and Their Primary Combinations." How could she read such a macabre thing? "You'd want to do that, anyway." I squeezed close to her, warming myself in her body heat.

"No. There are many pleasures I would not have wanted to give up before I saw Sophia Campbell fall out the window. Now my limbs are nearly frozen, and I am fatigued and suffering."

She felt warm enough to me, though I agreed with the fatigue. "There are monsters in between the pages of books, too."

She turned a page. "Yes, of course, but there is a queer sort of comfort in book monsters."

My nightgown rustled as I sat up to face her. "I don't know about that. Even book monsters don't always die in the end. Iago is still alive at the end of *Othello*. I think when something goes into one's thoughts, it can never truly be plucked out again."

"Yes, like that monstrous image of Shelley's assassin that he drew. I don't think I'll ever forget that," Mary agreed.

I blew out my candle, wanting darkness to hide the flush that crept over my cold cheeks. "Will you ever forget what has happened these past weeks?" I ventured in a quiet tone quite unlike my normal voice.

"I have just told you that I will not."

"How are we to go on if you do not?" I asked, my fingers stealing over her hip.

Mary's book banged shut, but she did not pull away from me. Maybe she needed my warmth, too.

"At least Peter Corn is free," I said.

"I suppose. I am happy we worked together to save ourselves, as well."

"Yes, we did." Something more seemed to be required. I attempted an apology. "Mary, I am truly sorry for every bad choice I made. I was trying to help."

"Only a child would think stealing could ever bring good," she snapped.

"How do I fix it?" I swallowed back tears.

Mary's fingers tapped the cover of her book. She surprised me by saying, "I am willing to disremember your part of it."

"Why?" Why would she not reveal what I had done to the bookshop? Mamma and Papa would be livid if they knew I'd been so dishonest, taken coins, and been a thief. In truth, I would want Mary to tell, except that there was no money to punish me by sending me away, and I did not want to think about the punishment that would occur with me staying.

"Why not?"

"Don't you want Mamma angry with me, so that I will stop being her favorite?"

"I will never be her favorite, even if you were dead, nor would I want to be."

How implacable she was, my Mary. She would never change her opinion of Mamma as an unwelcome interloper. But what about me? I didn't care what she thought of Charles, or even Willy, but she was my closest companion. "Does it matter? We will not live here forever."

"Mamma wants us to stay, to run the bookshop. Papa will not intervene in that."

"We'll go, Mary. I know we will." I pulled my hand from her hip as I closed my fingers into my palm. I vowed it; I really did. We could not stay here. This life that Mamma had built was not for us.

"I wish I could remember my life before you came into it, but I confess I cannot." Mary's words had a little growl at the ends.

I smiled. She'd offered me hope. "I cannot remember life without you, either. I would wish your mother to be as much my stepmother as my mother is yours, you know."

"It doesn't work like that."

"True." I touched the end of her braid, all fairy fluff and soft. "But I feel that it is so. You don't really know her except from stories and her books, any more than I do. Why cannot I claim her, too?"

"Instead of your own?" Mary coughed. "I wish Papa had never even met Mamma, but this is the life we have."

"We'll have a better life than this soon," I whispered. "We're nearly grown. You and I, Mary, we aren't like the others. Fanny can't do what we can. We have ideas."

"Your ideas might land you at the end of a noose yet," she said archly.

"I'll let you lead," I promised. "You will keep me out of trouble."

"I don't believe it. You must curb your headstrong ways."

She was the pot calling the kettle black, but I held out my hand, wanting to achieve something. "Truce?"

"I'll try to think of a way for us to escape, if you'll follow me. Truce." She shook my hand.

I lay back, happy as I had not been in a long time. She sighed and blew out her candle, then curled up next to me, her hand still in mine. My lips stayed smiling as I fell into sleep, secure in the notion that she'd always be beside me, my other half.

Acknowledgments

I want to thank you, dear reader, for picking up the first book in this new series. We authors live and die by our book reviews, so thank you so much for reviewing *Death and the Sisters* and anything else I've written. It has been so exciting to see eyes lighting up whenever I've mentioned this book project. Mary Shelley, who wrote *Frankenstein* as a teenager, lives large in our hearts to this day. I have enjoyed imagining what she and her storied family and circle were like when she was Mary Godwin, just sixteen years old.

Thank you to my beta readers, Judy DiCanio and Cheryl Schy, and I appreciate the emotional support provided by the Columbia River Sisters in Crime chapter. I took a wonderful class on Gothic literature through Regency Fiction Writers that really inspired me. Thank you, Dr. Sam Hirst! Thank you to my agent, Laurie McLean, at Fuse Literary. She went above and beyond for this one. Thank you to my Kensington editors, Elizabeth May and James Abbate; my copy editor, Rosemary Silva; and my communications manager, Larissa Ackerman; along with many unsung heroes at Kensington. This book gestated for over three years before I could write it, so thank you to anyone who helped with it over time.

While members of the Godwin family and Percy Bysshe Shelley are real people, my plot is entirely fictitious. *Isabella, the Penitent* is not a real novel, but I did quote Shelley and other poets accurately. Nearly everything Mary Shelley wrote before her late teens was lost, though that is a tale for another book. If you've read me before, you may know I'm a keen amateur genealogist. Discovering my distant cousinship to William Wordsworth meant I had to include his work, no matter Shelley's opinion of it, LOL. I worked from old maps to make the movements and locations in the book as accurate as possible. I also used William Godwin's journal to move real people in and out and around the story. A tremendous amount of material is available about this historical period in London, and I encourage readers to pick up some nonfiction on the topic.

While we cannot truly know what motivated Mary, Jane, and Shelley to do what they did in the summer of 1814, the consequences of their actions affected every one of the people in their lives, and I cannot wait to keep telling their story. Until the next one!

BOOK CLUB READING GUIDE for

Death and the Sisters

1. What did you know about Mary Shelley before reading this book?
2. How did Jane and Mary complement and antagonize each other?
3. The Godwin household was a complicated one, with each member of the younger generation having a different set of biological parents. How would this affect the sibling relationships?
4. How did Fanny, Mary, and Jane fit into the typical "oldest, middle, youngest daughter" roles?
5. Mary Jane Godwin was much maligned by Mary. Do you think Mary's stepmother deserved Mary's low opinion of her?
6. William Godwin was put on a pedestal by Mary. Do you think he deserved that? Contrast this parental role more than two hundred years ago with its modern-day version.
7. Mary Wollstonecraft, Mary's philosopher and novelist mother, has a presence in the book, as indeed she must have had in her daughter's thoughts. What do you think might have been different about Mary's life if her mother hadn't died shortly after her birth?
8. Mary's juvenilia has been mostly lost. Here some of her early writing has been fictionalized, based heavily on the Gothic literature of her day. Do you think *Isabella, the Penitent* is the sort of book she'd have been trying to write at sixteen?
9. Discussing characters' physical attributes, such as their weight, has become problematic in fiction as modern readers are sensitive to the perceived shaming of characters.

How do you think novelists should handle such information? For instance, Mary Jane Godwin's weight was used to belittle her in her own lifetime. How should it be handled in fiction?

10. Which of the real historical figures in this book are you most curious to learn more about?